MW00636640

Zen

To Caroline

Thank you
for your support.

Andrew Steele
2/27/22

Zen

The Anatomy of the Perfect Crime

The Griegg/Eastwood Mysteries

A WILSON STEELE

MOUSE HOLE FARM PRESS
DURHAM, CONNECTICUT

Copyright © 2021 by A. W. Steele

ISBN: 978-0-578-75868-8

The characters in this novel are fictional. Any resemblance to persons alive or dead is coincidental. Every effort has been made to depict the historical events surrounding the fictional story accurately.

Cover design by Andrea Steele and Willis Steele

Cover photography by:
Sarah Grote Photography, Cromwell, Connecticut, and
Stockwell Photography, New York City, New York

Printed in the United States of America
Signature Book Printing, www.sbpbooks.com

To my parents, Dorothy Eastwood Wilson and Harold Digby Wilson, who encouraged and supported my love of horses from an early age to adulthood.

ACKNOWLEDGEMENTS

I express my gratitude to the United States Equestrian Foundation for permitting the Hamilton Farm name and its history to be referenced in this novel. I am especially indebted to Bonnie A. Jenkins, Executive Director, USET Foundation, Inc., and Maureen K. Pethick, Communication Coordinator, USET Foundation, Inc., for taking time from their busy schedules to address my request. For more information about Hamilton Farm and to support the USET organization, visit www.uset.org.

I thank my friends and family who read the manuscript, reviewed the medical language, shared their thoughts on the cover design, and commented on the book's video trailer. Your feedback was essential.

Thanks to Huub van der Mark for appearing on the book cover. You were the face of Zen as I wrote.

In 2004, Mark Russell introduced me to Gillian Belnap when the Lyon's Press assigned her as editor for *Lessons in Lightness: The Art of Educating the Horse*. Since then, Gillian's expertise and commitment to excellence has enhanced all my audio, video, and writing projects.

I wish to recognize the horses and horse industry people that have impacted my life. These relationships helped me place the Zen mystery inside the horse community with accuracy, making use of artistic license in only a few passages.

I also welcome Candace Davis and Paula Murphy to the Mouse Hole Farm Press team as the Griegg/Eastwood Mysteries continue.

About the Griegg/Eastwood Mysteries

Zen is Book Two in the Griegg/Eastwood Mystery series.

While each book in the series stands on its own, the storyline and characters mature with each new mystery. To fully appreciate the nuances of each character and the plot development, reading in chronological order is advised. If you haven't yet read *The Trap*, not to worry…read it after *Zen*!

The following cast of characters from Book One, *The Trap*, come back to solve the mystery in *Zen*.

Alana Eastwood

Alana is an African American in her thirties. She graduated college with a double major in finance and fine art, which tells you that her adherence to facts and logic is enhanced by her imagination, ingenuity, and keen intuition.

That levelheadedness is put to the test when she finds an unopened letter, postmarked Berlin 1945. Opening the letter unleashes a chain of events that leads to murder and mayhem fifty years after World War II. Book One leads Ms. Eastwood to Sigmund Griegg and the adventure to solve the mystery of *The Trap*.

Sigmund Griegg

Sigmund is the Swiss investigator, who recognizes that the German police lack open-mindedness to connect a current murder investigation with events that occurred at the end of World War II.

In his forties, Sigmund is a brilliant investigator, but is still reeling from the tragic death of his wife seven years earlier. Griegg has a world-class team to assist him. That team includes his father, Andrew.

Andrew Griegg

The Griegg business of research and investigation has been located in the heart of Zürich's Old Town since the early days of the twentieth century.

Now retired, Andrew oversees operations using a steady hand to bridge conflicts between the strong personalities involved in each mystery at hand.

David Rosen

David Rosen is a Mossad agent, Israeli Intelligence. David crosses paths with the Grieggs from time to time. While both Sigmund and Andrew deem David a trustworthy colleague, their collaborations can be contemptuous when their self-interests collide.

The Griegg Investigation Staff

Ian Stewart

Expelled from Oxford University at eighteen, Ian landed himself in a British prison. He was convicted in England's most notorious computer hacking scandal in the modern era.

As computer science and technology bloomed in the 1990s, the Grieggs predicted that cyber-research would be critical in their line of work. They wanted one of the industry's best minds in their corner. They hired Stewart upon his release from prison.

Christopher Hutt

Hutt retired from Scotland Yard a decorated inspector. As one of the Grieggs' experts, he now offers research services to academia, governmental agencies, and corporations.

Christopher also assists police departments in their criminal investigations and runs quasi-spy operations amidst the underbelly of worldwide intrigue.

Sabine Bauer Hutt

Sabine earned a master's degree in drama from the Zürich University of the Arts. It might seem odd for an investigator to have a background in theater, but she can insert herself into any situation and extract information from the unsuspecting with cunning and finesse.

Sabine met Christopher on the job, and while he was many years her senior, they married soon after.

Boris Klondt

Boris came to work for the Grieggs from an elite branch of the German Federal Police force. As a skilled investigator, Boris also provides security expertise for the collaborators (who find themselves in tricky situations more often than they like to admit)!

J. Leopold Niedermeyer

Niedermeyer, as he is known, is a quirky fellow believed to be well into his seventies. Hired by the company's founder, Wolfgang Griegg, Niedermeyer is the librarian/archivist.

While he rarely leaves the building, he has yet cleverly procured a network of "street" connections that frequently produce vital information when it's most needed.

Other Helpful Information

There is one thing omitted from Alana Eastwood's background that is helpful to know. Throughout her life, she has experienced unusual dreams…unusual because they turn out to be true, an actual recapture of events that have happened in the past—occurrences in need of resolution.

Reluctant to consider herself psychic, Alana has always downplayed her visions. That is, until surviving the mystery of the trap, when it became hard to deny.

Having a character with such curious ability is inspired by the author's own experiences.

In addition, the character of the animal communicator is based on the author's encounters with people who can link telepathically to animals.

Fast-forward two years from when *The Trap* mystery was solved…a strange event spearheads Sigmund and Andrew Griegg to call on Alana Eastwood and David Rosen to help them unravel a new mystery that strikes at the very heart of the Griegg family.

Read *Zen* to see how it only takes one person to foil even the best-laid plans.

Cast of Characters

The Griegg Associates

Alana Eastwood–Former client now collaborating on a new investigation
Sigmund Griegg–Investigator
Andrew Griegg–Sigmund's father and retired investigator
William Zen Griegg–Equestrian and Sigmund's son
Sabine Bauer Hutt–Investigator
Christopher Hutt–Investigator
Ian Stewart–Investigator
Boris Klondt–Investigator
J. Leopold Niedermeyer–Librarian and Archivist

The True Crime Club

Trudie Rechsteiner–Ash's granddaughter
Viktor Harel–Palmer's grandson
Valentina Abbatelli–Mario's daughter
Remy Abbatelli–Tony's stepson
Rob Grazioli–Former club member

Operation Boomerang

David Rosen–Mossad agent
Palmer Harel–Art expert
Sara Mayer–Art expert
Yaffa Reis–Art expert
Joan Shulman–Retired Mossad agent, head of
Operation Boomerang

Cast of Characters (continued)

Additional Characters

Asher Rechsteiner–Animal communicator
Mrs. Rechsteiner–Asher's wife
Lara Bless–Coach, the Equestrian Federation
Melanie Pfenninger–Trainer, the Equestrian Federation
Paul Grazioli–Rob's father
Mario Abbatelli–Valentina's father
Tony Abbatelli–Mario's brother

Flying Oblique, AKA Tiger, was inspired by the real life horse Mylilsecret, AKA Miles, because of his size, coloring, and athletic ability. Miles appears on the book cover.

Tangential characters appear in cameo appearances throughout the book.

Like **Author Andrea Steele** on Facebook to talk about the Griegg/Eastwood mysteries, write a review, and read clues to solve the mystery.

Prologue

*D*o you know what it's like to have the talent to be the best at something? It doesn't matter what that *something* is. It just matters that the only thing holding you back is money.

You watch as less capable people succeed and it eats away at your very soul, knowing that without money, it will never happen for you.

Then, this ingenious scheme comes along…like it just falls into your lap—bam—there it is, enough cash to answer all of your dreams. It's the perfect crime: No one gets injured, and even better, you can totally get away with it.

1

Zürich, Switzerland, 1997

"Welcome to Tremblay's Auction House. Our celebration this evening is, '200 Years of European Art.'" The auctioneer struck a commanding pose as she pounded her gavel on the block with authority.

"Quiet in the room, please. We shall begin. Ladies and gentlemen, quiet please, as we begin the auction."

Her gavel hit the block again. "Lot number 50 is a water-color by Jan Ramseier titled *Venice Water Scene with Buildings*. I can start the bidding at…"

Sigmund and his father entered the eighteenth-century gallery in the heart of Zürich's historic Old Town. Hearing active bidding from the adjacent hall, they eyed the handful of people still milling about the lobby. Spotting a familiar face, they went over to say hello.

"Claus, it's been a while." Sigmund reached out his hand. The sparkle of a gold cufflink caught his friend's eye. "Are you bidding today?" Sigmund asked.

"Yes. The lot that interests me is one of the first to come to the block," Claus said in a quiet voice, as if he feared being overheard. "I'm using a bidding proxy," he whispered. "I fear showing my face in the auction hall will cost me more money. I arrived late, and now I'm hiding out here until the bidding on my lot is over."

Claus continued. "You are both looking well. I watched William jump at Saignelégier recently. He took home some money that day."

"Yes, it's been quite a season," Andrew said with a smile.

"I chatted with him after his ride," Claus said. "He told me he's in college now and is living at home. That horse he's riding is a stunner.

"You know my daughter is an artist, and doing a bang-up job painting horses on the circuit." Claus told them.

"Didn't I catch her work on the cover of H&H a few months back?" Sigmund asked.

"You did." Claus beamed. "I'm surprised you're reading horse mags, Sigmund."

"It's difficult to avoid the covers, Claus; they're spread all over the house," Sigmund said with a smile.

Claus reached into his coat pocket and handed Sigmund his daughter's business card. "If you are interested," he said, "she has a booth on corporate row at the major shows."

"Thank you, Claus." Sigmund examined the card. "I'll be at Hallenstadion with William next month. I'll make a point to see her."

"What's this Zen business?" Claus asked.

Sigmund smiled. "It seems my son has acquired a nick-name from his fans."

Then Claus paused, hearing the auctioneer's voice rise. "Are we all done at 250,000? Fair warning…the bid is 250,000 Swiss francs…anymore? I am selling."

The gavel sounded. "Sold to the lady on my left; paddle number 104. Thank you very much."

Claus grinned. "That's me! I'm paddle 104!"

"Congratulations," Sigmund said.

"I'm sorry, I've got to go. We'll talk after the auction." Claus rushed away.

The Griegg men took seats in the auction hall behind an associate they had arranged to meet there that evening. They observed the proceedings with interest, assembled with a hundred-plus attendees in the room.

A dozen or more people bid anonymously via Tremblay's staff using telephones set up along the mezzanine. Those phone lines opened the auction to all corners of the world.

Zen

The skilled auctioneer held the pulse of the room at her command. Both the pace and the number of bidders, made the men optimistic for the lots they'd come to oversee.

It was actually five lots that brought them to the auction that evening. Each one resulted from a case the Grieggs' company handled in 1995. The woman seated in front of them, Joan Shulman, headed a project for Mossad called "Operation Boomerang," which connected the Israelis to that same investigation. Shulman was equally eager to hear the bidding on those particular works of art.

The auctioneer announced the first of those lots. "Lot 61, ladies and gentlemen, is a drawing by Rodin. This is from his series of *Cambodian Dancers*. I bring your attention to discoloration along the right edge, as noted in our condition report."

She continued. "Auguste Rodin is considered to be the originator of modern sculpture—an accolade that can overshadow the innovative quality of his works in other media.

"Rodin created his series of Cambodian dancers in 1906, as he followed the royal ballet troop from Paris to Marseilles. With no drawing material with him, the artist purchased butcher paper and pencils to produce more than one-hundred-fifty drawings that captured the graceful hands, flowing tunics, and serene Zen-like energy of the dancers.

"We see here a charming composition from that series. Because of the damage, this drawing might appeal to bidders who thought a Rodin would be out of their reach.

"Can I start the bidding at 8,000 francs? Do I have 8,000 francs, 8,000…do I have 6,000…is there anyone at 6,000? Ladies and Gentlemen, can I have 6,000 francs for this lovely Rodin? I will have to pass…there; I have 6 on the phone. Thank you, Tamzin.

"Now I have 8,000 in the room. Do I have 10,000? Is there anyone at 10,000? I have 10,000 francs on the phone. Do I have 12,000?

"Is there any interest at 12,000 francs? I have 12, now 14, from the mezzanine." The auctioneer's hands danced as she acknowledged the bidders with clear rhythm and exact timing.

5

"Can I have 16,000 francs? Is there anyone at 16? Fair warning, I have a bid of 14,000 francs on the telephone. Is there any advance on that? I am selling at 14,000 francs..."

The gavel pounded.

The auctioneer said, "Sold at 14,000 francs. Can I see the paddle? That is number 139 on the sale of the Rodin dancer."

Sigmund whispered to his father, "That's a great price, don't you think?"

Andrew nodded. "There was significant damage."

"Next is Lot 62, a Federica Champoux oil painting titled *The Sewing Circle*." The auctioneer walked over to the painting.

"Ms. Champoux is an original member of the impressionist movement that started in Paris during the mid-1800s. Best known for her plein-air watercolors, *The Sewing Circle* is an example of her early works in oil.

"While unsigned, as many of Champoux's initial oils are, this painting carries a strong provenance, so we have validated this piece as a Federica Champoux original. Can I start the bidding at 8,000 francs? I have 8,000, do I have 10,000?"

Lot 62 was the second painting of interest to Sigmund and his father. The bidding shot to 16,000 francs, surpassing Tremblay's estimate. A telephone bidder dominated the room with rapid responses.

The room then went quiet as bidders shook their heads and laid down their paddles. The auctioneer announced fair warning before pounding her gavel.

"Sold at 16,000 francs to paddle number 139," she said.

That peaked Sigmund's curiosity. Tilting his head toward his father, he asked, "What are the odds that the same bidder would overpay for two of our lots?"

"Interesting," Andrew replied.

Up next was Lot 83. It was an early piece by the Dutch impressionist Johan Verhoeven called *Picnic Unspoiled by Rain*.

The auctioneer elaborated, "This charming genre painting depicts a fanciful young couple lying on a blanket under a storefront canopy. The artist deftly captures a turn-of-the-century village scene.

Zen

"Tremblay's presale advertisements have peaked interest in this lovely painting, so we can open the bidding at 150,000 francs," she stated.

Bidding ended at 325,000 francs, without notice from paddle number 139 on the telephone.

Likewise, Lot 94, another masterpiece, opened at 90,000 francs and sold at 165,000 without Tamzin raising her hand as directed by paddle 139.

The Grieggs' last lot of interest, Lot number 305, came next. The auctioneer started the bidding. "Lot 305 is by Swiss artist Anders Zaugg. It is a charming piece called *Lady in Gold*. Despite a recent restoration, our condition report makes clear that damage remains throughout.

"I can say with confidence, however, this is a fetching piece for anyone to display. I will start the bidding at 5,000. Can I have 5,000 francs?"

There was no interest, so the auctioneer repeated, "This is an Anders Zaugg, ladies and gentlemen; I'd like to start it at 5,000…anyone? Can I have 5,000 francs?"

Still, she could not generate interest.

Tamzin sat motionless, with the telephone's receiver fixed to her ear.

To her left, the auctioneer heard a patron utter meekly, "I'll go 3,000 francs."

Pointing her finger at the voice, she said, "I have 3,000 francs. Can I have 4,000?" The auctioneer looked around the room. "Is there anyone at 4,000?

"Are we done? Fair warning, I will have to pass at 3,000. I need 5,000, ladies and gentlemen."

Tamzin lifted paddle number 139, chased by an employee on another telephone line.

"I have interest from the mezzanine at 5,000. I recognize Tamzin, as I saw her paddle first."

The auctioneer looked at their other employee, sitting in the mezzanine. "Do I have 6?" That person waved her off.

Sigmund whispered to his father, "The bid is to paddle number 139."

The auctioneer announced fair warning. "I have 5,000 on the telephone…any advance? I'm selling."

Sigmund raised his hand and said, "6,000 francs." Not planning to buy that day, he had no paddle to display. The painting didn't interest him, but paddle number 139 did.

"I have 6,000. Can I have 7,000?"

The telephone bidder returned 7. The activity prompted another bidder in the room, to catch the auctioneer's eye. "I give priority to the room." She looked at Tamzin. "Would you like 8,000?"

Tamzin nodded.

"I have 8,000 francs from the mezzanine. Do I have 10,000?" The auctioneer canvassed the room. "I have 10,000 from the lady to my left. Do I have 12,000?"

Sigmund remained quiet with his eyes on the mezzanine until Tamzin raised paddle 139.

"I have 12,000. Can I have 14,000?"

Andrew watched as his son raised his hand.

Sigmund and paddle number 139 continued the to-and-fro in 2,000 franc increments until paddle 139 accepted 20,000, to which Sigmund shouted back, "25,000 francs."

The audience fluttered with excitement to see who had volunteered such an impressive bid for a damaged painting by an inconsequential artist.

Determined to keep control of the room, the auctioneer struck her gavel.

"Quiet, please. I have 25, do I have 30?"

That's when things went haywire. Tamzin gave a puzzled look to the auctioneer. Her phone line had gone dead.

The gavel ended any confusion.

"Sold to?" the auctioneer asked, straining to get a clear view of the bidder.

Sigmund stood to identify himself.

"I sell the *Lady in Gold* to Mr. Sigmund Griegg for 25,000 Swiss francs." She appeared mystified. Why would anyone as experienced as Sigmund or Andrew Griegg pay that amount for a damaged Zaugg?

Their friend from Mossad turned around with equal astonishment. "What's going on?"

"I have no idea," Sigmund said, "but my gut is telling me to find out."

Driving back to the office, Sigmund took a call on his cell phone. "Sigmund Griegg," he said.

"Sigmund, something's wrong with Niedermeyer. He's despondent; I think he's been crying. He won't talk to me, and Boris is out with a client. Ian and Christopher are in a meeting with BKW Energie."

"All right, Sabine, we're just ten minutes out. Stay with him until we arrive."

Andrew listened with concern.

"Sabine's worried about Niedermeyer. She thinks he's been crying." Sigmund told his father.

"Should we call our doctor?" Andrew asked.

"Let's see him first," Sigmund stated. He looked in the rearview mirror and pulled out into faster-moving traffic.

When they arrived at Ninety-Six Hochbaumstrasse, they found Sabine sitting with Niedermeyer as he rested his forehead into his hands atop his desk.

Andrew held his son back to take the lead. "What's going on, Leo? Talk to us."

That was the first time Sabine had heard anyone call him Leo. He was always Niedermeyer to everyone that knew him.

"I don't want to talk." Niedermeyer told Andrew.

"Well, you have to. We're your friends and we're concerned." Andrew pulled up a chair, placing his hand on his longtime colleague's back. "We're not going anywhere."

They kept silent until Niedermeyer lifted his head and, without eye contact with anyone, he announced, "Alexander Brandenberger has died." He choked as the words left his throat. "I'm sorry, but saying it out loud has made it so real."

"We're sorry, Niedermeyer," Sigmund said. "We know your friendship with Brandenberger goes back a long way."

Niedermeyer sobbed. "He was far more than my friend, Sigmund. I loved him, and I want you to call him Alexander."

"Excuse me. I didn't know Alexander, except in passing. But, Leo, your loss is our loss. Tell us how we can help," Sigmund said with sincerity.

Intensely private, Niedermeyer had never shared anything personal with his work family in the fifty-plus years he had spent as the Grieggs' librarian and archivist. Being enigmatic was a badge Niedermeyer wore with pride.

But once, perhaps ten years prior, Andrew had glimpsed the men in an intimate embrace during the friend's visit to the Grieggs' office.

It happened late one evening, when Niedermeyer believed everyone had gone home. In the darkened library, neither of the men saw Andrew's fleeting appearance in the doorway.

"It wasn't just that I loved him." Niedermeyer stumbled over his words. "We've loved each other for many years now. Alexander has no family outside of cousins in Germany, and they've never been close. In many ways, I was Alexander's only family.

"I will need to make the arrangements for his funer…" Niedermeyer couldn't finish his sentence.

"Let me help you," Sabina said. She wasn't comfortable calling him Leo. That would be a privilege left to the Grieggs.

"I'm embarrassed for you to see me like this."

"You are grieving a loved one," Andrew said.

"We want to help. Where is Alexander now?" Sigmund asked. "Is there anything we must handle tonight?"

"I don't believe so. I'm told that he died early this afternoon. An associate found him when making a delivery to his business. They've taken him to a funeral home." Niedermeyer burst into tears again and sobbed aloud.

Sabine looked up at Sigmund and Andrew. The anguish in Niedermeyer's voice generated concern for their friend and colleague who was older, with health concerns of his own.

"Alexander lived alone, and worked from his home," Niedermeyer rambled. "He kept a note card pinned in his kitchen. It listed his attorney's name and my name with our contact info in case of an emergency. The attorney called me a short time ago."

"Why don't you give me his attorney's number so we can put things in motion?" Andrew requested.

"I'm afraid you've caught me quite out of sorts. I now recall that Alexander prearranged his funeral. He once joked that all I had to do was show up...I wasn't thinking straight a minute ago. What's wrong with me?"

"You're in shock," Sigmund stated.

"Alexander was always so organized...like me. I find myself in a right state of confusion."

"I can stay with you tonight, if you like?" Sabine added, "I don't want you to be alone."

"Thank you, Sabine, but I'm fine on my own."

"Do you know what happened to Alexander?" Andrew asked. "Can you talk about it?"

"The police called the medical examiner to the house because Alexander had an injury from a letter opener found near the body. But that turned out to be inconsequential.

"With our business being what it is, I should say there was no evidence of foul play. He just died.

"Alexander's doctor concurred with the ME and listed the cause of death as heart disease without an autopsy. He collapsed while opening mail. He cut himself as he fell."

Niedermeyer wiped away more tears.

"After my health incident last year, we had talked about our physical conditions.

"Alexander discovered he had an irregular heart rate that put him at a higher risk for a stroke or heart failure, but he always felt so fit and healthy that he paid no attention and never took precautions.

"In recent days, he felt energized over the acquisition of a collection of rare books. That's his business, you know—buying and selling rare books and manuscripts.

"Alexander told me this particular buy was quite a coup. He had worked for several years to secure the deal when the collector called out of the blue, ready to make a quick sale.

"That was what brought the associate to his home earlier today. He was delivering the books. Alexander never got to see them; he was already dead on the floor.

"Daily life can make one lose track of the bigger picture," Niedermeyer mused. "One never imagines how swiftly death can come."

The group pondered that thought.

"I know my relationship with Alexander will come as a shock. He didn't care about secrecy; he lived openly and tried to get me to do the same. I couldn't do that."

Sigmund stated, "Leo, you have cloistered yourself in your library for far too long. It has been part of your charm, frankly, but the world has changed since you were a young man…much more than you might realize.

"The stigma over such relationships is not what it used to be. You must know Alexander was highly regarded in his field, as are you." Sigmund told his friend and colleague. "We approach the turn of a new century; few people still carry a bias for such personal matters."

"My business contacts still talk, Sigmund. People whisper behind the scenes, 'did you hear this, did you know that?' " Niedermeyer wiped his eyes again. "I could never bear to be the object of any person's dirty gossip."

Overcome by the day's events, Niedermeyer said softly, "I'd like to be alone now. With all that's happened, I suddenly feel tired."

"Sabine, you go home. We'll sleep here tonight." Sigmund rubbed Niedermeyer on his back. "We're upstairs if you need anything, my friend."

The building at Ninety-Six Hochbaumstrasse had been a home for the Grieggs since Sigmund's fourth generation grandfather moved his family from Scotland in the 1850s.

In search of a better life for his family, Andrew Webster Gow developed an alternative method for dyeing wool, which transformed the Swiss textile industry. Almost overnight, Gow became a wealthy homeowner. They still maintained an apartment above the offices.

As they entered their private space, Andrew told Sigmund of his past happenstance.

"And you never thought to tell me? I can't believe it," Sigmund responded.

"It was never my place to say," Andrew said. "It's always been up to Niedermeyer. I merely respected his privacy."

"It may sound morbid to mention now, but I'm glad to learn he had love in his life," Sigmund said. "Everyone deserves that, but for him think his relationship would trouble us is disconcerting."

"I don't believe he thought of it quite that way," Andrew said. "Niedermeyer lives in his own world; we'll never fully understand him."

The Griegg offices and research library shared the first floor of the building, separated by a grand entrance gallery.

The library was Niedermeyer's domain. It was open to the public by appointment, although only a few researchers ever ventured inside.

Several years ago, and, at the time, unbeknownst to the Grieggs, Niedermeyer had a bed delivered to the building. He began sleeping in a discrete alcove off his library several days a week.

At some point, he gave up the lease on the Zürich bedsit where he had lived for fifty years, bringing all his belongings to the library. Neither Sigmund nor Andrew objected.

Niedermeyer had been a key man within the organization since Andrew's father, Wolfgang Griegg, hired him. Together they created a business model around a modern-day vision of intelligence gathering and the analysis of intellectual material.

His photographic recall rarely failed him. He could recite minute details from those early cases with Wolf with the same accuracy as the particulars of current cases—that is, before Alexander's lawyer sent him into a tailspin. Now, he seemed a changed man. While the Grieggs often went out of their way to accommodate their bohemian friend, they knew he would need much more of their help in the weeks to come.

Days later, the Grieggs and their staff joined Niedermeyer at the funeral for his beloved friend. The small church was full. Niedermeyer needed a seat brought to the gravesite. Sabine held his hand, over the older man's objection. By this point, they all worried about their friend's state of mind.

Witnessing his self-imposed secret life spill out into the open proved too much for Niedermeyer to bear, particularly at his age. Emotionally drained and physically weak, there were no more tears to shed, just a lifeless stare when anyone came to pay their respects.

After the interment, Alexander's attorney asked Sigmund if someone would drive Niedermeyer to the Brandenberger estate, about a half hour outside of the city.

The other mourners would walk to a gathering at a nearby restaurant under Alexander's plan.

"Niedermeyer may not be up for that," Sigmund said.

"Yes." Niedermeyer overheard the men and volunteered his response. "I'd like my co-workers to come with me. Is that all right, Sigmund?"

Alexander's home was on the shore of Zürichsee, the lake of Zürich. The four-story historic mansion was built in 1826 by his industrialist ancestor six generations prior.

It served as the family's lakefront retreat at a time when most influential Zürich households kept a second home just a short distance from the old boundaries of the city.

Alexander grew up in lavish style. Then, changing with the times as such opulence became untenable, his father renovated the estate in the 1950s, selling off most of the land to finance its modernization.

After that, the family occupied only the ground-floor rooms. Luxury apartments and studios filled the upper levels, producing a good income for Alexander's thrifty father in his later years.

That was considered gauche back in the day. Nevertheless, it proved wise, as his son inherited the management of the estate.

Alexander rented the flats to like-minded artsy friends and associates. The address soon gained a reputation for its unconventional parties in the 60s and 70s, from which he smartly pulled back when AIDS emerged in the 1980s.

That was Alexander's wake-up call. He settled down and focused on what would become his life's work—the love of literature and historical documents. He had lived on the ground floor alone, immersed in his books, since his mother died in 1988.

Each time Alexander visited with friends in a fourth-floor studio, he would gaze out across the lake, remembering his mother curse, "I'll never view the water again" from what was, in her day, the ladies smoking lounge.

It was after his wild days ended that Alexander befriended Niedermeyer. They shared a love of books.

Niedermeyer was aware that Alexander came from a family of means, but when Sabine helped him from the car, the massive villa towering before them was unexpected.

"Wow," Sabine said.

"Alexander didn't like to talk about money," Niedermeyer explained. "He made it sound like the family wealth was long gone. He called his current lifestyle the 'comparative Dark Ages.' In hindsight, I guess that was misleading."

As they entered the foyer, the attorney asked the group to show themselves around while he spoke to Niedermeyer in the library.

"No," Niedermeyer voiced firmly. "These people are like family to me, and I'd like them to hear whatever you have to tell me."

"Very well," the attorney said. "Follow me." He signaled the group to walk past the floor-to-ceiling windows overlooking the back courtyard.

The water of Zürichsee appeared a deep blue over the pollarded centuries-old trees—a pruning method seemingly designed to accommodate such views.

When everyone was seated around the library's table, the lawyer said that Alexander Brandenberger had bequeathed all of his personal possessions to Jerely Leopold Niedermeyer.

In addition, he had given him the life use of his home. The lawyer stated that his practice handled all aspects of running the estate, including maintenance of the house, grounds, and rental apartments.

"Those provisions will continue," the lawyer said, "and you can live on the property worry free."

"Alexander wanted me to live here?" Niedermeyer asked in bewilderment.

"Yes," the lawyer stated.

"How is that possible? My home and my life are in the Old Town."

"You never discussed this arrangement?"

"No. I've never been here before." Casting his eyes across the bookshelves filled with volumes of rare literature and relics of antiquity, Niedermeyer said, "I am in disbelief."

"It is my understanding that Alexander expected you to catalogue his library and his artwork. Upon his death, he wanted you to place the collections at schools or museums, however you saw fit.

"The villa will, in time, transfer to his distant relatives. But Alexander didn't want any of his belongings to pass down to them. You can keep anything for yourself without concern over its value.

"In addition, your friend stipulated that his family would forgo any access to the property for as long as you lived here. He ordered that they must wait for you to vacate the home."

"Why did he never tell me?" Niedermeyer asked feebly.

"That's a question I can't answer," said the lawyer.

"I sleep in an alcove off my library. My entire life is there, in *my* library, in the Grieggs' office building." Niedermeyer's face was again drained of color.

"Alexander joked that he bought and he sold books for other people. But for himself—he only bought, never sold."

Niedermeyer looked to Sigmund. "I'm afraid I'm overwhelmed by all of this. Might I have a glass of water?"

"My apologies," the lawyer interrupted. "I should have offered refreshments when you arrived."

As the lawyer stood, Sigmund promised his friend that, "Nothing needs to be resolved today."

"Well, there's one more thing." The attorney took a letter from his pocket before leaving the room. "This is for you."

He pushed the robin egg blue envelope across the table. "It's from Alexander. No one knows its contents, not even me. Perhaps you'll find some assurances inside."

Niedermeyer took hold of the envelope inscribed *Leo* in Alexander's distinctive handwriting.

Returning to the library, the attorney said, "No doubt I've given you much to digest. Why don't you call me when you're ready to talk?" He gave Niedermeyer a glass of water and then laid a tray on the table with glasses for everyone.

Still holding the blue envelope, Niedermeyer said, "I can't open this right now." He folded the letter into the breast pocket of his overcoat. After drinking some water, he asked to go home...wondering if he was already there.

2

Months Later, Near Zürich, Switzerland

"Stop!" Zen yelled out, reaching for the woman's arm to bring her to a halt. "You shouldn't be leading this horse with a chain over his nose."

"What's the matter with you? I'm just taking him back to his stall."

"What's wrong is that I saw you snap the chain shank on his nose to slow him down." Zen cradled his horse's muzzle between his palms. The horse inhaled the constituents of the lavender oil that Zen rubbed on his wrists before working with his horses.

"Tiger is a sensitive horse. You should not subject him to such harsh treatment," Zen stated. "If you can't keep up with the stride of a horse his size, then you have no business walking him."

"Talk to the barn manager, I've got work to do," she said, flinging the lead shank at Zen as she turned away.

William "Zen" Griegg had come from nowhere to shoot up the ranks of the European show jumping circuit. William's practice of meditating in his horse's stall before an event, combined with his calm demeanor in the saddle, led *In the Ribbons* magazine to dub him "Zen" in their debut article on the young rider.

The moniker inspired onlookers to chant Zen the next time William entered the arena, no doubt irritating the more seasoned riders.

William placed a respectable third that day with clean rounds, but he squandered precious seconds in the jump-off when he drifted wide approaching the final fence.

When questioned in the post-competition press flurry, William asked his fans, "No—please remain quiet to respect all the competitors." Regardless, he remained known as Zen within the horse community from that day forward, and the chants continued.

"What happened in the jump-off, Zen?" asked *Euro Horse* magazine's Stacey Whitlamb. "I thought you had it won?"

"Stacey, watch the ride later on video," Zen said, as if everyone had his insight. "You'll notice that Tiger landed off balance from the oxer. I had to take him wide to the vertical." But no one could detect the horse's imbalance. It was something measurable only to Zen.

"Nevertheless, you traveled *so* wide," Whitlamb repeated. "Don't you think you could have balanced your horse and still squeaked out the win?"

"Perhaps that's what another rider might have done, but Tiger needed those extra seconds to finish," Zen responded.

Flying Oblique was Zen's mount—AKA Tiger. The 17.2 hand Thoroughbred gelding with a solid body hadn't always been a perfect ride. Tiger came to Zen with a checkered past.

In fact, some riders and trainers Tiger now competed against had rejected buying the horse in years past.

Despite his incredible athleticism when riderless in the jumping chute, Tiger had a history of panicking over fences with even the most experienced rider in the saddle. Similarly, there were times he couldn't contain himself to trot a low cross rail.

Labeled dangerous, no trainer wanted the risk of schooling the horse. In any outburst, Tiger could unseat his rider, putting the person out of commission for weeks or longer. Word spread that the horse was unsafe.

As the horse's asking price dropped lower and lower, Tiger found a home as a dressage prospect at the prep school William attended during his education in England.

Just by luck, William was the first rider to climb on Tiger shortly after he arrived. The bond between horse and rider was instant and palpable.

Despite Tiger's reputation over fences, William couldn't help himself. This was the horse of his dreams. He knew it. William called home to get his father's permission to buy the discredited horse called Tiger.

William started riding as a young child. His father had made sure that his son schooled on skilled horses to guide his riding education over the years. He trusted his son's judgement to take on a risky horse like Tiger at this time.

Perhaps his son would enjoy dressage and would not continue showing jumpers. It was William's choice. After all, the sensitivity both horse and rider possessed was an asset for dressage. While in the show jumping arena, sensitivity could be a double-edged sword.

It's true that you can have a sensitive jumper, but that sensitivity must be counterbalanced with aggressiveness and a ruggedness to navigate the big jumps and technical courses presented on the Grand Prix circuit. Few sensitive horses can perform at that level.

The fast pace of the competition combined with split-second turns and the necessity to jump from less than perfect distances will, more often than not, overwhelm a sensitive horse. The same is true for the rider.

This didn't concern William. Both he and Tiger were complex personalities, and they clicked. Once William got to know Tiger, he would decide which discipline to follow.

They spent their first weeks together hacking in the woods and grasslands surrounding the school. While other riders had clamped onto Tiger awaiting the next explosion, William relinquished the reins to allow the horse to experience the freedom conveyed by a trusting rider.

Tiger betrayed that trust frequently in those early days, but as William kept his composure and listened to his horse, they connected on a primal level. It was an approach William had been studying.

In the 1980s, a number of American cowboys started writing about a concept they called "natural horsemanship." The theory rejected the use of force, expressing a "kinder and gentler" approach to horse training, one that was developed by observing the animal's natural behavior.

These cowboys suggested that riders learn to copy the horse's conduct and mannerisms used when interacting with other horses.

By the 1990s, trainers had flooded the American market with their own versions of "natural" training. The approach sought to build harmony between horse and rider in a way that differed from what William's trainers taught.

William learned when the rider makes the wrong response difficult for the horse and the desired response easy, the horse will choose the easier path.

The cowboys wrote that horses don't make bad choices on purpose; they just misinterpret what they're asked to do. It's a simple concept, really—a natural concept. But simple doesn't make it easy.

In the early days, many trainers attempted to teach something they didn't fully understand themselves. It took time for the most talented among them to rise to the top.

To succeed, the rider must learn to connect with the horse at that innate level. It's not something every rider can do—but it's something William understood instinctively.

Then William found the writings of a little-known trainer named George Hodgson Reed. Reed's gift was in translating the works of the "old masters" of classical dressage into terms that the modern rider could easily follow.

Without disparaging natural horsemanship, Reed points out that in practice, many of the "natural" methods just forced the horse into submission by other means.

Reed's vision of the old masters, that included a distinct awareness of energy flow, made sense to William.

"When you learn to link to the horse's energy, the horse will respond in kind. That's when humans can enter the horse's domain, on the horse's terms."

William quoted Reed with a leap of faith, because he hadn't yet experienced that sacred bond with any horse. It was a bond based on energy flow.

"It's a spiritual connection akin to yin and yang, and for a rider, nothing compares to that feeling—it's a centaur-like union between horse and human."

Again, William articulated Reed's concepts with faith... because he trusted he could have that feeling someday...and it would be with Tiger.

The trainer explained that the horse was a prey animal. Thousands of years in the evolutionary process had imprinted a positive response, or a negative reaction to energy within their DNA.

When a horse perceives harm, it triggers a discharge from their nervous system—it's the "fight-or-flight mechanism." Humans have it, as well. It's just not as dominant.

When a rider repeatedly sparks that hard-wired prey-animal reaction to negative energy, it will, to some degree, break the animal's spirit. On the other hand, if you connect through their wired-in comfort zone, the horse will respond with positive energy flow. You move together—in a more natural union.

This was how William interpreted his horse's reaction to jumping with a rider on his back. Someone had tried to break Tiger's spirit. Putting it another way, Tiger's life-force had been too strong and couldn't be broken. The horse continued to fight back whenever he felt threatened.

When any horse has such a fierce visceral reaction, a peaceful union is unattainable. William knew he had to connect to Tiger on a different level. George Hodgson Reed presented the path for him to follow.

Equestrians like Reed have an instinctive ability to speak with horses. It's termed "whispering." And, while it's said that true whisperers are born and not taught, the link between species emerges through energy...and anyone can be trained to feel energy at a heightened level. This gives everyone the ability to strengthen their relationship with animals.

That's why William began practicing the disciplines of tai chi and qi gong. He believed that the slow grounded movement of these ancient postures would make his energy field more welcoming to his horses—all the while improving his riding through better breathing, relaxation, and balance.

William's decision to follow George Hodgson Reed put Tiger on the exact path needed to overcome his problems.

While William's goal was to one day compete in the Olympic Games, a group of students in Zürich were devoted to a very different game…

The True Crime Club

*I*t started as a lark in school. After reading legendary authors like Agatha Christie and Sir Arthur Conan Doyle, the notion of crafting a story around mysterious incidents or crimes captured the imaginations of a group of students. The Mystery Readers' Club was formed as they entered their third year of upper secondary school.

The only prerequisite to enroll in the club was a voracious appetite for reading whodunits. They read and dissected one mystery book each week. It was serious. If you didn't keep up, even during exam weeks, you were out.

If you dropped out, they did not welcome you back. Needless to say, their membership fluctuated.

In the club's first years, its founding members came of age as occupations in criminology reached new heights of sophistication. Science and computerization reigned supreme as forensic technicians joined police departments worldwide.

Documented in television programs like the CSI series, audiences were fascinated by the job of the criminologist, even if what they portrayed on the TV screen was skewed toward entertainment. Similarly, the Mystery Reader's Club was fixated on crime *as* entertainment.

So while the forensic revolution made getting away with a crime harder…the Mystery Readers' Club felt challenged to study the ways that criminals could outsmart even the best policing methods and scientific testing.

Simultaneously, another revolutionary transformation was underway. The global system of interconnected computer networks—"the internet" changed how we communicated. The World Wide Web was born.

The students realized they were no longer confined to the boundaries of their physical location. As they prepared to go off to college—the club hit the internet.

They created a simple website that attracted like-minded people from all walks of life, ages, and countries. They were stunned by how quickly their membership grew.

In recognition of their expanded audience, they made more changes. The students' focus shifted away from fictional mystery/thrillers to the budding genre of real, or true crime.

The club changed its name to the True Crime Club. Their website listed its mission as a passion for reading, dissecting, and solving crimes.

The True Crime Club's actual pursuit: How to plan and commit the perfect crime.

*I*t was about that time that William Griegg returned from England to attend college in Switzerland. He lived on the family's country estate, some twenty-five kilometers outside the Zürich metro area. He brought his three horses home with him.

Tiger shared the farm with Pendragon and Mylilsecret. The older horses now enjoyed semi-retirement, grazing on the lush grassy slopes by day and relaxing in the comfort of nicely bedded stalls each night.

Occasionally, all three generations of Griegg men would trek out across the mountainous terrain next to their small farm. It was a happy time.

While Pen and Secret had been excellent mounts to teach William to ride at an advanced level, it was Tiger's intelligence and athletic ability that drew the attention of the right people at the right time.

Tiger's recognition on the show jumping circuit was, however, more challenging than you might think. During the 1990s, trainers bypassed Thoroughbreds for the middle-weight breeds.

Called "warmbloods," these horses were bred to meet the needs of a particular discipline, rather than to perpetuate an ancestral bloodline of any specific breed. Warmbloods became jumping champions of choice, worldwide.

William never concerned himself with any disparagement of Thoroughbreds. It was those distinct qualities of energy, agility, and fortitude that made Tiger stand out from the crowd. No one could deny his athleticism—or the powerful connection he had with his rider. The training techniques of George Hodgson Reed worked.

To be honest, Zen's initial success with Tiger made him a bit arrogant. Highlighting their first big win, he removed the bridle and rode into the stadium to claim his award with just a strap around Tiger's neck. It was the first time any rider had attempted such a stunt, and both this horse and rider were cocky enough to pull it off.

As for the competition, it provided yet another reason for the other riders to dislike them. Let's just say William set himself up for many "frenemies" in his brief career. Although William was a very likable young man, he allowed few of his contemporaries close enough to find that out.

After a season "in the ribbons" at the big-name shows, William found himself with access to the best trainers. Lara Bless, head trainer for the Equestrian Federation show jumping team, kept a close eye on his progress and often commented on his rounds.

Zen

Soon after, William began riding with Lara's protégé, Melanie Pfenninger, under Lara's guidance.

They all got on well. Lara groomed William for the long term, and Melanie understood that William differed from her other students. She encouraged him to explore the spiritual aspect of his riding.

Admitting there was nothing she could teach "Zen," Pfenninger focused her efforts to bring increased style and sophistication to his jumping form.

William received his spiritual guidance from a man named Asher Rechsteiner. Ash was a seventy-something-year-old man who communicated with animals.

The Swiss riding community knew of Ash. That included Lara and Melanie. Few people took the old guy seriously. The amateur riders affectionately called him "quirky," while the professionals went straight for a term like "bat-crap crazy" to describe him.

Ash was not famous and didn't want to be. There were no Asher Rechsteiner books or videos to buy. A friend of a friend had told Zen how Ash had transformed an untrust-worthy dog into a child-safe family pet. Hearing that, Zen sought out Ash to help with Tiger…horses were Ash's forte.

To Zen's astonishment, Ash instinctively knew what George Hodgson Reed conveyed in his training. This made the fellowship between William and the older man immediate and intense.

Ash developed William's understanding of being "in the moment" with his horses. That concept is at the core of connecting with the horse, since it is how horses live—with no distractions from the past, or expectations for the future. It means living in the present, within your surroundings.

In other words, Ash taught William to communicate with Tiger as if he were another horse. Something promoted by natural horsemanship.

Still, Tiger needed time to reach his full potential because, while horses live in the moment, they hold memories of the past, both good and bad.

William had learned early on that applying a chain over Tiger's nose would unleash his worst conduct. This meant William had to train Tiger without causing him to relive any of the negative memories that had made him dangerous.

Building trust was the only pathway for Tiger to leave that behavior behind.

William's brilliance was how he blended aspects of natural horsemanship with the spiritualism taught by Ash, and the energy work of George Hodgson Reed, which included the art of classical dressage—what some call artistic riding.

The result of this fusion was still in progress, but it was elevating William and Tiger to an extraordinary level. Watching them ride now was like viewing art in motion.

Asher Rechsteiner lived a simple country life with his wife. Their children were grown and now had children of their own. Their home was tucked into the remains of rural life surrounding the Zürich metro area.

No one in Ash's family showed any interest in his work. His wife cared for their farm animals, but her interests lay elsewhere. So, working with Zen was a distinct pleasure. He was a kindred spirit.

While Asher's grandchildren found little time to spend with him, Zen made Ash his priority.

Their lessons involved walking the fields on the Griegg estate with Tiger in tow, as Ash enlightened Zen on subjects as diverse as meditation and spiritual energy, to baking bread, to living an honorable life.

It seemed Ash had knowledge and opinions on almost every subject. William had never met anyone like him.

Ash was just as captivated by their relationship. He knew Zen had only scratched the surface of his potential. Zen had undreamed-of abilities both on and off the back of a horse, and Ash assumed the role as his mentor.

Zen

One day, in the stall with Tiger, Ash told Zen, "Concentrate to lower your breathing into your pelvic core; you know this to be your center of balance. In addition, it's the body's central furnace and source of power. It's where 'Chi' lives.

"Now, in your mind, visualize your riding position and pretend to breathe down into your horse's spine. Bring all your thoughts down and, still in your mind, connect to your horse's body. This is how to speak to your horse."

That's when Tiger came over and lowered his head to nudge Zen's hip.

"Do you see what's happening?" Ash said. "Your energy has drawn Tiger to you. He wants to be close, just as horses like to stand close to each other. This is how you build trust with Tiger." That lesson was a defining moment for both of them. While others called him Zen, Ash taught him to *be Zen*.

Zen respected trainers Lara and Melanie and knew he wouldn't get to the top without their guidance, but it was Ash who unleashed the astonishing teamwork between the rider and his horse.

Tiger remained on the Griegg estate during the summer months, where Sigmund had installed a top-notch outdoor arena for his son. When the weather turned cold, Zen took Tiger to the Federation facility to take advantage of the indoor arena and consistent instruction.

Because Tiger needed less time training than the other horses, Zen had the opportunity to school on a variety of mounts and build his experience as an all-around equestrian.

As if being proclaimed Zen by the press wasn't enough, the circuit reporters also focused on the purchase price of his horses. All his successful show jumpers had cost a fraction of what others paid for their champion mounts.

Some trainers interpreted this as another swipe against them. The group that wanted Zen's shooting star to burn out fast, grew larger and larger.

That seemed unlikely now. Zen and Tiger were competing in the Olympic preparatory events sooner than anyone thought possible.

This is why Tiger had been trailered to an airport quarantine facility to undergo a health screening before boarding a flight to the United States with other Olympic hopefuls.

Zen knew that handlers who were unfamiliar with the horses under their care, would routinely use a chain over the horse's nose, especially when leading a big horse like Tiger. The practice was commonplace.

So, Zen had spoken with the quarantine barn manager about Tiger's particular sensitivities before his arrival. And that's why he was so put out to see the handler yank the chain shank down on Tiger's nose. William was mad.

"It won't happen again," said the barn manager. He was rightly embarrassed that he hadn't properly communicated with his staff.

That was little comfort to Zen, who was already apprehensive about putting his horse on a plane. Any relapse in Tiger's conduct could be catastrophic while traveling.

Zen had wrestled with the notion of air transport for some time. He knew it would be necessary to compete at the top level, but what if Tiger reacted badly under the control of strangers? The thought was frightening.

Tiger had traveled from England to Switzerland by train through the Eurotunnel, or Chunnel, as it's known. Intellectually, Zen knew the statistics of air transport safety. After all, inflight horse management was exceptional by the late-90s.

Long gone were the days when a panicked animal would be euthanized over the Atlantic to avoid spooking the other horses onboard the plane. Flying was now safe.

Being a member of the Swiss contingency also provided comfort…and, above all, Zen would be on board the plane with his horse.

When it came right down to it, riding in the Olympics was his goal. William had the dream early on, before his fans gave him the moniker of Zen.

With Tiger, he had a horse to take him there—that's when the dream became a goal and, like it or not, flying was part and parcel to fulfill his endeavor.

Zen

Zen allowed himself a brief window of time for competition. If he could prove himself in America, he might be on the short list for the Olympic Games in Sydney, Australia. To wait four years for Athens was a non-starter. He wanted to begin a career in his family's business.

Zen would always ride and keep horses, but he didn't want the lifestyle of a professional rider. He aspired to win big and then retire from competing.

Outside the horse world, William intended to become the fourth generation of his family to work at number Ninety-Six Hochbaumstrasse, the site of Griegg Informationsdienst und Forschungsbibliothek. (The English translation: Information Services and Research Library.)

It was his legacy to rise up through the ranks, learn the business, and someday take over running the company… putting his stamp on its operation in the new century.

Perhaps he would pass the company down to his own children, someday. Many factors drove William to succeed; both equine sports and business ventures motivated him.

William admired his father and grandfather, and wanted to follow in their footsteps. While he never knew his great-grandfather, Wolfgang, he'd heard the family stories so often he could recite them by heart.

In Wolfgang's day, the business didn't even have a name. It was a one-man spying undertaking that worked in the dark corners within the seedier side of Zürich life. It was a time when laws were few and dirty deals prevailed.

Men, and occasionally women, paid to gain any advantage within their families or their businesses. Wolfgang Griegg's services were for sale to anyone with cash.

But over time those assignments disillusioned Wolfgang. He soon rejected jobs at cross-purposes with his own ethics. Wolf would bend the rules, but he didn't like being asked to break them.

Once established, Wolf limited his work to a few known entities and set out to hone his skill set as an investigator and curator of information.

He employed Niedermeyer to add a Forschungsbibliothek (research library), into the business.

William perceived the spirit of Wolf in both his restrained but debonair father and his gregarious grandfather. He saw himself somewhere in the middle.

William grew up likening his great-grandfather, who he called Wolfie, to a contemporary English spy named Sidney Reilly. Made famous as *Reilly Ace of Spies* in a series of books by Robin Bruce Lockhart, William learned as much as he could about the real-life Reilly.

That included watching reruns of the British TV drama series of the same name. *My dad resembles the actor playing Reilly,* he thought.

Occasionally, Sigmund had to tamp down his son's wild fantasies of what might have transpired at number Ninety-Six Hochbaumstrasse in Wolfgang's day—perhaps ginned up by the company's display case, containing Wolf's now disabled Browning Model 1900 semi-automatic pistol.

Nowadays, their establishment claimed their services were limited to research, which wasn't quite true. Their clients included governmental agencies, academia, and independent businesses worldwide.

However, there was more than met the eye of any viewer on their website. At times, people finding themselves in dire straits would seek help from the Grieggs—perhaps reminiscent of Wolfgang's day.

It had been two years since anyone so troubled had asked for help. That was when an American, Alana Eastwood, had discovered an unopened letter while clearing out her deceased grandfather's home in Germany.

The letter, addressed to a relative who had died in World War II, made a troublesome plea to reveal a secret hidden in a place called "the trap." Signed with the single name Franz, the envelope provided no return address.

It painted a bleak picture, suggesting only Alana's great-uncle, Helmut, would know the meaning of the words "the trap." Alana's imagination ran wild.

Someone had sealed the letter inside a wooden box for half a century. Alana felt a curious family obligation to solve the enigmatic puzzle…she wanted to set right what she perceived as a dreadful wrong.

But Alana had nothing to go on. Who was Franz? What was the trap? Why had no one opened the letter? How would she even start to find such answers?

When she sought out the help of a professor at the local university, he turned up dead the next day. Fearful that the German police would never connect a fifty-year-old letter to a current murder investigation, Alana drove from Tübingen to Zürich to ask Sigmund Griegg to uncover the truth.

She posed to Sigmund, "What secret from the war would still be worth killing over?"

It was a harrowing ordeal, but Sigmund and his team of investigators prevailed. They uncovered the secret of the trap. This represented the company where William Zen Griegg wanted a career.

He couldn't, however, know how this long-solved case involving Alana Eastwood would come back to haunt him in the days to come.

William Zen Griegg

William endured one of the most devastating losses a child can bear: the death of his mother. Like other children who suffer this type of loss, William found it difficult to make friends. Horses took the place of human contact.

Sigmund knew the suffering. His own mother had died of cancer when he was about William's age. His father, Andrew, had done the best he could, but it was never enough.

When Sigmund lost his wife, his grief had been so deep; he couldn't allow his son to grow up without a woman's love.

Sigmund did what he thought was right. He sent William to spend his school years with his maternal grandparents at their home in England.

Then, mourning his wife's death, Sigmund buried himself in his work, just as his father had done a generation before.

Sigmund and Andrew visited England whenever possible, but family time in Switzerland was limited to summers and school holidays. As history repeated itself, that wasn't enough for William, either.

William was quiet, but he wasn't shy. His father had sent his son's pony with him to England. Riding taught him to be assertive, providing the leadership that equines desire. He came up through the levels of the local Pony Club and later became one of the youngest to hold an A Test certification.

When William wasn't riding, he played with the older neighborhood children. He deemed the kids his age childish.

Then an elderly vicar moved next door. William was at an age to ask about God. Many of his friends attended church services, and some stayed longer for religious studies.

While his father and grandfather were ethical men, they were not churchgoers. Neither were the grandparents who raised him. The last time any of them had been to church was for William's mother's funeral service. This created curiosity over the new neighbor.

Even in retirement, the man of God routinely wore his clerical frocks—usually an old-fashioned cassock. When the young William ventured next door, he asked the man why he wore a black dress.

The vicar answered that and seemingly endless other questions without complaint. He regarded the boy's attention a delight. The two became friends.

Having an official explanation of death from a man whose job it was to know such things was a comfort to the boy who had lost his mother. They discussed life, as well.

William grew up more sensitive than most boys and, perhaps with the vicar's help, without emotional baggage over his loss. He returned to Switzerland to attend college a smart and intuitive young man with a determination to succeed in whatever the future held for him.

William had dubbed his grandfather *Grandrew* as soon as he began to talk. Grandad Andrew quickly shrank to the more manageable Grandrew, and like his own nickname, Zen, Andrew's moniker stuck with loving approval.

Even when William returned to Switzerland as a college student, he still referred to his grandfather that way.

*O*n this day, Grandrew met his grandson at the quarantine facility near the Zürich Airport to work out any last-minute logistics for the pending flight to the United States.

To maintain medical protocols, Andrew couldn't enter the quarantine barn, so William came out to tell him that he had all the details sorted out.

William was accompanied by the young woman the Equestrian Federation had assigned to groom for him on the American excursion. William and Val, as he introduced her, planned to dine out that evening.

"Come have dinner with us," William insisted.

"Oh no, you two have a nice evening. I have the other horses to take care of," Andrew said.

Andrew and Sigmund would meet up with their young man at Hamilton Farm the following week. Home of the United States Equestrian Foundation complex in Gladstone, New Jersey, Hamilton Farm provided both a national and international venue for equestrian events throughout the year.

Andrew recognized Val from the current show circuit. She was a newcomer at the A-level shows. The fact that she was an owner/rider with no sponsor suggested to Andrew she came from a family of means, yet he had read nothing of her ascension in the equestrian press.

Why would a rider of that level be grooming for my grandson? he thought. An analytical mind like his was always curious.

Unlike the seasoned competitors, younger riders (usually female), followed Zen in awe of both his riding ability and his rugged good looks. Zen could model the equestrian line for any of the posh companies that sponsored the Grand Prix events each year.

In fact, William had offers of sponsorships from those businesses, but had declined at his father's request.

"Leave the money for the competitors who need it," his father had said.

So, it wasn't surprising to Andrew that the groom looked smitten with his grandson. William seemed taken with her as well. The name "Val" had come up in conversation since talk of the trip began.

Now, witnessing the two of them interact, Andrew put two and two together—they were, or would soon be, an "item." He smiled at the thought.

"It's been nice to meet you, Val. Is that short for Valerie?"

"No, Valentina," she said.

"What is your surname, in case I need to track you down in New Jersey?"

"It's Abbatelli."

"Ah, you're Italian?"

"My father is. My mother is Swiss."

"We must talk again when we see each other at Hamilton Farm," Andrew suggested. "I'll look forward to continuing our conversation."

"Tell dad not to worry about me," Zen said.

"I will. Give Tiger a big kiss and call me if you need anything, William," Andrew said.

*T*he True Crime Club's basic website matured into a stylish meeting place for crime story buffs in no time, thanks to a computer science major at the University of Zürich named Rob Grazioli.

The website offered tabs to write or read book reviews, join chatrooms to discuss infamous crimes of the past, or get information on current criminal activity hitting the broadcast news worldwide.

No other website offered such variety to their members, and Rob gave the site a professional look that would have cost the club money had he not been able to apply his work toward college credit.

The club then recruited content administrators from many colleges worldwide, each designated with their own area of expertise. This all-volunteer site was a testament to the widespread interest in true crime, and it worked with surprising efficiency.

Another unique feature of the True Crime Club website was that members could submit their own crime fiction. Club members would then scrutinize each plot, poke holes, and explain how the writer could, would, or should get caught.

The mission statement for that portal urged members to…"fantasize the perfect crime." The club founders cheekily defined the flawless act of lawbreaking as: "Vast monetary gain, no one gets injured, and of utmost importance—you can totally get away with it!"

The students intended this description to challenge the imaginations of its members. They wanted to foster out-of-the-box reasoning. They constructed it like a computer game. Members would judge the crime plots submitted and grade the author's aptitude for criminal activity. It generated fierce competition. Members vied for the "criminal mastermind" designation. The website was addicting.

Sounds like fun, right? The members thought so. But there was a hidden agenda. The founders were building a databank of crime and the fatal flaws that got people caught.

The website also contained a doorway to a password-protected chatroom where the founding members of the club could communicate privately.

The students even devised an encryption code—a way to talk freely amongst themselves. If someone ever hacked into their chatroom, the true nature of their discussions would be difficult to ascertain.

Seemingly, the True Crime Club website provided, on one hand, entertaining information on true crime, and on the other, an elaborate game to conceptualize crime.

Fixations can, however, spiral out of control when one hand doesn't know what the other hand is doing.

Minutes after finishing his meal, Zen's stomach churned. "I might be more anxious than I imagined. My stomach feels like it's just turned upside down." Zen told Valentina. "I ate nothing that should have caused a problem." He stretched up in his chair to relieve his discomfort.

In fact, Zen had stuck to his plan: a plain meal, nothing spicy, and no alcohol. He had been his usual calm self all evening, unlike Valentina, who had been jittery throughout dinner even after two glasses of wine. "This is my third flight accompanying horses. I'm not worried," she said, defying the obvious state of her nerves.

"Are you joking?" Zen asked. "You've been edgy since you arrived at the barn this afternoon."

"Maybe I'm just nervous about being with you tonight," she said.

"Really?" Zen questioned. "We'll be bunking for a few hours with the other riders and grooms. I don't think it will get romantic if that's what you mean."

"You never know. Perhaps Tiger's stall could offer us some privacy."

"Stop! I told you my mind has to stay focused on the competition. I want no talk of sex until after I ride...no matter how alluring you make yourself. My shields are up, as they say," Zen retorted.

"Isn't that the girl's line?" Val asked.

"What? Would a girl use Star Trek reference? I don't think so. Besides, as sick as I feel now, sex is the last thing on my mind." Zen requested the check, and they hurried off.

"Sorry to rush," he said. "I can't imagine what I ate to have brought this on. I'm hoping that walking, even just to the car, will settle things a bit."

It didn't. Less than fifteen minutes later, Zen was bent over the steering wheel. Now, along with the pain, his mind was playing strange tricks on him.

He pulled the car off the road and parked along the soft shoulder. He stood alongside the car, wanting to vomit, but couldn't make it happen.

"You need to drive." He told Valentina. "I need a doctor." Then he burst out in laughter.

Val got behind the wheel.

"You're acting strange," she said. "You're frightening me."

"Val, I don't know what's happening." Now crying, he said, "You have to get me to a hospital."

By the time they reached a nearby medical center, Zen needed help to get out of the car.

"Here, hold on to my cell phone." He told Val as a nurse took him away. "Call my father, but not until we know what's wrong. I don't want to worry him unnecessarily."

Zen looked at the nurse. "We were eating at a nice restaurant when I began to feel sick. The pain is unbelievable. I thought it could be my appendix, but now my entire body feels odd. What is wrong with me?" he asked, not expecting an answer.

"Just try to relax," the nurse said.

"I'll wait here," Val assured him.

Then, as Zen was out of sight, she frantically grabbed for her cell phone. "We are at the hospital." She jumped on the person at the other end of the call. "Zen is in terrible pain and acting very odd. You didn't prepare me for this." Val looked around to make sure no one could overhear.

"You said he would just get sick," she whispered into the phone, "like a stomach bug. That's what you told me!"

"Did you follow my instructions?"

"Yes. But I'm worried. We just wanted him to miss the flight...not end up dead. He's acting so weird, I'm scared. Could he die?"

"Don't be ridiculous. They will keep him overnight. He will miss the flight. By the time he gets to New Jersey, everything will be settled.

"Nothing can go wrong," the voice assured Val. "They won't find anything alarming, whatever testing they do. Continue with the plan."

"You talk like you knew he would be hospitalized, yet you didn't tell me," Valentina stated. "I thought he would just be in the ER long enough to miss the flight."

"Relax. Just do as I say."

Val now realized she couldn't trust everything she was told. But it was too late for any second thoughts.

She gave Zen's cell phone to the attendant at the reception desk, saying, "This cell phone belongs to my friend. His name is William Griegg. Please give it to him."

3

The Griegg Estate, Outside Zurich

Sigmund Griegg arrived home after an exhausting day at his Zürich office. Their firm's current project was representing Swiss business interests in the forthcoming handover of Hong Kong's sovereignty from Britain, to communist China on the first day of July 1997.

Negotiations were ongoing, but after today, the Grieggs' engagement had reached a brief lull. Breaking for the trip to New Jersey to watch William ride, fell at the perfect moment.

The thought of Hong Kong being returned to the communists weighed on Sigmund's mind. The Chinese couldn't be trusted. They didn't follow the protocols of negotiations as other countries did, and in Hong Kong, they held all the contractual cards. It led to heightened tension, but that wasn't Sigmund's concern.

The Grieggs job was to ensure that Swiss industry envoys understood the changing laws, taxes, and tariffs surrounding imports and exports under the new deal. They knew the Chicoms would take advantage of ignorance whenever possible.

In this, the Grieggs served their clients with years of experience in the business of trade.

Both men were drained after months of perusing contacts in countries with six-hour (or longer) time differences.

While Andrew's function was minor compared to his son's, they both relished the opportunity to support William as he pursued his dream in the show jumping arena. They were so proud of his accomplishments.

It was only recently that they realized those achievements might qualify William and Tiger as Olympic hopefuls. They rallied behind him.

Entering the kitchen, Sigmund found his father making coffee. He caught a whiff of hazelnut as he pulled two mugs from the cupboard. "Have you heard from William?"

"I left him at the quarantine barn a few hours ago. He is dining with Valentina, the young woman who will groom for him at Hamilton Farm."

"I haven't been able to reach him on his cell phone," Sigmund said, "so I was getting concerned. I guess I should relax. We can't compete with anyone named Valentina. He seems happy to team with her for the trip."

"Oh, that was obvious the moment I arrived this after-noon," quipped Andrew. "Everyone traveling on the plane will grab a few hours of downtime at the farm before leaving for the airport. I'm sure they'll be too excited to sleep, so they'll be partying.

"At their age, they can handle a sleepless night without skipping a beat. It's probably been too hectic for William to look at his phone."

"Yes, I suppose you're right. I had a late lunch, so I'll pass on dinner for now. I may fix something for myself later." Sigmund poured the coffee.

"That's fine." Andrew busied himself with pans on the cooktop. "Alana emailed, today. She'll be at Hamilton Farm to watch William ride."

"Will she stay at the Cranston Inn with us?"

"Yes, I booked a room for her when I made our reserva-tions. I counted on her joining us, and now she says she is 'all in' with the plan."

"I'm glad she will be there," Sigmund stated.

"She seems excited to be coming," Andrew said. "I don't think she gets much chance to leave her art gallery these days. She's calling it a vacation."

Late that evening, the two men were reading in the home study when the telephone rang.

"Hallo." As Sigmund interacted with the caller, his expression alerted his father that something was terribly wrong.

"Danke. Wir werden es so bald wie möglich." Sigmund told the caller. "Dad," he said, covering the mouthpiece of the phone, "William has been taken to a hospital emergency department with some sort of food poisoning."

"Is it serious?" Andrew stood.

"Wir sind auf dem weg." Sigmund told the caller they were on their way.

"They said he is resting comfortably," Sigmund said to his father. "I wonder what he could have eaten. Did William say where they would be dining?"

"No, and I didn't ask."

*F*orty minutes later, Sigmund and Andrew walked into the emergency department. A doctor came out to the reception area to speak with them.

"Gentlemen, I'm Dr. Böhmer."

Sigmund and Andrew introduced themselves.

"I'm sorry it took so long for us to contact you. The woman who brought William to the hospital left his cell phone at the reception desk, but when a staff shift occurred, I'm afraid it got lost in the shuffle for a time.

"First, let me say that when William arrived, he presented symptoms of a food-borne illness, but the pain was much more intense than we normally encounter. He also displayed cognitive dysfunction that, while odd, could have been a by-product of the pain. His condition alarmed every member of my team.

"Also troubling, was the symptoms appeared so soon after food consumption. This raised our suspicions, so we looked at his appendix, kidneys, gallbladder—but found nothing abnormal. Then, in a short time, the severity of his pain abated, and his mental clarity returned.

"We gave him an EKG and measured the arterial blood gasses to check for any damage or evidence of a chemical-based poison.

"At that point, we gave him sedation to allow him to rest while we observed his condition and conducted additional blood and cell analysis."

"Doctor, are you suggesting a crime? Has my son been poisoned?" Sigmund asked.

"It's too soon to suggest a crime—and most poisonings are accidental. A lesser number can be an attempt at suicide. After talking with your son, I ruled that out."

"Yes," Sigmund murmured as he thought who might want to harm himself through his son.

"You can rule out suicide," Sigmund said as his worst fears flooded his thoughts.

The family had been targeted with violence in the past. It happened in 1988, when they joined a team of Norwegians seeking to reopen the Camp David Accords (what would much later become known as the Oslo Accords).

It was the most high-profile project the Grieggs' had undertaken. They had wholeheartedly agreed to take part in the ambitious, perhaps world-changing, endeavor for peace in the Middle East.

As the Grieggs involvement stretched into a second year, terror struck. A car bomb, which everyone later believed was meant for Sigmund, killed his wife, Evelyn, instead.

The Grieggs believed reopening the Accords to be an honorable cause. Of course they knew what terrorists were capable of, but as tiny cogs in such a large wheel, they never imagined danger to themselves or their family.

The Grieggs' objective with the Accords was simple: They analyzed historical documents to find a common link that could be seen as a face-saving outcome for each of the factions involved.

What nerve had they struck to initiate the brutal attack? No one knew. The authorities downplayed the attack for the sake of maintaining a positive political outcome.

Had the terrorists gone after Evelyn to punish Sigmund, or was she just in the wrong place at the wrong time? To this day, no answers were apparent, and no one could ever give a reason for such depravity.

Evelyn's death permanently changed the way the Griegg organization operated. They no longer sought out projects with high risk. The Eastwood case in 1995 was an exception. And in that situation, the American was already in danger when she came to Sigmund for help—he couldn't possibly turn her away.

As Sigmund spoke to William's doctor, thoughts of their current project spun through his mind. But their involvement in Hong Kong wasn't controversial, nothing like the Accords assignment. Sigmund doubted any part of their work could be linked to what was happening to his son. Nevertheless, he couldn't stop the possibility from entering his head.

"Dr. Böhmer, when can we see William?" Andrew asked.

"I don't want to disturb him for another hour or so. We will have the additional test results by then. So, please, take a seat in the lounge down the hall and I will let you know when he's awake."

Sigmund stopped Dr. Böhmer from walking away. "My son planned to fly to the United States in a matter of hours. He is competing in a show jumping competition with his horse next week. What do we tell him?"

"Yes, he's told me. Even if the tests are all negative and he wakes without pain, flying that soon could be problematic. Perhaps postponing for a few days would be more sensible.

"Let's get the test results before we speculate. The fact that he's resting comfortably under sedation doesn't minimize the pain he exhibited earlier. Your son was in tough shape."

"Doctor, this may seem an odd request, but research is my business. Could we have samples of what you are testing? We may find an obscure substance not on your radar."

"Well, that's the first time anyone has asked me that question, and it's not one I can answer without checking. I'll see what I can do."

"I can talk to anyone you suggest."

"That may not be necessary," the doctor said. "First let me explore the options."

Sigmund and Andrew took seats in the lounge, discussing what to do about Tiger. If they pulled the horse from the flight when William could be fit to ride, it might doom his Olympic hopes.

Andrew proposed that he take William's slot on the plane. "But would the Federation coach approve?" he wondered aloud.

"Perhaps Tiger could take a later flight," Sigmund suggested, before realizing they might be over thinking things.

"We're only reacting this way because William is so protective of Tiger. The horse can fly alone, under the custody of his groom. It's unnecessary for William to be with him."

Sigmund continued. "I hate to say it, but the coach may actually prefer it."

"Yes, I was thinking the same thing," Andrew said. "But I don't want to say that to William."

When Andrew couldn't reach his grandson's coach by phone, he started out for the farm.

Coach Lara returned Andrew's call while he was en route.

"Andrew, the horses are already on the trailer and traveling to the airport. They may even be on the plane," she said. "Pulling Tiger from the flight is not an option."

That meant that getting Andrew on the plane with Tiger was also out of the question.

Lara added, "It surprised us when we didn't hear from Zen, but we couldn't wait any longer. I assure you Tiger will be fine."

She continued. "When he lands in New Jersey, the health officials must confine all the horses at the airport quarantine facility for two to three days, depending on where our group falls in their testing schedule.

"Zen can fly to the States in a few days when he feels better without missing a beat. He wouldn't have access to Tiger any sooner.

Zen

"This delay is not a game breaker. Zen just needs to be fit to ride when he arrives," Lara said. "Val has been working with Tiger, and I know William is happy with the way she handles his horse. You get your grandson better. We'll take care of Tiger. That's our job." Lara Bless was a professional, and she impressed Andrew.

"Thank you, Lara, your words are reassuring."

Andrew pulled the car over to call Sigmund.

"I'm with William now," Sigmund reported. "He's feeling a little better, and the tests have all come back negative for any known toxins. That means the cause of his condition is still a mystery. Because of that, we have to wait longer for the doctor to discharge him. I doubt we'll get home before late morning or early afternoon."

What Sigmund didn't say out loud was that he had already called Boris Klondt, one of the firm's researchers, to pick up William's test samples from Dr. Böhmer. The hospital had approved his request for an independent forensic analysis.

"Well, I understand that's mixed news, but good news all the same. Tiger is already on his way. I couldn't do anything to stop it, but I spoke with the coach and she made me feel comfortable with the situation. She explained that there is no rush for William to get to Hamilton Farm.

"I'll explain the quarantine timeframe in the United States later, if William hasn't done so already, but there is essentially two to three days of downtime for the horses at that end. William's late arrival will have no impact on the competition whatsoever," Andrew said.

"I'd like to drive to the airport and get on the next flight out to New Jersey. I think it will make William feel better if I am at least near Tiger until he can fly over."

"Yes, William heard you. He's a bit too groggy to show much emotion, but he's nodding in agreement with your plan, and I agree, too," Sigmund said.

"I'll need you to pack some clothes for me when you fly out. In the meantime, Lara Bless will keep me updated on Tiger and I'll pass everything along to you."

47

"Dad," Sigmund said, "thank you. I'll call you once I get William home."

"With all this turmoil now, let's hope everything goes smoothly from here out," Andrew said.

"Let's hope so." Sigmund ended the call.

*I*n another part of Zürich, a burner phone vibrated.

"Hallo."

"Das Flugzeug ist in der Luft. Er verließ Zürich vor ein paar Stunden. Alles ist im Zeitplan." The phone line disconnected.

The man repeated to his accomplice, "The plane has taken off. Everything is on schedule."

"Good," she said. "It's all in play, now. I thought I'd be nervous, but I'm not."

4

The Switch

"I'm sorry to disturb you, sir, but we're preparing to land."

Andrew leaned forward and looked about the cabin. "Thank you." He told the flight attendant. He was flying business class on American Airlines. It had been the first available seat to New York's JFK.

New Jersey's Newark Airport would have been closer to his destination, but that meant a delay getting in the air. He was at the rental car counter when Coach Bless called to say they had logged the horses into the quarantine barn and Tiger was fine.

"Thank you, Lara. I'll tell William."

"How is Zen feeling?" the coach asked. Having him ready to ride was important. Show jumping is like any other sport. Competing at the top level was big business and everyone had to produce their piece of the product.

"Much better, I'm told," Andrew replied. "He'll be at home resting by now."
"That's good to hear. The grooms have a digital camera to photograph the horses during their stay in quarantine. If you come out to Hamilton Farm, we'll be posting the pictures in our stall block. You'll see Tiger is content. There is no point driving out to the quarantine facility because only the grooms are given access to the horses."

Andrew called to assure William that Tiger had arrived in New Jersey and was safe. "Lara said all the horses are fine. Tiger is probably munching hay as we speak."

William had gotten the all-clear from the doctor, so he would be on the flight originally scheduled for his father and grandfather in two days. William didn't want to wait, but he accepted the doctor's advice that he needed the time to fully recover from whatever had happened to him.

As with access to Tiger, Andrew had limited interaction with Valentina while officials confined the horses in quarantine. Her lodging was next to the quarantine barn, and she had no international service on her cell phone.

William hadn't considered that they would be separated during the trip or he would have paid for the upgrade on her phone himself.

Andrew arrived at the Cranston Inn and checked into the room originally booked for his grandson. Since Sigmund was bringing his luggage, he had to go out for a few essentials and clothes to hold him over for several days.

Back in Zurich, William rested in their country home, recuperating. He ate only dry toast and drank herbal tea. By evening, he felt better.

His father made chicken soup for dinner. The day had been restful until evening, when Asher Rechsteiner called.

"Zen," he said. "How are you? Are things okay?"

"Everything is messed up. I got food poisoning and ended up in the hospital last night. I missed my flight with Tiger, so I am still here at home."

"I see…and Tiger, is he okay?"

"Yes, my grandfather flew over instead of me. He can't see Tiger during quarantine, but Lara assures us he took the flight in stride. He's in America, bright-eyed and bushy-tailed, as they say."

"Well, that's good…and you're feeling better?"

"Yes. It's just crazy, because I was in such pain. I can't even explain what was going on with my body. I couldn't think straight. I felt disoriented. Ash, at one point, I thought I was going to die. I made Val take me to the hospital. Now, less than 24 hours later, I'm well—back to normal, really."

"Interesting," Ash whispered.

50

Zen

Ash seemed detached from their conversation.

"Zen, I phoned because I sensed something was wrong. Is your dad with you?"

"He's walking the dogs and bringing the horses in for the night...wait a minute, I hear him coming inside. Did you want to talk to him?"

"I'd like to talk to both of you," Ash said.

"Go ahead, you're on the speaker."

"Ash, how are you?" Sigmund spoke loudly, to be heard from the far side of the room.

"Sigmund, I called because there is a problem with Tiger. I don't wish to alarm you, but Andrew must check on the horse immediately."

"Come on Ash, you know he can't do that." Sigmund admonished. "The horse is quarantined."

"I don't care. He must find a way," Ash snapped back uncharacteristically.

"Why are you upsetting William? The coach has told us that Tiger is fine. Perhaps you're reacting to William's visit to the emergency department."

"No," Ash said tersely. "I hate to upset you, but something is wrong. I can't say precisely what it is, but I sense trouble is brewing."

"Ash, I'm calling my grandfather to tell him. Bye-bye." William ended the call. "Dad, you don't know Ash as I do. He wouldn't worry me unless it was important. It can't hurt to ask Grandrew if there is something he can do."

Andrew called Lara to inform her that Ash had a concern for William's horse. "You appreciate the relationship William has with Ash. His anxiety will mount until I can assure him that Tiger is safe."

"Andrew, I don't know what more I can tell you. I've seen the pictures. Your horse is just fine. There's an entire staff of veterinarians at the facility, and Valentina checks on him continually. What more can we do?"

"Can I at least talk with Valentina?"

"Sure. The grooms are staying at a hotel down the road from the quarantine facility. I'll call you back with the telephone number."

Andrew didn't wait for her call. He drove to the hotel. When he arrived, Valentina came down to the lobby to talk.

"I'm so glad to see you, Mr. Griegg." Her eyes danced about, avoiding any direct contact with his. "I didn't know what to do," she said.

"Is there something wrong with Tiger?"

She pulled an envelope from her pocket and handed it to Andrew. "Someone pinned this to his stable sheet. I saw it earlier and assumed it contained quarantine documentation. It wasn't until I checked on him about an hour ago that I saw my name written on the envelope."

Andrew ripped it open. He pulled out a single page and read it aloud. "Do nothing. Say nothing. We will contact the Grieggs." He glared at Val and asked, "What's going on?"

"Mr. Griegg, the horse in the quarantine stall isn't Tiger."

"What?"

"He looks exactly like Tiger, but it's a different horse," she said.

"How could this happen? Didn't you care for Tiger on the plane?" he asked.

"Everything went haywire when Zen didn't show up for the flight. The stalls assigned to the horses changed due to the weight distribution on the plane, and I didn't get to see Tiger until he was here in quarantine…and then it wasn't him!" Val cried.

"I don't understand. You drove William to the hospital— you must have known he wouldn't make the flight," Andrew said anxiously. "Didn't you tell anyone?"

"Zen told me not to say anything. He said he would be there…no matter what. If he didn't make it to the barn, he said we'd meet up at the airport. I kept expecting him to walk onto the plane until the last minute. Once the doors were closed, it was too late to say anything."

The story she spun made Andrew's mind reel. William had relayed no such events when they talked by telephone earlier. Could he have been so out of it that he simply forgot the details? Andrew guessed that was possible. But it was more likely that Val was lying, and that was disturbing.

"I need you to tell me everything," Andrew said. "What happened at the restaurant?"

"We hadn't even finished dinner when Zen felt sick, so we started back to the barn. Halfway there, he asked me to drive him to the hospital.

"At the hospital, Zen told me to go back to the barn and he would catch up. He said they would give him something to settle his stomach, but since it might take a while, he wanted me to be with Tiger."

"You should have stayed with him," Andrew said. "Why didn't you call us?"

"Zen wouldn't let me! The ER was busy, and he didn't want to worry you. He couldn't say how long they would keep him."

"But you took his car. How did you think he would get to the farm?" Andrew asked.

"I don't know. I thought he would call you or his father to drive him."

This was ridiculous. She was lying, and Andrew's patience grew thin.

"When was the last time you're sure you saw the real Tiger?" Andrew asked.

"I loaded him on the trailer to go the airport."

"And you didn't see him again?" Andrew asked.

"They put the horse containers on the plane while I went to check-in. When I returned, Tiger's pod ended up at the other end of the plane. I was told to stay with the second pod of horses because that was the section they assigned to me."

"So, you can't say for sure that Tiger ever made it on the plane? This look-alike could have taken his place?"

Val shook her head. "The horses look so much alike—even more so when they're wearing a stable sheet. I had no reason to think anything was wrong. But in hindsight, I don't know if it was Tiger on the plane. All I know for sure is that it's not Tiger in quarantine. Please believe me."

"Why?" Andrew snapped.

"Why what?" Val asked.

"Why should I believe you?"

Valentina didn't respond.

"Where is the digital camera?"

"It's in my room."

"Have you taken pictures of this horse posing as Tiger?" Andrew asked.

"Yes," Val said.

"Go get the SD card. I want it."

Andrew walked outside the hotel and pulled out his cell phone. "Sigmund, there's a problem."

"What is it, Dad?"

"This will sound ludicrous, but Tiger has been abducted. According to Valentina, the horse in the quarantine stall is a dead ringer, but it's not Tiger."

"Surely it's a mix-up, and he's in another stall."

"No," Andrew continued, "there is a ransom note. It reads something like, 'say nothing, do nothing,' and they'll be in touch with us soon. I don't know what's going on."

"What about Valentina? Wasn't she on the plane?"

"Val was on the plane. Her account makes little sense. I know she's lying. We can't trust her. We can't be sure Tiger ever made it on the plane. They could have switched him on either side of the Atlantic," Andrew said.

"I'm speechless." Sigmund watched as his son entered the room with a look of dread across his face. "Hold the line a moment," Sigmund said to his father.

"Tiger is being held for ransom," William said. "I just got a call that said, 'We have your horse. We will care for him as long as you meet our demand. You will get instructions soon. They said, 'don't go to the police.' Then the line went dead."

"Son, listen to me. Your grandfather is with Val. She has confirmed that the horse in New Jersey isn't Tiger. It's a look-alike. They have a ransom note saying the same thing as your phone call."

William sank into a chair next to where his father stood. He stared into his father's eyes. "Ash was right."

"Son, clearly your trip to the hospital was intentional. Whoever is behind Tiger's abduction didn't want you on the plane. We must consider that Val put something into your drink at the restaurant."

"No!" William shouted.

"William, Val's lying to your grandfather. Dad, I'm putting you on speaker."

Andrew quizzed his grandson. "William, did you tell Val not to wait for you at the hospital?"

"I don't think so," he said.

"Did you tell her not to call us? Did you say to drive your car back to the farm? Is that what happened?"

"I felt so confused at the hospital. I don't remember what I said. Can we get on a plane now?"

"William, we can't say Tiger is in New Jersey—he may still be in Switzerland." Sigmund looked at his watch. "Dad, I will call everyone into the office and be back in touch with you from there."

"Okay. I'm getting pictures of the horse in quarantine. I'll upload them to you from the Cranston's computer."

Andrew then addressed his grandson. "Stay calm, we'll work this out. Remember, they have no reason to harm Tiger. He's not a person. He can't identify anyone."

"Pack whatever you need for America." Sigmund told his son. "I don't know if or when we'll fly to New Jersey, but we must be ready to leave on short notice."

"Why would anyone do this?" William asked.

"I don't know."

"I am so frightened for Tiger."

"Just remember what your grandfather told you, Tiger can't identify anyone. We'll get him back."

Sigmund said, "I've got to get ahold of Sophie to let her know she has to care for our animals ahead of schedule."

"Okay people, this one hits home." Sigmund called his staff meeting to order. "William's horse, Tiger, is being held for ransom. The abductors conveyed, 'We have your horse—do nothing, say nothing, and all will be back to normal soon.'

"Just a few minutes ago, as we were driving here, a second call came through demanding a painting by Anders Zaugg called *Lady in Gold* in exchange for the horse's safe return.

"The calls last only a few seconds, and the caller distorts his or her voice. William thinks the voice is male, but he can't be sure. The caller said the instructions to pay the ransom will come tomorrow. The caller stressed again that 'everything can be back to normal soon. Just do as you are told.'

"The ransom demand is puzzling on two levels," Sigmund explained. "First, we acquired this painting when Operation Boomerang consigned several pieces of art to an auction here in Zürich some months ago.

"Operation Boomerang, as you are aware, is the Israeli project to handle the treasure recovered in the Eastwood case. A telephone bidder had already purchased two of the five pieces of art consigned when the *Lady in Gold* painting came to the block.

"When the bidding far exceeded the market value of the painting, I decided to test his or her resolve. The bidder's phone line went dead, and I ended up with the portrait.

"We don't know what happened to the bidder with paddle number 139. Perhaps the call came over a cellular line and it just dropped off? Or did the caller hang up? We don't know," Sigmund stated.

"The second point of interest is that, even at the inflated price we paid, William's show jumper is worth much more. So why do they want this specific painting?

"It makes no sense unless there is more to the artwork than meets the eye. And what, if anything, does our horse's abduction have to do with Operation Boomerang? Those are the questions we must answer.

"I've kept the *Lady in Gold* in our office supply room since the auction. I'll get it out of storage after this meeting and make a close inspection."

The Griegg workforce included seasoned professionals with diverse experiences: Ian Stewart, Chris Hutt, Sabine Bauer Hutt, Boris Klondt, and J. Leopold Niedermeyer. All but one would give their all to answer the questions Sigmund posed. Niedermeyer was on a bereavement leave and would sit out this case.

Sigmund's father, Andrew, had been semi-retired from the company for two years, only dipping his finger in when a case or project interested him. But, as any business owner can attest, there's no such thing as retirement in a family venture—and never when a problem involves a loved one.

When Andrew joined the meeting via speakerphone from New Jersey, Sigmund uttered the words, *"Der Goldzug."* The office fell silent as each person recalled their own nightmare over the events that besieged those words.

Amazingly, in 1995, while solving the Eastwood case, the Grieggs discovered the legendary Nazi Gold Train treasure. The Grieggs then colluded with the Israelis to keep the discovery secret.

They trusted the Israelis to be the best people to reunite the treasure with its lawful owners. They believed involving any European government would have brought an army of bureaucrats, with all their inevitable expense, into the equation. It could have been a fiasco.

The Israeli's project was top secret, with only a handful of people aware of its existence. Everyone believed they could process the treasure quietly.

Yet, at this moment, meeting with their staff, Sigmund, Andrew, and now William, all suspected that the plan, no matter how well intentioned, had gone awry.

57

It was time to call the Israelis. Sigmund supposed the communication would need a delicate touch.

"We can't take our questions to Operation Boomerang directly," he declared. "Not if there's a criminal mole within the group. I'd rather contact David Rosen, but as you know, we didn't part on the best of terms two years ago.

"I think you should call him, Dad. David will be more amenable talking with you," Sigmund stated.

Rosen was the Mossad agent they teamed with on the Eastwood case, and Sigmund was right—it hadn't ended well. David vowed they would "never again meet as friends."

The reason for the kerfuffle was that Sigmund had demanded two million Deutschmarks to turn over the *Der Goldzug* Notebook to the Israelis. The notebook contained information on the Gold Train treasure and where to find it.

In the end, the Israelis agreed to pay the Grieggs' price— in part because Andrew, along with Alana Eastwood, nearly died retrieving the book.

Even so, David felt it was wrong for the Grieggs to, as he saw it, "profit" from the discovery. After all, they had found the notebook through a joint investigation with Mossad.

To the Grieggs, however, it was never about profit. The money covered their cost of doing business and risking their lives. Neither Sigmund nor Andrew could predict how David would react to their call.

In New Jersey, Andrew pulled an address book from his pocket to get David's number. He told the group in Zürich, "I must disconnect while I talk to David. I'll call you back."

The telephone rang in the agent's Berlin flat. "David, my old friend, it's Andrew Griegg. I'm afraid there's a problem that involves us both."

"Tell me, Andrew." David's tone was cautious.

"There seems to be a leak of information coming from the people handling the Gold Train treasure."

"Operation Boomerang…what makes you say that?"

"There has been a kidnapping, and the ransom demand is part of the treasure," Andrew said.

"That's ambiguous. I'll need more information."

Andrew told David the auction story. "Last year, there were families in dire financial need when your operation told them about their unexpected inheritance. The families asked if they could have cash instead of the artwork. Your people arranged for those pieces to be consigned to an auction.

"Sigmund and I attended the event, just out of curiosity, and noticed that a single buyer was picking up the Gold Train pieces. In a strange turn of events that I will give details on later, we ended up with one of the paintings.

"Now a horse is missing, and the ransom demand is that art from the Gold Train treasure."

"A horse?" David asked.

"Yes. A valuable show jumper," Andrew replied.

"Interesting, but why call me?"

"Because we trust you," Andrew stated. "Everything about Operation Boomerang is top secret. We believe a mole has infiltrated your organization. If not a mole by definition, a bad actor, and it will be tricky to investigate without tipping off the leaker."

"Let me refer you to someone you can trust," David said.

"Please, David, don't do that. This hits home. We are asking for *your* help."

"I've never heard of an animal being kidnapped. It sounds like a movie plot," David remarked.

"David, this involves my grandson. It's our horse that has been abducted. William is up for a spot on the Olympic team. The horse disappeared while traveling to a competition in New Jersey."

"Do you plan to pay the ransom?"

"Yes, that's the plan," Andrew said. "We'll worry about catching whoever is responsible for the crime once our horse is safe."

"What painting do you have?"

"It's an inconsequential portrait called *Lady in Gold* by Anders Zaugg."

"Never heard of him."

"Well, he's not Monet, but he's famous enough. The painting has damage and is not highly valued. Sigmund is looking into what could give the piece more significance than meets the eye."

"Like a Rembrandt masterpiece painted underneath?"

"Exactly," Andrew acknowledged.

"Why must this involve me? I don't want a repeat of 1995," David said with an air of contempt.

"David, please put that aside for now. Trust me. Something is wrong within Operation Boomerang."

"I'll see what I can do," David said.

"I'm in America. It will be better for you to speak with Sigmund from here out. We don't know if our horse's abduction took place before boarding the plane in Switzerland or after arriving in New Jersey."

"You don't make this easy for me," David said.

"That's not my first concern," Andrew responded. "The fact that they hold horses in quarantine is delaying us from seeing the horse for several days, but the groom handling him has confirmed it's a dead ringer—but not our horse.

"We believe that paying the ransom and getting our horse back is tied to the quarantine period, so we have to act fast.

"We've activated our entire team. It's all the same people you met on the Eastwood case a couple years ago, and I'm hoping Alana will join me here in New Jersey soon.

"The only thing I can share with you now is the name Valentina Abbatelli. She is a young woman assigned to groom for William at the competition.

"He was scheduled to be on the flight with his horse, but instead, he ended up in the hospital with food poisoning that Valentina must have given him over dinner.

"We can't push her until the horse is back in our hands… but then, like Charles the Fifth or the Corleone family, make no mistake about it—we'll go to the mattresses to nail the bastards involved."

"Okay, I understand." David took a deep breath. "Your people will hear from me soon. Take care."

Andrew got back on the line with Sigmund to brief him on the call with David and to continue their meeting.

Sigmund assigned priorities. "Dad, I want you to track the horses from the moment they landed until they arrived at the quarantine facility.

"Get the names of everyone that had their hands on the horses at your end. I know I don't have to say it, but we're looking for any breaches in security. I have no idea what level of security you'll find.

"Christopher, I want you to look into Valentina Abbatelli and her family's background. You need to trace where she gets her money. Competing on the show circuit is expensive.

"Ian, look into Operation Boomerang. We need to assemble bios on the team members. This will overlap with what David tells us, but let's develop our own independent information. Any discrepancy with what he shares might prove valuable down the road…trust, but verify, as they say.

"Boris, work your network of contacts to identify paddle number 139 at Tremblay's auction. There is too much coincidence here. We need a name behind the number.

"Sabine, I need you to contact Asher Rechsteiner. He makes his living as an animal communicator. He is William's friend and has been an enormous help with Tiger. Ash alerted us about trouble with the horse a short time before we heard from his abductors. Try to pin down when he first suspected something was wrong.

"I'm sorry, William, but Sabine must question Ash as a suspect. I want you both to understand that we can't divulge any information to Rechsteiner until we figure out if he's involved. We must see if any part of his story falls apart.

"I will remain close to William while the ransom demands come through," Sigmund advised. "He will shadow me until further notice. Our job will be to trace the horses to the airport and loading onto the plane.

"Valentina tells us she put Tiger on the trailer to go to the airport, but she's now a known liar who can't be trusted. We'll start by asking questions at the quarantine barn.

"Remember, our first priority is to get our horse back." Sigmund made his point clear. "No one acts on any criminal information until that happens."

Before Andrew closed the call, he said to Sigmund, "I'd like to contact Alana. She's planning to drive down before the competition next week, but her special talents might be useful sooner rather than later."

"I agree with you." Turning to his staff, Sigmund stated, "I'll acknowledge upfront that both Alana and Ash have abilities I find impossible to understand.

"However, we all remember our experience in Germany. We witnessed how Alana helped us solve her case. We must keep an open mind to what either of them tells us.

"All right, people, get to work. We don't have a lot of time left today, but keep me informed if you find anything critical. We'll plan to meet again as a group in the morning."

What Sigmund alluded to was Alana's dreams, which had helped them unravel the mystery of the trap in 1995. She was able to connect to past events in ways that normal reasoning couldn't explain.

Alana would dream about past occurrences as they related to the present day. These visions usually occurred after touching a physical object that was linked to an unsettled past.

She had never acknowledged any type of psychic prowess until the occurrences in Germany with the Grieggs made it difficult to deny. Since then, she has come to terms with the dreams as being part of who she is—and that required owning up to a psychic link to history.

Alana could never produce these dreams on demand. They just happened on their own...and hadn't resurfaced since uncovering the secret of the trap. Now, somehow, the mystery of the Nazi Gold Train treasure seemed to be in play all over again.

5

Working Both Sides of the Atlantic

"Alana, it's Andrew."

"Hello, Andrew. Your ears must have been burning, because I was just thinking about you. I'm all set to drive to New Jersey on Wednesday. I understand you…"

"Alana, I'm sorry to interrupt, but there's a problem. I'm here now."

"What's wrong?"

"Someone has abducted William's horse, he's being held for ransom."

"What!"

"I'm calling to see if there is any way for you to come sooner?" he asked.

"Yes, of course. I need time to adjust my plans to keep the art gallery open and get my dog settled with the sitter. I'll try to leave by noon tomorrow. Will that be okay?"

"Yes. You know I trust you, but I must say these words: You can't tell anyone that there's a problem."

"No worries. Can you tell me anything now?"

"No. We have so little information; it can wait until you get here."

"Certainly. I'll call when I'm on my way. Oh, I should ask—having come early, are you at the Cranston?"

"Yes," Andrew said.

"Andrew, this is unbelievable. I'm so sorry. I'll get there as soon as I can."

Alana had stayed at the Griegg's country home while convalescing from injuries incurred during her investigation. The ordeal had been life changing. When she came home to Connecticut, she couldn't resume her life as usual.

The inheritance from her grandfather's estate gave Alana the luxury, in her early thirties, to pursue a new vocation. With a rare double major in fine art and finance, she pivoted into entrepreneurship. She left a good career in banking and opened an art gallery off the center green in New Haven, in a historic district on the outskirts of the Yale campus.

It was a dream come true, for someone artistic but not quite talented enough to make a living as an artist. She bought a home along the shore of Long Island Sound where she lived with her German Shepard Disraeli (or Dizzy, as she'd nicknamed him).

The location of her gallery, halfway between New York City and Boston, meant her client base spanned what's called the northeast corridor, a region stretching from Washington D.C. up to Maine.

In two years, she had solidified her business with a unique eye to spot quality pieces by lesser-known artists—art she could sell at affordable prices.

Alana didn't want to be another hole-in-the-wall gallery with limited appeal. She also offered restoration services, and it paid off. Clients throughout the area opted for her shop, over trekking into New York City for cleaning and repairs.

Once there, people liked Alana's art stock and added to their collections. Her gallery was making a name for itself, thanks, in part, to referrals from the Grieggs.

Between the skilled art restorer in her employ and a Yale student who came in part-time, leaving the shop earlier than planned wouldn't be a problem. The issue would be the dog. When she called Disraeli's sitter, he was unavailable.

But nothing would keep Alana from helping the Grieggs. They had become a second family to her, and family was important. Both her parents had died from illness when she was in her twenties.

Andrew Griegg had replaced Alana's German grandfather as a fatherly figure in her life. In fact, she loved having all the Griegg men in her life.

It had been a rocky start with Sigmund, though. When they met, he was all-consumed with solving the mystery of the letter she had brought to him. People were dying and keeping her safe was job one. It wasn't until after the case ended that they got to know one another.

Even so, Sigmund still had an obstacle to over-come. He found Alana's psychic visions puzzling. As a skillful research-er, he analyzed facts…hard truths that did not include using someone's dreams as an investigative tool. Sigmund believed psychics to be hoaxers. He didn't know how else to think.

But when Alana's visions were proven true, he had to confront his skepticism. It still gave him angst.

After Andrew's telephone call, Alana sat on her deck with a cup of tea and her dog by her side. *Why would anyone kidnap Tiger?* she thought.

There were times when Alana's mind returned to 1995, so it was no surprise when the events of the investigation flood-ed her mind now. She pulled a blanket around her shoulders as she stared over the shoreline.

The energy released by the incoming tide intensified her thoughts. She couldn't prevent Andrew's whisper, "prepare to run," from sounding out in her head.

As she always did, Alana counted out two seconds before reliving the explosion in her bones. It was those two seconds that had saved her life and that of Andrew Griegg.

Alana told herself to stop, even though she never could. She had made a mistake back then that was difficult to over-come. Returning to the events at the church was always out of her control…no matter how hard she tried.

Already injured in a car crash, Alana had made her way into the church to call for an ambulance to help the others. Unaccustomed to carrying a gun, she placed it on the desk to make the call. In a split second, her nemesis confronted her, and she couldn't reach the gun.

Everything could have ended then and there, had the gun been in her hand. It haunted her to this day.

Her ex-military father had taught her to shoot as a teen-ager. Alana had no interest in guns, but she loved her dad, and going to the shooting range was something they could do together. They would target practice most weekends. In time, she became an excellent shot.

Even though Alana never carried a gun off the shooting range, her father instilled in her the responsibility of handling a gun. Yet, in a single moment, at a time of great stress, she had mistakenly placed the gun out of her control.

In her mind, that action meant she had let her dad down. It also meant she'd let the Grieggs down.

That night, as with countless others, she would struggle to clear herself of the guilt.

*S*igmund and William pulled into the parking lot outside the quarantine barn just minutes from the airport. It was late, but the manager lived on site, so they would try to get answers. Zen thought he might still have access to the barn, but his dad would not.

"You must be curious when you look around, William. Whether you're assigned a research project or investigating a crime, it makes no difference," he schooled his son.

"Our job is discovering and interpreting data. One never knows what will be important. Pay notice to everything, even the trivial. Something seemingly insignificant can turn into a critical element in the blink of an eye."

When William walked up to the barn, he heard, "Can I help you?" The manager appeared, then, seeing Zen's face, he said, "Oh, how are you? I heard you were in the hospital."

"Yeah, I'm good now. Thank you for asking."

"Val left your car keys in my office. This stall block is empty, so come in; I'll get the keys for you."

Zen ducked into Tiger's stall as he passed. Carlos kept walking. He had a minute to search the stall. Everything had been cleaned, but he spotted a single peppermint candy on the floor beneath the feed tub.

Carlos came back with his keys.

"Would you come out and meet my father? He's a bit of a control freak and wants to triple check that I'll have everything I need in New Jersey."

"No problem," Carlos said.

Sigmund got out of the car as they approached.

"We're so sorry to bother you, but I just want to be sure that all of William's tack and equipment got onto the plane. We will fly to New Jersey soon, so if Valentina left anything behind, we can take it with us," he explained.

"Well, everything from your group has gone. Each horse had with them their own show trunk and a barrel containing their tack," Carlos said. "Val took the suitcases from your car and put them on the trailer. So, as I said, everything is gone."

"And you're sure they loaded everything onto the plane?" Sigmund asked.

"When I arrive at the airport, a fleet service agent takes control of all the baggage. Once I turn it over, I can only assume it gets on the plane. But given that we pull the horse trailer onto the tarmac next to the plane, it's a good bet that your bags got on board."

"What about Tiger? Who loaded him onto the trailer?" Zen asked.

"Valentina did," Carlos stated.

"Did you admit any horses after I left for dinner?"

"No. I'm waiting for a trailer to come in now. When I heard your car pull up, I thought you would be part of that group arriving."

"Did you say that you drove the horses to the airport?" Sigmund probed.

"Look, I get that you're protective over your horse, but what's with the third degree? I supervised everything, and I drove the trailer to the airport."

"Please, Carlos," Zen said changing his tone. "I'm told Tiger cut his face. It's nothing serious—just a scrape, really. I'm just trying to understand what might have happened."

"Well, it didn't happen here. Your horse was 100 percent when he left my care. I didn't see Val walk him into the trailer, but she would have said something if he had cut himself.

"I had eight horses going to the airport. They were the four with the Federation, and four others traveling to the same event.

"Whenever we arrive at the airport, I back the trailer up to the airline container. The horses walk from the trailer into a pod and a scissor lift loads the pod onto the airplane. All the horses were quiet, and it was uneventful.

"I do the same routine four or five times a week. I know what I'm doing. But I didn't get close enough to see a cut on any horse's face."

Carlos hesitated, and then said, "Come to think of it, they loaded Tiger on another pod. That separated him from the other Federation horses. I didn't mention it sooner because it happens all the time. They have to balance the weight in each section of the plane."

"Thanks, Carlos, you're a good man," Zen stated. As they turned back to the car, William said to his dad, "I should give Ash a call."

"Ash Rechsteiner?" Carlos interrupted. "Sorry, I couldn't help but overhear his name. Ash was here earlier today."

"You know Ash?"

"I know *of* him. He's a crazy old coot, right? He drove off when I told him the horses had left."

William said, "Ash and I are friends. He likes to check on Tiger. He's harmless. Would you mind if I left my car in your parking lot until we return from New Jersey?"

"No problem." Carlos signaled good-bye.

In the car, Sigmund reached for his cell phone. The call went straight to voice messaging.

"Sabine," he stated, "we're leaving the quarantine barn now. I wanted you to know Ash Rechsteiner was here earlier in the day. There wasn't any trouble. He just asked about the horses and left once he learned they had already flown to the United States."

When Sigmund ended his call, William showed him the peppermint in his hand.

"Dad, I found this in Tiger's stall."

"What's your point?" Sigmund asked.

"Tiger loves peppermints. Grandrew gives them to him all the time. If he had dropped one, he would have searched for it."

"That's for your notebook," Sigmund said to his son. "It may or may not be relevant."

"When I found the peppermint, I thought Tiger must have been switched here," William said. "Then, after hearing Carlos, I thought the opposite."

"Welcome to your future job. You need to examine much more evidence before drawing conclusions," Sigmund stated.

He then called Ian. "Hold off on Operation Boomerang. I need you to look into the manager at the quarantine barn and the charter company, Pegasus Air Limited. They run the facility. They are one of three places that quarantine horses for flights coming in and out of the airport.

"The man's name is Carlos. We don't have his surname. Everything seems to be above board, but I'd like to you to confirm there's nothing going on behind the scenes."

"I wish you would let me talk to Ash," William said to his father. "I won't tell him anything."

"He hasn't tried to call you, has he? Just let it be."

*I*an Stewart had started gathering data on the Israeli's project to restore the Gold Train treasure to its rightful owners. They dubbed it בומרנג מבצע or Operation Boomerang (OB).

There were five permanent members on the restoration and research team.

Two workers were on loan from museums in Tel Aviv. They were the hands-on art experts chosen for the cleaning and restoration of the art and other items (mostly jewelry).

Two Mossad analysts and one field agent tracked the owners and created the false provenances needed so as not to expose finding the Gold Train. The team was headed up by a retired agent. While Ian didn't have names yet, David would provide them soon.

The notebook the Grieggs' investigation team turned over to the Israelis, detailed information on the treasure. It pinpointed its location to a tunnel beneath an old school-house in Poland. The OB team worked out of the same building where they had unearthed the treasure.

Ian found that a strange place to work until he realized that moving the treasure would have drawn undo attention to the project.

The cover established for the group described them as researchers opening a local history museum for the city and surrounding area. They could then conduct their work and move about the town without suspicion of their true purpose. The operation had to stay secret.

Ian temporarily put OB on hold to investigate the air charter service, as his boss had requested.

Sigmund tasked Boris to track down the name behind paddle number 139. He had made the same request at the time of Tremblay's auction, but other priorities intervened, and the question went unanswered. If Niedermeyer had not been on leave, perhaps the mystery surrounding the paddle would have already been solved.

When Boris picked up the trail, he found a familiar name heading up security at the auction house—Ros Wolfman. Ros had served with Boris at GSG 9, the German Federal Police, in the early 90s.

He told Boris that security at the auction house was tight. Answering Boris' questions could cost him his job, so he had to choose his words carefully. Still, he wanted to help his former colleague. It was good to see him again.

"Any buyer can transfer funds to Tremblay's before an auction," Ros said. "It happens all the time. They can then bid anonymously or under an assumed name, spending up to the amount of cash on account, but no more without a credit card number."

Boris' friend remembered paddle 139 from the auction in question because of an incident that took place on the loading dock after the auction.

"The woman who arrived to claim the paintings expected to pick up three lots," the friend said. "When she was told someone else purchased one of the lots, she didn't believe it and caused a scene. They called me in to defuse the situation.

"When I pointed out that the paperwork clearly showed two pieces, she took them and left."

"What was her name?" Boris asked.

"I don't remember, but I couldn't tell you if I did. Let's just say she was young, in her twenties…she wore a cap, so I didn't see the color of her hair. But she was a real looker—an athletic type. It looked like she could run a marathon."

Assigned to check out Valentina Abbatelli, Chris Hutt found that she graduated from an upper secondary school in 1994. She didn't continue her education. She had no police record or driving infractions.

An accomplished rider, Valentina worked as an assistant trainer and riding instructor at a top-notch show stable. She'd recently purchased a capable show horse and started competing at the "A" show level.

The costs to travel the show circuit were high, and seemingly impossible to cover on her meager teacher's wages. But Val also had an administrative job at many of the local shows, which meant that her finances were murky. But still, too low to buy a talented horse and enter competitions.

At her age, Val had little history of her own. However, her trail led Christopher to a treasure trove of information concerning her father. Mario Abbatelli, as his surname suggested, is Italian, and old enough to be Val's grandfather. The two of them had been estranged until recently.

The youngest of four brothers, Mario grew up on the boot of Italy. The siblings worked for their father in the construction business. They had a good life. Then came 1940, and everything changed. The brothers went to war for the axis alliance.

Months later, Mario celebrated his nineteenth birthday fighting with the Italian North Africa division in Libya. When his transport vehicle flipped over in a mortar attack, it threw him twenty feet out the back of the truck, right into the path of an oncoming vehicle. He sustained life-threatening injuries, but survived, minus his left leg. Back in Italy for the rest of the war, Mario took work wherever he could find it.

The construction business had taught him street smarts from a young age. Even before the war, his activities weren't always legitimate. Wartime then turned a young man living on the edge into a crook, by necessity. He ran merchandise for the black market in a utility van he had rigged to drive with a hand-controlled clutch.

Mario Abbatelli was what's called a "change of life baby." His brothers were sixteen, thirteen, and ten years his senior. A veteran of the Great War, his father was too old to serve again. That left Mario tending for his elderly parents, all the while struggling with his own injuries. Every morning, he dreaded waking.

He became obsessed with money. Accumulating treasure through his black-market connections was the only thing that kept him going. He soon realized that stealing required talent, and he was good at it. What else was there for him to do? He wasn't always proud of it, but then he'd recall the feel of his left leg, and he just kept looting.

While his mother and father were aware of their son's connection to the "mercato nero," he was careful not to flaunt his ill-gotten cash. His parents never grasped the extent of his criminal activity.

By 1943, he was looting anything of value he could grab. He stashed it all in a cold cellar beneath the family home. He bricked off the entrance to the hidey-hole after hollowing out a short access tunnel from the garage where the construction vehicles were stored.

It took months to excavate the narrow passageway while sitting in the wheelchair he sometimes used at home. He disposed of the dirt by filling his childhood wagon and hauling it out to the garden. Everything was hard for Mario, and each day that passed made him feel more entitled to do anything he pleased.

By the time peace arrived, Mario had filled his storage room with everything from silver spoons to Bellini masterpieces. Mario used his connections to find buyers for his treasure. People were ready to restore their lives, and many of them had the means to live big.

The buyers were mostly Americans. His treasure was smuggled out of Italy on ships, one piece at a time, and the police never knew his involvement—he pocketed over 575 million lire (the equivalent of one million US dollars) in 1945 alone. He bought the best prosthetic leg money could buy.

When his parents died within months of each other in 1948, there was no reason for him to stay in their home. Two of his brothers had died in the war and his remaining sibling, Tony, was married and running a construction business of his own in Rome.

Living the life of a wealthy playboy, Mario moved to be near his brother. When Tony asked about his obvious wealth, he was warned, "You don't want to know about it."

Mario married in 1977, when his Swiss girlfriend became pregnant. He was fifty-eight at the time; she was twenty-four. They lived together for a few years, but when he continually flaunted his infidelity, his wife moved back to Zürich with her three-year-old baby girl, Valentina.

Val's parents never divorced because Mario's Catholic faith prohibited it. Had his wife wanted to remarry, she might have pursued an annulment, but that never happened.

People liked Mario and excused his destructive behavior. "His war injury left him needing to prove his manhood," they would reliably say.

Most felt sorry for him, but deep down, his friends knew that his marriage had been the best thing in his life, and he'd blown it.

Mario didn't see his daughter after she and her mother moved away. While he provided a stipend for her upbringing, he wasn't generous with anyone but himself. His lifestyle revolved around him and what made him happy. He rarely thought of Valentina.

Then 1996 arrived to change Mario's life. Tony died. This shattered Mario to his core. After months of self-pity, Tony's death became a wake-up call for how he wanted to spend the rest of his days.

In his mid-seventies he took an interest in his daughter for the first time, even traveling to one of her local horse shows in Switzerland.

When limited to her mother's modest financial support, Val rode less talented horses that kept her out of the ribbons at even the small local shows. It wasn't until recently that she had the means to grab prizes at the big shows with a well-trained horse.

On first blush, it would have been easy to assume that Mario started using his ill-gotten gains to fund his daughter's equestrian endeavors. But Christopher found no evidence to confirm that.

Valentina flourished in her new success. "Where did she get the money?" Chris asked, but he couldn't yet link anything to Mario or Tiger's abduction. The banking system in Switzerland makes it difficult, yet not impossible, to follow the money. He just needed more time.

Ian found that Carlos was a Spaniard living in Zürich for fifteen years. He had worked for the charter airline for the last ten years. His name was Carmar "Carlos" Orgullo.

Orgullo's reputation was that of a skilled horseman. He had even competed on the Grand Prix show jumping circuit in his twenties until a terrible fall ended his successful career.

Carlos' body healed, but he never overcame the fear that lingered. As the months turned to years, he never rode again.

Instead, Carlos chose another way to earn a living in the horse industry. He loved caring for the horses that came to his barn. His position allowed him to meet many prominent riders and trainers, some of whom remembered him as a competitor. More a lifestyle than a job, Carlos enjoyed himself as a single man in his forties.

Ian found no irregular financial activity. Ditto with the charter air service: There were no problems on record. All he uncovered was praise for a well-run company with a talented team of employees.

Sabine spent the evening reading about Asher Rechsteiner before attempting to contact him. She read stories written about him, but only a few contained any quotes from him. Ash lived a simple life on his farm outside of Zürich.

Ash had a modest income as an animal communicator. His wife, a well-schooled herbalist, earned much more in her practice. The bulk of their money, however, came from their own line of artisan soaps and lotions that sold in the stylish boutiques throughout the metro area.

The Rechsteiners were quite wealthy. Like Carlos, Ash and his wife didn't have jobs—they lived their dream lifestyle. Money wasn't really a factor in anything they did.

When Sabine came in from a walk, she heard Sigmund's message on her phone.

It was late, so she got ready for bed. She didn't know if or when her husband, Christopher, would be home that night.

The next morning, when Sabine couldn't reach Asher by telephone, she headed out to his farm.

It was a scenic drive from the city. Chris had stayed the night at the office, so she phoned him to convey her plans to Sigmund. "Tell him I'll be in the office in an hour."

Ash and his wife lived in a small cottage on hilly terrain that provided picturesque views. They shared the charming clearing with their cats, and dogs, and the sheep and goats that produced the milk for their soaps and lotions.

When Sabine got out of her car, a woman, whom she presumed to be Ash's wife, was busy in the yard.

Hallo," she hollered, "is Mr. Rechsteiner about?"

Sabine unlatched the gate and let herself into the garden. The fragrance of herbs surrounded her. She reached out to touch the lavender.

"Don't let any of my animals out," shouted the woman in a gruff voice.

"I won't," she said, dodging two cantankerous goats. "I'm Sabine Hutt. Are you Mrs. Rechsteiner?"

"Yes." The woman held out a bucket of kitchen scraps to coax a black and tan goat onto a milking stand.

"I'm writing a magazine article about Zen Griegg and his horse, Tiger. Everyone tells me to talk with your husband."

"You can try, but that's not to say he'll talk to you."

"Is Ash here?"

"No. He went out last night."

"When do you expect him?"

"Ash isn't conscious of time, young lady."

"I'm sorry to just drop in…I tried to call first," Sabine said, stroking the forehead of a curious lamb.

Ash's wife didn't speak or even seem to listen.

"I'll leave you my business card if you would give it to your husband," Sabine said. She reached out to wedge her card into the top rail of the milking stand.

"This is beautiful," she stated, running her hand along the side rail that held the goat in place. "It's a work of art."

Made from the branches of Black Forest trees, the artisan had intertwined twigs of all sizes to form a stall to hold the goat still. The woman sat on a matching milking stool that positioned her at the exact height to reach the goat's udder with ease.

"Ash has made all of our furniture. He's quite proud of his work," Mrs. Rechsteiner said.

"That's amazing. Does he sell it?"

"No. It's just a hobby. Besides, he takes too long. He would never make money at it."

Sabine reasoned that the woman didn't appreciate what people would pay…not for a goat stand, but for household furnishings crafted in the same style. That wasn't her concern, however, so she turned to leave.

"Young lady," the woman shouted, even though Sabine was just meters away. "He took a suitcase with him, so you may not hear back for some time." Going back to her milking, she added, "He'll call you, eventually."

"Mrs. Rechsteiner, could your husband be going to the United States for Zen's competition?"

The woman didn't answer.

"Please, it's important." Sabine reflected on Ash's unusual existence and added, "Does he have a passport to travel?"

Again, the woman didn't answer or even interrupt the rhythm of her milking.

"I'm not a reporter, Mrs. Rechsteiner. I work with Zen, he's my friend. Ash told him that his horse is in trouble. Do you know what I'm talking about?" Sabine pleaded. "Please, we need answers. Will you help us?"

The rhythmic resonance of milk spitting into the metal bucket marked time like a clock. Without a response, once again, Sabine turned to leave.

"My husband has a passport, and he took it with him," the woman shrieked out as she heard the gate snap shut.

Sabine jumped into her car and reached for her cell phone. "Sigmund, I believe Rechsteiner is on a plane heading to New Jersey. I'll be in the office in thirty minutes."

"We're all in the conference room discussing what we've learned. Do you have your go-bag in your car?" he asked.

"Yes."

"Then head for the airport and take the next flight to the States. Call me with the details. Andrew is on the speakerphone so he knows you're coming."

Turning to William, Sigmund put his hand on his son's shoulder. "I'm trusting Ash. If he's heading to the States, that's where he believes he'll find Tiger.

"I've brought the Zaugg painting out of storage and a technician is on her way with a portable x-ray machine. We must learn what makes this lack-luster painting so important."

Sigmund then surmised, "They must want the painting delivered somewhere in Zürich. But it also makes sense that Tiger is already in the States. Both communications from his abductor, made a point of saying, 'things would be back to normal soon.'

"I may read too much into those words, but if the horse hasn't already crossed the Atlantic, it would be difficult, if not impossible, to ready him for the competition. That wouldn't get us back to normal. Keep that in mind as you continue to gather information. Let's get back to work."

Sigmund asked Chris and Boris to stay behind. Then he said to them, "We will need help surveilling the ransom drop. Contact everyone you know and bring them in.

"It's likely they will want William to make the drop. We'll need eyes on him and also be able to track whoever picks up the package. We'll need as many people as we can muster."

Sigmund continued. "I want everyone mic'd up to communication out in the field. This operation is completely out of our wheelhouse. I wish David could have provided the support of his people, but, at least for now, we're on our own. We have to step up our game."

6

The Ransom

*"H*allo."

"Andrew, I'm on my way. I should get to the hotel by noon," Alana assured him.

"Okay, I'll be here."

Jet lag had overcome Andrew. He'd been running on adrenalin since the day before, and now he felt totally drained. He found himself trapped in a void between exhaustion and dread. Any amount of professional objectivism was difficult, when William and Tiger were at the center of their case.

He was unable to clear his mind from something he had said to William—that there was no reason to harm Tiger; he couldn't name his abductors.

Andrew knew it was just as likely that the kidnappers wouldn't hesitate to kill the horse to get away with their crime. Logistics were critical in any criminal activity, so keeping and caring for a horse without detection could prove too difficult and not worth the risk.

For Andrew, staying put until Alana arrived was out of the question. He couldn't relax, and he had yet to learn when Sabine would arrive.

Getting up and driving out to check on Valentina seemed his best option. As Andrew turned onto the street leading to the quarantine facility, he saw Val walking back to the hotel. He pulled up alongside her.

"Get in the car, Valentina." Andrew told her.

"What do you want now?"

"What is your father's occupation?"

"He's an old man, he doesn't work."

"Well, how did he earn money when he was younger?"

"We didn't communicate back then. We're not even close now. The family worked construction or something. I've just always known him as retired."

"Your mother never talked to you about him? How he supported you?"

"Mario never supported me. My mother did...now I support myself. What does this have to do with Tiger?"

"Maybe nothing, but I can send someone to your house to talk to your mother if you're not straight with me." The tone of Andrew's voice threatened Valentina.

"Why would you do that? She doesn't know anything!"

"She doesn't know anything about what?" Andrew asked.

Valentina fell silent, starring out the car window. Andrew saw the reflection of tears in the glass.

"I don't want to upset you, Valentina," Andrew said drawing in a deep, audible breath.

Val shouted, "My mother doesn't know anything about Tiger. I don't want you to worry her. She'll think I am in trouble or something."

"I get that you don't want to worry your mother. But you *are* in trouble. You've been lying to me," Andrew stated.

"You're not listening to me. I don't know what happened to Tiger," Valentina said.

"I don't think you're aware of how *we* earn *our* money," Andrew replied.

"Zen said you run some kind of library, researching stuff for schools or something like that. He plans to work there after winning a gold medal."

"In addition to research we are detectives, Valentina. And we employ a team of investigators who are very good at their jobs. If Tiger doesn't come back safe and sound, every one of us will come down on you like you can't even imagine.

"Do you go to the movies?" Andrew asked.

"Of course I do."

"So maybe you *can* imagine what's in your future if we don't get Tiger back. Do you understand me?"

Valentina kept silent.

"We've learned a lot about your father, and I'm certain he doesn't want us snooping around in his finances."

"My father? You people are crazy. How do you think Tiger's abduction involves my father?"

Andrew felt her anxiety build. "Because we know how he earned his money."

"Then tell me, because I never got money from him."

Andrew supposed that, sitting in New Jersey, Valentina felt vulnerable and isolated from the others involved in the scheme. He knew she would break; he just needed to apply the right amount of pressure without endangering Tiger.

"This is not how it's supposed to work," Val said. She bit at her fingernails while she stared out of the car window.

"Why don't you tell me then, how is it supposed to work?" Andrew asked.

"You give them what they want and Tiger comes back and no…" She stopped talking.

"And no what?" Andrew pulled her arm, forcing her to look at him. "And nobody gets hurt? Is that what you were going to say?"

Val wouldn't answer, but then said, "I just meant that's how kidnappings work, right? Someone asks for a ransom, you pay it, and get your horse back."

Andrew glared at her. He clearly rattled her.

"Please, just give them the painting," Val cried, "and Tiger will come home."

Bingo. That's what Andrew wanted. Valentina exposed, knowing about the painting. She was all in, involved with the plot full bore.

Realizing her mistake, Val jumped from the car. "Fuck off. I'm done talking." She slammed the door.

Andrew picked up his cell phone. "Sigmund, the groom let slip that she knows about the painting.

"I doubt the involvement extends to her parents, though. She sounded truthful, saying neither her mother nor father knew anything about Tiger. Have you heard from David?"

"Not yet, but Ian said the calls to William's phone came in from two different public phones in the railway hub.

"He found Rechsteiner booked on a Swiss Air flight scheduled to land at JFK soon." Sigmund added, "Ian also confirmed a connecting flight to New Jersey on American Airlines flight number 934. That plane arrives in Newark at 1:45 your time.

"Sabine is en route now. She will arrive in New York early afternoon. I told her to rent a car at the airport, so she should get to your hotel by 3:00."

"Okay. I'm heading back to the Cranston now to wait for Alana. We'll get to Newark in time to greet Ash."

*D*avid sat in his office, putting off calling Sigmund. He had taken the Grieggs' concerns to the head of Mossad, who then assigned him to the case.

David was briefed on all Operation Boomerang's activities to date. He was told that specialists from the art industry were brought in to authenticate, clean, and restore each piece of treasure. They worked side by side with Mossad agents.

Those civilians had to pass the same background checks as any Mossad operative. "We didn't let just anyone in." David would later tell Sigmund.

David had the names of art experts: Sara Mayer, who handled the paintings, and Yaffa Reis, who managed jewelry and other sundry items.

At the end of the project, Israel could decide to go public with the general story of finding the Gold Train and the distribution of its treasure.

The Grieggs and Ms. Eastwood could elect to reveal their involvement or remain anonymous—Mossad didn't care.

Even before the discovery of the Gold Train, lost art turned up in many places each year. In fact, the OB team had used some of those finds to insert pieces from their treasure. It was an ideal situation. It meant no one would ask troublesome questions that could disclose their operation.

To illustrate, when lost paintings were uncovered during a home renovation in Amsterdam the year before, the OB team had used Mossad operatives to sneak pieces of their treasure into another section of the building for certain discovery. The team only needed to tip off the rightful owners to claim their paintings. They never needed false provenances.

In addition to casual discoveries, research on lost art from World War II was already out in the public domain. It began with an American Army unit established in 1943, nicknamed the Monuments Men. Like those people, others have been searching for, recording, and returning stolen treasure to its lawful owners for well over fifty years.

OB piggybacked on the work of others when possible, but they returned most of the treasure through their own research. Regardless of how the beneficiaries were found, none of them would ever learn the truth about their inheritance.

That was the attraction of the plan the Grieggs suggested to the Israelis and was then implemented by Operation Boomerang. They kept the Gold Train secret. Israel, Mossad, and the Grieggs all assumed the process was functioning with perfection, until now.

David Rosen didn't want to find a crook or a mole within the operation. However, if someone had gone rogue, it was his duty to bring that person to justice. One of the civilians became a likely suspect.

Sara Mayer was a fine art expert, in her second year of work on the treasure. Yaffa Reis just started less than six months ago. Reis replaced Palmer Harel, the original jewelry specialist assigned to the team.

Harel had fallen ill at his workbench last year. He left the project on an emergency medical leave and soon after that suffered a fatal heart attack.

David recalled a disturbing history with Palmer Harel. He sucked in his gut to inform Sigmund.

"Hello, Sigmund, can we meet in Poland? I'd like us to review Operation Boomerang together, from the ground up."

"David, I can't leave Zürich until the ransom is paid and William's horse is safe. We are still waiting for instructions to deliver the painting, but I will meet you as soon as I can.

"We've x-rayed the Zaugg, which confirmed that there's nothing underneath the surface of the *Lady in Gold*," Sigmund explained. "I mentioned before that the painting had damage and therefore was of little value, so what worth it has to the individuals holding our horse is still baffling."

"I'm sure you'll find out," David said. "I can give you the name Palmer Harel." He added, "I played no role in his security clearance for OB, but hearing his name now, I recall meeting him back in the 1980s.

"It's funny what makes you remember people. Harel had a tiny dachshund named 'Kendryek' that was always by his side. The dog used to pee on the Persian rugs displayed in his shop. Kendryek was our dachshund's name when I was a child. It's a common name for that breed.

"Anyway, Parmer Harel skirted the law when working in the antiques trade throughout Europe as far back as the 1960s. He was just a tangential player, mind you; he avoided any hard-core misconduct or an arrest record. Even so, he was a slimy character with a bad reputation with the police.

"As I read his security clearance dossier prepared in 1995, agents had discounted those questionable years because he had redeemed himself to become a well-respected museum expert in Tel Aviv. The recent glowing references earned him his place on the Operation Boomerang team.

"I won't say people can't change, Sigmund, but I believe it was foolish to put Harel in OB.

"A short time before the art auction in question, Palmer Harel took ill and subsequently passed away. He could have been our troublemaker inside OB, but he's dead now. He can't play any role in what's going on with your horse.

Zen

"I'll be back to you when I know more." David hung up.

Andrew drifted off to sleep in a comfy chair on the veranda at the Cranston Inn. It was a tranquil time of day. Most of the guests were away, many of them involved with the events at Hamilton Farm. At just about noon, Alana Eastwood pulled her SUV into the parking lot right on schedule.

Andrew awoke to something nudging his fingertips. He opened his eyes. "Oh, Disraeli, what are you doing here?"

"I couldn't get a sitter," Alana said sheepishly. "I hope it won't be a problem. When I called the inn, they told me this was hunt country and dogs were welcome. Apparently they have kennels behind the hotel."

"Oh, Disraeli will be fine, won't you?" Andrew rose to hug Alana. "I'm so pleased that you're here, my dear. I'm afraid you caught me napping."

Rubbing his forehead, he said, "I can't shake this jet lag." Sitting back down, Andrew grumbled, "I'm getting old."

Alana sat next to him. "You look wonderful. You never show your age," she said with admiration. "You're feeling the stress of the investigation on top of jet lag, that would bring anyone down."

It reminded her of a particular conversation she'd once had with her German grandfather. She loved them both.

"What can you tell me, Andrew?" Alana pulled her hair into her signature ponytail. Fitting in with the horse crowd, she dressed in a vintage sweater handed down from her mother, blue jeans, and black leather boots.

Andrew said, "There's not much to tell. We believe that the horse in quarantine isn't Tiger. That's what the groom tells us. She is clearly involved in the abduction, but we have no other choice than to believe her right now.

"Whoever is holding the horse is demanding a painting that was on the Gold Train."

Alana questioned, "The treasure?"

"Yes. The painting came up to auction last fall. Curious over the actions of a single bidder, Sigmund jacked up the price. The other guy dropped out, and we ended up with an expensive portrait we didn't want...so, for that painting to be Tiger's ransom is just mindboggling. It's somehow connected to the distribution of the Gold Train treasure.

"There's also something about that painting that we must not understand," Andrew stated. "It's not valuable—nowhere near what a horse like Tiger is worth. Sigmund is trying to find the answer."

"I'm sure he will have the piece x-rayed."

"Yes, of course. He may have done it already. I haven't had an update in several hours. Sigmund is waiting for the instructions on when and where to make the ransom drop.

"Our team is doing what they do...you saw how it worked on your case. In the early stages, it's like assembling a jigsaw puzzle. They're just scanning mounds of data for a piece that fits.

"As for me, I'm tasked to trace the horse's steps from the airport to the quarantine barn. We're looking for any breech in security, but something else has surfaced that has more importance." Andrew continued. "William has this...for lack of a better word...guru, called Asher Rechsteiner. Have you heard of him?"

"I think Sigmund has mentioned him. Is he the animal communicator that helped Tiger?"

"Yes, and he's quite a character. Ash alerted us that something was wrong with Tiger a short time before we had heard from the abductors.

"Sigmund sent Sabine out to talk with Ash, only to learn he had already boarded a plane to New York.

"That suggests Ash thinks the horse is on this side of the Atlantic, but frankly, we don't know how anyone got their hands on Tiger." Andrew glanced at his watch. "Our first job is to meet Ash at the Airport. His plane lands at 1:45. Let's check you in so we can get on our way.

"Sabine will arrive here later today. I hope you don't mind sharing a room with her. If not for a cancellation, we'd be asking the staff to set up cots for both of you in my room." He chuckled.

"Mr. Griegg, I do apologize, but I'm afraid our server went down, and the file you asked to be emailed has been delayed." The desk clerk reported. "The technician is getting us back online now and your email will go out momentarily."

"It is critical that my email gets transmitted." His voice conveyed the urgency. "I'd like to speak with your expert."

"Certainly, sir."

The technician told Andrew that his work would be completed within the next few minutes. "If, for any reason, I can't bring the server up, I'll send your email from my office just five minutes away."

Andrew handed the man his business card and asked him to call if there was any further delay.

In the car, Andrew updated Alana. "The horses are in quarantine until tomorrow. Only the grooms are allowed into the barn. I haven't pushed to see Tiger; we don't want to alert anyone to a problem.

Andrew continued. "The Federation assigned a young woman named Valentina Abbatelli to groom for William. As I said, we don't trust her, yet she's the only person who has seen the horse.

"She says it's a look-alike, but it's not Tiger. As a matter of routine, the grooms take pictures of all the horses in quarantine, and as you just heard, those pictures haven't reached William yet."

"Andrew, I'm so sorry to hear all of this. I don't know what to say. How's William?"

"Well, that's a whole other part of the story you haven't heard yet. The Federation had scheduled William to fly on the plane with Tiger, but someone, probably Val, put something in his drink at dinner, which landed him in the emergency room long enough to miss the flight. The hospital didn't ID any poison, but we are retesting.

"We've been keeping it low key with Val until we get Tiger back, but when I questioned her earlier, I pushed too hard. She stormed out of my car, after revealing she knows about the painting.

"Having William and Tiger at the heart of this case is testing my composure. I'm breaking my own rules. Kidnapping is not something we've dealt with before."

"Don't be too hard on yourself," Alana said. "I'll assist in any way I can. But I'm not sure I'll be able to help at all.

"You know the visions I have are not like a light switch. I can't turn them on and off. I never know if or when anything will happen."

"It's just good to see you." Andrew looked over at her. "Alana, there's no pressure. I appreciate that you dropped everything to be here.

"Before we get to the airport, I should warn you that this Ash character is a loose cannon. We don't want him poking around asking questions. He could unwittingly disrupt Tiger's return or derail any part of our investigation.

"Frankly, we're not sure which side he's on—ours or the abductors. It's possible that alerting us to a problem was part of the captor's plan.

"I hope he's not a bad actor, because that would devastate William. He thinks the world of Ash."

"Yes!" William answered his cell phone. His father stood at his side, listening.

"Wrap the *Lady in Gold*, in its frame, in brown packing paper, and bind it with a natural twine. Go to the Zürich Hauptbahnof station and board the 5:18 train to Baden. Get on the train alone. We will contact you on the train." With those instructions, the line disconnected.

"I'll update everyone." Sigmund told his son. "This is positive, but we have little time to prepare."

William sat alone in his father's office; he stared at the portrait called *Lady in Gold.*

Before long, Boris joined him. "Hey, William, I'm here to wire you up so we can communicate on the train and anywhere the ransom drop takes us."

William pulled his shirt from his trousers. He was tall and thin, like his father. He resembled Sigmund, but with the Basque-like complexion of his Welsh mother. His almost black hair and deep blue eyes offset chiseled facial features that any artist would be eager to interpret on canvas.

"Your dad embedded a microchip transmitter in the painting's frame," Boris explained.

"Is that wise?" William questioned.

In a matter-of-fact tone, Boris chatted while he taped a thin black wire to William's chest.

"As a police detective, I assisted in a kidnapping case. I can tell you what I was told by the people in charge—if the abductors are rank amateurs, they won't discover the transmitter. If they're more sophisticated, they'll expect one to be there." Boris educated his new colleague.

"Either way, it's worth trying to fool them. There would be an enormous upside for the investigation if it works, and really no downside if it doesn't."

Sigmund shouted, "Where the hell is the photograph of the horse? We're running out of time."

As Boris tested William's microphone, Sigmund appeared with a map of the train lines.

"The train you'll board originates at the Zürich hub, so you can board as soon as you arrive. When you walk out onto the platform, you will be at the tail end of the train…here." Sigmund pointed to the platform on the map.

"Board the car that is the third from the end. That will put you at the midpoint of any platform when you exit. Sit on the same side that you enter. Take your seat facing forward.

"There are nine stops between Zürich HB and Baden— that's the end of the line for this train. We don't know which station they'll ask you to depart from, but it's likely they'll want you off somewhere within the greater metro area. Boris will board the train after you are seated."

"We'll have someone positioned at each station," Boris acknowledged. "Wherever you get off, I'll get off, and we won't be alone."

Sigmund couldn't regard the young man he spoke to solely as his son; William was now one of them, and he needed the facts, just like any other member of the team. William was a colleague.

"People will crowd onto the train at this hour, so be careful communicating with us." Sigmund told his son. "Assume anyone could be an enemy."

Then, in a rare show of emotion during any investigation, Sigmund couldn't resist saying, "William, I wish I could do this for you, but it's got to be you."

William looked at his father and nodded.

"I want you to remember that whoever's doing this has no reason to be violent. As your grandfather said, Tiger can't identify them. I'm hoping the exchange will take place inside one of the train stations.

"If you are sent to another location or told to go someplace remote, we may ask you to pull back. Trust us. We want both you and Tiger home safe."

"I do trust you, all of you," William said. "I'll follow your instructions to the letter."

"Good."

"I'm okay," William stated. "I remember you talking to Grandrew a long time ago. I assume whatever you guys were working on wasn't going well. You said, so calmly, 'I must play out the hand I've been given—I've got no choice.' I can tell you now, I'm okay. I'll play out my hand."

"I know you will."

Ian rushed into the room, handing William the picture of the horse in quarantine. Even though the enlarged image became grainy, William looked at it and said with confidence, "It's not Tiger. It's all about the hair swirl that is on every horse's forehead.

"Think of it as a cowlick," William explained. "This horse looks remarkably like Tiger, but the hair swirl is wrong. Tiger's is lower and larger than the one in this photo.

"I asked you to blow up the face when the file came through because these swirls are as good as a fingerprint for identification. It's unmistakable—this is not my horse."

The ransom drop could take place knowing that, in fact, the horse in the New Jersey quarantine barn was not Tiger.

William's horse was missing, and they had no clue when, where, or if he would be located. Following the instructions given by the garbled voice on the phone was their only hope to get Tiger back.

A short time later, William boarded the train. He took his seat, on the same side as he boarded, and faced forward, just as his father instructed. The *Lady in Gold*, wrapped in brown packing paper and bound with a natural twine, sat balanced on his knee.

The painting measured just 30-by-40 centimeters, (roughly 12-by-16 inches). It felt heavier than he'd expected because of its ornate frame.

The fact that the abductors requested the painting remain in its frame didn't go unnoticed. Sigmund had examined the frame and found nothing of interest, but he wished now he'd had time to have studied it further.

William sat and waited for something to happen.

He wondered if he might catch a glimpse of whoever was behind this ordeal...was anyone looking at him? Did anyone suspicious follow him onto the train?

Someone took the seat next to him as the train car filled to capacity. He recognized a disguised Boris board the train. They made no eye contact.

Standees crammed near the doors as William heard a conductor call out, "alles an Bord, alles an Bord, all-aboard, all-aboard," in a rhythmic tone. A buzzer sounded, and the doors closed.

William felt his muscles tighten as the train jerked forward. The movement felt measured until the train cleared the complex of rails within the station.

Once the tracks split, the rolling movement that came with speed filled William with anticipation. He felt his phone vibrate in his pocket. He held it to his ear and said, "Yes."

"Get off at Schlieren. As you leave the train, a woman will bump into you. She will grab for your parcel. Let her have it. She will push another package of similar size into your hand. Take it and walk away. The instructions to retrieve your horse are inside that package. Do you understand?"

William said one word, "Yes."

"We are watching you," the voice said. "Stay in your seat until Schlieren. Do not talk or put your hands in front of your mouth. Do not look around or communicate with anyone. Don't shake your head. Don't cough…you pick your nose and the deal is off. Your horse will not come home. Do you get what I'm saying?"

"Yes," he said.

"Good, then everything will be back to normal soon." The phone line disconnected.

Like the previous calls, the voice was distorted, and provided no benefit to the investigation. The only difference this time was having the person speak longer convinced William it was a man.

William took a few deep breaths. Boris faced him on the opposite side of the car. William looked in his direction, but not at him. Boris would have seen him take the call.

This wasn't the plan. He had been told to pass along his instructions through the wire. He knew now that he couldn't risk it.

His father had said: "If you find you can't communicate, so be it. Just do what you're told, and we will keep up. The mission is simple—all we want from the exchange is the information to bring Tiger home. Everything else comes later."

William had memorized the stations to Baden, but he looked at the map, anyway. Schlieren came first. It was barely five minutes outside of Zürich.

The exchange would happen fast. *How can I make Boris aware*, he wondered? But he forced that thought from his mind. He had to stay focused on the exchange, and besides, he had no experience to improvise anything.

Instead, William visualized how he would step from the train and look for a woman with a package. Should he leave the train right away, or wait for the crowd to clear? The voice on the phone hadn't said.

Struggling to decide, his heart pounded, making him question if he was up to the task. At twenty-one, William had to step up to do something unimaginable. He had to maintain his composure—play out the hand he was dealt, as he had told his father he would.

Suddenly, Rechsteiner's voice sounded out inside his head, guiding him as he had done before his jumping competitions. Ash told him to ground himself and stay relaxed.

"Think of how you communicate with Tiger," the voice advised. "You're no good to anyone when you're tense or nervy…you must stay grounded—connected to your brain. All your actions must come from thought. Never allow an incoherent nervous system to drive your actions. You can do this, Zen."

This wasn't telepathy that William experienced—it was memory. It was how Ash talked. He could now envision the transfer of the package, as he had visualized jumping while meditating in Tiger's stall.

The thought of Ash's words continued, *Ride first in your head, then ride in the arena*. William focused his mind and galvanized his resolve. When he opened his eyes, Zen was ready to leave the train and make the ransom drop.

When the announcement sounded out over the intercom, "Nächsten Haltestelle Bahnhof Schlieren, next stop Schlieren station," Zen's fingers tightened around the twine holding the package together.

As the train stopped, Zen stood immediately and shuffled down the crowded aisle. Walking by Boris, he told himself to remember, *Boris has my back. My dad has my back.*

Zen stepped off the train with purpose. He immediately felt a bump. Bam! Before he realized it, the package in his hand was lighter. All he saw was a hooded brown coat scurrying away.

Zen supposed that Boris wouldn't have seen the exchange since he was still aboard the train. *It all happened too fast!* he thought.

Then, amid a swarm of rush-hour commuters, dozens of schoolgirls dressed in identical hooded brown uniforms surrounded William and pushed him forward into the station.

It was a classic ransom exchange scenario played out throughout history—to use ordinary events for unintended purposes: The crowd of schoolgirls would have flooded that station at that time on every school day.

Even though he hadn't seen the exchange, Boris knew the plan instantly. He looked at the students, knowing any one of them could hide the small painting beneath their cloak. There wasn't anything he could do. There was no one girl to follow.

Tiger's abductors had plotted a skillful exchange. From timing to location, each aspect put the Grieggs at a disadvantage. Every member of the team knew it, and felt helpless.

Zen spotted an off-the-path corner, where he ripped open the package. Inside was a piece of plain artist's cotton duck, held taut by four stretcher bars found in any art supply store throughout the city.

Written on the white canvas, with a bold black marker were the words: "Miami Airport quarantine facility." Copies of a horse's passport and travel documents were pinned to the canvas. He read the horse's name aloud for the benefit of the others. "Big Broon, Miami Airport quarantine barn. They've given Tiger a new name and identity."

"Okay, William," Sigmund said. "Good job."

Sigmund added, "Boris, the transmitter embedded in the painting has gone dead. They must have enclosed the painting in a metal container. It appears these people are smarter than we thought. They've outmaneuvered us."

"Everything happened so fast, Sigmund, I saw nothing," Boris reported.

"No worries," Sigmund noted, not liking they had just been played.

"We have what we came for; let's get back to the office."

7

Where's Ash?

Sabine pulled into the parking lot of the Cranston Inn. Alana and Andrew walked out to greet her.

"How are you, Sabine?" Andrew asked.

"Traveling is exhausting, but I'm fine." Sabine always dressed to impress. The former actor wished she had left her home in casual slacks. It had been twenty-four hours since she slipped into a tight dress and heels, believing she would drive to the office after questioning Ash Rechsteiner.

Alana hugged Sabine. "I know it's a cliché, but I wish we were meeting again under different circumstances."

"I know. Have you heard anything new?"

"We've paid the ransom. Tiger is in quarantine in Miami."

Sabine pulled her small "go bag" from the car.

"Sigmund called in a favor, and he and William will be on a private jet to Miami soon. Perhaps they are already in the air. I don't have their ETA yet."

"I wonder how many calls it took for that to happen," Sabine joked.

Andrew smiled. "All he said was that it's good to have a long list of corporate clients."

"You guys treat your clients well, so it's good someone was able to step up," Sabine said.

"The important thing is that they have the passport and other travel documents to claim Tiger. I just hope they're met with no resistance," Andrew said.

"I take it Ash is still in the wind?" Sabine asked.

"That's right, and it grows more troubling by the hour."

"Ash landed in New York with a connecting flight to New Jersey. We were at the airport to meet the plane, but he wasn't on board.

"I alerted the Swiss coach to tell me if she sees him. Ian's doing what he can to track him down."

Andrew continued. "The people behind Tiger's abduction are well organized. They orchestrated the ransom drop with precision. To use Sigmund's term, we were outmaneuvered."

"This is not a normal case, is it?" Sabine questioned.

"No, nothing about it is normal," Andrew said.

"I seem to recall a discussion we once had concerning the pursuit of smart adversaries versus stupid ones. We listed the pros and cons either way."

"Well, I prefer smart people. The stupid ones may be easy to hoodwink, but they're unpredictable," Sabine responded.

An hour later, over coffee, Andrew told Alana and Sabine that with Tiger in Miami, there was no point to trace the horses from the Newark airport to the quarantine facility as he had been assigned. We'll go to the quarantine barn in the morning. "We'll see what happens when Lara Bless takes control of the horses.

"The horses will wear stable sheets coming out of the barn, and also have a protective helmet on their heads, and shipping wraps on their legs. I don't want to say anything to Lara, so I hope all this cover-up will make the look-alike a good enough match to fool her.

"If Tiger's exchange happens without a hitch, we may not have to admit to any problem. That's the ideal situation."

Sabine said, "I'm worried about what will happen when Ash surfaces. No blanket, on or off any horse, will fool him. What if he talks to the wrong people and screws things up before we can intervene?"

"I hear you. I'm worried, too," Andrew admitted.

"Why wasn't Ash on the plane?" Alana asked. "He booked the flight; he just wasn't onboard."

"Was the trans-Atlantic flight on time?" Sabine asked. "Perhaps he just missed the connection."

"That's unlikely," Alana said. "The Zürich plane landed well ahead of the New Jersey flight. I don't like it. It makes no sense."

"I hate downtime like this," Sabine said. "It feels like we're just waiting for something to happen."

"I'd like to drive over to see Valentina again," Andrew said. "Perhaps she can shed some light on Ash. While it's unlikely, he could have changed his plan and rented a car in New York. We can also look at Hamilton Farm. Who knows where he'll turn up."

"Sabine," Alana said, "I had to bring my dog with me to travel on such short notice. I need to walk him before we leave. I won't be long."

"Alana seems quiet, she's not acting herself."

"Yes, her demeanor is downright subdued," Andrew said. "I fear she's worried we will depend on her to 'feel' something to help the investigation."

Andrew continued. "I think everyone recognizes she can't turn her visions on and off, but that doesn't ease her burden. I hadn't considered the pressure she would be under when I asked her to help."

Sabine replied, "That's understandable. I'll have a chat with her later."

Alana walked Dizzy down the lane and turned into a wooded path that circled behind the hotel. She put her dog into a kennel. Her every movement felt mechanical. Her mind was elsewhere…where's Ash?

Sabine asked Andrew, "How do you think they separated Tiger to get him on a different plane?"

"I have no clue. The team will work that out. I keep saying that getting Tiger back in the morning is just the start of our investigation. In the meantime, I'm with you. I hate being in limbo. I want someone to pursue."

Sabine said, "I wish Ash had been on that flight. His disappearance is an unneeded distraction. I doubt if he travels much. Do you think he could he have gotten confused and missed the plane, despite having plenty of time?"

"Let's hope it's that simple," Andrew said. "I want it to go smoothly tomorrow and this Ash situation is complicating that from happening."

Andrew looked at Sabine and said, "You've seen William and Tiger together. It will shatter him if anything happens to that horse." Andrew sat back. "And it's not just William—it would devastate all of us."

"I just thought of something interesting...what if Ash flew to Florida?" Sabine asked.

"If he had sensed something in Zürich, then he was wrong...at least about the horse's destination. To me, that suggests he's not in on the plan.

"Now that he's vanished, what if he found out, or sensed by other means, that Tiger is in Miami?

"What if Ash wasn't on the New Jersey flight, because he changed his ticket to fly to Florida? He could be there now, looking for Tiger."

"That's a brilliant point," Andrew said. "I'll pass it along to everyone."

When Alana returned, Sabine shared her idea that Ash might be in Miami.

Alana agreed, "That would make sense."

"We should be able to get confirmation on that fairly soon," Andrew said.

In the meantime, they drove to Hamilton Farm. They walked over to the stall assigned to Tiger. His name was already on the door.

Andrew introduced the women to Lara Bless and Melanie Pfenninger. He reiterated their excuse for why they needed to speak with Ash.

"William's heard that Ash has this crazy notion that the flight has traumatized Tiger. Apparently he's so concerned that he has flown over to be of help. We don't want him to be disruptive, so if you see him, just ignore him. Once my grandson arrives, he can bring Ash back down to earth."

"We know all about Ash Rechsteiner, Mr. Griegg, and we pay little attention to him under any circumstances." Melanie chuckled. "Frankly, we've never understood your grandson's devotion to him."

Melanie told Andrew that he didn't need to show up at the quarantine facility in the morning. "You could wait for Tiger here."

"Wait here!" Andrew jested. "You must be crazy! William would never forgive me if I didn't follow his horse every step of his journey.

"By the way," he continued, "I'm curious how Valentina Abbatelli came to groom for Tiger. Did you know her prior to this trip?"

"Yes." Lara confirmed. "Val has been on our groom list for quite a while. It's funny you should ask, though, because when she called she specifically asked for Zen, as most of the horse people call him.

"The other riders had long-established relationships with their grooms. So we matched them up right away. Have you noticed they seem to be—help me, Melanie…how should I put it?"

"They're besotted with each other," Melanie said with a smile. "I assumed Val was on a mission when she asked to groom for him."

"I like besotted. It's better than what I was thinking," Bless said with a grin.

"Ah, yes," Andrew bantered. "If you were thinking of a horse metaphor like 'hot to trot', that hasn't gone unnoticed."

*U*pon leaving Hamilton Farm, they drove out to check in with Valentina. Andrew said to her, "We're looking forward to seeing the horses in the morning."

Andrew introduced Alana and Sabine as friends who came to watch William ride. He acted upbeat and natural with Val. But when the women walked back to the car, his tone changed in a heartbeat.

"What *will* take place in the morning, Valentina?"

"I don't know. But if I were you, I'd try to keep Lara and Melanie away from the horse," she said. "Once I get him into his stall at Hamilton Farm, you're home free.

"Everyone will be too busy to pay close attention to the horses in their stalls. I'll still be the only person handling him. The other riders will preoccupy Lara and Melanie until Zen arrives. Do you know when that is?"

"Not yet," Andrew said. "But how will the horses be switched back? Where is Tiger?" Andrew didn't acknowledge that he knew Tiger had been flown to Florida.

"Mr. Griegg, I haven't been completely honest. There's something I've been afraid to tell you."

"What is that?"

"I overheard something at the airport in Switzerland. It meant nothing at the time until I found the note about Tiger being kidnapped—then it made sense.

"I wanted to tell you, but you acted like I was involved. I was terrified to say anything."

"What did you hear?"

"A man was talking on his cell phone. He said something like 'we get the painting, they get the horse.' I couldn't hear everything, but I think he said Miami Airport."

"What did he look like?"

"I don't know. He had his back to me. I had no reason to pay attention to him."

"Okay."

"That's why I told you to give them the painting. I remembered that conversation. I should have told you sooner, but I was scared. You were treating me like a criminal. I just wanted to get out of your car and run away from everything."

"Fair enough. I admit my temper flared. "You're right, Tiger was flown to Miami. William and his father went to pick him up and trailer him here.

"Could this man you heard on the phone have been Ash Rechsteiner?" Andrew asked.

"I don't know."

"Did you know Ash is here?"

"No."

"He flew over, but we can't locate him."

"Then I suggest you find him and keep him away. He's the only one who can screw this up now," Val said testily.

Andrew didn't know what to make of Val's claim, but he saw no harm in acknowledging Tiger's whereabouts.

He called Sigmund to say, "I don't believe her, as you well know; cons often make up stories to legitimize themselves. I played along, because until we get Tiger back, communicating with her is useful."

The one point everyone could agree on was that having Ash on the loose was dangerous. He could screw things up big time—so where the hell was he?

Ian called to say Ash had booked no flight to Miami. They were back to square one, and the clock kept ticking.

Mossad agent David Rosen arrived in Walbrzych, Poland, home of the Israelis' Operation Boomerang. The busy city was situated deep in the Owl Mountains, near the popular tourist attraction, the historic Książ Castle.

For many years, treasure hunters believed Książ to be the most likely place to find the legendary Nazi Gold Train—and they were almost right.

Talk of a gold train had spread through Berlin in the spring of 1945 as the Nazi war effort deteriorated. They called it *Der Goldzug*. But when the war ended, so did the chatter and any curiosity over a gold train soon died.

It wasn't until the late 1950s that people started talking in the form of deathbed confessions. They claimed they had seen or played some role in hiding the "gold train" or "ghost train," as they sometimes referred to it.

Any serious research produced nothing of substance, but it didn't stop people from dreaming and searching for remote railroad tracks that could support such a tale.

By the 1960s, the treasure legend ballooned, and fortune hunters from all over the world looked for places where train tracks that existed in 1945 might lead to a site suitable to conceal a buried train car.

The viable locations were endless, and with the advent of geological technology every few years, the search area just kept expanding.

As the internet took hold in the 1990s, the number of fortune hunters continued to increase. Gold Train seeking became a cottage industry.

Over time, even with no fortune found, people profited from the mere idea of a treasure…and the Owl Mountains provided endless locations to bury a train car.

As far as the castle being involved in the legend, it was off limits to searchers. The known complex of tunnels beneath the compound, however, just bolstered the notion that the Gold Train was real and just out of reach.

Historical records revealed that, in time, those tunnels would have extended under the city of Walbrzych. Alas, that never happened. The Nazis simply ran out of time when the war ended.

The legend story, however, was real. And, thanks to the Gold Train notebook that Andrew and Alana had found two years earlier, Israeli agents discovered the treasure in a tunnel smack dab in the center of Walbrzych.

The Nazis never intended to bury the train at all—just its contents. If the Nazis themselves floated the rumor of a treasure-laden train car buried in the surrounding area, it was a brilliant redirect.

The notebook told the complete story. The Nazis packed the treasure in wooden crates, transported it by train to Walbrzych, and then buried the crates in a passageway attached to the basement of a run-down schoolhouse.

No one with any actual evidence of the Gold Train talked because they had died after the event, fled to South America in 1945, or needed to hide their participation in war crimes. Only rumors were left behind.

Representatives from Israel purchased the school building and surrounding property in 1995. They immediately opened the tunnel and began cataloging the treasure.

Since the tunnel had served as a secure repository for fifty years, they left the treasure in place while their work progressed. Operation Boomerang was born.

The Grieggs and the Israelis restricted the number of people with knowledge that the Gold Train had been found. They called for a quiet resolution to the legend. There would be no fanfare. After all, the treasure owners had a right to privacy before the war. Why should they be obliged to go public now?

The Walbrzych city records designated the building over the tunnel as "Budynek Fabryki Porcelany," after the wealthy porcelain magnate that constructed it. A capstone bearing that name adorned the main entranceway; it became known as Porcelain House.

The three-story brick structure, erected in 1810, first opened as a school. It was large. The impressive façade boasted 400 square meters (over 4,000 square feet) of interior space. In the early 1900s, an adjacent two-story addition more than doubled its size.

Since its construction, the building also served as a general store, a guesthouse, and a tavern. It reverted to a school for wayward teens before the Nazis occupation during World War II.

Abandoned prior to the Israelis' purchase, the building had fallen into disrepair. The entire district had languished for many years, coinciding with the Soviet occupation and the post-war economic downturn.

But now, by the late 90s, Walbrzych was a lively tourist destination for visitors to the castle and the many outdoor activities offered by the Owl Mountains.

Ecotourism boomed and became a catalyst to rejuvenate the region. Eco jobs replaced lost businesses. The legend of the Gold Train, and the arrival of treasure hunters played no small part in adding to the attraction.

Once the Israelis secretively took ownership of Porcelain House, their shell corporation made it known the building would reopen as a local history museum. The timing couldn't have been better as an apt cover to restore the treasure.

Over time, both missions would come to pass. Another group of people were busy to make the museum a reality.

In the meantime, that cover story concealed the goings-on within the building.

To make things more secure, the core members of OB lived on-site, which enabled the staff to log long hours and complete their mission in record time.

Mossad granted David the highest security clearance to conduct a forensic audit of their operation. That clearance extended to Sigmund Griegg, when he arrived.

"We expect your cooperation with anything they require. We have given both men complete access to our undertaking," Joan Shulman, who managed OB, said.

She did not, however, indicate any breakdown of security. Her people believed that Rosen and Griegg were conducting a routine examination, but, as anyone who's been the target of an audit can attest, there's nothing routine about it.

David expected everyone he spoke with to be standoffish, so he listened with care when Yaffa Reis volunteered her long-held belief that she had found a breach in security.

"I've had this anxiety since soon after I arrived," Yaffa explained. "The first task of any operation like this is to establish an index to record each item. OB based their index on standard protocols. It represents an inalterable 'bible,' if you will, to control all aspects of the work processing the treasure.

"We mark the index when any item leaves the tunnel," she said. "Anyone can scan the pages at any time, to view, in chronological order, every action taken on each individual piece of the treasure—research, cleaning, repair, owner ID, provenance—you get what I'm saying. We record it all.

"As I said, it's our bible, and serving that purpose, means accuracy is paramount. So when I found a logging error, it was alarming.

106

"Please explain," David said.

"It involves the cataloging of a specific group of coins," Yaffa said. "Understand that Sara and Palmer faced a monumental task. Fifty years ago, the Nazis dumped the treasure here and then sealed the tunnel. No one would have expected such a lengthy delay before it was reopened.

"Had the war ended differently," she said, "the Nazis would have uncovered it immediately. Thankfully, history provided another outcome.

"Fortunately, the tunnel remained dry. That was a miracle in itself. The tunnel and the treasure survived unscathed.

"Once reopened, the experts applied proven protocols to handle the treasure, as I said. But the sheer size of the hoard would have overwhelmed two people. While they could have made a mistake, what I uncovered is no blunder."

"Why do you point to a problem with coins?"

"Well, there are two reasons for concern. First, the index shows only one line item for coins. It lists 'a pouch of gold coins,' without specifying individual coins within the pouch.

"When I arrived, the pouch contained a dozen unrelated gold-plated coins. Yet, as I said, the index listed 'gold coins.'

"This language is telling because at the time the antique coins were minted, the value of metallic money came from the commodity itself, along with its weight.

"By contrast, we use representative money today, which has no intrinsic value. It represents a specified amount for the sake of legal tender.

"In other words, gold coins are pure gold, and no expert would ever record gold-plated coins as simply gold.

"Not listing the number of coins in the pouch is also a problem. That would be a breach of protocol under any indexing system."

"Who made the index entry?" David asked.

"It was Palmer Harel," Yaffa said.

"Second, and likely more significant, I found one loose coin on the tunnel floor by accident. It happened soon after I arrived. The coin was an aureus medallion, an ancient Roman gold coin that would sell for 750,000 US dollars—trust me, I looked it up on the internet. It is very rare."

With that, Reis had David's attention.

"You *found* the coin?" he asked.

"Yes. In the tunnel…well, I should explain that when any of us uses the term *tunnel*, we are referring to our vault. That's what the tunnel represents to us. It's secure, and it's where everything is stored when not in use.

"Anyway, one day, I went into the tunnel to bring out a small box of jewelry I had started cleaning the day before. When I bent down to lift the box, my fingers felt the hard edge of an object stuck in the dirt floor. I brushed back the loose dirt and found, wedged in a crack between the wall and floor, one of the rarest Roman coins known to exist.

"I ask you, what are the odds that a single Roman coin would be part of the vast Gold Train treasure? Or then, to have that coin omitted from the index? It's ludicrous."

"I'm listening," David said.

"The only coins cited as part of the Gold Train treasure are the ones inside the pouch. And I encounter a coin on the floor? We're not that careless. I can't say it in stronger terms, something is wrong.

"I've had time to think about it, so I don't say this lightly. The coins in the pouch are old, but not rare or particularly valuable, and are not on par with the rest of the treasure. I don't understand why they would have even been on board the Gold Train to begin with.

"The pouch is old—much older than the coins inside— and is far more likely to have held the aureus medallion that I found on the floor. So I asked myself, has someone switched the coins? You know, stolen them?"

"But," David interjected, "if what you say is true, couldn't the coins have been switched before the treasure was put in the tunnel?"

"Yes, I suppose that could be true. But then, how do you explain the coin on the tunnel floor? Or why the index would be so ambiguous?" Yaffa asked.

David nodded in acceptance of her argument.

Yaffa stated, "If I were logging the pouch today, I would list twelve gold-plated coins circa whatever date—I don't recall—and I would give the country of origin. I would also refer to the pouch as a purse, a leather purse circa 1600."

"Wouldn't that make the pouch, or purse as you call it, a different age from the medallion?"

"Yes. The medallion is 300 CE, but we seldom see purses from that period outside of museums. They're not found in the hands of coin collectors."

"I see," David replied.

"I've told this to my superiors, Mr. Rosen. The problem they have is the same problem I have: If someone stole any coins, how could they have gotten them out of the building?

"You are the first auditor to come in, so I felt it my duty to tell you my story. I say that despite the fact no one else has taken me seriously. I'm not complaining, but I'm hoping *you* will take me seriously."

"Well, your story is fascinating. Thank you for sharing your concerns," David stated, all the while reflecting that her testimonial validated not only Sigmund's worry for OB, but his own unease learning that Palmer Harel had been involved. Like Yaffa, he now believed something was wrong.

"It's a locked-room mystery Mr. Rosen," Yaffa said with a slight grin. "If anyone had theft on their mind, coins could be brought into the building with ease. What I can't explain is how any coin could be smuggled out?

"If I'm right, coins akin to the medallion could be the single most valuable pieces in the entire treasure—and we can't know the number of coins involved."

"Ms. Reiss, you make a compelling case that I *do* consider serious. You can trust me to follow up. But now, I have other questions for you to answer."

David interviewed each of Operation Boomerang's team members. He then reviewed their security procedures with the Mossad agents, all the while weighing the plausibility of Yaffa's coin mystery.

He approached the person in command of Operation Boomerang, Joan Shulman, and then spoke with the head of Mossad. They were well versed in Yaffa's story, and they each concurred: OB security seemed airtight.

Only the museum experts handled the treasure and had access to the tunnel vault. Mossad agents provided protection 24/7. Everyone, including the guards, went through a pat down and a metal detector scan when leaving the section of the building where the treasure was handled and stored.

It seemed unlikely that any Mossad security agent would conspire to steal the coins—no matter how much they were worth. But it wouldn't be the first time an agent went rogue.

Yet, no one could satisfy Yaffa's concerns, or explain the loose medallion she found in the tunnel. It seemed something had gone wrong.

To do his job, David had to consider everyone a subject of his investigation. That is, if he even had an investigation. But he kept returning to one certainty: The *Lady in Gold*, Palmer Harel, and a Thoroughbred horse named Tiger were all connected, and the only apparent link was the Nazi Gold Train treasure.

*T*hirty-six thousand feet over the Atlantic, Sigmund allowed himself to accept a whisky from his friend, American software developer Deroy Jones.

"If you called five minutes later, I'd have been in the air," Jones said.

"Well, Deroy, William and I are indebted that you could wait for us to get to the airport. As you know, my business doesn't allow me to discuss the events that put us in such dire need to get to Miami."

"No explanation necessary." Deroy turned to William and asked, "What can I get for you?"

"I'm going to surprise my father and follow his lead."

"Then it's whisky all round. I've had dinner in Zürich, but I'm sure I'll find a snack for you," Deroy said.

He returned with William's whisky, a few bags of chips, and several chocolate bars.

"Thanks, Deroy; it's been a tough day."

"Well, there's nothing like the feeling of flying to leave the stress behind...what do you think about my jet, William?"

"Yeah, you know how it's done. Maybe I should come to work for you instead of my father."

"Oh, you're working with your dad, now? I didn't realize that. So you're out of college?"

"Well, I'm through with school soon, and it's not official that I will work for my dad. I have a big commitment to show jumping for the next few years, but I'd like to start training at the company part-time...just to get my feet wet."

"So there's still time for me to steal you away?" Deroy teased. "Sigmund, would you still be my friend if I convince your son to work for me?"

"I think I'm good with the family business." William sipped the whisky with caution, hoping his stomach would handle the alcohol.

"You should listen to the man." Sigmund ribbed his son. "We haven't discussed your salary yet—Deroy might have a better offer."

The jet maneuvered into its flight path for Miami.

Undaunted by the angle of the plane as the pilot banked, Deroy asked, "Now, Sigmund, how much are you traveling these days? I bought this plane a few years ago when I started schlepping across the United States at the drop of a hat.

"Now I'm crossing the Atlantic several times a month. This flight's on the house, but we *do* take paying customers, if you're ever interested."

"I travel a bit, but I'll tell my dad. Andrew is the globe-trotter, these days." Sigmund told him.

"This is a Falcon. People look at me and assume I brought myself a toy, but it's the best investment I've ever made. It's removed all the barriers I faced with commercial travel." Deroy continued. "My wife drops me on the tarmac alongside the hanger and I'm off. It's complete freedom."

Now, if you have an impression of Deroy Jones as some geeky elitist who came into a gazillion dollars by taking a gaming software company public, you'd be wrong.

Deroy is a former college football tight end turned Navy seal. After losing both his legs above the knee in Desert Storm, he formed a company to develop computer-assisted prosthetic limbs.

Deroy put everything he had on the line and it paid off. His was now the most advanced technology company in the field worldwide.

He started out to improve mobility for amputees, at a time when his client base was growing exponentially. For the first time in history, soldiers were surviving war with the most profound injuries.

Deroy set his mission to restore as much of their lives as humanly possible. He was both an owner and a client. When he said, "I feel your pain," he meant it.

Most of his success to date involved forearms, hands, and fingers, but looking down the road, anything was possible. He employed a talented group of scientists and engineers.

After chatting over drinks, Deroy checked with his pilot for their ETA in Miami. Then all three men reclined their seats to drift off to sleep.

When they landed, Sigmund held out his hand to his friend. "I hope to repay you someday, Deroy—or at least be able to explain the situation."

"Glad I could help, Sigmund. Call me anytime. I'll always be in your debt for helping me start my business."

"You're forgetting you paid me for that. You don't owe me anything."

"A fraction, Sigmund, that's what you charged me…you know that. Money is meaningless if you don't do good things with it—I learned that from your actions, buddy."

"Yeah, I think you've got the do-good market cornered, Deroy. So I'll just thank you again."

"William, it was good to see you. My job offer is serious, so make sure your dad pays you well." Deroy winked.

"Throw in use of the plane and you got a deal." William shot back.

Sigmund rented a car, and the two of them checked into a hotel at the airport. It would be several hours before they could claim Tiger from quarantine. William was on the phone to horse transport companies to book Tiger on a truck as soon as possible.

The winter horse show season had wrapped up, so he expected it to be difficult to find an open stall with so many horses heading north.

A rig with an air-ride system was optimal. Otherwise, Tiger might stress his legs during the lengthy trip. They both had to be ready to jump a high-stakes Grand Prix course within days.

On the fifth call, he caught a break. He found a cancellation. It was for a single stall, and not the stall-and-a-half size William would have preferred for a horse as big as Tiger; but beggars, as they say… he booked it on the spot.

The trucking company was Equi-Air/Ground Transport. They were international and William had heard of the name.

The timing couldn't have been better. The van was taking horses from a training track in Ocala to Belmont Park in New York. The drivers had waited overnight in Wellington to pick up a show horse, but as that order canceled, Tiger would fill the open stall.

The van was now en route to the quarantine barn near the Miami Airport. After stopping in Ocala to pick up the racehorses, it would travel non-stop to Hamilton Farm.

William presented the travel documents at the quarantine office, pushing the paperwork under the Plexiglas shield at the counter.

The woman flipped through the papers with experience. "Your horse is Big Broon?"

William nodded in agreement.

"We were wondering when you'd show up. Your horse was the only one with no one asking about him." She glared as if he didn't care about his horse.

William ignored her snide comment.

Sigmund noted his son's maturity. His aptitude for the Griegg business was being tested under an emotional firestorm when it should have been the most exciting week in his young life.

"Where are you taking the horse?"

"He's going to New Jersey," William said. "The Equi-Air truck is outside waiting for him."

"What's the horse doing here?" the clerk asked. "Why the heck didn't you fly him into New York?"

"It's a lengthy story that's not your concern. We just want to get on our way." Sigmund interrupted.

They went outside to wait for their horse.

As Tiger walked toward them, Sigmund saw how easily a dead ringer could be found. Tiger was dark brown with a small white star on his forehead. While the shipping boots he wore now covered the white hairs around his left front hoof and the white sock on his right hind ankle, any white could be added, or disguised with a little hair dye.

Breeders have cultivated Thoroughbred bloodstock to produce his body type and characteristics over and over. Tiger is just a little larger than most.

In fact, he was big at 17.2 hands and over 600 kilograms (or about 1,400 pounds). He was in "good flesh," as they say. While tall and heavy, there wasn't an ounce of extra fat on his bones. Tiger looked fit and ready to compete.

A smile covered Zen's face the second he saw Tiger. He reached for the small bottle of essential oil in his pocket.

When Tiger noticed Zen, even Sigmund recognized his look of acknowledgement. Soon they could all take a breath and relax.

Taking hold of the lead rope, Zen allowed his horse to breathe in the familiar scent of lavender oil on his wrists. He then took a moment to cradle Tiger's head and draw him into his shoulder, as he would often do at home.

When his horse pulled back, wanting to absorb the newness of his surroundings, Zen paid little attention. There would be ample time for Tiger to settle at Hamilton Farm. "It's okay, buddy, I'm here now." Zen scratched his horse's neck instead.

After loading Tiger into the van, Zen found relief for the first time since he'd taken that call from Ash. He could now concentrate on the competition…except for wondering when Ash would turn up.

As much as he wanted to remain part of the Griegg team, he accepted he couldn't do that and ride at the same time. Tiger would pick up on his stress, and neither one of them could compete with that albatross hanging over them.

When they got in the rental car for the drive to North, Sigmund reiterated that point to his son.

"You need to be totally focused on your riding. I can't even brief you." He told William. "Don't feel left out; it's the only way for each of us to function."

"But I'm worried about Ash, Dad. Where is he? What could have happened to him?"

"I can't answer that now, but I promise to tell you whatever we find out. I understand what Ash means to you."

"I'm not sure you do, Dad. You know it's difficult for me to make friends. I mean, there were a lot of guys and girls that I knew at school in England, but only a few that I felt close to. There's a big difference when you let someone get close. You expect them to be there forever.

"Maybe not forever, but you expect friendships to last a long time." William searched to find the right words.

"Is this about Angela?" his dad asked.

"You know about her?"

"Yes, your grandfather told me when the two of you broke up."

"That's part of it. When you share your life with a friend, you disclose things about yourself. Things you don't tell to just anyone.

"I left all my English friends a few years ago. Soon I'll be leaving my college friends behind as well. Ash came into my life when I needed a friend. He's been a constant in my life.

"You might think that's weird because he's Grandrew's age. But the things Ash has taught me have felt right. Even just seeing how he lives his life has been worthwhile.

"You've made me aware that I've had the benefits of money growing up, but I shouldn't let it influence who I am as a person. You've said to judge people by their character and their actions. But some people don't give Ash a chance.

"I know people think he is silly. But they're wrong. I think he's brilliant. Teaching me to meditate and practice tai chi has been beneficial—and not just for my riding, but for everything I do.

"That training helped me yesterday during the ransom drop. It enabled me to remain calm and focus my mind on the job at hand. I feel I'm a better man because of Ash."

Sigmund let his son reflect without interruption.

"You and Grandrew teach me as well, and I'm grateful, but it's different coming from Ash."

"William, I'm glad you have Ash as a friend. I'm keeping an open mind about him. But, you must see that we have to solve this case before I can trust him completely. Your safety has been at risk."

"I know. Ash makes it difficult. But I wouldn't be riding at Hamilton Farm without his guidance. No one would call me Zen if not for him. I know that for sure."

"The way you talk about Ash," Sigmund stated, "reminds me of the vicar that lived next to you in England. He arrived at another time when you needed spiritual guidance.

"I think of Ash in the same way. People come in and out of our lives. They can bring stability, or create change…some will become friends and we have to appreciate them, knowing that they may not always be there. It's important for you to

understand this William, because you will have the same impact on other people."

Sigmund continued. "I'm not trying to make light of
Ash's disappearance. I'm as concerned for his welfare as you
are. But people have committed a crime. One of the first
things you'll learn working with us is that bad and unexpected
things happen during the commission of any crime.

"The longer Ash remains missing, the more troubling it
becomes. You must prepare yourself for several outcomes:
That Ash is involved, and he's gone into hiding, that he isn't
involved, but hiding anyway, or the possibility that something
terrible has happened to him.

"The abductors poison you, William. Ash is older and
may not have been able to survive similar treatment. I don't
want to scare you; I just have to be honest with you."

8

Reunited

Andrew pulled his car into the parking lot at the quarantine facility just behind the truck and horse trailer carrying the Federation trainers Lara Bless and Melanie Pfenninger.

"Good morning," Andrew shouted over to them.

"Hello!" Lara waved back.

Andrew walked over to Lara as Melanie entered the door marked *Office*.

"Valentina is already here with the other grooms, getting the horses ready. They'll be out any minute," she said.

"It's crisp today." Andrew shivered, zipping up his jacket.

"Yes," Lara agreed, "but no rainfall. The footing in the schooling arena will be in nice shape for the horses to get moving and ready to jump."

Soon, Melanie joined them, arranging a stack of discharge papers in her hands. "The horses will be right out," she said.

As Val had suggested, Andrew planned to keep Lara and Melanie talking when the grooms came out and loaded the horses into the trailer. He glanced over at the barn and saw the doors opening.

That was the signal for Alana and Sabine to get out of the car and walk over to say hello.

Even with his foreknowledge, the horse Valentina led out looked so much like Tiger, Andrew was sure no one would suspect an imposter. *So far, so good,* he thought as they latched the trailer doors shut.

The same was true when arriving at Hamilton Farm. Val hurried the horse into the show barn before anyone was the wiser. She implied to Andrew that the truck carrying Tiger should not arrive before nine PM. After that, the barn would be quiet.

As Andrew drove back to the Cranston Inn, he tried to envision where Tiger's truck would be at that moment. With two drivers, they'd go non-stop to New Jersey, as would his son and grandson, following behind.

Andrew speculated William would take the wheel for parts of the trip, even though, at his age, he couldn't legally drive a rental in some of the states. Andrew called Sigmund to tell him the time schedule Val had indicated.

"The imposter is in the stall at Hamilton Farm," Andrew said. "It went off without a hitch. Valentina had bundled the horse up, as they do for shipping, but even so, he's a dead ringer for Tiger.

"Val arranged for his stall to be at the end of the block assigned to the Federation. It's up against a hard wall. There will be no passersby."

"Okay, Dad. We were delayed several hours in Ocala when the race horses weren't ready to travel. We won't reach New Jersey until the early hours. The barn manager knows 'Big Broon' is coming. He agreed to let us arrive at five AM, but no sooner.

"We had to ask the truck drivers to slow down. They grumbled until I assured them they would be well compensated for the extra time."

It was exactly five o'clock when William walked Tiger off the van. Following the instructions pinned to the canvas at the railroad station, he put his horse into the stall marked Big Broon. He left all the travel documents thumbtacked to the wall inside the stall.

William walked back outside to see why his father hadn't followed them into the barn. He found his dad chatting with the drivers and paying them the generous tip.

When they returned to the stall, William said, "This isn't Tiger." They rushed to the Federation's block and found their horse standing in the end stall. Thankful they were finally back to normal; William hugged Tiger again. They drove to the Inn for a short rest.

The Griegg group planned to meet for breakfast at eight o'clock. As William walked into the dining room, he found Alana and Sabine already seated.

"Hello," he said. "I can't believe I'm finally here. It's good to see you," he acknowledged.

Everyone smiled happily for the first time in days.

"Is Tiger okay?" Alana asked.

"Tiger is fine. I'm so relieved."

"It's such a long drive from Florida." Sabine asked, "How did it go?"

"I enjoyed it. I looked at the back of the horse van the entire way, knowing Tiger was safe inside," William said. "The stress was off. My dad and I got to talk. It was nice."

"Male bonding?" Alana asked.

"Yeah, we rarely get the chance for that," William said. "Dad's a good listener. When I was at school in England, my friends would complain about their parents, but I've never felt that way. I actually like spending time with my family."

"Speak of the devil," Sabine said.

Sigmund walked in and poured himself coffee. Andrew followed close behind.

"I had the best rest last night," Andrew declared as he sat at the table. "It's amazing how good I feel this morning."

"I think we all feel good this morning," Sigmund stated for everyone.

"I'm in a hurry to get to Hamilton Farm, so who wants to drive me?" William asked.

"Eat breakfast first, and then I'll drive you over," his grandfather said to him.

"The rest of us will stay here and talk to Zürich about the investigation," Sigmund said. "And, for everyone's benefit, William must concentrate on the competition, so he'll have no involvement with the case until he is back in Switzerland with Tiger. We'll keep him informed on Ash's whereabouts, but nothing else."

"I've been thinking about telling Lara that I don't want Valentina to groom for me," William said. "Grandrew can take over."

"No, William, you can't do that. You must act normally around her," Andrew said to him.

"Your grandfather is right. It has to be business as usual between you and Val."

"But, Dad, you understand that Val and I were…"

"I understand perfectly. We all do. It won't be easy," his father said. "Val has had contemptuous moments with your grandfather, so she will be on edge with both of you.

"Just ignore all that. If you must say anything, tell her the only thing on your mind is the competition and that you don't want to talk about anything else."

"Acting plays a role in our job as investigators," Andrew suggested. "You'll team with Sabine during your company training, she will teach you a lot in that regard. As you know, she spent several years in the theater, that's how we met.

"In the meantime, I'll be around to help you avoid any uncomfortable interactions with Valentina," Andrew said. "Just act like nothing is wrong."

When William arrived at Hamilton Farm, the other riders crowded around to wish him well. Even the somewhat cold competitors sounded concerned over his health. Some were, after all, teammates. It was no time for petty differences.

"Zen, you look great!" said one groom. "It's so weird, what happened to you, right? Val has been taking excellent care of Tiger for you."

Another asked, "Are you fit to ride? We're not a team without you."

"Yes, I'm fine," Zen said. He was back around horse people; he acted naturally, all the while dreading the inevitable encounter with Valentina—but she never showed.

"What have I missed here?" Zen asked.

A rider's husband said, "It's been quiet."

One rival walked up. "Except we schlepped your crap halfway round the world for you," he wisecracked. "You're

Zen

welcome." They gave each other a half-handshake, half-hug, as competitors do.

Another rider assured him, "Seriously, Zen, I know you were worried about Tiger flying, but all the horses were fine. The flight was uneventful."

Lara Bless walked in. "Zen, you're here," she said, hugging him with genuine affection.

"Yes, here at last," he said.

"Melanie will arrive any moment. I need you up on Tiger and out in the schooling ring in fifteen minutes, understand?"

"I'd like to walk the grounds with Tiger today, just to get him moving," he said, forgetting that, for them, "Tiger" hadn't just arrived a few hours ago.

"Valentina did that yesterday. I want you in the saddle," Lara instructed with the stern voice of a coach. "Is there any reason for you not to ride?"

"Truthfully, Coach, I think I need another day to be 100 percent. But, walking will help me."

"I don't need you at 100 percent today," Lara stated. "If you can ride later in the day, do it. If Tiger was a different horse, I'd have someone else up on him already. Don't force my hand."

"I know that," Zen said. "Just as you know that putting another rider on Tiger would be a mistake. I'm here to do a job, and I plan on doing it."

Andrew overheard his grandson's rather heated exchange with his coach. Tempers will flair at these events. It didn't concern him; he said nothing.

With just a few days before the competition, Zen and Andrew walked Tiger several times that day.

One of those walkabouts took them by Big Broon's stall block. Zen asked his grandfather if he had a peppermint in his pocket.

"You know I do," Andrew said.

"See if Big Broon will eat one," he asked.

"Looks like this horse isn't interested in mints."

Zen smiled.

The next time they passed Big Broon's stall, it was empty.

"Where do you think he is?" Zen asked.

"And where is Val?" his grandfather responded. "Big Broon's name is off the stall, so he's not coming back."

"I assumed Val was avoiding me. Perhaps she's taken the imposter away."

"That would make sense," Andrew said. "If we had gone to the police, the last thing she would have wanted is the dead ringer stalled a few blocks away from Tiger."

Zen did not ride Tiger that day.

"I'm afraid Valentina has been under the weather today." Lara told Andrew later that evening.

"Nothing serious, I hope."

"A migraine, she assures me she'll be fine tomorrow." Andrew assumed Lara demanded Val be back on the job.

"I'm sure Val is just as apprehensive to come face to face with you, as you are with her." Andrew later told his grandson. "Whether or not she trailered Big Broon somewhere, the stress she's under could have made her ill. No matter how difficult it may be, you must keep your cool."

"Yeah, I'll do it. You can stop reminding me." Zen changed his tone and added, "I'll do it."

When Zen arrived at Hamilton Farm the following morning, Valentina was busy grooming Tiger.

Andrew broke the ice. "Good morning, Val. I hope you are feeling better?" he asked.

"Yes, all better. I had a migraine," she said, without looking in his direction. As Zen came over, she added, "I let him trot on the lounge line after breakfast. He's moving fine."

"Thanks," he acknowledged.

"Are you going to ride? Should I saddle him?"

"Yeah, I guess we're both up for that."

"Okay. I'll tack him," Val said. But before she could tighten the girth, she felt her face flush, and she ran to the first open stall to vomit.

She hadn't expected this reaction to face Zen. The club never discussed it in all their planning. It took her by surprise.

Zen

Even though Zen was uncomfortable around Val, he didn't share her reaction. He had the advantage of the moral high ground and easily maintained his calm demeanor.

Zen wanted his father and grandfather to be proud of how he handled himself. But no one had ever deceived him as Valentina had done; it wasn't easy for him to face her.

They had been close to a relationship in Zürich. He had kept it in the flirtation stage. He hoped it would go further in New Jersey, after the competition, when he was free to either celebrate or need consoling.

Yeah, Zen liked Valentina. What was not to like? She was quite pretty, she had a killer body, and she was a formidable rider. Perhaps she was not his intellectual equal or shared his sense of morality, but also important was that Tiger liked her. She handled him well, and William didn't have to worry.

The young William had dated lots of girls while he was at school in England, yet there was no one particular girl he wanted to introduce to his father and grandfather. Those dates had been casual nights out to the movies or dinners with other mates.

Then he met Angela Lancing-Mogg. Under no circumstance were their dates ever casual; it had been an intense sexual relationship from the start. They were inseparable.

But when the school semester ended, so did their four-month romance. She dumped him. It devastated William. He felt broken.

Angela had said, "I like you Wills, but it was just a bit of fun." She could have stopped there, but she didn't. "Grow up. It's not like we would have gotten married and spent our lives together," she said lightheartedly.

But that's exactly what he thought. Angie was perfect. William loved everything about her. He'd thought she would be the one he'd bring home, knowing his dad and grandfather would love her too.

William had dated after Angela's rejection, but meeting Valentina was different. As equestrians, they had so much in common. He felt ready to plunge into a new relationship.

Now, knowing Valentina's attention to be part of an elaborate criminal scheme, Zen felt violated.

Val's actual boyfriend, and crime club member Remy, had been on her case for weeks leading up to the trip. "Are you sleeping with Zen?" he'd asked.

"No. he's the old-fashioned type. He wants to get to know me better, I guess." She had told Remy. "But you agreed to the plan. I can't say it won't happen."

Valentina loved Remy—at least, at twenty years old, she thought she did. Neither had dated other people for a year, but now was not the time to be possessive.

Despite his apparent jealousy, Remy wasn't as committed to their relationship, but the stakes in the club's scheme were high, and he didn't want to make waves while the plan was in play. He could see Valentina was caught up in her role as a seductress. He didn't like it, but he let it go.

Valentina tried to act cool around her boyfriend. "It's just a job. Don't think of it like I'm cheating on you," she added. "Tell me you wouldn't shag a girl for what we're being paid?"

In reality, Val had been trying to get Zen into bed from the start. Getting paid for this wild scheme empowered her, like an actor playing in a movie. She wanted it to be exciting.

Valentina's role was to seduce the young hunk, and she desired the full experience. The True Crime Club had always involved role-playing and make-believe. While in New Jersey, Valentina had expected to live out her fantasy.

Along with that dream, however, came an unexpected nightmare called Andrew Griegg. He had caught Valentina off guard from the start. His attacks on her and her family were frightening. No one had said he was a private detective.

Their website mentioned nothing of the kind, and her friends didn't tell her. Did they know? Could she trust them? They had deceived her about the powder she was told to stir into Zen's water—it was much more potent than they'd led her to believe.

Valentina had imagined her interaction with Zen would be normal throughout the trip. The club never thought she would be connected to the abduction. That was naïve. It may have been the one problem with their plan.

She was scared. Zen probably knew what she let slip to his grandfather. Did Andrew believe that she'd overheard the call at the airport? Val thought her cover story was brilliant. She had to think of it on her own, and she had done it. Yet she couldn't judge Andrew's reaction. Did he buy it?

Who were all the investigators working for the Grieggs? Had they documented her involvement by now? Did they know about the club? Their names? What would happen when she returned to Switzerland?

All of these thoughts suddenly spun through Val's head. She was falling apart. She dreaded having to face Zen and his grandfather. She had to keep up the charade, but how?

The plan called for only one communication. That had happened after the ransom exchange. Valentina had time to think, and she now believed they weren't paying her enough. The others didn't have the same responsibility…and they left her to fend for herself. She threw up again.

*W*hen William got in the saddle that morning, Tiger felt good, but he needed to burn off his pent-up energy. Zen put him into a canter to quiet him down. They lapped the large warm-up arena. Zen monitored his horse's respiration rate with his legs. Every rider learns to feel the horse's ribcage expand and contract with each inhale and exhale.

This is easy to detect at the canter or gallop, because the horse takes one breath with each stride, (a phenomenon called respiratory-locomotor coupling).

It's this ability to synchronize stride with breath, and when paired with their tremendous lung capacity, it makes the horse an amazing athlete.

Zen regulated his horse's respiration between strenuous and moderate as he lapped the arena. Once his horse was warmed up and supple, they trotted and cantered a few low fences with their normal grace and style. Zen then asked Tiger to canter some larger fences. Everything felt good. Zen was relieved to be back in the saddle and have it feel like nothing had gone wrong.

Andrew observed their confidence from the rail. Against the odds, they had salvaged what seemed so unlikely just days ago. William and Tiger would jump at Hamilton Farm.

Sigmund joined his father along the fence. "Are they ready, Dad?"

9

The Investigation Ignites

Christopher Hutt's inquiry into Valentina Abbatelli linked him to her internet activity, where a familiar surname popped up in his search—Rechsteiner. It was Trudie Rechsteiner, who he identified as the granddaughter of Asher Rechsteiner.

Valentina and Trudie knew each other. This wouldn't seem strange if Trudie shared her grandfather's interest in horses, but she didn't. Chris found no evidence of that. Trudie wasn't into horses.

The investigation ignited when Chris linked Val and Trudie to Viktor Harel, the grandson of Palmer Harel…the name David Rosen had passed to Sigmund in their phone call days ago. Palmer had been part of Operation Boomerang until his death.

Then another name, Remy Abbatelli, appeared as an internet link. For the investigator, that sounded alarm bells.

The connection was still just tangential, however, until he discovered the website for the *True Crime Club.*

Christopher announced his find to the rest of the group with one word…"Bingo!"

In Christopher's style, he walked well into the weeds as he perused the club's mission statement for his colleagues. "It reads, in part…to fantasize the perfect crime.

"They defined that as: Massive monetary gain, no one gets hurt, and most importantly—you get away scot-free!

"It's an amusing use of the idiom *scot-free*." Chris told the group. "In contemporary language, the term insinuates you get away with something—particularly a crime.

"But in its origin in twelfth-century England, a *scot* was a municipal tax. Hence, if someone avoided paying taxes, it was said that they got away scot-free.

"With the True Crime Club," Chris tutored, "it's a double entendre. They want to get away with a crime and, by default, like most criminals, they don't pay taxes on the money they steal. It's a lofty goal for university students!"

"You're sounding like Niedermeyer, Chris. Make your point," Sigmund requested.

"Members of the website talk about true crime books and the like, but they also fantasize their own versions of crime to see if they hold up to scrutiny by the other club members.

"The crime club's founders are Trudie Rechsteiner, Ash's granddaughter, Viktor Harel, Palmer Harel's grandson, Val Abbatelli, we know, and Remy Abbatelli. I don't know how the Abbatellis are related, but I will find out.

"I noticed that chats from four members ended abruptly a few months ago. It was about the time of the art auction. I asked Ian to help me hack through a firewall into what looked like a private portal within the site.

"I couldn't do it myself, but I knew it would be easy for someone who had once hacked MI-5."

"I was a foolish teenager, Chris. Will I never live that down?" Ian asked.

"It's why we love you, Ian. You should know that by now!" Chris exclaimed.

"Nevertheless," he explained, "Ian breached the site, and that's where we hit upon private discussions among a smaller group of people.

"While sentences in the private portal were readable, they didn't make complete sense until we spoke with Sabine. She recognized they were referencing the children's book, *Nikki Goldshimmer*. Ian believes the members concocted a code to communicate in private. He needs some time to crack it."

"I've confirmed Viktor and Remy attend the University of Zürich.

"I found another club member of interest, his name is Robert Grazioli. He spent one semester as an international student at the same school. He is no longer active on the site, but as a computer science major, he seems to have developed the club website.

"Rob, as he calls himself, has a curious personal story. He grew up in New York City, in a family with ties to organized crime. Apparently, being so far away from his home and family gave him a level of comfort to talk openly.

"I didn't dig for this information," Chris noted, "the kid posted it right in his bio on the website. Rob claimed he had no intention of following in his father's criminal footsteps.

"Rob wrote, 'My father doesn't consider himself a crook. He calls himself a facilitator. He moves merchandise from point A to point B, or he connects person A with person B, and he doesn't ask questions.

'The police have come to our house as far back as I can remember. They know about his involvement in crime, yet they never charge him with anything.

'Maybe he's a snitch. I don't know. I don't care. I'll never be part of his criminal lifestyle, but I'll play your crime games because I find the complex analytics you guys go through are really fascinating.'

"The website has thousands of members. It's going to take a while to grasp what's going on," Ian said. "I'm highly suspicious of the names Chris uncovered. There's no doubt this connects Operation Boomerang to Tiger."

Beginning in the 1990s, the internet was rapidly becoming a database of information and personal stories. Chris soon discovered that Valentina and Remy Abbatelli were related, but not by blood.

Remy's mother married Valentina's Uncle Tony when Remy was ten years old. His biological father died when he was a baby. The much older Tony had been a widower for some time. Tony adopted Remy soon after the marriage.

131

Remy and his mother had a pleasant life in Rome until Tony died without warning in 1995. Like Rob, Remy knew all about growing up in a family that shirked the law.

When Tony took a second chance at fatherhood, it was to overcome a perceived failure the first time around. He doted on Remy in a way he never had with his own children. His kids grew up in the 1940s and 50s, when his construction company struggled to provide enough money to put food on the table.

Tony learned the construction business from his father in southern Italy. After World War II, he moved to Rome, where he found access to jobs. He labored around the clock to rebuild his life, while rebuilding his country. Most working families operated in the same fashion.

Men in that day brought home a paycheck; their wives kept the home and raised the children. If he tried to do more, his wife put him in his place. "You want to do more, go earn more money," she'd say. He wasn't happy, but he obeyed.

He entered his second marriage already an old man, but fit and healthy, content with his life, his new wife, and his adopted child.

Soon afterward, Mario confided to his brother how he obtained his wealth. Tony wasn't surprised. Nothing else could have accounted for his brother's lavish lifestyle.

The confession came after Mario had burned through most of his cash. What he called his "export business" of the post-war period had been his only profession, and he didn't want to think about what would happen if the money ran out.

Mario was too old to work at any job, but he had held back some of his wartime spoils and asked his brother to help him liquidate what he now referred to as *their* "inheritance."

Sympathetic to his one-legged brother's circumstance and with a new family of his own, Tony needed cash himself. He agreed to help.

Mario's larger merchandise had all sold years ago, but he kept a stash of "smalls," that included items like silver cutlery, tea services, and jewelry.

The jewelry was a mix of silver and gold and included precious and semi-precious stones.

Smalls referred to the size of the items, not the value. Mario stored the smalls in huge steamer trunks, also stolen in the 1940s. He had opened the trunks just one time over the years. That was to find the diamond ring and wedding band set he gave to Valentina's mother.

Mario couldn't remember where he had stolen the rings, and they became a sore subject. He felt that his wife had pinched the expensive jewelry from him. After all, he would never have married her, if not for the baby.

When his wife moved back to Switzerland, Mario often wondered if she had sold *his* rings—it enraged him. It was one of few regrets in his life.

He became obsessed with the value of the rings, which may have been far less than he believed. Still, in his mind, the rings belonged to him. Had he ever asked, he would have known that the rings were in safekeeping until the time they would be passed down to Valentina.

As the brothers opened and emptied each storage trunk, Tony was careful not to ask questions. The men focused on the future, not the past. The obsession with money clouded any guilt over the illegality of their actions.

But times had changed since Mario had packed the trunks. He knew he couldn't move the merchandise as he had done after the war. And neither man wanted to go to jail.

During 1945–46, markets were in chaos. It took little expertise to operate as Mario had. Buyers didn't ask questions. They just ponied up the cash—usually American dollars, and the merchandise shipped on boats. There was nothing left behind to tie Mario to any crime.

Now, all these years later, the people who had helped Mario back in the day, if he could find them, would be too old, or dead. The brothers had no clue of the value of what they had in their possession. They needed an alternate plan and new connections.

Tony took charge.

He often shouted, "Legittimo, Mario, legittimo." Well, that was deceiving because, to the brothers, legittimo just meant not getting caught.

Mario had two numbered Swiss bank accounts he'd opened in the 1940s on the advice of one of his black market connections. One account held what was left of his fortune. The other carried a small deposit that he had planned to give to his daughter at the time of her birth. He never did.

Mario mulled over depositing any new money into that unused account, but instead, he revisited the notion of giving the account to his daughter. But the mere sound of saying the words—"his daughter," still didn't resonate with him. So, *now wasn't the time*, he said to himself. He left the account inactive.

Mario's focus at that moment was on creating the *legittimo* business Tony demanded. (Evidence they were in denial of the facts.) A friend of a friend introduced the brothers to an import/export antiques dealer named Palmer Harel. He was in Rome on a buying trip.

People called Harel smart, and he was…brilliant, in fact. He had a degree from a notable university and was skillful at running his business.

Most who said Palmer was smart, however, didn't point to his art history degree. They meant he had street-smarts. He knew how to work people and he did it with ease.

Palmer reacted to whatever vibe emanated from the "street" and then profited from it. He didn't make a fortune, so he was always in search of that one special piece that would make him rich.

That happened to people in the antique trade back then. It still does. Dealers less talented than Palmer would hit on a garage sale gem. It infuriated him. Fairness didn't seem to play a role in success. *I'm just not lucky*, Palmer continually consoled himself.

Back then, Palmer specialized in jewelry and *objets d'art*. His items from the late nineteenth and early twentieth-centuries were not quite posh enough for main street sellers, but they sparkled in the eyes of the less affluent who wanted bobbles to display. As a practical man, Palmer bought any product he might move at a profit. And his instincts for that were spot on.

The life he lived in his later years, however, was chalk and cheese to the younger Palmer Harel…which wasn't even his true name. His life story was quite remarkable. Born during World War II to an unwed Jewish mother in the ghettos of Belarus, Palmer never knew his biological father.

His mother had nothing. They survived off the generosity of others when everyone was stretched to sustain themselves. At times, amid grave death and destruction, certain people rise above the odds to save one particular life (or, in this case, two lives).

Thankfully, such stories have existed throughout history. You've heard them. Palmer's rescuer was a driver aligned with the Red Cross. He snuck Palmer's mother across the Swiss boarder disguised as a medical worker. Her baby came with her, hidden in a crate marked "therapeutic supplies." They had sedated the infant to ensure that no sound would endanger their lives.

Sometime later, the benefactor came back with a phony marriage certificate of a man named Palmer Harel, killed on April Fools Day in 1944, when the Americans bombed the Swiss town of Schaffhausen by accident.

The child assumed the name Palmer Harel Jr. and within a few years; it was the only name the boy remembered.

The allies had targeted a chemical plant in the German city of Ludwigshafen, 235 kilometers north of Schaffhausen. This mistake made in the fog of war provided a cover story that legitimized Palmer and his mother to live in Switzerland. It would alter their entire future.

Years after the war ended, Palmer's mother remained poor. If he grumbled, she would scold him by saying, "We would both be dead if not for the courage of a man I didn't even know."

Perhaps this is not what a parent would tell their children today, but in those days, the war left its imprint on everyone.

It was commonplace to make even the youngest children fully aware of their circumstances.

With falsified papers, Palmer's mother never applied for the widow's pension she appeared qualified to receive. The young mother and son lived in an overcrowded apartment with other war refugees.

She shared her bed with Palmer in a room with two other women, one with a child of her own.

There were days she went hungry to give all her food to her son. Mrs. Harel was twenty-three, with a six-year-old son. She spoke only a few words of the language of the country where they lived.

It wasn't a normal existence, but it was better than anything Palmer's mother had hoped for. Everything in her memory was worse. She was grateful to be alive.

Their lives improved a little when his mother found a job cleaning at a library in Zürich. It was the night shift, so she took Palmer in tow. He educated himself reading books until he fell asleep between the stacks. Sadly, it was not an uncommon story in post-war Europe.

When a letter arrived at the apartment addressed to Mrs. Palmer Harel, it frightened her to open it. She recognized the words *United States of America* emblazoned across the envelope, but she didn't know the words that followed…*The War Office*. Folded inside was a letter in both English and German, but she read neither.

Palmer's mother took the letter to the library, hoping to find a translator. She spoke the language of Belarus called White Russian, so it was a tall order indeed.

After days of trying, someone finally told her what the important-looking document said. It was an official apology for the accidental bombing that killed her husband. The letter explained America would compensate the victims of their tragic mistake.

The translator attempted to explain how to apply for the recompense. But the words only frightened Palmer's mother.

"Bad…bad," was her only means of expression.

"No, this letter is a good thing," the librarian assured her. "You don't realize what I am saying."

Palmer's mother feared responding to the letter would expose her fraud. She couldn't admit that to the translator.

Sensing such a problem, the librarian made it her mission to find the right person to communicate with the frightened refugee. It was too important to let it go.

She found a Belarus student who also tried to convince Palmer's mother that replying to the letter was worth the risk.

"I have too much to lose," the young mother said in her native tongue.

"No, you're wrong," the translator said. "There's so much to gain." He then chose his words skillfully. "Even if there is reason to consider it wrong, it would give you a fresh start in life. How can that be bad? A man named Palmer Harel is dead, let something positive come from his life. Let this be his gift to you and your son."

This act was yet another life-changing event for Palmer Jr. His mother's filing met with no resistance and she claimed her survivor's benefit. The payment wasn't a fortune, but it was enough to change the trajectory of their lives.

His mother met and married another refugee. They moved into an apartment of their own. Having been poor for so long, however, left the child obsessed with money.

Years later, in the late 1980s, Palmer Harel helped the Abbatelli brothers sell their remaining treasure.

When items arrived wrapped in newspapers from 1940 to 45, he knew how the Abbatellis had come by their hoard. When he cashed his last commission check, he'd had enough of life on the edge.

When an opportunity to work at a museum in Tel Aviv arose, he applied. They recruited Palmer as a costume jewelry expert in 1988. He jumped at the chance to distance himself from anyone who knew his checkered past.

Harel moved his family to Israel. That included his wife, his married son- and daughter-in-law, and their eleven-year-old son, Viktor.

Several years later, Viktor's mother and father moved back to Zürich so he could enroll in secondary school and go on to college in Europe.

Viktor revered his grandfather. He missed him dearly. In 1995, when he learned his *opa* would take a temporary job assignment in Poland and would be in Zürich most weekends, he was so happy. It meant that Viktor and Palmer would be together again.

*V*alentina and Remy Abbatelli had met each other many times in Rome as teenagers after Mario took an interest in her life. The two teens were smitten with each other, even then.

Unrelated by blood, Valentina and Remy joked they were "kissin' cousins." When Remy arrived in Zürich for college, he called Valentina right away. They hooked up that same evening in his dorm room. It developed into a full-fledged relationship while Remy continued his education.

One night, Remy confided in how his stepfather, Tony, had earned a living. "When Tony married my mother, we had a decent life, but we never had much money," he explained. "Then he went into business with your father. Suddenly, Tony bought a nice car and showered my mother with gifts.

"He put money aside for my education. That's how I got to come to Zürich for my degree."

Growing up in Tony's home, Remy knew exactly what the men were up to. They didn't hide anything because they had convinced themselves that they were just selling what Mario continued to call their inheritance.

But their story didn't hold up—not to a bright teen. Remy saw the trunks full of jewelry and ornate silverware. He read the dates on the newspapers, just as Palmer Harel had done. Then, just like Harel, he kept quiet.

"I would have given anything for your childhood." Val once told Remy. She had always liked Tony, and she didn't care how he earned his money. "He sent a card every year on my birthday," she said. "That was more than my father ever did. I don't think he even remembers my birth date."

Remy had to make it clear just how illegal their parents' activities had been. It amused him how Val cared for Tony, yet loathed her father. She didn't seem to grasp what "illegal" really meant.

"I didn't grow up poor," Valentina said to Remy, "but middleclass girls rarely win horse show medals. It requires a fancy horse. It didn't matter how well I rode, my horses lacked the panache to win blue ribbons.

"Since reconnecting with my father, all I can think of is the type of horse his money could have bought. That's all I've ever dreamed of—winning trophies in the show ring."

In an attempt to atone for his absence, Mario finally gave Valentina that Swiss bank account. He deposited just enough money for her to enter horse shows, but that was it. He gave nothing extra for the fancy horse.

Mario promised that his attorney would deposit more money into the account under his last will and testament. "But don't kill me," he joked.

While a nice gesture, it outraged Valentina. She lived for the moment. A promise of money in the future didn't change her life that day, so she paid little attention to her father's gift. She accepted the bank account, though, and she even said, "Thank you."

"He was helping himself, not me," she said to Remy. "He's feeling guilty for never paying attention to me. Still, he's kept all his money for himself." She hated him.

Valentina had the optimal body for a woman rider. At 1.73 meters (5'8") and 54.4 kilograms (120 pounds), she had excellent muscle fitness, and her legs had the length to wrap around the big horses she rode.

Her tall stature placed her half-seat in perfect balance over the girth of a big warmblood. Horses felt comfort in her strength and stability.

Riding came easy for Valentina.

Surprisingly, Val didn't start riding until thirteen. That was late. Most advanced riders begin at four or five or earlier. Her mother, however, had enrolled Valentina in dance classes at a young age. She started riding with a superb sense of balance and a significant range of motion in her riding position. Luckily, that prior training put her on the fast track to an excellent riding form.

Valentina learned the basics of horse health and care, but what she loved most was the excitement of flying over huge fences. She rode without fear. The adrenalin rush of jumping empowered her.

Val was also conniving, however, determined to achieve success at any cost. This made her an ideal candidate for the inner sanctum of the True Crime Club. It meant fantasizing about having the money to buy the horse she deserved wasn't just a pipedream. With the perfect crime, it was possible.

Over the years, the casual members of the True Crime Club, and all the viewers of their website, thought Viktor Harel spearheaded the activities. That was because his name and likeness were prominent on the website. While Viktor became the face of the club's website, he was no leader.

Viktor wasn't handsome, but he could strike an appealing posture. He turned out to be smart enough, athletic enough, funny enough, and polite enough to be likable, and people genuinely liked him. But for anyone who got close to Viktor, "enough" didn't cut it. His friends soon learned he was lazy.

As Trudie once defined him, Viktor was an empty suit. He was skating through life, looking for the easiest way to get ahead. It was Trudie Rechsteiner who worked hard and supplied the brains behind the successful club.

Long before there was a website, Viktor knew Trudie by name; they had shared classes in school as teenagers. He had a crush on her and joined the Mystery Readers' Club to get closer. He tried everything to get her attention; including reading every mystery book she could think of. He would have done anything to impress her.

Viktor fell in love with Trudie before their first date. But he didn't fully commit to the club until it transitioned to the genre of true crime and became a blueprint for the perfect crime. Then the club was compelling, and before long, it was all-engrossing for Viktor. He thought of nothing else.

Trudie's petite, childlike appearance belied her maturity, intellect, and self-possessed personality. Strong-minded and forceful, she was fiercely competitive in everything she did. Second place, for Trudie, was the same as losing.

Trudie felt she had to be assertive to offset her four-foot-eleven, ninety-pound body. People found her personality off-putting and rude. Viktor saw Trudie differently, he saw her as irresistible. He was totally smitten.

Trudie saw herself as a high-powered business executive after college, though her obsession with the True Crime Club exhausted much of her energy that would have been better spent on her studies.

She was a B student, but to be fair, she carried a heavy class load each semester. Undeterred by her grades, Trudie always considered herself the smartest person in any room.

Besides the crime club, she got involved in online stock trading while studying at St. Gallen University. It had become a craze in the United States in the 1990s even though, due to cultural differences, "day-trading," as it became known, was not common in Europe.

Trudie studied money management in an intro business class and immediately thought she could master what day traders were achieving online—an accumulation of wealth through a high volume of small capital gains.

Trudie opened an online trading account in the American market by taking the equivalent of 6,000 US dollars from an account meant for her education.

She began analyzing tech stocks, and within days, she started trading. The time difference between Wall Street and

Zürich meant that Trudie was at her computer every weekday at 3:30 in the afternoon to catch the market as it opened in New York.

Trudie bought and sold multiple stocks within hours, each day. Every small gain increased her funds to trade even more. Soon 6,000 dollars turned into 8,000 dollars, then 10,000 dollars. That was peanuts for a seasoned trader, but for Trudie, it was a solid start and it added up fast.

Reaching her goal meant realizing small capital gains each day the market was open while holding no stock overnight—hence, the moniker "day trading." She became hooked on the thrill and power of what was essentially gambling.

The 1990s offered the precise economic setting to create day trading. Tech (technology) stocks soared by multiples at lightning speed, even though the underlying companies never turned a profit—or even projected one.

It's what then-Federal Reserve Board Chairman Alan Greenspan labeled "irrational exuberance" when he warned of a looming financial disaster.

But Wall Street didn't listen…and the day traders didn't care. Why should they? The Nasdaq index, where most of the tech stocks traded, kept rising. Traders may have known it couldn't last, but as long as it lasted that day, they could continue to make money.

Since traders didn't hold their positions overnight (they held positions from minutes or hours) they believed they couldn't lose. It didn't matter if you were a momentum player, buying on a dip, or actually researching the companies you wanted to buy, each success story, real or exaggerated, drew more people in to try their "luck."

But Alan Greenspan was right, and the tech bubble came under pressure. (In the years before the bubble burst.) During those dips, Trudie fell into the two-phase trap that swallowed up most of the amateur traders along with many seasoned professionals.

Phase one: When the market had a down day, Trudie resisted selling her positions at a loss. She broke the rule. She held stocks overnight. Sometimes an individual stock would rebound the next day, but as time passed, more and more of her portfolio traded below her cost.

Avoiding losses meant she had no available cash to buy fresh stocks. With no new positions, she couldn't dig her way out of the hole in which she traded. This was all because, in her mind, realizing a loss on any stock meant acknowledging a mistake.

Phase two: She started trading on margins. This meant she borrowed against her stocks that were already underwater. It was her only source of cash to continue trading.

As the value of the margined stocks dropped lower, the margin would be "called"—to pay off the loan.

That's exactly what happened. Over time, Trudie's stocks and their values were gone. Hence, the fate of many a day trader—she lost everything.

Trudie didn't think she had done anything wrong. The problem was she lacked the funding to ride out her losses. All she needed to fulfill her dream was more money.

It's easy to see how "gaming" the perfect crime would run wild through the vivid imaginations of people like Trudie Rechsteiner and Viktor Harel, and how they could pull Remy Abbatelli and Val Abbatelli into their true crime adventure.

Then a linchpin event changed the state of play for the True Crime Club...Palmer Harel died.

10

The Competition

"Welcome, sports fans." The announcer was cheerful and eloquent. "I welcome everyone to the Grand Prix Jumping Championship here at Hamilton Farm, home of the United States Equestrian Team and the USET Foundation.

"The riders have finished walking the course that will challenge them today. So, while they ready their horses, I'd like to tell you the history behind this beautiful equestrian complex that America's team calls home.

"The saga begins in 1911 when financier James Cox Brady purchased the original 180-acre property for 18,000 dollars...I bet you would have liked that deal. I would have snatched up acres at that price!"

Laughter and applause filled the stadium.

The announcer said, "Brady began construction as soon as the ink dried on the contract, and he continued to add acreage over the next decade. His magnificent barn, still in use today, housed outstanding specimens of dairy and beef cattle, sheep, pigs, chickens, ducks, and geese."

A poignant pause allowed a bubbling hubbub to rise up from the audience.

"What's wrong?" the announcer queried. "Could I have left something out? Let me look at that list again..." He repeated, in rapid succession, "Cows, sheep, pigs, dah-de-dah-de-dah...oh my, did I say HORSES?"

The crowd roared.

"Yes, ladies and gentlemen, that's why we are all gathered here today—the Grand Prix Equestrian Competition, and I can announce with absolute certainty that no cows will jump today. Although, I'm told that cows are talented jumpers…they just can't find willing riders!"

Laughter filled the complex again as Sabine Hutt scanned her military-grade binoculars across the seats in the stadium. She was hoping to see the face of Asher Rechsteiner. Andrew eyeballed the crowd from another angle.

The announcer continued. "In 1961, this opulent farm became the home of America's equestrian team. Ever so many famous riders, you know their names by heart, defined those early years to shape the sport of show jumping—American style!"

His rousing pronunciation of "American style" drew more cheers from the crowd.

"Throughout the past thirty-plus years," he said, "riders, fans, and industry professionals alike have walked these grounds to advance equestrian sports to the highest level. Whether it's your first time here, or you're a regular patron, I encourage all of you to breathe in the history of Hamilton Farm as we sit here today.

"Ladies and gentleman, as they say across the pond, let's give it up for these talented riders, their horses, the teams, and of course, for our wonderful Hamilton Farm."

The spectators erupted into a thundering applause as the announcer stood and clapped in appreciation. The prolonged clapping electrified the stadium as the first horse and rider entered the arena.

The announcer said, "This is a technical course of eleven obstacles, including one double, one triple jump, a wall, plus a water obstacle, which can be difficult for horses to negotiate.

"The horses will gallop a distance of 420 meters, which is just shy of 1,400 feet. We expect the horses to complete the course in seventy-five seconds, with a limit of eighty seconds without time faults.

"Anna Powell and Vinnie Van Go are in the stadium."

Zen

"This Dutch warmblood is one of the smaller horses in the field, standing at 15.3 hands. But don't let that height fool you, this horse is a competitor. His coloring is what's called a blood bay, and he paints a stunning picture as he now gallops the arena."

Quiet blanketed the crowd as the announcer lowered his voice. "Powel takes the first oxer in excellent form. Choosing the shorter route to the next jump, Vinnie is over the vertical with ease. Powel cuts a hard turn to the oxer...oh...tapping behind, but the rail stays up."

An audible "uh" comes from the stands.

"Powel recovers for the gallop to the water...and well done, she's clean. A daring tight turn to the next fence, the in-and-out...and she makes a quick pace, ladies and gentlemen. Very nice! Powell is over 6 and driving on to the triple oxer.

"Powel keeps checking her horse on the approach. She doesn't want to get strung out over this one...and, yes, that was marvelous, they're both handling this course with ease.

"Powel is over 7—again, an ever-so-light tap on the rail, but it stays in place.

"Her horse is strong leading up to the next oxer...and Powel is over. Well done! She's clean over the big wall and now making the long gallop to the triple combination of 10a, b, and c, along the north rail. Checking, checking, and over the third...well done! One fence remaining.

"Will they go clean? Coming in nicely, yes! It's a clean round for Anna Powell and a fine way to kick off today's competition. A clean round for Great Britain's Anna Powell and Vinnie Van Go."

Applause filled the stadium.

Sigmund arrived at the balcony where Andrew, Alana, and Sabine sat around a table overlooking the arena. Wine and water glasses on the table twinkled in the sunlight.

A server spread bottles of sparkling water and a tray of finger sandwiches across the blue linen tablecloth. A bottle of wine had been opened and placed into the wine cooler next to Andrew.

"I saw no sign of Rechsteiner in the stable yard or the warmup area. William is riding tenth in the field of twenty horses," Sigmund stated. "He's happy with that position.

"I take it that no one has seen Ash from this vantage point?" he asked.

"We've scanned the crowd every few minutes," Sabine reported as the second competitor navigated the jump course.

"While Tiger looks fit and ready to go, I'm worried about William. He says he's okay, but he's not eating as much as he should. I can't argue with him. His stomach may not be back to normal yet." Sigmund reached to pour himself a tall glass of water.

Ignoring the horse on the course, Sigmund sat back in his chair. "William just needs to get through today. I hope he can have a nice round, but with all that's transpired, I wonder if that's possible."

Sigmund stopped talking, and the group focused on the announcer. "That is twelve faults for Alan Mandell, captain of the Canadian team, on his young horse Cinnamon Prince."

"You're being quiet, Alana," Sigmund said as he stood to offer wine.

"Am I?" she said. "I'm taking in the ambiance, Sigmund, these horse shows are impressive. Sipping wine and grazing on salmon mousse sandwiches is an absolute delight."

"Well, this isn't the normal show, by any means," Andrew suggested. "We spend much more time in our wellies in cold and muddy tents. This is a treat for us, too."

When the audience gasped, their attention turned to the jump course. Domino had refused the third oxer of the challenging triple combo. "Tough break for the Americans," said the announcer.

The horse jumped clean on the second attempt, finishing the course with four faults.

"I see you ladies have been shopping," Sigmund stated, as he looked at Sabine in a smart blue dress and matching coat.

"We had to, Sigmund. Sabine's 'go-bag' had nothing suitable for a gala event like this," Alana said.

"The desk clerk at the Cranston put us on to shops just around the corner from the hotel," Sabine said.

The two women wore different style clothes, each looking at ease with their choices. Sabine, stunning in her posh two-piece ensemble, Alana less formal in a black turtleneck and black trousers matched with a camelhair blazer. As always, Alana wore her simple gold chain necklace given to her by her father.

"Well, put it on your expense account."

"Already done." Sabine smiled back at Sigmund.

The group watched the next few horses jump the course with growing anticipation for William's turn. The men gave some necessary explanations of the rules.

"It appears that the water at jump number 4 and the triple at 10 are creating the most problems for the horses," Sabine said. "Only one horse has made it around unscathed."

Andrew stated, with family pride, "William's horse excels over the water."

"William liked the course when he walked it," Sigmund announced. "The coach warned him about keeping track of his time, as she always does."

Turning to Alana and Sabine, Sigmund explained his comment. "William lets Tiger set the pace on the course. Lara believes William should do it.

"What concerns William is the landing at 9. He must check Tiger up fast to make a turn in front of the first jump. That will make the route to jump 10 shorter. He says he'll have a nanosecond to decide whether to go long or short.

"The longer route will add several seconds to his time. I heard the coach snap at him, 'Tiger is not a novice any longer and neither are you.'"

"Competing at this level is cutthroat," Andrew explained. "William will do the best he can. He's impervious to what the coach tells him.

"Don't misunderstand—he'll try to follow her directive, but in the end, it's him and his horse making quick decisions as they experience each moment of the ride."

"Lara and Melanie know that," Sigmund acknowledged, "and they all get on well."

Andrew looked over to Alana and Sabine and said, "Time isn't a factor in the first round, as long as you stay within the allotted limit. But saving the horse from unnecessary galloping is essential for energy conservation. The horse must retain enough vigor to clear the last fence."

"I saw Tiger from a distance as we came up to our seats. He's a beautiful horse," Alana said. "I hope I get a chance to meet him after the show."

"We'll all go down after William rides," Andrew said. "I don't want confusion when they come into the ring. Tiger's registration name is Flying Oblique, so that is the name the announcer will use. Tiger is his stable name."

The announcer called out the next competitor. "Malcolm Cummings on Gift For The King. This is an eleven-year-old Hanoverian, and one of the two gray horses in the field today.

"A massive stallion, this horse and rider team has been on everyone's radar for some time. They were European champions last year, and now contenders to ride for Britain in Sydney. Ladies and gentlemen, Malcolm Cummings on Gift For The King."

With an eye on the horse in the arena, Sabine repeated the rhetorical question, "Where the heck is Ash Rechsteiner?"

No one could sidestep the issue. Sabine picked up her binoculars again to peruse people standing near the entrance to the stadium. It would be like Ash to want to get close to Zen before his ride.

"Did you know Ash crafts beautiful furniture?" Sabine asked. "He could make a fortune selling it, but his wife says he's too slow to turn a profit.

"They live on a beautiful farm. It's a bit run down in spots, but still." She spoke, while eyeballing a section of nearby bleachers. "They have the cutest little baby goats."

"I haven't been to Ash's farm, but it doesn't surprise me he would make furniture," Andrew replied. "Ash has many talents, but all people see is a quirky guy who thinks he talks to animals. William came home with bars of the goat's milk soap that his wife sells. It's wonderful. I'm told she produces many different soaps and lotions.

"The things Ash tells William are truly thought provoking." Andrew explained, "He recently commented about a saddle William purchased. Without getting too technical, it had to do with how the saddle fit on Tiger's withers.

"The purchase was controversial because his coach had rejected the saddle out of hand for sitting too far forward, but when William rode in it, he bought it anyway.

"Ash knew nothing about a new saddle, yet, out of the blue he told William that Tiger liked, not only the way the saddle felt on his withers, but all the way down his body.

"Can you believe it? William knew the saddle was a good fit when he rode, and then Ash confirmed it…what would prompt Ash to have said anything without Tiger's help? It was like having confirmation straight form the horse's mouth, if you believe that sort of thing." He ended with a chuckle.

Andrew raised his eyebrows. "It makes you think. You've got to meet him, Alana. He looks like a mad scientist with this mass of curly hair and an overall unkempt appearance…I like the guy.

"Coach Lara called him bat-crap crazy when we spoke the other day." Andrew laughed.

"Malcolm Cummings and Gift For The King have a quick pace approaching the last fence…can they go clean?" The announcer paused as the horse galloped closer. "Yes! It's a clean round for Cummings!"

Sabine said, "It makes no sense that Ash flew across the Atlantic at a moment's notice, yet fails to surface for days and doesn't come to see William ride in the competition. What's going on that we don't understand?"

"It *is* puzzling," Sigmund acknowledged. "We're doing our best, but he's simply vanished."

The group watched a stunning chestnut mare enter the stadium. The horse let out several bucks before coming under the rider's control.

Sigmund said to Sabine, "I'd hoped your idea on Florida would have been right, and Ash would have turned up there." He added, "Then there was the business about Val overhearing a conversation at the airport, which conveniently gave her an excuse for knowing about the painting."

"That's preposterous," Andrew interrupted, "now that we know about the True Crime Club."

Focused back on the announcer, they listened as he said, "After a wild start, it is a clean round for the American Jillian Sanders, riding Stars Beyond."

"William is next," Sigmund advised the others.

They heard his name over the sound system, and everyone turned their attention to the arena.

The announcer read from the schedule. "William Griegg, riding Flying Oblique are in the stadium."

They heard a small contingent of European fans chant Zen as William walked to the center of the arena and picked up a canter.

"Zen is the nickname given to William Griegg—and you can hear his supporters in the stands today," the announcer stated. "But I must ask for you to be quiet, please.

"This horse and rider could have a trip to Sydney in their future. They need a good round here at Hamilton Farm.

"In fact, many of our competitors will have their Olympic dreams extended or unraveled, during this competition. As we watch both the newcomers and seasoned professionals, we must respect what's on the line as they ride this difficult course today.

"Every competitor has faced years of training, massive expense, and the odds of being matched with the right horse.

"Some might call it providence, to have all these factors culminate at the exact time to compete in the Olympic Games. That will be on Griegg's mind as he readies his horse.

"Flying Oblique is over the first fence with ease as they pivot to navigate the shorter route to the next jump...and they are over the vertical with room to spare. Looking good tracking to jump 3, he is over that big oxer. Griegg now has

152

the long gallop to the water jump, which…the young pair handle like seasoned competitors."

Andrew just smiled.

The announcer continued. "Griegg goes wide and gallops to the in-and-out with a tap on the oxer, but it stays up. He's coming in fast to 6…but no matter, they are clear. Turning to jump 7, this is a polite horse…I'm told he is rarely rattled.

"Now, over 7 and approaching 8, we see Griegg's relaxed jumping style as he takes the big oxer with ease. This horse is galloping strong again to the wall, and he's clean. Oh my! This is the first rider to cut inside fence 1.…"

The announcer watched as Tiger elevated his chest to maintain perfect balance while navigating the tight corner. Then he drove into the approach for the triple combination.

"Griegg is clean on 10a…clean on 10b." The crowd roared. "Again clean at the triple, with a fast approach to the final fence. He's clean!

"This gives us the fourth clean round today, as we move into the next group of competitors."

It was smiles all around the Griegg table as they clapped for William amidst a few chants of "Zen." Sabine wanted to join the vocal group, but didn't.

"I think I held my breath for the entire ride!" exclaimed Alana. "That was so exciting."

"I think we all held our breath," Andrew responded.

Sigmund smiled, not taking his eye off William as he walked Tiger from the stadium. "He's come far in such a short amount of time. I'm just so glad he found the right horse in Tiger. There couldn't be a better match."

"What a ride," Andrew said.

Andrew said to Alana and Sabine, "William knew the first time he mounted Tiger that he was the horse for him. And Tiger was wild! Untrainable, by the accounts of other riders, but William took his time and the two of them worked out any problems together. It's a lovely story."

"His first two jumpers were reliable, well-trained horses; we made sure of that." Sigmund added, "As with any sport, you need time to learn and build up confidence. Now that he has Tiger, the two of them are charting their own course."

Andrew commented, "Much of that is because of Ash's influence. That's what makes his disappearance so disturbing. He should be here celebrating with us."

"Dad, let's not pile on accolades until we're sure which side of the fence Ash is on," Sigmund said.

"Fair enough, but if he comes out of this investigation clean, you need to apologize. It would make William happy for you to acknowledge Ash."

"No worries. I want Ash to be clear of any wrongdoing. You know I don't want William disappointed. That's the very reason for my apprehension."

Andrew and Sigmund explained to Sabine and Alana what would happen after all the riders complete the first round.

"That's when things get really exciting!" Sigmund stated. "They shorten the course by blocking off certain jumps. The riders with clean rounds in this first segment will return for a jump-off.

"That's when time counts. Assuming more clean rounds on the second effort, the one with the fastest time will win the competition." Sigmund told them.

"No more talk about the investigation," Andrew said. "It's William's day, let's give him our undivided attention." As if any of them could avoid thoughts of Ash from entering their heads.

As the second bottle of wine arrived, they were readying for the jump-off. Two more competitors had ridden clean rounds after William, so there would be six horses and riders vying for the prize.

The announcer told the audience that they would block jumps 1, 4, 7, and 11 for the second round. "It's the infamous jump-off, ladies and gents. I'm told that the course designer has made this next round quite challenging.

"The emphasis will be on fence 3. The shorter route, takes the horse in front of two of the blocked off fences, which creates a tough angle to navigate that big oxer. Anyone who can ride that line, and jump clean, will have a strong time advantage for the rest of the course.

"But 'clean' is always the operative word. Any fault will send the team down in the ribbons. Every rider must decide if they will go long or short to approach jump 3—and they'll have a split second to decide.

"This is quite a challenge," the announcer said. "Testing the horse and rider teams so early in the round is the trademark of Claudio Faustino, who has designed the Grand Prix courses throughout this competition."

For the benefit of newcomers to the sport, the announcer added, "While the riders are permitted to walk the jump course before round one, that opportunity is not extended to the second round jump-off.

"The competitors must jump cold, demonstrating their skill to navigate the new course. It is a definite challenge for these incredible athletes.

"For both the riders and the horses, it's all about judging the horse's length of stride. The rider must help the horse find the exact spot needed to take off and clear each fence.

"Finish up whatever you are doing and hustle back to your seats, because, ladies and gentlemen, the action is just moments away. You don't want to miss a second of today's championship event."

"William will ride fourth, with two horses behind him," Sigmund said. "How are you holding up, Dad?"

"I've never been so thrilled for William," he said. "But we must remember every rider is out there to win."

"Anna Powell has entered the stadium on Vinnie Van Go," the announcer said. Powell cantered a tight circle before riding through the start flags.

"The horse is on the clock." His voice picked up with the faster tempo of the riding. "Over 2…and she cuts to the inside! Approaching 3, it's a refusal!

"It seems the horse could not overcome the angle at fence 3. That is the question for every rider to come—will they risk going short?

"Powel is clean on the second attempt and on to the next jump…which is also clean. No problem at 6, and then an easy cut in to set up for jump 8, also clean…galloping to the big wall, and over with ease.

"Because of the refusal, Powel is not pushing her horse. She has galloped around jump 1 and is now approaching the triple at 10—over a, now b, and c, and galloping to the finish.

"A tough break for Anna Powell and Vinnie Van Go, the British rider finishes the course with four faults and a time of 55.11 seconds.

"Jump 3 will drive the competition through this jump-off and it's why only a few elite horses and riders reach this level of competition," the announcer stated.

"Next up is Malcolm Cummings on Gift For The King, the gray Hanoverian. Will Malcolm attempt the shortcut with a horse this size?" the announcer asked. "Cummings is over 2, and he's cut in! He's over 3—he's tapped it—oh, the rail is down! That's four faults for Cummings."

Like the previous rider, Malcolm Cummings rode a good round after his mishap at jump 3. He finished with four faults and a time of 49.47 seconds.

"This is no doubt a tough course today," the announcer said. "Some might say, too difficult. The riders will answer that question as the competition continues."

Jillian Sanders and Stars Beyond came up next and took the wide approach to jump 3, finishing clean with an otherwise fast pace of 50.03 seconds.

"Sanders has set the time to beat—just a fraction over 50 seconds." The announcer sounded cheerful, to finally report a clean round.

Sigmund and Andrew smiled at each other, waiting to see William enter the ring. They heard a single cry of "Zen," that was followed by several whoops.

"Quiet, please, quiet," the announcer instructed. "William Griegg and Flying Oblique are the next competitors on the jump course.

"They are on the clock."

Zen

Tiger galloped over jump 2 and, in perfect unison with his rider, turned right and barreled toward jump 3 in what was proving to be an impossible angle.

William felt a tremendous thrust, and he knew Tiger was over the fence clean. The crowd applauded and shouts of Zen rang out as William and Tiger continued to gallop the jump course.

"Silence," the announcer demanded.

William also asked Tiger to navigate the shortcut in front of jump 1 and then jumped the triple at 10a, b, and c, with enough stored energy to gallop across the finish line with a time of 48.10 seconds on the clock.

The crowd roared as chants of Zen rang out as he walked from the ring. They were in the lead, and two competitors away from winning: Germany's Marc Tresch on Caspari was next. Then, Claire Faust on Last Dance, from William's own Swiss contingent, would close out the competition.

"Griegg has set a high bar for Marc Tresch and Caspari," said the announcer. "Are they up to today's challenge? Tresch and Caspari have dominated in Europe, leading up to this event. Everything is on the line for them today.

"The clock has started, and Caspari gallops to the first fence…he's over and yes! Tresch has turned for the short approach…can he do it? Tresch is clean on 3, with Caspari making that delicate angle look easy."

Everyone at the Griegg table sat bent forward and breathless. They watched Caspari clear one fence after another until he approached the final jump. Caspari dragged one hind ankle a hair too low, and the rail on 10c went down.

The rider showed obvious disappointment as his horse flew between the finish flags.

"That's a tough break for Marc Tresch. Caspari clocked the fastest time with 47.62, but four faults puts him in third place. William Griegg remains at the top of the leader board," the announcer stated.

Claire Faust walked Last Dance into the arena. She had no choice—ride the short-angle to jump 3, or accept defeat.

To make Faust's task more challenging, her champion horse, Lochinvar, had to stay behind in Zürich, recuperating from a painful hoof abscess. Faust was paired with the less experienced mare, Last Dance.

The crowd fixated on the red head covering worn by the novice. Hypersensitive to sound, Last Dance wore earplugs and a bonnet to muffle the stadium noise.

The mare galloped between the start flags. She cleared jump 2 nicely. Then, Faust checked her horse to make the infamous hard turn to 3, albeit with less finesse than the prior successful horses.

At the fence, Claire let out an encouraging yelp to her mount—it worked, Last Dance had done it! She cleared the angle with room to spare!

The crowd gasped.

"What a display of athleticism from this horse that is a newcomer to the international circuit," the announcer said with an upbeat voice.

Last Dance had been considered an "also ran" for Claire. They brought the mare to Hamilton Farm to deepen her experience. Now, they were jumping for the win.

Also taking the shortcut to the triple combination, Faust and Last Dance breezed over 10a, b, and c, as they galloped on and through the finish flags with seemingly endless energy.

The announcer's voice hesitated while he awaited their time…"They've done it!" he exclaimed. "48.01 is the time for Claire Faust and Last Dance!

"They have won the championship!"

"Ladies and gentlemen, that is a fraction of a second faster than her teammate William Griegg and Flying Oblique. It's an advantage of just nine-tenths of a second to give them the win…Unbelievable!

"Clair Faust is the champion at Hamilton Farm! What an outstanding performance from Last Dance, the inexperienced ride chosen for Ms. Faust at the last minute."

The crowd's applause was deafening as Last Dance stood with Claire's arms wrapped around the horse's neck.

Everyone at the Griegg table had wished for a different outcome. They sat silent.

Sigmund gulped the last swallow of wine from his glass and said, "It doesn't mean he won't go to the Olympics. He had a fantastic performance. Let's go see him."

The applause from the crowd continued.

After the dignitaries handed out the awards, William walked Tiger over to where his father and the others waited.

"Well," William said with a forced smile, "we almost did it." He cradled Tiger's muzzle between his hands.

"We are so proud of you." His father hugged him.

"Alana, please come and say hello to Tiger. You haven't seen him since your convalescence at our farm." William said, "He's matured since then…I guess we both have."

"Well done, you two. He's such a beautiful horse," Alana stated. Then, the moment she touched Tiger's neck, she was overcome with the sensation that Ash Rechsteiner was dead.

She gave Sigmund an upsetting look, but he didn't notice.

"Are you okay, William?" his grandfather asked.

"Yes. Not to worry, I'm just fine," he replied. "I wanted to win, but we had the ride of our career out there, and I'm thrilled. What's a fraction of a second between friends?"

"Do you want us to wait here for you?" Sigmund asked his son.

"No, you guys go ahead," William said. "I guess we are all meeting up for dinner. I'll meet you at the restaurant. It's a huge deal for the Swiss riders to place first and second in the competition, so we'll be celebrating. Then I'd like to have some quiet time with Tiger."

Lara Bless walked over beaming with her team's success. There were hugs all around. What a day!

At the restaurant that evening, the group ordered appetizers before William arrived. Alana had waited for an appropriate moment before she said, "When I touched Tiger after the competition, he told me that Ash is dead.

"I can't explain it; I don't even know how people communicate with animals. But the instant my hand stroked his neck, this feeling of dread washed over me. I don't want to say anything to William, since I can't be sure."

"That same attempt at compassion didn't serve me well when we were solving your case, did it? You have to tell him," Sigmund said to her.

"Right, I get your point," Alana said reluctantly.

When William joined them, Sigmund said to him, "Son, you know Alana can sense things at times."

"Sure, she's like Ash. I can't wait for her to meet him. I've been so wrapped up in the competition, but I thought about him today. Why hasn't he shown up? Were we wrong to think he was here? Maybe he never flew over."

"Well, he did fly over, William," his father said. "We've confirmed his flight into JFK in New York."

"Then why isn't he here? What's happened?"

"William." Alana looked into his eyes. "When I touched Tiger after the competition, I sensed that Ash has died."

"He's dead?" William asked.

"I don't know. I can only say what I experienced."

"No. If Tiger told you Ash is dead, then I think he is. Ash and I would talk for hours on end about how he was able to communicate with animals.

"Ash said it was all about energy—what he called subtle or spiritual energy forces. It travels endlessly throughout time and space.

"Ash said you had to also think in terms of the energy frequency and vibration. Animals are attuned to vibrations naturally, so it's how people can connect with them—through subtle energies. The rest of us deny or don't know how to connect to energy at that level. It's mystifying; I can't claim to understand it.

"In your case, Alana, I believe touch is what triggers your connection. Am I right?" William asked.

"Yes," Alana agreed.

"But sometimes you just 'know', don't you?"

"Yes, but to be honest I wish I had been able to talk to Ash to understand it better myself."

"Do we have any idea what could have happened to him?" William asked.

"Open mind, William." Sigmund placed his hand on his son's shoulder. "We don't know anything has happened, not yet. But, as promised, I couldn't hold back any information."

"We all share a concern for Ash." Andrew told the group. "But," he said, "we've gathered here to recognize my grandson. Before we plunge ourselves back into the case, let us all toast William, for a job well done."

"Here, here…to William." The group raised their glasses into the air.

"We're so proud of you," Sigmund told his son. "I know a lot can happen between now and Sydney, but I should think your performance today will serve you well toward your Olympic dream. We are behind you all the way, son. It's such a delight."

"I'd like to toast Tiger—he did the heavy lifting today," William said with a smile. "To Tiger!"

The group responded.

William said, "I did some soul searching with Tiger this evening before I came out tonight. I have something to say, and I'd like you to hear me out before you react. I've decided to drop out of any more competitions."

"Is this about Ash?" his grandfather couldn't help but question. "Don't make any hasty decisions. We'll solve this case soon, and then you can consider your future."

"It's not about Ash, and while it may be hurried, I believe it's based in reality. The Olympics are for riders like Claire," William said. "I went out today and rode as I always ride. That's all I know how to do. I'm so proud of Tiger. Heck, I'm proud of myself. I mean, we killed that course!

"Tiger came to me as a broken animal that no one else would even ride. Many of my competitors tried and failed.

They labeled him dangerous and untrainable. Yet together, we overcame his fears and proved them wrong. That was a brilliant accomplishment.

"But look at what Claire Faust did this afternoon. She took an untested and inexperienced horse—no one even knew the mare's full potential. Yet she produced a winning performance. That mare never jumped like that before…and it's all because of Claire's will to win.

"Years ago, I had a dream to compete in the Olympics before I understood what it would take to get there. As the time passed, my success with Tiger clouded over any serious sole searching on that very question—what would it take to become an Olympic equestrian?

"Competing at Hamilton Farm has crystalized not only the question, but the answer. Do I have Claire Faust's will to win? The answer is no.

"I've never had the same kind of drive as riders like Claire possess. Yes, I've wanted to win every one of my show jumping classes. Coach Lara and Melanie have tried hard to instill that competitive spirit in me. But it's not *in* me—not at the level that's needed to be an Olympian.

"Both coaches know it. They coax me on and try their best to make me more like Claire. The truth is, I'm just a good rider with an incredible horse.

"So my decision to stop competing was easy. Today was my Olympic experience," he said, with a dry eye and an upbeat voice.

"Losing Tiger for a few days has made me realize that what I want now is to ride on our family farm, take care of my horses, and work with my dad and grandfather." He looked over at Sabine. "And work with you and the others. I want to be part of *your* team, not an Olympic team."

Everyone at the table was silent. There wasn't a dry eye, except for William. He seemed undaunted by his decision.

The women felt like intruders on what should have been a private family moment for the Grieggs, yet they wouldn't have wanted to miss it.

William raised his glass again and said, with sincerity, "I want to make two more toasts: The first one is to Claire Faust." Everyone lifted their glasses and said, "To Claire."

"Now I'd like to reflect on my friend Ash." Zen lowered his tone. "I know Alana is probably right. He would be sitting here now, unless the unthinkable has happened. But I want to leave hope on the table tonight. So, against the odds, let's lift our glasses to Ash, whether in body or in spirit."

Everyone followed along solemnly, "To Ash."

"Now," William slammed his fist on the table and stated with conviction, "let's get the bastards who took Tiger and find out why they did it.

"I'm new at this business, but I'm getting a taste for what the organization goes through on a regular basis. We have all been through hell this week. It might sound naïve, but the bad guys can't win. We have to find them."

"Here, here."

"I feel like we should fling our glasses against a stone fireplace or something," William said, to lighten the moment.

"I'm just so angry over the events that put us in this investigation. Valentina played me for a fool, but she didn't do it alone. Don't get me wrong, I don't want revenge. I want justice for what happened to us, and to Ash."

"We'll do our best, William," his grandfather said.

Sigmund leaned back in his chair, watching and listening. He couldn't have been more proud of his son than at that moment in time.

William had come home from England a well-rounded teenager…now he was on track to finish his college degree early, while simultaneously attaining the pinnacle of success in his equestrian pursuits.

He did it all without drawing undue attention to himself. He had emerged from the week's events as an admirable man…and it wasn't over yet.

But Sigmund couldn't spare any more time with his son right now. As William had said, there were criminals to bring to justice. The investigation needed him in Europe.

Within hours, Sigmund boarded a Swiss Air flight back to Zürich. Mossad agent David Rosen had completed his work at Operation Boomerang in Poland. They planned to meet at the Griegg office the next day.

11

The Griegg Office, Zürich

"Good morning everyone, our investigation takes on new life today," Sigmund stated. "Is the phone line open to our group in New Jersey?"

"We're all here," Sabine replied.

"As you all know, Alana believes Rechsteiner to be dead. I've asked my father and Sabine to stay put in the United States until we can determine what's happened to him. Ash's fate may very well reveal other angles of the investigation that lie on that side of the Atlantic.

"Alana will remain with them for the time being. William will fly home soon. He must stay at the farm with his horse until they board the air transit.

"Let's recap what we have documented, starting with how someone could have switched the horses. What can you tell us, Chris?"

"We have more information since we last spoke. When Big Broon vanished from the show, someone, probably Val, trailered him to an auction in New Jersey, where he sold for 35,000 dollars the following day. I'm told that is a fair price for a horse with his talent and training.

"It's no longer our concern, but I'll mention that they planned the consignment of the horse well in advance, as confirmed by advertisements placed in industry publications in the month prior to the competition.

"I asked our colleagues in America to drive over to the auction stable. The horse had already left for his new home, but I wondered if Ash had any involvement. They found no sign that he had been there. I see no need to continue this part of the investigation. It's closed.

"We are, however, still interested in a man named Paul Grazioli. His name appeared on Big Broon's import papers. Grazioli is a name we already knew.

"His son, Robert Grazioli, studied in Zürich last year, where he joined the True Crime Club. Rob has returned to Long Island to finish his education at a local college."

"Outstanding." Sigmund gave a wide smile. "I believe you reported that Rob was the club's web designer, am I right?"

"You are," Christopher said.

Ian added, "He's quite talented, Sigmund. The website he designed is brilliant."

"Dad, it would be helpful for you to visit the Graziolis. What's their address, Chris?"

"Somewhere on Long Island," Christopher said. "I'll get that information to Andrew. I'm not sure if the son lives at home or on his college campus."

"Impress upon the Graziolis, they're in a bit of trouble," Sigmund advised.

"This means the son, Rob, knows Trudie, and possibly her grandfather," Andrew said.

"You're right. See if either of the Graziolis can shed light on Ash's situation," Sigmund said.

"For the record," Chris continued, "we believe they switched the horses at the Pegasus Air Limited barn after William and Valentina left for dinner. It seems the company's security is adequate by their industry standards, but we found a snag on the night in question.

"A one-hour lapse occurred at dinner time, which is a quiet period on any day. The vet and her technician were at dinner. Carlos was alone when his barn worker reported car trouble, and the group flying with the Federation horses wasn't scheduled to arrive for several hours.

"We envision a scenario where Big Broon was walked up the short secluded driveway leading to the quarantine barn, and then Tiger was whisked away in the trailer waiting on the quiet road.

"We estimated that just five minutes would be needed for such a switch—and accomplished by simply drawing Carlos to the phone in his office at the far end of the complex.

"All other scenarios required an accomplice at the airport. Since we have Tiger back, the exact details of the switch seem immaterial. We only demonstrate how a switch was possible.

"We have closed this part of the investigation. I will pass along to Ian to bring us all up to speed with what he knows about the True Crime Club."

"Thanks, Chris. The last time we met, we talked about finding a private chatroom portal within the club's website.

"I hate to confess this, but it appears that these university students have devised a low tech, but still sophisticated two-tiered quasi encryption scheme that is proving difficult for me to crack.

"Here it is, in a nutshell," Ian explained. "Each of the four founding members has multiple online personas within their private chatroom. Every identity chats normally within the context of their discussion, but only certain chat streams apply—the rest is subterfuge.

"I'll give you a simple hypothetical: Login ID 'A' says let's go to dinner tonight. IDs 'B' thru 'L' throw out the names of restaurants, but only those who know which ID codes matter will show up at the right place."

Ian said with frustration, "It's been impossible to follow. All of our decryption software is useless in this case.

"Then I got a break. As we already noted, the chatroom had been silent for some time, but after the ransom drop one post appeared.

"That post was from the username Annika and reads: 'Grabbed the book *Ice Angel* by Ann Rose that someone dropped on the train today. It was easy. I smiled all the way home.' " Ian then explained, "The following day, username Aunt Lauren logged in to read the post."

"Recently, username Teddie read it."

Ian explained, "*Ice Angel* is a best-selling murder mystery from 1938. The plot is that someone kills a college professor, and the suspects are identical twins. The police could never prove which of the twins committed the brutal act, so they made no arrest. Reviews of the book, back in the day, said it was the perfect crime.

"The theme of look-alike characters, and reference to a perfect crime, does not go unnoticed, but it's irrelevant.

However, having the usernames, Annika, Aunt Lauren, and now Teddie, attached to a post that we understand is important. It tells me which dialog streams to follow. Hopefully that will help crack the code.

"One username is still unidentified, and I don't know which ID belongs to each of the four founding club members." Ian added, "I can, however, use the three usernames I have to piece together their posts. The fourth username may become apparent along the way. It will take time."

"Okay, Ian. That's good work," Sigmund said. "David, what about Operation Boomerang? How does any of this tie to the Gold Train treasure?"

"There is hearsay that valuable coins are missing from the treasure stockpile, but I have no evidence to prove it."

"This rumor has circulated for some time, when a project member named Yaffa Reis found a Roman coin on the floor in the OB tunnel vault. She makes an intriguing argument, and although unverified, I'm afraid it's all we have.

"Reis' claim was considered a nonstarter until you shared your story of the *Lady in Gold*. When put in context with Harel's work on the treasure, his grandson's participation in the True Crime Club, and the ransom demand for your horse being a Gold Train painting, it's clear that something criminal occurred within Operation Boomerang.

"With the elder Harel dead, we must get ahold of these university students for answers," David said.

"They have gone dark," Sigmund declared. "That is, all but Valentina. Just for the record, she's not actually a student, but we are calling them students as a group.

Valentina remains in New Jersey with William. I see no need to involve the American police. She'll be coming back to Switzerland on the same plane with my son, and we can pick her up then."

Sigmund asked David Rosen, "Do you want to disclose anything to Swiss law enforcement?"

"Let's hold off," David said. "As we've already hashed out, we need to confirm if there's any knowledge of the Gold Train treasure before we hand any crime over to the police.

"Even without knowledge, involving the police could be problematic. We must tread carefully in that regard. Telling the police is a decision we can make down the road."

"We are on the same wavelength," Sigmund stated.

"I tracked the OB log entries for the artwork consigned to Tremblay's auction. Sara Mayer worked on each of them. She cleaned all the canvases, and she did extensive restoration work on your *Lady in Gold*.

"Each piece then went to Palmer Harel to examine the frames. The log shows he repaired four frames, three of which tie back to the items that paddle 139 either bought or attempted to buy at the auction. That path is clear.

"I asked Mayer if she recalled anything notable about those pieces. She said no."

Sigmund interjected. "When our painting was x-rayed, I took the first shot of the canvas and frame. Then I removed the frame for another shot, so I could see right up to the edge of the canvas.

"My initial focus was on finding a more valuable painting hidden underneath our mediocre portrait. Historically, that's been the most obvious crime.

"When that wasn't the case, I thought the painting might conceal some sort of message. Again, I saw nothing, but any-thing hidden or coded on the canvas would be difficult, if not impossible, to discover without more information.

"I also looked at the frame. Everything seemed above-board. It was actually quite nice. The style was baroque. The artisan had carved the wood with the typical flourishes of the period. I'm not an expert on value, but the frame seemed quite expensive.

"It felt solid, made of a heavy wood. Brass L-brackets supported the four corners on the back of the frame. I've seen this construction method before. The x-ray revealed nothing of interest."

Sigmund continued. "David, can you tell me the diameter of the coin that was found in the tunnel?"

"Yes." He checked his notes. "It's 20 millimeters."

"Well," Sigmund said, "those L-brackets were too narrow to hide a coin from the x-ray."

Sigmund asked, "What has the OB team been told about the Gold Train?"

"We told them everything," David stated. "We had to. The size of the treasure made it necessary. These people are not stupid.

"Besides, it involves them. They are in charge of creating the false provenances; they needed to know the truth. These people all passed Mossad security clearances and signed non-disclosure agreements."

"So, Palmer Harel knew about the Gold Train," Sigmund said. "But we don't know who, if anyone, he told. If Viktor knows of the treasure, what information has he shared with the True Crime Club?"

"Again, Sigmund, I advise you to tread carefully," David said. "We don't want to reveal anything about the Gold Train that's not yet known. That, my friends, is job one." With that, David left the meeting.

*T*he team in the States drove to Long Island with addresses for Paul Grazioli and his son, Rob. They went to the college first to track down Rob.

Sabine went in alone and asked where she might find him. A student said he worked at a convenience store on the main road where they turned onto the campus. "If Rob's not in his room, you might find him there. Other than the library, he doesn't go out much."

Sabine went into the store. "Rob?" she asked, identifying him from a photo sent by Ian.

"Yeah," Rob said.

"Hi. I'm here from Switzerland. I can't believe I tracked you down." Sabine flirted a bit. "Maybe you've heard of me as Lindgren."

"I have no idea what you're talking about."

"I'm Lindgren, Rob—you know, the True Crime Club. That's the name I go by online…the whole thing about using Nikki Goldshimmer characters, you know, to identify the club's inner circle from the rest of the members.

"Come on Rob, admit it, you know how much fun it is. I get so caught up in it; I don't get all my class work done."

"I haven't taken part in that chatroom for a long time, and I was never in the inner circle," Rob said.

"Yeah." Sabine knew that. "I just thought since I was here at the college, I'd say hi.

"I'm here for my Masters, this semester. I've been out of school for a few years, and I'm finding it a bit daunting. I don't have friends here, so I wanted to look you up…you know, because we have stuff in common, with the True Crime Club and all."

Rob wasn't buying it.

"How come you didn't stay active?" Sabine asked, "I think it's a blast."

"I'm just not interested any longer."

"Wow, it's riveting now. We should talk about what's happening. Val is here, we could all meet up."

"Valentina is at the college?" Rob questioned. "What's she doing here?"

"She flew to New Jersey on club business…you know, what they planned…what I can't say."

"Not interested. I have to get back to work, so please leave me alone."

"Sorry, Rob, I'm not being honest. I'm here to ask for help. I just didn't want to blurt it out." Sabine took a chance and said, "Things have gone haywire with the deal to fly the horse over from Switzerland, and Valentina needs help. She's in trouble."

"Valentina? I told Trudie I wanted nothing to do with the horse. I'm not getting dragged into anything to do with the True Crime Club."

"Oh, should I talk to your father?" Sabine asked.

"What?" Rob appeared shocked. "Please don't tell me they involved my father in their scheme?"

"Well, yeah. Your dad signed for the horse."

"That fucking bitch. I told Trudie to leave me alone. I had no idea she turned to my father."

"I didn't know they kept you out of the loop," she said.

"Get out!" Rob motioned Sabine away. "I can't take any more of you people."

"Hey, calm down. I'm sorry. I thought Trudie might have given you a heads up that I'd be coming. She told me you would help. We all need your help, but I'm asking for Val because she's alone, and all strung out."

"My help!" Rob said. "Why would Trudie think I would help? The club was fun until I realized what was really going on." Rob spoke with emotion. "Look, I'm not my father…do I have to live that down for the rest of my life?

"Whatever trouble the club is in now is not my problem," he said. "Get out!"

"Okay, I get you don't want to help us, but what about helping your father?" Sabine asked.

"I won't get dragged into anything illegal. My father can take care of himself. There is no perfect crime. I hope you understand that now."

"Can you at least tell me where Ash is?"

"Ash who?"

Sabine left the store.

They drove to Paul's house about ten miles away. Andrew banged on the door.

"Yeah, what do you want?"

"Paul Grazioli? Andrew asked.

"Who wants to know?"

"Andrew Griegg, USDA," he replied. He flashed an ID card printed in the hotel's computer center.

Paul looked baffled.

Andrew said, "I'm from The Department of Agriculture, Mr. Grazioli. We need to talk about the horse you imported." Andrew pretended to refresh his memory by flipping through his paperwork.

"The horse's name is Big Broon." Andrew looked up. "May I come in?"

"No. All I did was sign some papers for a friend. I never set eyes on the horse."

"Well, that's unfortunate, since your name is on the legal travel documents…"

"Get the hell outta here." Paul tried to shut the door, but Andrew stuck his arm out.

"Talk to me or talk to the police, Mr. Grazioli," he said, glaring into the man's eyes. "It's your choice. I have just a few questions…no cops."

Paul opened the door and Andrew walked inside.

Sabine and Alana watched the exchange from the car.

"I'm sorry I didn't fly over for your wedding last year," Alana said. "I wanted to."

"I understand. It was too soon after your case," Sabine said. "Andrew's worried he's put you under a lot of pressure by inviting you to join our team, but honestly, I'm glad you're here," she admitted. "Have you had more thoughts on Ash?"

"No," Alana said. "In fact, I just feel numb. I'm not even sure if what I felt yesterday was real. That sensation of dread vanished. It's confusing.

"This is the first time in my life that I've tried to tap into a psychic episode. I'd like to be of help, but I'm in disarray. Perhaps I'm trying too hard, I don't know."

"Well, I can only imagine what that feels like; just know there's no pressure." Sabine told her.

Sabine and Alana were on tenterhooks for ten minutes until Andrew emerged from the house.

When he sat back into the driver's seat, he said, "Chris was right. He's a two-bit crook used to buckling to the police.

"Trudie contacted him six weeks ago about the horse. In exchange for his signature on the import documents and con-signing the horse to the auction, he got to keep the proceeds from the sale—he netted almost 25,000 dollars.

"I'm sure it's the biggest deal of his life." Andrew shook his head. "He doesn't know Ash. Just like his son, Paul had no reaction to his name. He knew Trudie, but not Ash.

"I'm sure he knows nothing about the rest of the scheme. The club just needed his name on the horse's papers so they could keep their noses clean.

"The students knew Rob's father was on the wrong side of the law just by reading his bio on their website. He had held nothing back.

"It was just a convenience for the club to have someone on this side of the Atlantic. The only thing Paul seemed wor-ried about was his son finding out what he'd done."

"I've been trying to talk with Ash's wife again. I've left several messages," Sabine said, pulling out her cell phone. "I'll try again now."

"Mrs. Rechsteiner…it's Sabine Hutt." She gave a look to convey *finally, she picked up.* I spoke to you a few days ago, looking for Ash."

"Yes, I remember you."

"I'm at the horse show in New Jersey. I thought I would run into Ash here, but I haven't caught up with him."

"No, you won't find him. He's not there."

"Can you tell me where he is? We're all worried."

"My husband is in the hospital."

"Oh, I'm so sorry to hear that. What's wrong?"

"I'm not going to give you more information. I don't know you."

"Mrs. Rechsteiner, if you'll recall, I am a friend of Zen Griegg. I'd like to tell your husband that we found Tiger. He was worried that something bad had happened to the horse. Don't you want him to know that everything is okay?"

There was no response.

"Can I visit him in the hospital?" Sabine asked.

"No, you can't. His condition is serious."

The line went dead, but Sabine called right back.

"Please talk to me, Mrs. Rechsteiner. Zen is so worried. Just tell me what happened."

"No, leave me alone."

"Mrs. Rechsteiner, Zen was poisoned before his flight to the States," Sabine said. "He recovered. Is it possible someone poisoned Ash as well? I can share information that might be valuable to the doctors. Please let me help."

"You are putting me in a difficult position."

"How, I just want to help?" Sabine asked.

"I was told Ash was bent over in pain on the flight to New York. By the time the plane landed, he had slipped into a coma," said Mrs. Rechsteiner. "Apparently he had a variety of herbal remedies in his baggage. The doctor implied Ash had been taking dangerous amounts of medicine, yet I knew nothing of any illness. She said he may have cancer."

Mrs. Rechsteiner continued. "That's ridiculous! I never gave him anything harmful. Everything the doctor said was absurd. I'm working with Swiss doctors to bring him home."

"Ash is a good friend of Zen. We want to help. What hospital is he in?"

"Just mind your own business, young lady."

"I can't. I might be able to help Ash. He may have been poisoned. I have to try to help him."

"I'm an herbalist. I know all about medicinal herbs and poisons. God help me for thinking this, but I'm worried that my granddaughter may have done something stupid.

"Trudie has grown up with an interest in herbs. She thinks she's an herbalist, but she's not. It's like everything else she touches; she thinks she's an authority after little effort.

"A journal recording my twenty-five years of work as an herbalist went missing. I know she has it. I don't trust her.

"The American doctor spoke of potions that I don't use, and never prescribed to Ash. Then, to have the doctor talk of cancer…I just don't know what to think. I fear Trudie has unwittingly given my husband something dangerous.

"I couldn't admit this to the doctor because I don't want her to get into trouble."

"Well, I don't want to get your granddaughter in trouble, either," Sabine said. "But we have to help Ash. Is there anything else?"

"Trudie quarreled with him the day before he left for the horse show."

"What did they argue about?"

"Ash wouldn't tell me," Mrs. Rechsteiner said.

"Trudie's not answering her phone. She sent a message to her parents saying that she is away with friends and would be back in touch soon.

"We are all worried about her. She doesn't know what has happened to her grandfather."

"Please tell me the name of the hospital…Thank you, Mrs. Rechsteiner. I'll try to help."

Sabine said to Andrew, "Midline Hospital, fast."

"I saw the exit sign for the hospital when we were on the highway," Alana said. "I guess I was wrong about Ash, he's just ill."

When they arrived at the hospital, they were told that Ash was in the ICU. Andrew spoke with his physician after flashing an official-looking Interpol badge and ID card that he'd carried for many years.

Dr. Nelson explained that while she couldn't discuss her patient's particulars, she could speak in general terms about his condition.

"A man arrives at the ER in a coma," she said. "He is geriatric. His clothing suggests vomiting and removing his shirt reveals pruritus and bruising on his upper body. This suggests liver disease.

"He carried a tote bag containing a multitude of homeopathic remedies, none of which would help his condition. Among them was lobelia. A handwritten note taped to the bottle instructed him to take a dangerous level of the herb."

The doctor slipped, making a personal comment: "I speak a little German; but I checked the internet to confirm my suspicion. It is likely the lobelia is what's causing the man's coma. It's then complicated by his underlying problems.

"A patient could recover, but why would anyone be self-medicating for such a serious condition? We've confirmed he has cancer. In plain talk, Inspector Griegg, I would say the patient's prognosis is bleak."

"Thank you for your information doctor.

"Why are the police involved?" Dr. Nelson asked.

"One of our people was poisoned before a flight to New Jersey a few days ago. He is a friend of Mr. Rechsteiner. Our man is young and healthy and he recovered within twenty-four hours.

"The case involves a kidnapping. Whether your patient is the perpetrator of a crime or trying to stop one isn't clear, but he's a person of interest.

"Given his current circumstance, I think it might be the latter," Andrew said.

"Inspector," the doctor explained to Andrew, "this would appear as an accidental overdose to anyone treating him. The cancer was not advanced. He could have functioned quite well until ingesting the high level of lobelia.

"As is often the case for older patients with preexisting conditions, the overdose ignited a chain of interconnected events that is difficult to stop once in motion. The man is in a very bad place."

"I understand," he said.

Andrew continued. "We've been trying to locate Mr. Rechsteiner since his plane landed in New York. We couldn't find him, the trail was cold."

"Yes, that's understandable. I'm afraid his wallet and passport did not arrive with the patient. We later received a wallet with no cash or ID, as if he had been robbed. Even the herb containers he carried were not labeled with a name.

"The EMTs only recently matched lost identification documents to our patient and delivered them here."

"What are the chances Mr. Rechsteiner could answer my questions soon?"

"Slim," she said.

The doctor ignored her patient's confidentiality and said, "He's been in and out of a coma several times since he arrived, but never lucid. He doesn't respond to his name, now that we know it. As I said, his condition is dire.

"I asked his wife to come to New York, but she declined. She did, however, seem shocked to learn of his illness. She's speaking with her own doctors and trying to fly him back to Switzerland against my recommendation.

"I should tell you that Mr. Rechsteiner lapsed into cardiac arrest yesterday afternoon. We resuscitated him, but it's been touch and go. It's all part of the spiraling down I mentioned. We don't know what could happen next.

"If he survives the next few days, it's possible you could talk to him, but I wouldn't bet on it."

Andrew gave the doctor his cell phone number. "We will fly back to Zürich soon, but would you let me know if Mr. Rechsteiner's condition changes?"

"Certainly."

"Thank you, Doctor."

Walking to the car, Andrew turned to Alana. "You were right. Ash *was* dead yesterday…and he may be again, soon. Once again you amaze me with your curious talents."

Heading back to the Cranston, Alana decided to take her dog home to Connecticut and fly to Zürich on her own. She now believed she could contribute to the investigation.

While at the Cranston, Dr. Nelson called to say Ash had passed away. It wasn't clear to the Grieggs if this was now a murder investigation.

Zen

When Sigmund heard that Alana would fly over, he made arrangements for her to land in Poland. He would meet her there, and together they would visit Operation Boomerang headquarters in Walbrzych.

David explained that Palmer Harel's room had been left untouched. His people had searched for anything to do with the coins, but found nothing of substance. He wondered if Alana might pick up on something that others had missed.

12

Beginnings

*W*hen Alana Eastwood landed in Kraków, Poland, Sigmund was waiting. Watching her uneven stride as she walked toward him brought Sigmund's thoughts back to the explosion at the church where Alana and his father found the *Der Goldzug* notebook. They both could have died. It still haunted him, especially now, as the Gold Train case had resurfaced.

Alana disliked flying so she was glad the last leg of the journey would be by rail. They boarded a first-class train car to travel four hours west to the city of Walbrzych. David would meet them there the next morning.

During the train ride, Sigmund was in what Alana called his "case mode." Reserved and serious, his every word revolved around the investigation. They discussed the details uncovered since her last update.

Jet lag caught up with Alana, and she closed her eyes for perhaps forty-five minutes. When she woke, Sigmund's tone had changed.

"Are you still seeing John?" he asked.

"It's Jim, and no." Alana pulled her hair from its ponytail. "Long-distance relationships are difficult."

"Remind me how you met."

"Jim purchased a set of antique horse racing prints from my gallery. They were by a British artist named Cole Elliot. It was a big sale."

"Ah, yes. He is the veterinarian."

"Correct," Alana said, "from Saratoga Springs, in upstate New York. William would like him. Jim lives and breathes horses. He took over an equine clinic near the Saratoga racetrack from his father.

"Vets are so busy—even more so with a practice like his. When the racetrack meet is in session, he is on call 24/7 for weeks at a time.

"I never got to see him unless I drove four hours. I have my own life in Connecticut. It was exhausting. Besides, he was too young for me." She smiled.

"What about you, Sigmund?" Alana asked. "Is there a special woman these days?"

Sigmund looked at his watch. "Why don't you rest your eyes again? You must be tired, and it's another hour to the Walbrzych station."

Alana grinned as she leaned into the comfortable seat. *Same old Sigmund,* she thought. Had Sigmund not fallen back into his case mode, he might have said that he'd dined out with several women friends when they were in Zürich. Nothing had changed. Alana knew his MO. He couldn't allow himself a normal relationship with any woman.

Sigmund was so charming when no investigation loomed. It made her wonder why there wasn't more between them. Sigmund clearly liked her.

Since her case ended in 1995, he had visited when he had business in New York. It was an effort to trek to Connecticut from the city, yet he always made the trip. Sigmund enjoyed showing up at the gallery or her home, unannounced.

"I like the look on your face when I surprise you," he once said. "I don't need an appointment, do I?"

They got on well…but it always ended with laughs and hugs and a goodbye peck on the cheek. "Until next time," he'd say, but their relationship went no further.

It wasn't just Sigmund, as she said, long-distance relationships didn't work for her…and Sigmund would never be a relationship guy until he overcame his guilt for the death of his wife—or at least allowed himself to love someone else.

Would Alana ever become one of those dinners and… women? One who spent a night with him a few times a year?

No, that wasn't her style. Their friendship was too important for that.

Besides, there was more to consider. Andrew, and now William, felt like family—a family she chose, other than by birth. Alana was loyal to her friends, and the Griegg men meant too much to risk an affair with Sigmund. For Alana, a relationship with any man had to be all or nothing.

*T*he next morning, Alana woke hearing Sigmund's gentle taps on her hotel room door. "Alana, David is here. We'll meet you in the breakfast room."

"Okay! I'll be right down," she shouted from the bed. Alana reprimanded herself for not setting the alarm correctly. Cutting her morning routine to just a few minutes, she pulled her hair back into a ponytail and hurried downstairs.

David was David. He made her uncomfortable. This time, however, she wouldn't allow him to dismiss her from the investigation, as he had done in the past.

She had flown over as a member of the team, and during the journey she swore she would confront him if he didn't give her the respect owed to a colleague.

Before long, Alana, Sigmund, and David walked through the door at the soon-to-be Walbrzych Local History Museum. A colorful signboard announced the Grand Opening events beginning in January 1998.

David provided a tour without introducing Sara Mayer or Yaffa Reis or any of the Mossad agents. "This is the work area," he declared.

Alana gave a friendly smile to the women occupied at their workbenches, flanked by a display of H-frame easels holding museum-quality works of art.

"Follow me to the tunnel." David walked down a hallway to a door leading to the basement.

At the bottom of the stairs, they saw a vault door covering the opening to the tunnel.

"I'm told the Germans had rebuilt this entire wall. It was solid when the Israelis arrived, with no sign of a tunnel on the other side," David said.

The guard who accompanied them downstairs opened the vault and allowed them to stand inside. Alana ran her hand along the chiseled rock wall as she walked into the passageway. "How long is the tunnel?" she asked.

"It's just what you see here—about twenty meters or so. It appears to turn off to the right," David said, "but that's where the tunnel ends."

Alana examined the crates stacked along the wall.

"There were many more crates when our people started," David said, watching Alana dig her fingers into the loose dirt and stone dust along the edge of the tunnel floor.

"Where was the coin found?" she asked.

"That was over here." David bent down. "Yaffa Reis found the coin wedged between the wall and floor, in this area. I made sure I could be exact with you."

Alana joined him to poke around in the dirt.

David asked the guard for the coin.

"This is the gold aureus medallion that Yaffa discovered," he said. "I wanted you to hold it."

"Thank you. I've never held a precious coin. It's thrilling, actually." Alana cupped the coin in the palm of her hand and rolled it around. She scrutinized the profile of the Roman emperor Maxentius. Then she asked Sigmund, "Would you like to see it?"

Alana walked the length of the tunnel, imagining both the people who had dug it and those who had labored to carry the treasure inside.

The diggers would have had a very different experience from the delivery crew. In preparation for her trip, Alana had read the history of Walbrzych and its famous castle.

She knew the Nazis used slave labor to dig tunnels under the castle at the top of the mountain; no doubt they would have utilized those slaves to excavate under Porcelain House, where she now stood; the thought was unnerving.

But nothing invoked any spiritual energy. Not even as she held the coin in the palm of her hand. *That didn't matter,* she told herself. A vision could come later, when her mind was quiet. That was how her visions came to her in the past.

"I'll show you the treasure index when we go back up to the workroom. Then we'll go upstairs to Palmer's room." David seemed to hurry them along.

As they left the tunnel vault, Sigmund returned the coin to the guard.

Upstairs, David opened the logbook. "This is what they call *the bible,* as it is an inalterable record of OB's history with the treasure.

"There are two sections: The first lists the treasure as it was originally logged. As you run your finger across the line, you can read all subsequent activity on each piece of treasure.

"The second section is a calendar listing the date and time that any item is taken in or out of the tunnel vault."

Yaffa overheard the words "pouch of coins" as David turned the pages.

Alana noted the different handwriting of the entries. Palmer Harel's writing slanted to the right. The two women wrote vertically. It was just a curiosity, but penmanship can speak volumes about the author.

The logbook resembled an old ledger, like one seen in an office a hundred years ago. It was covered in a blue corduroy fabric and measured 40-by-30 centimeters (16-by-12 inches).

Long silver screws held the hinged front and back panels together, allowing for pages to be added as their work continued. The hinged feature also permitted the ledger to lie flat when fully opened—a convenience for logging updates throughout the day. Alana revisited the coin pouch page.

Examining the antique-style ledger pulled Alana back in time. The artists listed were talented painters; she recognized some from her college days and now from owning the gallery, but only a few were the masters that others would know.

When she touched the pages of the "bible," there was no chill or tingling in her fingertips…the telltale sign when she connected to an unsettled past. Alana wanted to feel it again. Yet nothing happened.

Soon, Alana made her way upstairs to the staff quarters. The accommodations were nicer than she'd imagined for temporary lodgings. The cozy rooms reminded her of the small German hotels she had stayed in years ago.

A whiteboard attached to the wall made known that the team members took turns cooking in a well-equipped kitchen. Alana imagined the comradery of a small military-style operation. Mossad was highly structured; *the civilians were no doubt obligated to fit in,* she thought.

David and Sigmund were talking in Palmer's bedroom when Alana appeared in the doorway. She walked about the room, running her fingers across surfaces. She stopped at Palmer's window, which overlooked a quiet side street.

"We've sent Palmer's clothes and some personal items to his wife." David told them. "He took the overnight train to Zürich almost every weekend, so there wasn't much here.

"He kept a few handwritten notes on this pad. And then there's this journal." David took a small leather-bound diary from the bedside table. "We've looked through it. I'm told there are curious lines, but, no smoking gun." David handed it to Alana.

Sigmund informed Alana that he'd spoken with Boris. "He's looking for an uptick in chatter within the collectible coin market worldwide.

"The numismatic community is limited for high-value coins, if that's what's involved in this case," Sigmund said. "Those collectors can typically afford to buy when something new comes up for sale.

"There used to be one or two experts for us to turn to, and to some extent that's still true for the local market. However, the internet has amalgamated collectors into one worldwide group.

"That's good for the collectors, but it makes our job more complex because the data can be duplicated across multiple websites and every listing must be checked."

Zen

Sigmund continued. "While we know which of the local experts to trust, a spiffy website can make any amateur appear as a seasoned professional.

"At least we have a specific time frame to work with—the date of Tremblay's auction is our starting point," he said.

Alana sat on the bed, reading through Palmer's journal. He entered his notes in his native German. Alana's German was tenuous at best; nevertheless, she usually got the gist of whatever she read. This wasn't true paging through Palmer's journal. She didn't recognize words. Something was wrong.

Alana recalled how helpful Marta Voss had been to translate "the trap" letter, yet reading Palmer's writing now, made Alana doubt if even Marta would know the words that gave her pause.

It seemed an obvious attempt at subterfuge, and it didn't sit well with Alana. It made her question why David's people had communicated nothing of consequence when they read the same pages.

Even calling Palmer's notebook a journal was misleading. It was mostly a to-do list for his wife to get books to and from the library, or make his dental appointments. He made notes of what to include in his trips home. Trips, as David correctly noted, he'd made almost every weekend.

It all seemed mundane, on the surface that is, excluding those lines she couldn't translate without help.

Perhaps David's people hadn't looked at the titles of the books Palmer was reading. There were several volumes on cognitive dissonance—the necessity to justify one's actions. There were medical books on heart health, how to control your blood pressure, and dealing with stress. He was writing about his anxiety as "the deadline gets closer."

There was no time to read every word right now, but one word—"Benommenheit"—caught her eye. It meant light-headed in English. Other entries also recorded his declining health over a period of months.

Days before his collapse, Palmer entered: "Focus! Not much longer." Another note said, "Chest pains again today,

187

but I calmed myself and they subsided. I have to hold on just a little while longer."

Alana again recalled David's comment about no smoking gun and she questioned, *how is this not a smoking gun?* She reminded herself that she's not a trained investigator, but it still didn't sit right. She continued to flip through the pages.

The journal was mostly blank after 15 September until 6 November where the word "Frist" appeared. Alana ran her finger across the line. The English translation—"deadline."

Alana scurried downstairs to check the index. She turned the pages back to November. Day 6 listed the five pieces of art for shipment to Tremblay's auction house.

With that in mind, other lines in the journal held deeper meaning. It now appeared that Palmer had planned his entire schedule around that vital date.

David and Sigmund waited for Alana at the cafe just across the street from Porcelain House. It was where the team ate whenever it had been Palmer's turn to cook dinner.

The hostess called David to the telephone. It was the OB security guard. He was asking permission to let Ms. Eastwood take Palmer's journal out of the building. David agreed.

The director of OB, Joan Schulman, joined Alana as she entered the restaurant.

Alana showed them the interesting "frist" entry as soon as she sat down. "Let's work backwards," she said. "When did you commit the art to the auction?"

Joan took out her appointment book and flipped to the prior year. "I first contacted Tremblay's in August. We had to wait for the right auction. I committed the pieces on the first of September."

"Tremblay's held auctions once a month at that time of year. Our pieces fit in with the broad theme of the November event: Two-Hundred Years of European Art.

"November 6 was the date scheduled to ship the art to the auction house."

Alana turned to September 1 in Palmer's journal. It was blank. "But," she wondered aloud, "he had already completed work on each piece of interest to paddle 139. The index was clear. So why did he work on them again before the auction? Sara logged each piece out and Palmer logged them all back in, noting work on the frames."

Joan responded, "That's not alarming in itself. I think you will find that Sara also looked at the other two pieces that went to the auction. She would have checked them out to crate them for delivery. It's likely Palmer would have helped.

"The fact that Palmer noted work on the frames might be as simple as a double check before sending the art to a place as prestigious as Tremblay's. Once crated, the art would have gone back into the tunnel to await transport.

"I asked Sara if she recalled anything particular about the works in question. She remembered them because sending the art to Tremblay's was unusual, but nothing else stood out as strange. She noted that David had asked her the same question. We can talk to her again, if you like."

Alana stated, "I don't know if that's important. Sara's log entries show she crated the last painting on September 15.

"Palmer wrote one word in his journal that day…'Fertig,' meaning 'finished' in English. A short time later, he collapsed at his workbench and never returned.

"The journal also makes note of recurring health issues throughout the summer and into September." She told them. "Palmer chalked it all up to stress. He wrote that he would ask to be taken off the project in December; he said he would call it necessary because of his declining health."

"None of us picked up on his health issues," Joan said with assurance. "Palmer was likable, but intensely private. I'm not sure any of us got to know him. His notes in the journal, however, make the auction an important event for Palmer."

"That might be an understatement," Alana noted. "We've just said that the index revealed he repaired each of the frames of interest to paddle 139 just before they crated them for delivery to the auction. That can't be a coincidence."

Sitting between Joan and David, Alana pointed them to the journal's puzzling words. Look how his handwriting changes from when he's assigning mundane tasks to his wife, to these words that I can't read. It tells me these entries were made under stress.

"Well, I don't know about that, but the words you're pointing to look like Russian," David said with just a glance. "I know a little Russian, so it's an obscure dialect...one I can't translate."

Joan asked to see the journal.

"Palmer's security clearance uncovered that his mother was from Belarus. They escaped to Switzerland during World War II. The file reads like a movie script.

"Palmer spoke five languages. There are several languages spoken in Belarus. Some are dialects of Russian. One is called White Russian. That's what he might have used in his journal. I can have the words translated."

"If I may," Sigmund said, reaching for the book. "I may be able to get it done faster."

"Regarding Palmer's security report," Joan said, "it turned up instances of poor judgement in his younger days, but nothing that precluded him from our project. His time in Tel Aviv was exemplary."

"Yes, David has mentioned that," Sigmund said.

Alana appeared deep in thought.

"What are you thinking about?" Sigmund asked

Alana pulled an American quarter from her pocket and placed it on the cafe table. "Even though I don't understand some of the passages in the journal," she said, "this vision keeps coming into my head. I see a coin in a flat position, like this, to standing upright on its edge, like this."

She held her finger on top of the coin to keep it on end. "In this position, the coin isn't visible behind my finger. I'm not sure what it means, maybe nothing. I just keep seeing the quarter vanish from sight when it's behind my finger."

"Well, that's interesting," Sigmund stated. "I assumed any metal would have shown up on the x-ray of the *Lady in Gold's* frame. It seemed that the L-shaped corner brackets were too narrow to hide much of anything.

Zen

"To be honest, I didn't consider the option Alana's just brought to light. With what she says, a coin could stand upright, with the narrow edge of the coin directly behind a bracket in such a way that it's invisible on the x-ray, all you would see would be the mark of the bracket itself."

"I only took one head-on shot at the frame," he said.

"Oh my, with four corners and three frames, that means Palmer could have smuggled twelve coins out of Porcelain House," Joan said.

"I think it could be worse than that," Sigmund stated. "Both the stem and the leg of the L bracket could hide a coin from view." Sigmund added, "We could be looking at up to twenty-four coins taken from the treasure."

"Yes, of course," Joan admitted. "Either way, if true, it would be an untold fortune."

"We had little time to explore the possibilities surrounding the *Lady in Gold*, as the fate of William's horse hung in the balance. I'm sorry, David; it seems that I have let you down," Sigmund acknowledged.

"There's no blame," David said. "The case had barely begun when the ransom was paid. There was no talk of coins at that time, or where the mystery might lead."

David summed up what now seemed obvious. "Palmer Harel came across a stash of highly valuable coins in the treasure vault. It was more wealth than he could imagine—and he could hold it in one hand.

"In an instantaneous flash of thievery, he logs the coins into the inalterable bible using ambiguous wording.

"Next, he postpones working on the coins until he can replace them with ones of lesser value. As Yaffa Reis noted to me, he could bring coins into Porcelain House with ease. Our security focuses on no piece of the treasure getting out—but Palmer found a way.

"He bypasses security by concealing the coins in the frames of artworks he knows will go to auction. He chooses the pieces he could afford to purchase."

"Oh my," Joan said.

191

David continued. "He arranges to bid anonymously via a telephone line and voilà—he would have stolen a fortune in the rarest coins on the planet…but the guy dies!

"Whether he involved his grandson in the plot from the beginning is unknown. I doubt it. Regardless, the students take over. And, if the telephone line had not gone down," David said to Sigmund, "you wouldn't have ended up with the *Lady in Gold*. Admit it; it's brilliant!" David chuckled in a grating way that often annoyed people.

Alana added, "It would have been the perfect crime…if not for greed."

The others looked at her.

Alana explained, "The students already had the fortune from two frames in their hands." She added, "They pulled off everything the True Crime Club set out to achieve. All they had to do was let the *Lady in Gold* go." She smiled.

"They had the coins, nobody got hurt, and they *would have* walked away scot-free, if not for greed. They wanted it all, and now they're busted."

"What about Sigmund's son…they poisoned him," Joan interrupted, "so they hurt someone."

"No, you're not following." Sigmund shot back. "The poisoning wouldn't have been necessary if they hadn't come after our painting."

"My mistake, you're right. It really is amazing."

"So who planned it?" Sigmund asked, "Palmer Harel alone, or were the uni students in from the start?

"David could be right. Perhaps Viktor was only told about the plan after Palmer's collapse…as his grandfather feared death. That would mean the True Crime Club was late to the game. The crime, as we know it, could have taken shape after Palmer dies." Sigmund deduced.

Joan said, "Typically we crate the art outside of the secure area and ship it immediately. The art going to Tremblay's, however, was crated in advance and put back in the tunnel.

"Palmer marked the location of the brass brackets on the crates, and since the crates were screwed together, we took them straight from the tunnel to the van waiting on the street. We bypassed the metal detector all together. It now appears Palmer had been steering us in that direction all a long."

"Well, hindsight can be made perfect, but no one would have thought those brass corner brackets problematic at the time," David said.

"It makes me think Palmer drilled the slots in the frames early on, and then inserted the coins when they were crated for the auction," Alana said. "That puts the log entries in a logical order. David's scenario ties everything together and a brilliant plan falls into place. The students' strength was in planning crimes, so maybe they were in on it from the start."

"Catch them, Sigmund. I must leave now to attend to other business." David stood up, tossing his napkin on the table. "It seems I've solved things for you."

"Leave?" Sigmund asked, ignoring David's quip.

"You can access the OB building as long as you like, but I have to go to Berlin."

"But, David, we need you. Can't Berlin wait?"

"You know my business, Sigmund. It can't wait. Your mission is to catch these students without revealing the Gold Train. I have yet to imagine how that will play out, but you, Sigmund—you and your father masterminded how to deal with the treasure two years ago, and you can do it again."

David put some cash on the table. "Lunch is on me. Just find those students, Sigmund…don't let them outwit you again," he said.

Sigmund gave a half-hearted smile. David's snide remark about the ransom drop didn't concern him.

Sigmund and Alana walked around Walbrzych after lunch. They talked about the case and how to deal with the True Crime Club.

"How many people would have made Palmer's choice?"

"Probably more than you'd think," Sigmund supposed.

David allowed them to keep the journal, and they had sent the alleged White Russian wording back to the Griegg office for translation.

They passed a sandwich board sign outside a bar. It was promoting the "Gold Train Walk Tonight, at Nine O'clock." It read: "Learn about the legend of the treasure from a local historian…become a treasure hunter, yourself!"

Sigmund laughed when Alana wanted to sign up.

"It will be fun," she said. "We're not leaving for Zürich until the morning. What's the harm?"

Sigmund humored her and went inside the bar to add their names to the reservation list.

"I hope you don't mind, but I asked Sara Mayer if Palmer did anything special during his downtime." Alana confessed.

"No, not at all. What did she say?"

"That Palmer traveled home most weekends," Alana said. "When he stayed in town, he bicycled out to an old ruins site called Zamek Stary. She told me Palmer detested the opulence of the castle up the mountain. That's understandable, given the Hitler connection. I would have no interest going there."

The castle Alana referred to was Książ, long rumored to be the hiding place for the Gold Train treasure.

During World War II, the castle underwent an enormous reconstruction project with plans to house Hitler in the post-war era. They also intended the complex to provide a military redoubt for Hitler's Nazi henchmen. Hitler had stayed at the castle on occasion to oversee the operations.

Since neither of them wished to tread in Hitler's foot-steps, they made use of bicycles at their hotel and trekked out to see the landmark that had captured Palmer's attention.

The ruins of Zamek Stary were sparse. They were com-prised of cornerstone walls, some stretching eight meters or higher, with just a scattering of rubble stones in between. Only one section survived intact, that of an outbuilding.

"It's sad," Sigmond stated. "A once great feudal complex is now a teen haunt strewn with beer bottles and cigarettes."

Zen

The ruins weren't an organized tourist site—just dirt paths leading into the woods where the long abandoned stronghold lay, conquered by time.

"Still, I'm glad we came." Alana told him. "It tells me so much about Palmer Harel."

"And what is that?"

Kicking her sneaker over the cigarette butts covering the ground, Alana said, "Palmer wasn't happy about what he was doing in Walbrzych. He wanted to hide in the past. Unless you're a teenager, there's nothing to do here but meditate."

"Feelings of guilt or not," Sigmund said, "Palmer Harel was a flawed man. He tried to hide it for many years, but in the end, he succumbed to his dishonest impulses. There's no excusing that."

"I'm not excusing anything," Alana said. "I'm just saying that he found himself deeply conflicted."

"Between good and evil?" Sigmund asked.

"I'm not sure he would put it so succinctly, but yes. It's probably what killed him."

"So, Palmer achieved his goal but paid the ultimate price? I don't waste time thinking like that. My job is to solve the mystery," Sigmund said with confidence. "Humanizing Harel is of no interest to me."

Alana continued to push her toe in the dirt.

"Watching you kick those cigarettes around has made me realize something," Sigmund said.

"What's that?"

"That David has quit smoking. He couldn't have avoided a cigarette outside the restaurant if he was still smoking. We talked for some time, and he didn't light up."

"Good for him." Alana hesitated, then said, "I haven't cared for David, as you may have guessed long ago, but he's acting differently toward me this time around. I hadn't expected him to change.

"I planned to confront him if he didn't regard me as a member of the investigation, but he's treated me well—now I regret judging him so harshly."

"David knows you better now," Sigmund said with a smile. "There is no neo-Nazi zealot trying to kill you this time around. He's more relaxed. But don't feel badly. David takes some getting used to."

"I know I'm not an equal part of the team. I'm just here to help, but I wanted him to show me some respect. He didn't do that two years ago."

"Like I said, he knows you now. With William and Tiger safe, even I can unwind, if only to traipse around the hinterland for an afternoon." Sigmund told her.

"Never doubt your value to our team. You bring a unique perspective no one else can offer, David knows that as well."

Alana didn't respond.

Sigmund changed the subject. "How will your ankle hold up to walking this evening after bicycling all afternoon? It's several miles back to the hotel."

Alana grimaced. "I never think about it until it's too late. I might need to take a couple of aspirins."

"We could cancel?" Sigmund volunteered.

"No! I'm not letting you off the hook," Alana said. "We rarely see each other, and never like this—two people enjoying time together. It's nice."

"Just don't make me carry you back to the hotel."

"Yeah, I can guarantee you that won't happen."

She paused, mustering the courage to say what was on her mind. "Neither of us finds it easy to talk about personal things. I hope you realize that I'm forever in your debt over Germany. It sounds awkward to just throw it out there like this, but there's never been the right moment to tell you.

"I said things back then that I now regret. I've come to terms with the decisions you made…at the end of the case… if you get what I mean."

"I know exactly what you mean. I find some words aren't necessary between friends. I like to think that, anyway," he said, not looking at her.

"I did what I thought was right, for everyone involved. I've never regretted my decisions, but I am sorry I wasn't up front with you. You deserved to know the truth, and I kept it from you. I know now I could have trusted you. I didn't know that at the time. I'm sorry."

Alana wasn't expecting his candor.

"I find it easy to talk with your dad," she said. "He's been a rock in my life since my grandfather died. Does he share that with you?"

"No details," he said, "but, yes, I know the two of you are close. Believe it or not, you are as much of a rock for him. Maybe you are the daughter he never had. That's how I think he feels about you."

"We once joked that if he was twenty years younger, or I was twenty years older, there would still have been an age difference, but things might have been different between us.

"I did some soul searching after the experience at the church. I can say without a doubt that meeting you and your dad was a pivotal moment in my life. It may seem foolish, but you guys are the closest thing to family that I have."

Alana felt tears build in her eyes and wished she hadn't said those last words.

"Alana Eastwood…that's one of the nicest things anyone has ever said to me."

A group of teenagers emerged from a side trail, breaking the moment.

13

A Bit of Fun

Sigmund and Alana enjoyed their afternoon in the country-side and arrived at the bar that evening early enough to order pub grub for a relaxing dinner before the Gold Train walk.

They ate bigos (a traditional Polish hunter's stew—Alana ate an all-vegetable version). Sigmund mentioned his father was dating a fifty-something widow, and that she was at their country home more often than not in recent months. I like her very much, but it's taking time to get used to having a woman in the house.

"Should I even use the word dating? It seems a silly word when you reach my father's age."

"Do you mean Elizabeth Croy?" Alana asked. "We met last year."

"You what?"

"I met her last fall."

"I can't tell you anything, can I?" Sigmund wisecracked. He ordered another beer.

"Elizabeth accompanied your father to his last lecture at Yale. Andrew brought her to see my gallery one afternoon, and we had dinner together. I liked her very much. Do you know she has a pilot's license?"

"I think she is an impressive person, but I didn't know she is a pilot."

"We need to talk more often. I could keep you up to speed on what goes on under your own roof.

"You're a world-class investigator, Sigmund, until it comes to your dad!" She laughed. "Did you know Elizabeth would be with Andrew now, if not for a family wedding? I think it's a distant cousin who's getting married in the Austrian Alps."

"No, I didn't know that either." Sigmund leaned back and fiddled with his napkin. "This Hong Kong business has taken so much of my time. Still, if it hadn't been Hong Kong, it would have been something else.

"I'm glad we didn't rush back to Zürich today. We learned a lot, and your vision of the coin hiding behind your finger inspired David to render a decent account of the crime. I think we'll find he's spot on with his analysis. We can resume with fresh eyes in the morning."

"It has been an enjoyable day." Alana sipped her wine.

"You'll think this odd, but the last time I spent a day like this, William was a young child," Sigmund admitted. "Evelyn and I took him to see Caerphilly Castle in Wales. We were visiting her grandparents.

"I remember William going on and on about wanting to see the dungeon. He was disappointed when the tour guide said the castle didn't have one. He kept asking where they put the naughty people.

"That evening, Evelyn booked us on the town's ghost walk. We met at a pub, much like this one, and walked the village streets listening to ghost stories.

"Evie loved it because growing up in the area; she had heard many of the ghost tales before. You understand the guide tonight will just recite made up stories, right?"

That was the first time she had heard Sigmund call his wife Evie. "Well," Alana leaned in to whisper, "I certainly don't think he'll tell us the actual story of the Gold Train."

They both laughed.

"Sigmund, it's just a little bit of fun, after what—fifteen years since your trip to Wales? You can take having fun again, right? Even if it is silly?"

About 8:45, a scruffy-looking man came through the door dressed in a navy blue pea coat, work pants, and well-worn boots. Stringy, unkempt hair crept out from under an official-looking railway cap.

Alana caught Sigmund's eye and raised her chin, signaling him to look. "Our tour guide," she said.

"Yes, and he looks just like the guy in Wales." He smiled. Sigmund watched the man as he greeted the bartender and ordered a beer.

The rule was that the tour guide couldn't discuss his enterprise inside the bar, so at nine o'clock sharp, he emptied his stein and headed outside to stand by his sign.

Another couple left their table and followed Sigmund and Alana outside.

"Dobry wieczór," the man said. He watched a group of college-aged boys walking up the street and waited to see if they were the last people booked for the tour that night.

"Witamy w złotym pociągu spacerować." He repeated in English, "Welcome to the Gold Train walk. Are there English speakers in our group?"

It surprised Alana to see everyone raise their hands. The tour began in English.

"It's the spring of 1945, and my job is baggage handler at the Walbrzych train station." The guide spoke in the snarly voice of an over-worked, aging laborer of the war era. His presentation was effective and made even better by his thick Polish accent. He performed his job well.

"First, let me tell you the history of our lovely city. People settled in Walbrzych in the ninth century. It became a city by the 1400s. Everyone's heard of the castle, but Walbrzych has always had so much more to offer. It's been a coal mining and weaving epicenter since the 1500s.

"After the First Silesian War, the Kingdom of Prussia annexed the city in 1742. It joined Germany in 1872. Our city was lucky to have survived the 1940s unscathed.

"With Germany's intentions for Książ Castle after the war, it makes Walbrzych the perfect destination for the Gold Train and its staggering treasure.

"Many treasure hunters believe it is here," he said.

"It wasn't until after the Second World War that the city was reunited with Poland. Have you been up to the castle?" the guide asked.

Everyone but Sigmund and Alana raised their hands.

"It's beautiful," someone commented.

"The castle is where the ghostly part of my talk begins. Princess Daisy lived in Książ Castle until the Nazis evicted her. Daisy was a great beauty, and she loved her status in high society. As people say today, the girl loved to party!

"Daisy married Hans Heinrich, Prince of Pless, in 1891. They received Książ as a wedding gift." The man paused. "My in-laws gave me the bill when I married their daughter. What did you get?" he asked, looking at Sigmund.

Everyone laughed.

"Daisy became a social reformer and militant for peace. During the First World War, she served as a nurse, and while that was commendable, not every historian paints Daisy in a glowing light. She was a notorious anti-Semite.

"Sadly, and nothing to do with her anti-Semitism, Hans divorced Daisy in 1922, after which she published a series of tell-all memoirs from her journals that totaled over 600,000 words. That was a lot of writing.

"Can you just imagine that stack of diaries?" The guide motioned with his hand, to suggest the journals would pile up from the ground to his waist and then up above his head.

"The published books were widely read in Europe. Daisy created quite a scandal for Hans back in the day, as people from all walks of life read about their escapades.

"Then, in an outcome no one deserves, Gestapo agents captured, tortured, and murdered the princess in 1943. It was a horrendous event that Daisy did not deserve. Her servants buried her body near the castle.

"While burial is usually the end of the story, sadly, that was not the case for Daisy. Fearing the Soviet troops would plunder her casket, the same faithful servants dug up her body and moved it so many times that her final resting place has been lost to history.

"This occurred because rumors spread that Daisy had been laid out for all eternity, adorned in jewelry, worth millions. That's what happened in those days. I tell you the truth.

"Perhaps this made Daisy's soul restless. People say that her spirit is alive, and she haunts the castle to this day." The guide's voice took a sinister tone as he told his captive audience, "...understand that some ghosts need fearing, but not Daisy's ghost. I believe her spirit remains here to welcome visitors into her home, as living at the castle was the best time of her life.

"Tourists tell me they feel they are being watched as they stroll through the grand galleries and halls of her castle. Some have even seen Daisy's image in a mirror!

"Others get a whiff of her favorite perfume—a blend of sweet jasmine. A fragrance her husband had commissioned especially for her after their wedding...you can buy vials of the perfume in the shops in town."

Sigmund rolled his eyes at Alana.

"You roll your eyes," Alana said softly, "but this man's story makes me think about all the ways that fortunes were stolen. Look what we learned about Mario Abbatelli.

"Forget about the Gold Train treasure," she questioned, "how many people like Mario were there? No one will ever know the massive transfer of wealth that took place, during and after the war."

Sigmund nodded in agreement. Alana was right.

"Follow me across the street to the train station," the guide advised. "Stay together on the sidewalk."

They regrouped in a quiet corner of the station. The guide positioned them away from the bustle of people coming from the tracks, as trains were still arriving that evening.

"Now remember, it's the spring of 1945, and a night much like tonight," the guide said. "I'm a baggage handler, and I work the late shift in the dark of night. Fighting is in full swing all over Europe. Some nights, we would hear the bombs exploding in the distance. The allied forces could have targeted our city at any time. No one felt safe.

"Then, late one evening—a buzz arose from the people scurrying along the platform…they were whispering about a special train, or special people on their way to Walbrzych. The stories were different, but they all predicted something unusual was about to happen.

" 'What's going on?' I heard fellow handlers and even some passengers ask. 'What have you heard? What can you tell me? Don't ask me,' they'd say. But the questions kept coming. Everyone was curious.

"Then, just before the last train was scheduled to arrive, the German bigwigs came out of their offices and told us to go home. Just like that—get out, don't ask questions.

"Some of us decided to hide in the trees, just up that hill," he said. "An hour we waited, sitting quietly, like soldiers…we didn't even light a cigarette for fear they would see the burning tobacco.

"If they saw the light, we thought they would kill us. We was real scared," he said, using poor English grammar.

"Then, we heard it…the sound of an in-coming train. We held our breath, anxious for it to pull into the station."

Sigmund rolled his eyes again as Alana poked him to stop.

"But the train never arrived," the guide commented, "the sound ended abruptly. Just then, we watched as a convoy of automobiles pulled up to the front of the station. SS officers got out and talked amongst themselves. We never saw such a group before.

"The Germans stood over there." He motioned. "One was a general, he was. Another had the green insignia of an SS-Oberführer. That man had a loud voice.

"We could hear him talking about a railroad track, hidden from view, which led into the mountains. The Oberführer kept repeating, 'Wir verstecken einen Waggon,' meaning 'we are hiding a train car.'

"One soldier grumbled, 'Impossible!' The general told him to bring workers down from the castle. 'Zerstöre die Strecke, wenn wir fertig sind,' he said, 'Demolish the track when you've finished—leave no trace behind.'

"That was the Gold Train plan: Bury a train car full of treasure and then erase all traces of it," their guide said. "People are looking for the train to this day."

The tour guide recited an exciting, albeit wrong, adaptation of the Gold Train legend…and, for the tourists, drinking in the bar before the walk, his theatrics made for an amusing evening to remember.

To his credit, the guide sparked the imaginations of unlikely treasure hunters to wonder if the Gold Train *was* real. The walkers would marvel at the notion of finding an old coin or other relic of history while rambling along the ancient paths abundant throughout the mountainous terrain.

Afterward, Sigmund and Alana stepped into the bar for a nightcap before heading back to their hotel.

Later, as Alana lay in bed that night, images of the coins flashed through the recesses of her mind. She had no new visions, but she felt certain that the coins left Porcelain House in the artwork just as she had described—perfectly positioned behind each of the narrow L-shaped corner brackets.

Sigmund lay in bed in the adjoining room. The evening had stirred memories of his life with Evelyn, when, fifteen years ago, he had spent a day exactly like today.

Tears dampened his pillow.

Sigmund arrived for breakfast impeccably groomed and dressed in a blue suit with a narrowly striped tie. He had arranged for a private jet to fly them back to Zürich.

After eating, Sigmund asked, "Are you sure you wouldn't like to go back to Porcelain House?

"The pilot can wait."

"I'm good," Alana said.

Later that day, the usual group met around the conference table in the Grieggs' Zürich office.

"Where are the university students?" Sigmund asked.

Andrew said, "William called to say that Valentina has disappeared. He doesn't think she will be on the flight home. She gave an excuse to Lara Bless, which Bless didn't share."

"Well then, all the club members have gone dark now," Ian replied. "I'll do what I can to track Valentina."

"Do you think this was their plan, or has something made them change their plan?" Sigmund asked.

"I think Andrew had an impact on Valentina."

"Come on, Chris, tell it like it is," Alana taunted. "Andrew scared the crap out of her."

"Perhaps, but there is no evidence she communicated with anyone. Wherever Valentina is now wasn't planned as a group," Chris replied.

"So," Ian said, "as I like to say, let's follow the money. Viktor Harel dropped all his classes at the university after his grandfather took ill in September. He was in constant contact with Palmer during the last weeks of his life.

"We've tried to link into Viktor's finances, but, as you know, in Switzerland, that's difficult. I did, however, find that paddle number 139 had a cash reserve of 50,000 Swiss francs on account at Tremblay's for the now-infamous auction.

"The transfer came from a numbered account, but even without a name behind the number, it gave us another lead," Ian said. "Before he died, Palmer liquidated a German bank account of the equivalent of 50,000 francs.

"That account was from the antique store he ran before moving to Israel. It had sat idle for years and now seems the likely source of funding for paddle number 139.

"The buyer spent 30,000 francs to pick up the first two items, the Rodin and the Champoux. Then, when the bidding for the *Lady in Gold* exceeded 20,000, whoever was bidding ran out of money.

"I think it's safe to say the bidder believed, as did Palmer Harel, that the funds in hand would purchase all three pieces of art, and was surprised when the bidding surpassed 50,000 francs. In any case, if it was Palmer's money, it was all the bidder had. I'll have more about the money later."

Boris said his contact at Tremblay's had described the woman that collected the artwork. "His description matched Valentina Abbatelli.

"Interestingly, she expected to pick up all three items, and caused a stink when she was told there were only two. That tells me they weren't communicating in real time, even in the early stages of the plan."

"Thank you," Sigmund stated. "Any update about the Russian words in Palmer's journal?"

"Yes," Boris continued, "but first I'd like to talk about the toxin that made William ill.

I wasn't getting answers within the customary channels, so I tracked down a German biochemist I knew during my military service. His specialty was structural biology. I won't use the term biological warfare, but feel free to think it.

"He believes the toxin William consumed was a derivative of helenalin, found in the arnica plant.

"Last year, nut jobs in Africa began altering helenalin with a hallucinogenic psilocin extracted from mushrooms.

"Their intent was to create a recreational psychedelic drug akin to LSD, but much less potent and safe to use.

"The resulting drug had wide-ranging effect on people. Some got a little 'trip' that was pleasurable, but most felt no mind-altering sensation at all; instead, the drug caused gastric pain—occasionally at the level that William experienced. No surprise that there's no market for that kind of product," he joked. "Still, some people found a use.

"Curiously, splicing the constituents in the helenalin with the psilocybin mushrooms created another, more surprising reaction. After the initial trip/pain, the drug goes through a cannibalization process that neutralizes its effects. This explains why William recuperated so quickly, and had no toxic residue in his test samples.

"The bit about cannibalization is what attracted military attention. My friend found one telltale enzyme in the test sample I gave him. That convinced him that William ingested the helenalin concoction.

"He assures me that there will be no repercussions from being given the drug a single time.

"Next, on the Russian dialect, I'll pass along the full transcript after this meeting. It doesn't advance the investigation past what we already know, but it confirms facts and provides interesting details.

"Palmer wrote about his difficulty acquiring the antique L-shaped brackets that would be correct for each frame. He never, however, divulged hiding coins inside those frames.

"He mentions losing one coin. He used the term disc. As we know, he was sick for some months. He suffered dizzy spells, which left him confused for short periods of time.

"Perhaps Palmer documented his journal as he did, fearing he would need a reminder of what had transpired during those muddled minutes.

"It seems odd that his coworkers never picked up on his health issues, but his notes indicated he was fine 99 percent of the time with just momentary lapses in cognition.

"I know he died of a heart attack, but I think an autopsy might have revealed another condition, perhaps the early stages of a brain tumor.

"Anyway, about the gold medallion found in the tunnel. Palmer explained that he had the 'discs' at his workbench to take their exact measurements. He felt a dizzy spell coming on and rushed them back into their hiding place in the tunnel. The next time he retrieved the discs, one was missing.

"Palmer freaked out. He feared someone would find it. He searched, but obviously it remained lost until Yaffa picked up her box of jewelry."

"What more do you have on the money trail, Ian?"

"We found that the doppelganger, Big Broon, cost 25,000 francs in December of last year."

"Where do you think that money came from?"

"I can speculate," Ian said. "The students had money from reselling the Rodin and the Champoux. They sold them about a week after Tremblay's auction—if we're right, after removing the coins hidden in their frames.

"I traced the art to two galleries, one in Bern and one in Interlaken. It's unlikely those dealers would have paid anywhere near the auction prices, but the students would have received something.

"Don't forget, Sigmund, there were expenses to board the horse until the flight—the airline ticket price and related vet fees. That could have added 10,000 francs to the equation.

"It's likely the students would have had to sell one or more of the coins extracted from those first two frames."

"Good point. Is the art still at the galleries?"

"The Champoux is still in Bern. The Rodin was sold to an American living in Zürich."

"Let's buy the painting from Bern. Send someone to pick it up," Sigmund stated. "I'd also like to have access to the Rodin, so find a way to make that happen."

Chris continued talking money. "We know Rob Grazioli's father, Paul, was paid to sign the horse's import papers. When Big Broon went to auction, he kept the proceeds. That appears to be his only role in the scheme.

"Andrew confirmed it was unlikely that he had any other information, and technically," Chris said, "I don't think what Paul did was illegal. However, as is usually the case with ill-gotten gains, he could face tax issues that get him in trouble."

"I think you're right, on both counts," Sigmund said.

"So, we are still asking the same question—did Palmer put together the original scheme, and the students only took over because he died?" Sigmund asked. "The plan to switch horses was fairly sophisticated for uni students to concoct."

"But these aren't typical university students, are they?" he said. "They're crime aficionados. Knowledge of an obscure toxin that leaves no trace, except for an innocuous enzyme, could have come from just reading their crime plots."

Sabine took over. "We know that Trudie learned about herbs from her grandmother, including the deadly ones.

"As Sigmund pointed out, it's likely she also read about chemical compounds, like the toxin Boris uncovered, just by studying the crime scenarios played out on their website.

"I could argue that, at least in their minds, giving the toxin to William met their edict of not harming anyone in the pursuit of their perfect crime.

"I understand that there are different opinions about Ash. Whether or not he's involved, he's unpredictable, and the students wouldn't have wanted him at the New Jersey show.

"They could have drugged Ash to keep him off the flight, just as they did with William. It worked once, so why not again, but their timing was off, and he boarded the plane."

Alana interrupted. "I see your point, but I'm not convinced Ash had any knowledge of the club's plan. What if he *did* pick up on Tiger's perilous situation intuitively—that's what he did for a living.

"The doctor said that Ash's coma was likely the result of the lobelia in his system. That could have been accidental and led to his demise with no other intervention. Why does Ash have to be involved?"

"Okay," Chris said. "Let's move on."

But Alana couldn't. "If Ash knew his granddaughter was part of this wild scheme, wouldn't he have told his wife? But he didn't. He boarded a plane to New York, not Florida.

"What was he doing, if not going to Tiger's aid? However misguided that may sound to you, there's no evidence that Ash's motivations were criminal.

"Put yourself in his head. He *felt* something had happened to Tiger…and he knew Tiger and William were showing in New Jersey."

"But, Alana," Sabine reasoned, "the similarities between what happened to Ash and William are so strong. Ash's wife said he argued with Trudie before he flew, and even she thought her granddaughter was up to no good."

Chris interjected himself into the conversation. "Okay, let's put Ash's circumstance aside. I don't think it matters any longer. With Ash dead, we may never learn the truth."

Distracted by the vibration of his cell phone, Boris said, "Remy has resurfaced at the university. Coming out of hiding may mean he isn't involved in criminal activity, either.

"Although he may know something to help us; I can talk with him after this meeting."

"Hold off on that, Boris," Sigmund advised. "Let's keep monitoring his online activity. Remember Val has gone dark. She may try to communicate with him. We need to know what she's up to as well."

"No problem. Moving on," Boris said. "When we first heard about the gold aureus medallion, I looked to see if any coins had come up for sale following Tremblay's auction.

"We have proven that the group needed money early in the game...and remember, Val purchased a horse for herself.

"In addition to Big Broon, she purchased her own show jumper. That tells me they had already divided some money among themselves. For that to happen, they had to have sold at least one coin.

"I found no aureus medallions sold at auction, but that doesn't rule out a private transaction. When I looked deeper, I noticed other high-valued coins changing hands after our key auction date.

"The first is an Edward III florin from 1344," Boris said. "Only three of those coins were known to exist until a fourth surfaced in late November. It sold for 685,000 Swiss francs from a dealer in Berlin.

"Another coin, the 1787 Brasher Doubloon, is a gold coin made by the American goldsmith Ephraim Brasher. One specimen coin sold for 800,000 dollars in New York at about the same time.

"It may be a stretch to link that transaction to our crime, but there's a third coin with an interesting backstory that might connect to the Gold Train.

"That coin is a 1933 American Double Eagle," Boris said. "Fewer than 450,000 of these twenty-dollar gold coins were minted, but they were never circulated because the American Congress passed a law in 1934 that outlawed gold coins as legal tender.

"The American mint melted down the coins, but it's well documented that some were stolen. That's where a link to the

Gold Train comes in. Numerous stolen double eagles circulated amongst collectors in the United States until federal agents started seizing the coins in 1944.

"The rumor mill, at the time, was that one or more coins ended up in the hands of a buyer in Germany. The alleged customer was Bruno Weiß. He boasted to have double eagles and aurei medallions in his collection.

"Bad for him, SS assassins killed Weiß in January 1945. It stands to reason that his valuable coins could have ended up on the Gold Train.

"If double eagles exist, and if Weiß had any, the coins would be worth millions in today's market. In addition, owning and selling these coins is no longer a crime. The statute of limitations has expired. They can be traded openly.

"With more time, we could find what other coins Weiß held in his collection. As you know, I put the word out that we are curious about any coin sales within our time frame. That message revealed the chatter I picked up on earlier.

"But the collector community is always skeptical of any newcomer asking questions. It's hard to get them to talk. Even the internet dealers depend on client confidentiality and don't talk openly about sales.

"This is not my area of expertise. Niedermeyer is our authority and the only one with solid connections. How would you feel about bringing him in?"

Sigmund looked over at Boris, and said, "You're the one closest to him, now. What do you think?"

"There are days when he struggles. He no longer looks frail, but his mental stability still concerns me.

"He's winding down his responsibility as the curator for Alexander Brandenberger's estate, and it's giving him time to dwell on his loss. Rekindling memories may have started the grieving process all over again."

Sigmund wondered aloud, "Perhaps he'd welcome a distraction at this time. I know Niedermeyer likes to keep busy."

"He might. He's delving into Alana's genealogy, so he has the time," Boris said.

"You're kidding me?" Alana seemed shocked. "I once mentioned something in passing, but I had no idea he was conducting any research on my behalf."

"That's Niedermeyer, he's a surprise," Boris said.

"When he started his bereavement, he constantly asked about my work and what everyone was doing at the office, but he hasn't done that lately. He's been doing his own thing.

"Heads up, Alana," Boris said, "he's found something of intrigue in your family tree. He's got papers spread all over the library where he's living."

Sigmund interrupted. "Can we discuss Alana's ancestral trail at a later date. Let's tackle one mystery at a time."

"Sorry. The bottom line is, I think Niedermeyer could manage work on the coins," Boris responded.

"Okay, why don't you go out and talk with him. Let's not give him more information than he can handle. All he needs to know is our interest in the coins." Sigmund inferred, "Researching rare coins with astronomical values at play is just the sort of mystery Niedermeyer will love.

"Where are we on passports? Have Trudie and Viktor left the EU?" Sigmund asked.

"The short answer is, we don't know," Chris said.

"There's been no passport activity, except for Valentina, obviously, and as we now know, Remy has surfaced at the university…but Trudie and Viktor could be anywhere in the EU, or have left from any EU country under fake passports.

"Ian turned up talk about forged passports in the open forum portal of the club's website. Participants, also deliberated travel to non-extradition countries should a crime go wrong, and they needed an escape.

"Even though this was commentary about true crime in general and not necessarily posted by the students we're looking at, the posts were well argued and would educate anyone reading the site.

"In fact, they designed the site to approve or block specific members. This filter means that members only see the posts of the members they trust. It's brilliant.

"I'm fascinated by the sophistication of the website. The knowledge and research that people put into their posts is also impressive. Some post are anonymous, but others list their credentials. Many have backgrounds in law, law enforcement, or academia, if you believe them. Regardless, the posts are from well-educated people and many of them are skilled writers.

"Anyway, back to our subject. Cuba surfaced as a destination should things go wrong with any crime. Contributors to the discussion believed they could bribe their way to a good life in Cuba."

"Yeah, good luck with that," Sigmund said. "Let's find these people before they get spooked and run off to paradise."

"Are we done for now?" Sigmund asked.

The meeting ended.

Ian and Sigmund stayed behind to make plans to access the Rodin drawing located in Zürich.

"I need an excuse to examine the frame. We need to confirm our suspicion that each frame concealed coins. It's the only thing that makes sense."

14

The Snare

"Frau Lambert?" Sigmund asked.

"Yes. I'm American, do you speak English?"

"Yes, of course," Sigmund replied.

"I'm sorry. I'm taking German classes, but I'm afraid it's not going well."

"No worries. German is a difficult language. I'm Sigmund Griegg." He held his hand out. "This is my colleague, Alana Eastwood. Alana is also here from America."

"Hello, Mrs. Lambert," Alana said.

"Oh, please, it's Susan. You are from Tremblay's about the Rodin I purchased, right? I received a telephone call that said you would be coming."

"Yes," Sigmund said. "Even though you didn't purchase the drawing from Tremblay's directly, it sold at one of our auctions recently. I believe you spoke with Ian Stewart?"

"Yes," Susan replied. "He told me your company restored the frame and that you needed to check on something about the workmanship. To be honest, I wasn't clear."

"It's quiet embarrassing, really," Sigmund said. "We pride ourselves on 100 percent accuracy with each restoration, but it's possible we mixed up the screws used to reassemble your frame. If anything is amiss, I can replace the hardware."

He held up a container with screws inside. "May we take a look? Here are our credentials."

Susan didn't look at their fake IDs. She opened the door.

"Come on in. The Rodin is hanging in the living room to your left."

Alana had a small square of quilting folded over her arm, and she carried a professional-looking tool kit.

As Sigmund lifted the artwork off the wall, Alana spread the quilt over a table and he placed the frame, face down, on top of it. It appeared they had partnered together for years.

"I find your work so fascinating," Susan said. "It's nice of you to drive out to do this for me."

"It's Tremblay's guarantee of service," Alana said, handing Sigmund the correct size screwdriver from the toolkit. She saw the frame had the same L-shaped corner braces that Sigmund had found on the *Lady in Gold*.

To distract Susan, Alana asked, "What brings you and your husband to Switzerland?"

"It's my husband's job," Susan said. "He works for an international finance corporation. The company operates out of the World Bank building in whatever country needs his service. He's here on a special project."

"Our home is in New York City, but we've lived in Rio and Cape Town prior to this placement."

"Since we stay in each country for such a short time, it's difficult for me to find employment. I'm enjoying myself touring about and occasionally buying something nice to take home. I've never been to Europe before, so it's such a treat."

"What a wonderful opportunity for you. My home is in Connecticut, we're almost neighbors," Alana said.

"Wow, small world, right?" Susan replied. "I've been trying to do my research, but I just buy what I like, if the price is right. Do you think I got a deal on the Rodin? I paid 7,000 francs. From what I'm told, that's a good price."

Sigmund said, as he unscrewed the frame, "This Rodin sold for 14,000 francs from Tremblay's."

"Oh my, I got a great deal," Susan said with a smile. "I'll be able to brag to my husband."

"It's as we suspected, Susan, I must change the screws." He then asked, "Might I trouble you for a glass of water?"

"Sure, it's no trouble, but would you prefer coffee? I have a pot brewing now."

"Thank you," he said.

"I'll be right back." She walked away, beaming over the price of her Rodin.

As soon as Susan left the room, Sigmund whispered, "Alana, look at this."

He showed her that under each end of each L-shaped bracket was an expertly drilled slot, lined in paper-thin brass plating, to conceal the coins from any angle. "It's as we thought," he said, "eight coins left OB inside this frame."

Moving quickly before Susan returned with the coffee, Sigmund measured the length, width, and depth of each slot with precision. They were identical.

When they returned to the car, Sigmund called Ian. "Talk with Joan at OB and have her measure the coin pouch. See if it's possible to estimate how many of the coins on our radar might fit inside.

"There were eight identically drilled coin slots in this frame." He gave Ian the dimensions and asked him to see which coins might match up.

It was time to talk with Palmer Harel's widow. David was free earlier than expected. He would pose as a Swiss police detective to ask her questions.

"Jana Harel?" David asked.

"Yes," the woman said.

"Detective Randall Landon," David said, flipping open a fake badge wallet.

"Ach du lieber Gott, has something happened to my grandson? Why are you here?" the woman sounded frantic.

"Frau Harel, these people are from the museum where your husband worked. We'd like to ask you some questions about Palmer and Viktor."

They sat around the apartment's kitchen table. Jana faced David, Sigmund, and Alana.

"We're sorry for your loss. What do you know about the project Palmer was working on when he passed away?"

"I know very little. We never discussed his work He was on loan from his job in Tel Aviv to open a history museum in Walbrzych, Poland. That's all I know."

"You moved here when Palmer started work in Poland?" David asked.

"Yes. I could have stayed in Poland with Palmer, but we lived in Zürich before moving to Tel Aviv some years ago. Our family is here, and it's where I wanted to call home.

"My husband had to be in Walbrzych during the week, but then he came here most weekends."

"Did Palmer like his job?" David asked.

"That's a strange question. As I said, he didn't talk shop, as they say.

"I know he was lonely in Poland," she said. "I believe it was too much work for him. I could tell he was under stress, yet he wouldn't say why.

"Living on the premises meant he worked around the clock. There was nothing else for him to do. He was not one to socialize with the younger members of the group."

"Alana and I work at the museum's corporate office. We didn't know your husband, but Palmer was invaluable to the museum's team."

"I never understood what was so crucial about Walbrzych history that required my husband to work so hard. Coming here on weekends was his only escape.

"Look, I am not a well-educated woman," she admitted. "I didn't understand my husband's work in Poland. Family is what matters to me. My husband is dead, so tell me what you want with my grandson?"

"No one has seen or heard from him in a week or more," Sigmund replied.

"Viktor is away with some friends. I don't know why that is your business. But you didn't answer my question."

"The university is in session. He has not attended his classes," Sigmund said.

"He's a young man. Who can justify some decisions that people his age make? My grandson is a brilliant student; it makes little difference for him to miss a few classes."

"Do you know he hasn't attended classes since Palmer took ill?" Sigmund asked.

"No," she said with surprise. "I don't believe you. Viktor loved his grandfather. He idealized him and was devastated by his death.

"Of course Viktor missed classes last fall, but he assured his parents he would make up the work. You must be mistaken. Have you talked with his parents?"

"Not yet," David said.

"Did Palmer do any work at home? Is there an office or workbench here?" Sigmund asked.

"This apartment has no space for anything like that. The work in Poland exhausted my husband. He slept on weekends. We led a very boring life. Palmer said everything would change once we moved back home. He even talked about vacations and travel.

"I will remain in Switzerland, now. Viktor promised to help me arrange selling our house in Tel Aviv and shipping my belongings here."

"Did Viktor receive any kind of inheritance from his grandfather's estate?"

"No. We have no money—other than what I need to live on. I don't understand these questions. Please explain why you are here," Jana demanded.

"Palmer may have taken some documents when he left the museum in Walbrzych," David said.

"That's ridiculous. What would he take?"

"May we look through his papers?" David asked.

"No. I want you to leave. You can't come in and accuse my husband of theft. What is your proof?" Jana was annoyed.

Sigmund instructed, "Mrs. Harel, Jana, you misunderstand. The detective's words were misleading. There was no theft. We wondered if your husband brought any work home, and then, because of his death, items were never returned to the museum."

"I'm not aware of any items that belong to the museum," Jana said. "I want you out of my house." She stood up. "Palmer did nothing wrong, and it's none of your business if Viktor is not in school."

As they got up to leave, Alana spotted a book on the kitchen counter. "Are you a coin collector?"

"No. That is…that was my husband's interest."

"I'm a coin collector," Alana lied, picking up the book. "I have nothing of any real value, but I always keep my eye out for something rare," she said. "Where is your husband's coin collection now?"

"I don't believe he ever had one. I never saw any coins. I'm sure he would have told me. My husband read books because of his job. Palmer's interest was learning new things; he always had a book in his hand."

"Was Viktor interested in numismatics?" Alana asked, spotting a hand written note tucked into the book.

"I don't know. Palmer began studying antique coins after we came from Tel Aviv. I know because I went to the bookstore for him. I also checked books out of the library. Then, before he died, he gave his books to Viktor.

"My grandson left that one behind the last time he visited. I put it out to remind myself to give it to him, but he hasn't been back."

Alana turned around to place the book on the counter.

"Coins were one of the topics Palmer researched for the museum," Sigmund ad-libbed. "Walbrzych's history is steeped in antique coinage because the region came under the control of several empires over the years.

"Palmer was developing an exhibit of historic coins of the territory. I'm afraid that's just part of the paperwork that is missing from the museum. He compiled documentation on other displays as well. We can't pinpoint with certainty what is lost, so our questions are regretfully vague.

"His records are invaluable to us, and they will be difficult to replace. We just want to be assured that he didn't bring papers home.

"You say Palmer didn't socialize with his coworkers, but he spoke frequently of Viktor. Since he was so devoted to his grandson, we wondered if he gave his journals or any other materials to Viktor to return to the museum. Your grandson could be unaware of their value and simply forgot about them," Sigmund said.

This explanation changed everything.

Palmer's widow allowed them to look around the house, but there was nothing of interest. They would have to move on to Viktor's parents.

In the car, Alana read from the paper she'd removed from the book. "Telstra's 83, 22 November."

"That's Tremblay's address and the date of the auction," Andrew said.

"What about Am Rank 92, Fürstweg 4 A, or Ginsterweg 23 D?" Alana asked, showing Andrew the notepaper.

"Those are addresses. I don't recognize the street names."

"What about Gen Global?" she asked.

"That's a private jet service," Sigmund advised.

"I know the owner," Andrew said, "so do you, Sigmund. His name is Alain Barth."

"I know Palmer's writing from his journal; the writing on this notepaper must be Viktor's," Alana said.

When they arrived at the parents' house, it was obvious that the grandmother had telephoned ahead. The parents appeared guarded until Sigmund repeated the account of how Palmer's valuable papers had gone missing.

"We wondered if Viktor had brought Palmer's papers here, without realizing their value to the museum," Sigmund explained. "No one is being accused of any wrongdoing. We just want to speak with Viktor."

Both parents turned cooperative, and it was clear that they knew nothing about any coins. Their son's absence, however, did concern them.

"Viktor never went more than a few days without calling home, but that changed after my father died. Viktor changed. He dropped all his friends, except for Trudie Rechsteiner.

"They became inseparable," the father said. "He never brought her here because my wife doesn't care for Trudie."

"They're not interested in that," the mother said. "I don't care about any papers, but I care why Viktor is not in school.

"You've made me worry that Viktor has eloped with that girl. Is that why he is away? And why is he not in school?

"Trudie is strange. I don't understand what he sees in her. Viktor told me to get used to her because they would marry."

"It's not our intent to worry you; we just want to talk to Viktor," Sigmund said.

David asked, "Did Viktor ever talk to you about the True Crime Club?"

"A crime club?" his mother asked.

"No, no, it's a book reading club." Alana jumped in. "They discuss true crime books."

"Viktor has always been an avid reader. I know he joined a book club in secondary school. That's where he met Trudie.

"He called that club a modern-day version of the Tuesday Night Club championed by Agatha Christie in her novels. Viktor loved reading murder mysteries, but he never mentioned a crime club."

"Tell me how this concerns the museum, or the police?" the husband asked.

"It's a stretch, I know, but Viktor's friends are so absorbed in reading, is it possible one of them took Palmer's papers to read?" Alana asked.

Their line of questioning had veered off track, and the parents became irritated.

"Viktor lives at his college," the wife said. "He has done so for several years. There is nothing like what you are talking about, belonging to Viktor or Palmer, in our house."

In the meantime, Boris had gotten into Viktor's dorm room at the university, everything had been cleaned out. He wasn't living there.

Zen

Chris called on Sigmund's cell phone to inform them that Ian had broken the chatroom code. He was piecing together their posts and could follow how the crime was planned.

"We're on our way," Sigmund replied.

*A*t the office, Ian explained, "The condensed version is—everything started after the Tremblay's auction. Viktor posed a puzzle for the inner circle of the club to solve. 'The quest is to steal a painting,' he said. 'The problem—you don't know where it is.'

"He gave them our website URL using a conventional code. The students never connected that we were investigators. They only accessed what we make available on our website—our public persona.

"Remember, these exchanges were in the club's private chatroom, not in the open forum. It was for their eyes only.

"Sabine's connection between the students' login names and the Nikki Goldshimmer book characters was central to breaking the code. The inspiration to mix truth and fiction in their posts came right out of the book's storyline.

"Each of the four founders used multiple logins to make accurate and conflicting posts. It's only after I identified the 'real' logins that I could follow their actual plans.

"After Viktor challenged the group," Ian explained, "they began discussing how they could commit the crime.

"The first problem was they didn't know if the painting was at the Griegg's' home, their office, or another location.

"Valentina wasn't active in those early stages. It wasn't until Remy recognized the Griegg name from attending her horse shows, that they connected William to our company.

"After she learned about Zen, which is what the horsey set calls William, Valentina became vigorously involved in the discussion. She was the one who threw out the idea of holding Tiger for ransom.

"At first they humored Valentina. They didn't take her idea seriously. They just went through the motions. Frankly, Valentina wasn't known for her ability to conceptualize crime—not like the others.

"As they hashed out abduction scenarios, however, it soon became clear her kidnapping scheme was brilliant—they didn't have to know where the painting was, if they could get it delivered to them as a ransom demand.

"Their initial thought was a simple kidnapping. They planned to dye Tiger's white markings brown. Disguised, they could hide him in plain sight at a rural stable. They tested the dyeing process on another horse to prove it would work. They agonized over every detail to plan even a fantasy crime.

"Viktor never tells them about the coins. He insinuates that there was a valuable painting hidden beneath the *Lady in Gold* portrait. Even though Palmer's expertise was jewelry, Viktor told them his grandfather was an art restorer. I guess that gave credibility to his claim of a hidden masterpiece.

"Viktor disclosed no part of his grandfather's theft. He says only that the elder Harel planned to buy the nondescript painting when it went to auction and then sell off the un-named hidden work of art. Then everything went wrong when the Griggs outbid his grandfather for the painting.

"I can't believe a group of students thought they could pull this off," Sabine said. "It's a complicated crime."

"Yes, I'll give my thoughts about that in a moment. But, remember, so far this is just another club game of plotting crimes. This is how it worked. Someone would throw out re-alistic events, and they would go to work to plot a realistic crime," Ian said. "They considered it fun."

"Then, well into the plan, Viktor tells them the plot is re-al. His grandfather was dead, and it was up to him to carry out the theft...but he couldn't do it alone. He offered each of them100,000 Swiss francs if they helped him pull it off.

"Hearing the monetary details was a wake-up call. Viktor made them declare if they were in or out. They all said they were in.

"Remy, Valentina, and Trudie would each receive 25,000 francs up front, with the balance paid when the job was done.

"That's when William's American trip came to light and the abduction plan, as we know it, took shape. Val told them Tiger would fly to New Jersey. She said she could get on the team traveling with the horses. She also told them about the dead ringer—and he was for sale. While Val theorized the plot, it fell to Remy and Trudie to sort out the details.

"When Val was given the money to purchase the horse known as Big Broon, everything became real. Their posts turned intense. While it was Viktor who initiated the scheme, it was Trudie and Remy who took charge; and the hierarchy of command went unchallenged," Ian said.

"At the time these discussions took place, Val had already picked up the two other paintings from Tremblay's. I found no discussion of why Viktor asked her to do that, or if Trudie or Remy knew.

"Val should have put two and two together and realized Viktor wasn't telling them the entire story...but nothing like that was debated in the chatroom. Perhaps she thought it wasn't her business. I can't explain it. Viktor could have picked up the art himself, but he didn't.

"The club's challenge was only about getting their hands on the one painting...the one that the Grieggs took home from Tremblay's.

"Going back to Sabine's comment earlier, I'd like to share my hypothesis after reading all their posts in their entirety," Ian said. "When Viktor presented them with the challenge to plan a real crime, one they would actually commit, they continued to treat it like any other club game.

"I believe their mission was about more than any painting or any amount of money. It was about how living out their fantasies online had disrupted their ability to function as normal people in the real world.

"Analyzing crimes, and meticulously plotting their own versions, had become an enormous part of their lives. Each of them had obsessions that made them addicted to the club.

"The fact these clever people didn't question the name or value of the painting supposedly hidden beneath the *Lady in Gold* seems odd, but it reinforces that they viewed Viktor's challenge as a game. No doubt they were all obsessed with money, but the perfect crime was equally compelling. The more complicated the better, because they believed they could pull off any crime they planned. They all muddled the lines between fact and fantasy—especially Valentina.

"Then, Valentina, the least likely among them, assumed the major role. She came up with the horse kidnapping idea, she flew to New Jersey with the horse, and, of course, she poisoned William.

"Within the group, Trudie Rechsteiner is a manipulator. The fact that Val wasn't detail-oriented wasn't a problem. Trudie told her what to do, and Val was happy to do it.

"Rob Grazioli wasn't part of the crime, but he had been the brains behind their website and the encryption coding.

"Remy and Trudie dug into the minutia to plan all the details. Remy fiddled with the farmworker's car to make him late for work. Then, having handled Val's horses, Remy, along with Trudie, switched Tiger at the Pegasus Air barn and took him to the airport to board the plane to Florida.

With falsified travel documents naming him as Big Broon, they sealed the trailer shut with stolen quarantine tape— which had to be intact when the trailer arrived at the airport. Big Broon traveled normally under Tiger's paperwork.

"Trudie made the ransom exchange at the station. Her petite size allowed her to fit into the crowd as a schoolgirl.

"They worked out all the details online without meeting face to face. They made a dry run before the abduction, in which Viktor managed the action via burner phones.

"This says volumes about Viktor. He put himself behind the scenes every step of the way. He didn't plan or call any of the shots; he simply telephoned in from a safe distance.

"Clearly, Valentina is vulnerable, but it's Viktor who is the weakest link for us to break."

"Amazing," Sigmund said.

Then Sigmund asked, "If I wanted you to insert a message in the secure and private chatroom, could you do that?"

"Sure, but don't forget the students haven't been using the chatroom since they went dark—just that one time, after the ransom drop."

"They might if we urge them," Sigmund said.

"What are you thinking?" Ian asked.

"Let's shake them up a bit," Sigmund said. "Let's turn their chatroom against them."

"How so?" Ian asked.

"We say, for example, we know everything and will help them get away scot-free…we could say we want a cut of the ransom. Scratch that," Sigmund mused. "Make it first person I know what you did. I could send you to jail."

Then Sigmund asked, "Could you make a post disappear? To be exact, could you add or delete entries in the chatroom, regardless of who posted them?"

"Yes," Ian said.

"What would happen if the police came looking? Would they find anything?"

"O k a y…" Ian intoned while contemplating the task. "It depends on how hard they look…I'll do my best to clear any trail…perhaps the best way is to create a false trail. I can send anyone trying to trace the posts on a wild goose chase."

"Perfect," Sigmund stated.

"Where are you going with this, Sigmund?" his father asked with interest.

"I'm not sure yet, we need to keep talking."

"I like the notion of messing with them and I agree to make it personal…with Viktor. Let's get inside his head. We could mess him up big time."

"I agree," Andrew offered. "But don't forget, we must find out if Viktor knows about the Gold Train. If he doesn't, then we don't have to worry about the others. We can push all we want."

Christopher stated, "We also want to divert any suspicion away from us."

"Why don't we play out that Palmer Harel had a partner?" Sigmund beamed with that idea. "Let's say this partner wants his cut of the action. We can make it ambiguous at first. Then adapt our messaging after we read how Viktor reacts. Our posts could take any number of paths."

"That would distract thoughts away from us," Sabine said. "I like it."

"Yes, I like it too." Andrew explained, "We stay anonymous. There's no reason for vengeance down the road. Our noses are clean."

Ian said, "It would also allow us to prod him about what he knows of OB, if anything."

"Yes," Sigmund acknowledged. "Let's do it."

"Post this: 'Palmer and I were partners. I want my cut. We need to talk—now.' "

Ian said, "I'll need time to sort out the details of adding and deleting posts without leaving any linkage back to us. I can do it, I just can't rush it…I need time for proper testing."

"How much time?" Sigmund asked.

"A few hours," Ian said.

"Okay, but time, as you know, is of the essence. Get back to me as soon as you're ready," Sigmund replied. "Thank you, everyone, we're done here."

*A*n hour later…

"I thought I might find you out here." Alana walked into the stable. "Hello Pendragon." She stroked the horse standing on the cross ties.

Andrew walked out from brushing Pen's tail. "Does my son need me in the house? I had hoped I could slip away for a short time."

"Yes. Ian and Christopher have been working nonstop. They've asked for a conference call in about thirty minutes," Alana said. "We have a little more time."

"I come out here whenever I feel overloaded," he said. "It's my sanctuary."

"Grooming the horses clears my head and rejuvenates my body," Andrew said proudly. "I remember the day we learned William was coming home from school in England. It was much sooner than either of us expected.

Andrew handed Alana a peppermint for Pendragon.

"William told his father he had qualified to leave his prep school early and that he wanted to go to college in Zürich. Not only were we not ready for him—we weren't prepared for the horses he brought with him.

"Sigmund had asked, 'Are you prepared to care for horses again?' and I responded, 'Always. It will be a pleasure.' What I hadn't realized, at the time, was just how gratifying it would be to care for the horses at this stage in my life."

Alana recounted, "I looked out my bedroom window this morning and watched you walk the horses out to the pasture. When you took off their bridles, they galloped off, kicking up their heels. It was a beautiful site."

"Now, Alana, I have to correct you." Andrew took hold of Pen's head. "This is a halter. Bridles are hanging in the tack room...with the saddles."

"Yikes! I should have known that!" she admitted.

"I could turn you into a horsewoman in no time." He laughed. "I'm just teasing you."

"Feel this spot," Andrew said, "right here, along the side of the nostrils. This is the softest spot on the horse's body.

"When William was a child, even before he had his first pony, he watched a mare pinch this area of her foal's soft skin and hold it between her lips. It was a bonding moment for the mare and her foal. From then on, William has mimicked what he learned from that mare," Andrew said.

"You can watch him, to this day. He likes to rub essential oils on the horses—usually lavender. They love it. Sometimes he will gently pinch that soft part of the muzzle with his lips.

"It says everything about his love for horses...but, it also reflects their bond with him."

"It's why he's called Zen, Andrew," Alana stated. "I think he's proud of that nickname, you know.

"I know he is."

"Why is it that you and Sigmund don't call him Zen?"

"I've never thought about it. It's not that we choose not to. It's that he has always been William. We rarely shorten it to Will."

"Zen will have a lot to deal with when he arrives home," Alana said. "Look at everything that's happened in the past week…Tiger went missing, Ash's death, losing the jumping competition, his decision to stop showing, wanting to work for his dad…I could be leaving something out. He won't have had time to digest all that's happened. It will hit him once he's home."

"Yes, that's not lost on us." Andrew told her. "He will have our support. "There's also the fact that he left all his school chums behind in England and will lose friends again leaving college."

"Oh, Andrew, I don't doubt your concern. I envy the close relationship the three of you share. I just want him to hang on to Zen as part of William during this transitions."

"You have raised an insightful issue," Andrew acknowledged. "We must consider how William will deal with all these changes through the lens of being Zen in the horse world for so long. Thank you for pointing that out."

Alana smiled at Andrew.

"You know, Sigmund and Evelyn bought William his first pony for all the noble reasons for a child to learn to ride. They had no idea how Princess Buttercup would capture his heart," Andrew said.

"William was addicted to riding from the start. Gosh that was a happy time. I wish you could have known us then. You would have liked Evelyn…and Sigmund was—well, not as structured as he is now.

"Sometimes I feel like my son carries the weight of the world on his shoulders. He's afraid if he ever lets his guard down, something bad will happen to someone he loves."

"I shared his burden when I was younger." He offered Alana a soft brush, and they began grooming Pen together.

"We both rode with William when he started. Evelyn didn't. She led the pony around and cheered us on.

"I played polo in college. Sigmund went to the same school and played a bit, himself. He didn't stick with it, but he understands the special relationship with horses…it's unique.

Andrew professed, "When you wrap your legs around a horse…your bodies are linked together to move as one.

"It's a spiritual connection between species that has enhanced our lives with pleasure and economic considerations for thousands of years. There is no equivalent.

"People have tried to articulate that connection from the beginning of time. Personally, I don't believe mere words can capture the essence of what it means to love horses…though I'm sure many great people have come close."

They finished brushing the horse.

Andrew stroked the Pen's face. Still thinking of William, he said, "The horse's eye is a marvel of anatomy. I've heard it said that looking into the eye of a horse is like looking into their soul. William has a different take on that notion. You won't believe what he once told me."

Alana listened to Andrew with interest.

"He said, 'When I look into a horse's eye, it's like peering into my own soul. I perceive everything from kindness and vulnerability, to wisdom and doubt, to frailty and strength. Each physical layer of the eye seems to coalesce, forming a tunnel that draws me inside…it's where I feel safe and whole, as a person.'

"It's a powerful belief for anyone to express, but William was just a young teen when he said this."

Alana replied, "Zen always amazes me."

"Yes. I think he amazed us all with his speech after the competition," Andrew said. "I wish he could have been an Olympian. Yet, he sees it differently and no one can doubt his reasoning. Still, he'll make his mark in another way."

"I'm sure he will," Alana said.

"I wonder if he would have reached the same conclusion had Tiger not been taken. I know he says he would, but how can he be sure?"

"I listened to him Andrew; I've never heard anyone so sure." Alana told him.

"I hope you are right." Andrew took a deep breath. "Well, enough said, when I'm down here, anything going on in the house feels a million miles away, but we have a crime to solve before William…before Zen arrives home," Andrew said, correcting himself.

"We've got a reply in the chatroom," Ian declared. "And, by the login, I'm 100 percent sure it's Viktor."

"Let's have it," Sigmund commanded.

"He says, 'There is no partner. Who are you?' " Ian read.

"Okay," Sigmund stated. "Let's discuss how to reply."

"If we say anything about the horse, they could connect it back to us," Chris said.

"Well, is mentioning the *Lady in Gold* also out?" Ian asked.

"It would seem so, but tell us, what you are thinking?" Sigmund asked.

"To let on that we know about the coins," Ian said. "That should rock his boat a bit."

Chris replied, "We could just respond with three words: gold aureus medallion."

At that moment, Boris and Niedermeyer called in to join the meeting.

"Apologies for lateness, we've just closed a call with one of my contacts," Niedermeyer explained, sounding like his old self. "We have a bombshell, Sigmund."

"Well, what is it?" Sigmund asked

"The numbered account we have on record from the Tremblay's auction was used to transact a coin sale last year. My contact bought the coin himself.

"He paid 500,000 Swiss francs for an American Double Eagle last December. He dealt with a man unfamiliar with the collectibles market.

"My contact controlled the negotiations from beginning to end. The seller had no understanding of the "art of the deal"—something that most collectors take seriously. How the *deal* plays out is an integral part of what makes these coin collectors tick.

"This particular seller just threw his cards on the table and cashed out. My friend sited the rather vulgar sounding cliché of: slam, bang, thank you...I won't finish repeating the phrase, as I think you get my point."

Niedermeyer added, "He went on to describe the bizarre way in which he picked up the coin. The seller left the coin in a locker at Zürich's rail hub. A messenger delivered the key to his office. He felt like James Bond, looking over his shoulder the entire time!

"My friend has been dealing coins for forty years. He can tell some of the wildest stories, but nothing like this has happened before. Since he closed the deal at a bargain price, however, he's not asking questions. My friend has checked the coin, and it's 100 percent."

"This is great information, Niedermeyer. It's good to talk with you," Sigmund acknowledged.

"It's both of us, Sigmund. Boris couldn't shut me up... I've been out of the game too long. I thought I would burst in anticipation."

"Well, like I said, it's good to have you back, even if it's only temporary," Sigmund stated. "I speak for everyone when I say you've been missed."

"Getting back to our chatroom response, why don't we take Chris' suggestion, but change the words to American Double Eagle?" Ian asked.

"I like it. They would have no reason to link that back to us," Sigmund said.

Andrew suggested a change. "Let's repeat that Palmer had a partner, and add that he wants his cut on the double eagle and every other coin. This way, we drill down on the partner angle while divulging that we know about the sale of the first coin—including the exact coin sold."

"Agreed. Put that into the chatroom. Thank you both. Call when you get a response," Sigmund said.

But as they continued to chat, a response came back before they closed out their call.

The following line appeared under Viktor's login: "Big fucking deal. Go to hell."

"That's feisty," Andrew said.

"Yes, any ideas on how to respond?" Sigmund asked.

"Is Viktor bolder than we thought?" Sabine asked.

"I don't believe so," Ian said. "It's easy to be provocative posting in a chatroom."

Sigmund proposed they respond: "See you there, Viktor." His father nodded.

Chris said, "Viktor read it and then logged off."

"Okay. Did you delete all the comments?"

"I'm handling it now," Ian said.

"Let him brew on that." Sigmund ended the call.

15

Disruption

"*T*rudie, wake up." Viktor shook her.

She rolled over and asked, "What's wrong?"

"Someone is posting in our private chatroom. Whoever it is, knows I sold the double eagle…and even though I'm posting as Tommy, the person called me Viktor. Who would betray us?"

Trudie sat up and said, "No one."

"Trudie there are four people who know I am Tommy—you, me, Remy, and Valentina."

"Well, clearly someone else knows," she snapped.

"The post said he's Palmer's partner."

"Partner? What are you talking about?"

"That's what he said. I assume it's a he, but it could be a woman. Anyway, the person claims to be Palmer's partner. He wants a cut of the money I got for the double eagle. Maybe it's the man who bought the coin?"

"How?" Trudie frequently talked down to Viktor. "You only talked over a pay phone in a public space. No names, and payment came into the numbered bank account. How would he know your grandfather, and why would he claim to be his partner?

Trudie continued. "We put the coin in the locker, and I delivered the key to an office. The man never saw either of us. He didn't even learn where the coin would be exchanged until he had the key."

Viktor just stared at her, and then he exploded. "Well, someone knows!"

"Who could know about our private chatroom, and how did they get in?" she asked.

"I have no idea!"

"Is there a way to trace the login?" she asked.

"I don't know," Viktor said.

"There must be a way," Trudie said.

"I'd have to contact Rob." Viktor told her.

"We can't do that," she said.

There was a chink in their perfect crime, but they had handled chinks in every crime scenario that they played out. It was the exact reason for the open forum chatroom…to be schooled in how to answer any flaw that surfaced during any crime. It was no big deal.

Trudie got up and paced the room. "Reflect back to when you arrived at the hospital on that final day. I need you to tell me every word your grandfather said. Be very specific, don't leave anything out."

"My grandmother called for me to come to the hospital, by that point we knew he was dying, but we didn't realize it would happen so fast.

"When I arrived, people were going in to say goodbye one at a time. When I went in, he was incoherent. While I can't recall exactly what he said, I know he didn't mention any fucking partner…if that's what you're talking about."

"What about your grandmother, or your mother or father, or doctors or nurses? Could any of them have overheard your conversation? Maybe he talked to one of them before you arrived? Think about who could know what he did."

"You think he rambled something to my family and now they are posting on our chatroom? They know nothing about our website—they don't even use the internet."

Viktor continued. "You think he told a nurse or doctor about an elaborate theft and they somehow found our private chatroom, hacked in, and are now demanding money? Trudie, it killed my grandfather to admit what he had done." Viktor grabbed her by the arms. "You weren't there. It literally killed him to admit he had committed a crime."

"You're still not telling me what he said."

"I've told you before."

"Then tell me again," Trudie snapped at him.

"What, you think I'm not telling you everything?"

"I'm not saying that." She tried to calm down. "We have a problem, Viktor. I'm just suggesting that saying it again might bring something new to light."

Viktor acquiesced. "First of all, we *were* alone. No one could have overheard. My grandfather mustered the strength to talk lucidly. He admitted he stole the coins from the Polish museum where he worked. He said he hid them inside the frames of paintings that would go to Tremblay's auction.

"He told me he had transferred enough money to buy the art. He gave me the key to the safe deposit box at the bank on Badenerstrasse.

"Then he gave me a choice: I could do nothing, or I could carry out his plan. Trudie, he didn't say anything about the rest of his plan! He closed his eyes and died!"

"Are you sure you're not leaving anything out?" Trudie lost patience again.

"I'm not!" Viktor shouted

"Was his death really that quick?" she asked. "You don't remember anything else?"

"What, like, he had a partner." He blasted again. "You don't think I would have remembered that!"

Viktor asked Trudie, "What about you? Who have you talked to?"

"Who would I have talked to? I want to get away with this. Since this whole thing started, I've only left one message in the chatroom.

"I told Val that we had the painting," she said. "That's it. We've been together 24/7 ever since."

"Well, that's not quite true," Viktor said. "You went to visit with your grandfather."

"Yes, I saw my grandfather, but nothing happened."

"I'm sorry. The breech of our chatroom has me spooked. How can we find out who hacked us?" Viktor asked.

"You're asking me? The chatroom is your deal,"

"What—something goes wrong and now it's *my* deal?"

"That's not how I mean it," she said.

"It's just that I wasn't involved. The website was something you mastered with Rob's help."

"And you're insinuating that I made a mistake!"

"No Viktor, I'm not saying you made a mistake…but we've been hacked, so clearly something has gone wrong."

"I've shared everything with you," Viktor said. "I don't know what's gone wrong and I don't know how to find out."

Trudie sat quietly before telling Viktor, "We need to call our parents. We told them we would be away for a few days, and that was up days ago. They might be concerned. We need to know if anyone has asked about us."

"It's too late to call my parents now. They'll be in bed," Viktor said.

Trudie picked up her cell phone. "My mother will be up." He heard Trudie say, "Hallo, Mamma."

"Trudie, where are you?" her mother shouted. "We've been worried sick."

"I'm fine. Why would you worry?"

"You didn't say where you were going, and you turned off your cell phone."

"We've been up in the mountains. I didn't have service until now. I'm sorry it's late."

"Trudie, I hate to say this over the telephone, but your opa has passed away."

"What!" Trudie was shocked.

"He flew to America, worried about that horse ridden by Zen Griegg."

"Why would he do that?" Trudie asked.

"You know how he is. Your grandmother said the horse told him he was in trouble, and your grandfather just packed up and left.

"We didn't learn for some time that he died."

"Died of what?" Trudie asked.

Viktor looked at her with alarm, hearing only her side of the conversation.

Trudie glanced at Viktor. "My grandfather, Ash, has passed away."

He felt relieved by the news.

Trudie's mother continued. "The doctors said he had cancer. He never told anyone he was sick. Now we learn he was self-medicating with herbal remedies. Apparently, one of them, called lobelia, caused his collapse of the plane."

Trudie cried out, "I'm sorry!"

"There's nothing for you to be sorry about. We need you to come home, now. Your oma is frantic. She has fallen apart. She won't even say if she knew he was sick."

"I have to call you back," Trudie said.

"Trudie, we need you to come home."

"I will come home for the funeral. I will call you tomorrow for the details."

Trudie ended the call and powered off the phone. "My grandfather died after flying to New York, believing that something was wrong with Zen's horse."

"You told him about the horse!" Viktor shouted.

"No! I told you he communicated with animals."

"I thought that was bunk."

"Me too," she admitted.

"You didn't tell me he flew to New York."

"I didn't know!" Trudie screamed.

"But you saw him."

"Yes," Trudie said. "He told me months ago that he was sick. He had gastrointestinal issues. He hadn't wanted to worry my grandmother, so I have been treating him with herbs, based on her notebook, along with ideas of my own.

"The American doctor told my mother he had cancer. I didn't know. He wouldn't go to a doctor. I only tried to help.

"When we met the other day, it upset him to learn that I had my grandmother's journal. He told me I had to give it back. I told him I would, but we quarreled.

"He told me I disappointed him…now he's gone."

Trudie sat wondering if she had killed her grandfather. *No*, she thought. *It's sad, but it has nothing to do with me.*

"You better wake your parents. Tell them you're okay." Trudie walked into the bathroom.

When she came out, Viktor told her that people from the Polish museum had been to the house and questioned both his parents and his grandmother.

"They wanted to know my whereabouts," he said. "What if one of these people is the partner?" he asked. "It would make sense for any partner to be connected to the museum, right? I was afraid to ask their names."

Trudie said, "I don't know, let me think." She paced the small hotel room, again. "Val could be back in Switzerland by now. The plane carrying the horses wasn't a scheduled flight, so I'm not sure when she was slated to arrive."

"I just called her," Viktor said. "If she's here, she has her phone turned off.

"We can't post a message in the chatroom—not if some stranger is monitoring everything we write. I think we should take the chatroom offline," she said.

"We can't. We don't know what would happen if our hacker couldn't communicate with us. The chatroom must remain active," Viktor said.

"Try Remy. He'll tell us if Val is back yet," Trudie said.

"I already tried. Both the burner and his regular cell phone are off."

"That's not good. He should have kept the burner on."

Viktor blew up. "I'm scared! I can't believe this is happening? Everything went according to plan. We switched the horses without a hitch. The coins are in the safe deposit box, except for the one I sold. How does anyone know what we've done? It doesn't seem possible."

"Calm down," she said.

Trudie was tempted to say "What do you mean *we*?" It had been her and Remy who made all the plans and switched the horses, but she let it go.

Instead, she explained, "This guy posting in our chatroom can't go to the police."

"You don't know that."

"Even if something *is* exposed, what could he prove? Nothing! You just say you inherited a coin from your grandfather and sold it. No one could know about the safe deposit box, or where it's located. Nothing that we've done can be traced…it's still the perfect crime.

"You can't be scared or you'll act irrationally." Trudie picked up the *Lady in Gold* and pushed it into Viktor's lap. "Get rid of it," she demanded.

"How?" Viktor barked.

That made Trudie want to put her fist through the wall. Instead, she stood with her back to him while she collected her thoughts.

"I'll go downstairs to the reception desk and ask for a screwdriver and a pair of scissors," she said.

When she got back, they broke the frame into pieces and discreetly tossed one chunk at a time into a fire burning in the hotel lounge.

Afraid that burning the artist's canvas might make a smell or create strange smoke, they cut the canvas into tiny pieces and flushed them down the toilet a few bits at a time. It took hours to finish.

When they were done, Viktor said to her, "There's one thing I haven't told you."

"Oh God, Viktor, what is it?"

"When I opened the safe deposit box for the first time, there was a gun inside."

"What did you do with it?"

"I brought it back to the apartment."

"Do you know how to use it?" she asked.

"No, do you?" he asked.

"Yes. There were times when my grandmother had a fox problem on her property. A skulk of foxes could kill off her chickens, baby goats, and lambs in a single day. It was a huge deal to keep them safe.

"A farmer she knew from Kollbrunn would come over and kill any fox for her. When he got older, she asked him to teach me how to shoot.

"I was the only one with the guts to pull the trigger. It was a secret we kept from my grandfather. Where is Palmer's gun now?" she asked.

"I put it in the nightstand next to the bed."

"Is it loaded?"

"I don't know."

How does he not know if it's loaded, she thought.

With the painting destroyed, Trudie felt relieved that their plan was okay. The chatroom intruder was a setback, but not a game breaker…as she said, no one could go to the police or prove anything. She just had to keep her cool with Viktor. Once he paid her off, she would never have to see him again.

"I will have to go to my grandfather's funeral, but I don't want you to come with me."

Trudie lay back on the bed. "You know what we never thought about?"

"What?" Viktor asked.

"What to do once we pulled it off…our perfect crime. How do we go back to our lives?"

"Come here." Viktor pulled her into his arms and they rolled over on the bed. "I love you. Why would we go back to our old life?" he asked. "We have new lives now, together. We can do anything we want."

He kissed her; Trudie stared at the ceiling with her eyes wide open.

"Not now, Viktor. I'm not in the mood."

David arrived at number Ninety-Six ready to learn how they would bring down the True Crime Club.

"Before we begin," Sigmund said, "we have *The Sewing Circle* and found four coin slots drilled into the frame. There were eight in the *Cambodian Dancer*. Depending on how many slots were in the *Lady in Gold*, there could be sixteen to twenty coins in total."

Sigmund added, "We consulted with Joan and determined that unless some of the coins are quite small, it is doubtful twenty coins would have fit into the purse.

"While it's not exactly scientific—our gut feeling is that sixteen is the number. We know one coin was dropped in the OB tunnel and one coin was sold. That leaves fourteen coins still in play."

"Now, for the topic of the day, we've conceived a sting operation." Sigmund explained, "Our objective is to convince Viktor that his grandfather had a partner.

"We've hacked into the club's private chatroom. We've already introduced Viktor to his new coconspirator.

"The backstory is that the partner was up in the air when Palmer died. He didn't know the status of the coins until the first one came up for sale.

"That's when the partner realized someone had taken over Palmer's plan. We will present this guy as a bad actor—a real malcontent, someone willing to do anything to get his share of the coin hoard.

"This phantom partner can take any number of paths as the chats progress. The point is that this partner knows everything. We want to scare the hell out of the students."

"I like the way your minds works," David stated.

"As I said, we've taken control of their internet chatroom, which is how the students communicate. We can add and delete conversations at will, so we have the ability to pit the players against each other.

"The goal is to create confusion and mistrust—complete chaos. If we disrupt their communications, we can contradict or deny anything they tell each other. We can confuse and destroy any cohesion between the members."

"How do you explain this partner finding out about the chatroom? How would he have gotten in?" David asked.

"We don't have to explain anything," Sigmund said."

243

David looked confused. "How do you mean?"

"We're in and already threatening them. It's fruitless for them to wonder how it happened. The only hitch is convincing the Israelis to have faith in the plan," Sigmund said.

"You're running the show," David said. "Why care what the Israelis think?"

"We need them to front five million Swiss francs for the sting. If all goes well, they'll get it back...but, of course, we give no guarantees."

"It always comes down to money, doesn't it?"

"Everything is always about money, David. Will you get it for us?" Sigmund probed.

"I hate being your piggybank, Sigmund." David stood up to leave. "If you want millions of francs, you must ask for it yourself.

"My superior in Zürich will contact you—that's as far as I will go. We can talk later."

16

Confusion

*V*alentina couldn't sleep. She was afraid to fly back home to Switzerland. She had enough cash to board a train to New York, then go on to Montreal and book into a hotel.

Andrew had left her unable to think clearly. She was afraid to use her credit card or buy international usage for her cell phone. Paranoia had set in.

Her decision to go to Canada was impulsive and foolish, but being left to her own devices had driven Valentina crazy.

The students' complex scheme demanded there be no communications between any of the members for two weeks. Yet knowing she had let slip about the painting, and not knowing if Andrew believed her cover story, Val feared he had already figured out the truth behind their plan.

He may no longer be content with just getting the horse back, as he'd said. He might turn her in to the police. She needed to talk to someone. When the train stopped in New York, Val took a bus out to Long Island to visit Rob Grazioli. He was her only source of advice.

It didn't surprise Rob to see her. He had almost expected it, after his previous visitor. When he said that Trudie had sent a woman to see him, Valentina asked, "Something went wrong? What went wrong?"

"The woman didn't say, and I didn't ask."

"What was her name?"

"She didn't give me her name. She told me her chatroom logon. Lindgren."

"There is no Lindgren. What did she look like?"

"She was Swiss or German. I don't know accents well enough to tell. She looked in her thirties, blonde hair, kinda hot looking.

"When I turned her away, I saw her get into a car driven by an older man."

"What did the guy look like?"

"He was old," Rob said, "my grandfather's age."

It had to be Andrew, Val thought. He introduced her to two women outside the hotel. She saw them again at the quarantine facility. One had blonde hair.

How did they know about Rob? Why did they come to his school? She kept rehashing Andrew's voice in her head, saying he would bring hell down on her. How could she not be afraid?

"You have to help," Valentina demanded. "I am all alone. I'm afraid to contact anyone else.

"I have money in a Swiss account that I don't know how to access from here…and the cash in my pocket won't last long. I don't know what to do. I need someone to tell me what to do."

"Why are you even here?" Rob questioned. "Is it about the horse you conned my father into importing?"

"Don't ask."

"You won't answer, yet you want my help?" Rob asked. "There's another thing, Val. An official from the USDA went to see my father about that horse. So, he's scared too.

"My father didn't want me to know what he had done, but then he read in the newspaper that a man named Asher Rechsteiner had died in a Long Island hospital while visiting from Switzerland.

"The man from the USDA asked my father if he knew a guy by that name…that's Trudie's grandfather, right?"

Val looked devastated. "How did he die?"

"I have no idea!" Rob shouted

"I can't believe we're even having a conversation about a dead person."

"But the paper would have said if they suspected foul play, right?"

"I heard this from my father, Val, and he didn't say." Rob added, "Look, I feel bad for you, but you can't involve me in any of this."

"Would you at least let me use your computer so I can get ahold of Remy and my mother?"

"I'll take you to the library," Rob said.

*T*he following day, lying on a bed in Canada, Val continued to feel utterly lost. She told her mother that there would be a delay flying the horses home. That bought her more time to figure out what to do.

Remy wasn't online when Val used the computer at Rob's school. She left a message in the club's chatroom for him to be online at noon that day—six in the evening Zürich time.

She had computer access at the Canadian hotel, so she was just hanging out until it was time to log on. Val had no way of knowing that Chris and Ian would be lying in wait. They had deleted her message after Remy read it, so Viktor and Trudie would be left in the dark.

Val's mind ran wild while as she waited to go online. In her darkest fears, she remembered reading about Cuba in the club's open forum chatroom. They talked about hiding out there if a crime went bad. She knew she couldn't go there alone. *Remy wouldn't be on board for that,* she thought.

Besides, she had received only one quarter of the cash Viktor promised…and she had spent most of that to buy her show horse, even borrowing money to come up with the full purchase price. She was dependent on the rest of the money before deciding anything.

It was yet another example of her impulsiveness.

At ten minutes to noon, Montreal time, Valentina pushed the elevator button for the hotel lobby and its computer room. She found Remy logged into the True Crime Club's private chatroom. His login ID was Teddie. Valentina logged on as Aunt Lauren, as usual.

Aunt Lauren: "I want to go to church, but I've been away so long, I'm afraid to go back."

Teddie: "What are you talking about? There is nothing wrong with going to church. Don't be troubled. I'm just hanging out, reading a *Dancing at Midnight*."

Aunt Lauren: "Yeah, I heard that is a good book. I'm reading book 45 from the club's catalog. I just took 74 books off my personal wish list."

Teddie: "That's a total surprise...I don't even know what to say. Just go to church."

Aunt Lauren: "Should I read *Dancing at Midnight*?"

Teddie: "That would be good. I don't understand your hesitation."

Aunt Lauren: Maybe I'm reading too much. Do you remember the book, *The Killer Following Me*?"

Teddie: "Just stop reading and go to church. *Dancing at Midnight* has a happy ending."

Aunt Lauren: Logged off.

Teddie: Logged off.

Christopher and Ian told Sigmund that Valentina was in Montreal, Canada. She had revealed the city's geographic coordinates—45° N, 74° W—within her message to Remy.

"Montreal? What the heck is she doing there?" Sigmund asked them.

"Yeah, that's a bit of a shock. It appears she is fearful of being caught if she returns to Switzerland. Remy seemed as surprised as we are. He's given her the green light to fly home as soon as possible," Ian said. "We deleted all their posts."

"If you recall, we talked about the Cuba option being discussed in the club chatroom. This was in the context of any crime going wrong. That's what the reference to the book *The Killer Following Me* was all about—retreating to Cuba," Chris said. "I found no evidence our students took that seriously, but I guess Valentina did."

"Well, they didn't plan for every contingency—namely, us," Sigmund said. "Tell me the flight Valentina is on, and my father and I will meet her at the airport."

Valentina calmed down after her online "chat." The posts, at least for a little while, served to reunite her with Remy and the club. Her sense of abandonment subsided.

Remy Abbatelli was a curious character. He grew up in a crime family, but unlike Rob, he lacked the moral compass to lead a law-abiding life.

The fact was, Remy liked living on the edge. The others saw the perfect crime as the means to an end—financing a better life. It was a one-shot deal.

Remy, however, saw the club's activities as his life. After all, it had worked out for Mario...and then, when his father, Tony, was pulled into a life of crime, it worked for him as well. There was no going back for Remy. He was where he wanted to be.

He knew Valentina loved him, but once the lust of dating died down, he no longer felt the same. Their relationship became convenient; it was about sex and the True Crime Club.

He planned to tell Val she couldn't move in with him after the American trip, and he wasn't sure if he would stay involved in the club if this scheme was just a one-off deal.

Remy's link with Viktor and Trudie was about money and the True Crime Club. Sex and money were the two most powerful motivators for people like him.

Remy interpreted the empowerment he gained through the True Crime Club activities as strength. When in fact it was weakness, he couldn't resist the allure of money.

Valentina was also weak. She sold her soul for the horse of her dreams. She thought the perfect crime scheme would set her up as a world class equestrian, but in reality, she didn't think past winning the next jumping competition.

Posting in the club's chatroom, however, was a mistake for both their ambitions. It fed into a series of engineered communications to divide the club in ways that the students couldn't conceive.

It was almost too easy to divide Val and Remy against Viktor and Trudie. The sting fell together with ease.

"What a difference a day makes." Those words were immortalized by the Dorsey Brothers back in 1934. Their song tells a timeless tale of inspiration for love and life and how fast any bitterness can heal…that is, unless the problem cuts so deep, that it can't be nursed by the light of day.

Trudie awoke in the same despair that plagued her sleep. It was now apparent she hadn't planned for life after their perfect crime.

If she had made a plan, it wouldn't have included Viktor. Why hadn't she grasped that he had fallen in love with her? He never said it before last night. All the signs were there, but she had been too wrapped up in herself to notice.

The moment "I love you" passed his lips, Trudie knew she was screwed…but there were more than mere feelings to consider. The bulk of her payoff was yet to come.

What if Viktor pressed her to say she loved him? Their crime games involved role playing, but that was online. Could she pull off lying face-to-face? Would the balance of her money be in jeopardy if she didn't say it? She recalled that old adage, "no honor among thieves."

They had committed to the perfect crime scheme as a group, but Trudie was in deeper than Remy and Valentina. She knew the truth.

Trudie knew about all three pieces of art—the truth that Palmer had hidden coins inside each of the frames. She knew that the coins, worth millions, were squirreled away in a safe deposit box at a bank on Badenerstrasse.

She knew there was no masterpiece hidden beneath the *Lady in Gold*—they'd burned it…and most disturbing of all, she knew that Palmer Harel's gun was tucked away in the nightstand in Viktor's bedroom.

Val had brought the artwork to Viktor's dorm room, but it was hours later when Viktor and Trudie ripped open the packages and unscrewed each frame's corner brackets.

They were alone when Trudie held the coins in her hands as Viktor pried them, one by one, from the slots drilled to conceal them. There were four American Double Eagles in *The Sewing Circle* and eight small South African Een ponds in the Rodin.

"Fantastic." Trudie had relished. "What are they worth?"

"I have no idea. My grandfather didn't tell me."

"Well, let's find out. It must be millions!"

"Probably," Viktor had said.

"What do we do now?"

"We put the coins in a safe deposit box."

The same thing happened with the *Lady in Gold*. Viktor unscrewed the frame to reveal four aurei medallions. Those coins were dropped into the safe deposit box as well, and that painting would have been sold, had fear not intervened.

What started out like any other club fantasy had, in fact, never been a game at all—it was a mission, and Trudie thought she had worked hard for the money.

Part of her 100,000 francs payoff would fund her online trading. Trudie intended to become wealthy in her own right, not through a relationship with Viktor, or any other man.

But Viktor's declaration made her think—he had come into an untold fortune...and he loved her. When Viktor came out of the shower, Trudie called him back to bed.

"Did you say you loved me?"

What a difference a day makes.

Waiting beside the baggage carousel at the Zürich Airport, Val's heart sank when she saw Andrew walking toward her.

"How did you find me?" she asked.

"I told you, we're investigators," Andrew replied.

"Are you the police?" She scowled at Sigmund."

"Oh, he's much worse than that, Valentina. This is Zen's father," Andrew said. "You didn't meet him in New Jersey."

"You have your horse back. What more do you want?" she asked. "You said you would leave me alone."

"We don't want anything," Andrew said. "We're here to warn you to watch your back."

"Screw you." Valentina grabbed her suitcase and rucksack from the platform and walked away.

"We've uncovered an unscrupulous character," Sigmund said. "He knows about you and the True Crime Club."

Valentina kept walking.

"He was Palmer Harel's partner in crime," Andrew said. "He wants his cut of the money...and he won't take no for an answer. This man is a bad actor and you don't want to cross him. What he is capable of is beyond your grasp."

Val still didn't acknowledge them.

"It's why we are backing off," Sigmund stated. "You beat us. We would have never hurt you, but with this nameless partner involved, you must ask yourself—is the money worth your life?"

Valentina stopped short and turned. "I have no clue what you're talking about."

"Okay, I hear you," Andrew said. "But when you figure it out, don't call us. I'm afraid this partner may see you as the weak link in the chain, so be prepared.

"While we hate what you did, you don't deserve the kind of trouble that is barreling your way."

The Grieggs walked off. If Remy had cooled Val's fears in Canada, they were red hot again now.

What are they talking about? Val thought again. Now frightened, she rushed to Remy's apartment on Kirchenstraße (English translation: Church Street).

Like Viktor, Remy had moved off campus after pocketing his share of the scheme's down payment money.

When Val unlocked the door, her emotions burst and she broke into tears.

"What's wrong?" Remy asked.

"The men that own the horse were at the airport."

"The Grieggs?"

"Yes. They said Viktor's grandfather had a partner, who wants his share of the money.

"They came to warn me because he might come after me. Andrew acted like the guy might kill me or something. What's happening to our perfect crime?"

"Calm down, Val. Tell me exactly what they said."

"Okay, I'll try." But she couldn't stop crying.

Remy couldn't understand a single word. After a few minutes of sobbing, she tried again.

"They said they were over what we did to them. They got their horse back, and everything was cool.

"But, they were investigators, and they discovered this other person—they called him a 'bad actor,' who was some-how involved…and I'm the weak link." She cried again, "I'm so scared."

"What are they talking about? Val, nothing went wrong. We did it…we pulled off the perfect crime. It's over," Remy assured her.

"Then who is this bad actor?" she asked.

"It's nobody. They're messing with you. Viktor will send the balance of our money soon. We're home free, you should be happy. Don't cry."

"Is that what Viktor said?" she asked.

"I haven't talked to him. You know we're not supposed to communicate yet."

"Not even through the chatroom?" she asked.

"No. Viktor stated no communication for two weeks. We broke the rules when we chatted online."

"Do you know that Trudie's grandfather came to New York and now he's dead?" Val asked.

"No." Remy was taken back. "What happened?"

"Rob just said he was dead. He didn't know any more."

"Rob? Rob Grazioli? When did you talk to him?"

"I took the bus to his school because that Griegg guy frightened me. I was afraid to come home. I guess it sounds stupid now, but I just couldn't wait in New Jersey. I felt like a sitting duck.

"Rob told me that Trudie had sent some woman to tell him I needed help. She made out like some part of the plan had gone haywire. The woman might have been a friend of the Grieggs, I'm not sure."

"Did you ask the Grieggs about that?"

"They mixed me all up. I haven't been able to sleep…I can't think straight. We could go to jail!"

"Val, everything is fine," Remy repeated, but now, with the knowledge that Ash was dead, he wasn't sure if that was true. "If it will make you feel better, I'll call Viktor," he said, needing reassurance himself.

When there was no ringtone on Viktor's cell phone, he wasn't surprised. They were supposed to keep their regular cell phones turned off during this period on incommunicado. His burner phone wasn't holding its charge, so he logged into the chatroom to ask him to talk.

Ian called Chris to his desk, "The chatroom has a visitor."

"Who is it?" Chris asked.

"Remy is on as Teddie, asking to talk to Tommy, which is Viktor's character."

"Do you want me to call Sigmund?" Chris asked.

"No," Ian replied. "We can handle this. I paused all post notifications from Remy being sent to Viktor. We can chat without Viktor knowing."

Responding as Tommy, Ian typed: "What do you want? We shouldn't be talking online."

Remy typed: "Val thinks someone knows about us? What the hell is going on?"

Ian typed again as Tommy: "We can't talk without the encryption code."

Remy typed: "I'm done with your secret codes. Val says Ash is dead."

Ian typed: "What are you talking about?"

Remy typed: "Is Ash dead?"

Ian typed as Tommy: "Ash? Where did she hear that?"

Remy typed: "Paul Grazioli read it in the newspaper."

Ian typed as Tommy: "Why would she talk to Paul?"

Remy typed: "Because you're not being straight with us…did Palmer Harel have a partner? You're not answering my questions…why are the posts disappearing from my computer screen?"

Ian typed as Tommy: "Because we're not using the code, you idiot."

Remy typed: "Don't screw with me." He hit the cap lock. "TELL ME WHAT THE FUCK IS GOING ON!"

Ian typed: "Okay, calm down. I'm paying you to do a job, that's it. Nothing else concerns you."

Remy typed: "If Val feels threatened, it concerns us."

Ian typed: "Look, we agreed not to talk for two weeks, but I'll call you on the burner phone. Just get off the chatroom." Ian had Remy exactly where they wanted him.

Valentina wasn't the only one freaking out now.

17

The Sting

*T*rudie told Viktor to simplify. "I suggest you transfer the balance of money due Val and Remy. They've done their jobs. It's best to have no further contact with them for a while."

"What about your money?" Viktor asked.

"Sure, if you wish. I just assumed we had other plans to think about." Trudie placed her hand on Viktor's chest.

Viktor disregarded the rule and logged into the chatroom to tell Remy about the payoff. Again, Chris and Ian lay in wait…watching and reading.

Viktor typed as Tommy: "I suggest the book *Living Paycheck to Paycheck*. Goodbye."

Remy typed: "You said you would call me. Why are you posting now?"

Viktor typed: "What?"

Remy typed: "You posted a few minutes ago that you would call. I've been waiting."

Viktor typed: "What posts? I haven't posted."

Remy typed: "Yes, you did. I demanded we talk because Val is freaking out…now I am too."

Viktor typed: "What are you playing at Remy? There are no posts."

Remy typed: "You deleted all the posts—because we weren't using the encryption coding."

Viktor typed: "I am paying you and Valentina the balance of the money. We're done for now. I will contact you when we can talk again. Just be cool."

Remy typed: "What's going on?"

Viktor typed: "Get offline." Viktor logged off.

Remy typed: "If Valentina or I get threatened, we're going to go to the police. Understand?"

Viktor was off line. Remy doubted he'd read the last post...but that was a moot point, as all the post lines disappeared before his eyes.

Knowing Remy's nerves were fried, Chris and Ian let the exchange stand without any addition.

A short time later, the "partner" logged into the chatroom and waited for Tommy.

Ian typed: "I've made the decision to take all the coins off your hands."

Soon after, the following line appeared on Ian's screen. "*You* have decided?"

Ian typed: "Yes. I value the coins at ten million francs. I will pay five million to buy you out. You sold one. Consider it a gift."

Viktor didn't acknowledge.

Ian typed as the new partner: "What's the hesitation? This is nonnegotiable. My offer is more money than you ever imagined. You turn over all the coins and I turn over five mill in Swiss francs—end of story."

Viktor typed with confidence: "I am in no hurry to sell. I control the coins."

Ian typed: "You control zilch. You are an ignorant punk. Five million is a fair price. Agree or be sorry. I'll be back online in one hour."

The partner logged off, and Viktor watched the post lines disappear before his eyes.

Trudie glared at the now blank computer screen. "What is happening?" she asked.

"I don't know." Viktor shook his head.

"Well, obviously your grandfather really had a partner," she shouted.

"I guess."

"You guess! Are you kidding me? That's what you have to say? You guess!"

"What do you want? This is not my plan."

"Your plan? Your plan was for me to do everything," Trudie snapped at him. "I've been planning our perfect crime every step of the way. Now you guess your grandfather had a fucking partner!"

"Well, then, if you're so smart—what do we do?"

"I can't believe you don't know what the coins are worth. You had plenty of time to find out."

"I wasn't planning to sell any coins right away. Except for that one coin—and in hindsight, I let it go cheap. My grandfather gave me his books, but I haven't read them, and I don't have them with me."

"Viktor, we have one hour. There's no time to read now, and you don't get a current market price by reading a book. There must be a way to stall this so-called partner."

Trudie felt trapped in the hotel room with a fool. It was difficult for her not to say how she felt in no uncertain terms, but locking into a larger share of the fortune meant she couldn't speak her mind.

As the end of the hour neared, "I'll take the five million," Viktor announced.

"No! I told you to stall this guy. I need more time to think," Trudie demanded.

The partner's post lit up Viktor's computer screen.

Ian typed: "I'll take my money now."

Viktor typed: "No. I need more time."

Ian typed: "If you want more time, give me two words that describe where your grandfather's coins came from?"

Viktor typed: "I don't understand."

Ian typed: "Maybe this will help—Two words that say where the coins came from or I will go after your friends."

Viktor typed: "What! What words am I supposed to know? I don't know what you are talking about? I need more time to think."

Ian typed: "I want two words, you idiot. Two words from 1945—type them now, or Remy and his girlfriend will meet with an unfortunate demise."

Viktor typed: "What words am I supposed to know? My grandfather never told me anything about the coins. I don't know where they came from. I didn't know he had a partner. Don't hurt anyone."

Ian typed: "Your choice is simple, deal or death. You must decide. The deal is five million Swiss francs for all the coins…you know what death is. If I log out of this chat session, the consequences will be sealed. I'll count to three… one…two…"

Viktor typed: "Okay! Okay, I'll take it…I'll take the deal." He was frantic to type before *three* appeared on his screen.

Ian typed: "Wise choice."

Trudie watched all the posts disappear from the screen and realized that Viktor was right. They had no choice. Five-mil would be enough.

Sigmund had entered the room and watched the exchange take place. "The students know nothing of the Gold Train," he said.

*T*he next morning, David mingled with those assembled at the cemetery for the burial of Asher Clement Rechsteiner. He believed his disguise looked so natural it would fool Sigmund.

A neo-pagan minister read from his notes. "Ash endeared himself to animal lovers from all walks of life," he said, looking over a crowd that embodied that very diversity.

From the super-rich to those who paid Ash their last few francs, the mourners turned out in the rain to say adieu to a dear friend.

Some brought their dogs, believing that the animals could reach out to Ash's spirit. The ceremony did not disappoint. It both honored and poked fun at Ash's quirky life.

When the minister concluded his sermon, the individual eulogies began. Each tribute illustrated how, by helping their animals, Ash brought families together in amazing ways, a feat those who dismissed him as bat-crap crazy failed to value.

David sought out Trudie at noon.

Following her instructions, Trudie moved away from her family. She stood alone, clutching a small brown paper bag.

"I'm sorry for your loss, young lady," David said. "Do you have something for me?"

"Someone is watching us, so don't try anything stupid," Trudie lied.

"My dear, the mere fact that I am here is stupid. I want my merchandise. *My* merchandise, do you understand what I'm saying?"

Trudie offered him the bag, but David refused it.

"Let's not do this out in the open. We must walk farther away." David indicated a mausoleum several meters behind the crowd.

The man unsettled Trudie, but she complied.

The clouds drifted off and the rain ended, allowing David to shut his umbrella. He removed a jeweler's eye loupe from his pocket to examine each of the fifteen coins in the bag.

An expert had tutored him on what to look for. It was a risk, but one he had to accept. After all, it was unlikely the coins were fakes; and the sting seemed to have little danger of losing the payoff money.

David looked for slight variations on the edges of the coins. Perfect symmetry or large disparities would be equally suspicious. He also knew variants in the patina should be irregular, yet uniform on each side of the coin.

When David recalled something about bubbles in a molded coin versus a minted coin, he realized any attempt at validation was pointless. He couldn't do it. He just looked at each coin for an adequate amount of time and then handed the bag back to Trudie.

David then made a cell phone call in which he muttered the word, "Go."

That word sent the disguised Boris walking through the Zürich train station. He carried a large attaché case in his hand. Boris placed the case in a locker and discretely slipped the key to a passerby.

A disguised Ian then bumped into Viktor, standing where he was told—at the gate to tracks 21–23.

"Excuse me," Ian said, pretending to pick up the key. "Did you drop this?"

"Yes," Viktor said.

Viktor pulled the case out of the locker and pressed it against the wall to open it. He found the attaché filled with circulated 1,000 Swiss francs banknotes banded in 100,000 franc currency straps.

Amidst the commotion of station, Viktor closed the case immediately. The plan allowed for him to scrutinize the pay-off in the privacy of the bank's safe deposit box room.

Viktor called Trudie and said, "Phase one is complete."

Boris watched to see the call take place.

David initiated a cell phone call from his pocket, counted to five, then disconnected. This confirmed that Trudie had taken Viktor's call. The sting was on.

Viktor turned to walk around the corner to the bank on Badenerstrasse, where he would call Trudie again. She would wait for the "all clear" before handing over the coins.

But before Viktor could take a single step, an over-packed baggage cart slammed into him. He fell to the ground.

A group of soldiers outfitted in TAZ 90 fatigues encircled him to help.

"My case! I need my case!" Viktor exclaimed as he flailed about the floor. Reaching for the attaché at his side, he locked his fingers around the handle.

The soldiers took ahold of his arms and pulled him to his feet. Viktor barked out, "Where's my cell phone! I had it in my hand." He pushed the soldiers aside; as he shouted again, "Where is my cell phone?"

"I'm afraid it's damaged." A soldier handed him a shattered phone. "Are you okay, sir?"

"This isn't my phone!" Viktor shouted out, throwing it against the lockers. His mind raced as he tried to grasp what was happening. "Where is my phone?" He repeated. "Where is my phone?" The soldiers dispersed around him.

Viktor looked down at the attaché in his hand…it wasn't the same case. He opened it…it was packed with newspapers.

Panicked, Viktor scanned his eyes across the station's large concourse. The man who'd passed him the key, was nowhere in sight. The soldiers were gone. He had no phone. He had no money. Reality set in: The mysterious partner had duped the True Crime Club. There was no perfect crime.

Meanwhile, at Ash's funeral, Trudie and David waited for the sound of Viktor's "all clear" call. The seconds ticked off in Trudie's head. Standing beside David was awkward. She didn't look at him.

Boris had estimated it would take twenty minutes for Viktor to walk around the corner to the bank, enter the safe deposit room, and be satisfied that the payoff was all there—despite the fact he couldn't possibly count it all.

The team had to maintain a convincing timeline. Viktor and Trudie would have come to a comparable assessment. She looked at her watch again and again. A friend walked over to give his condolences.

"Thank you, but please, I'd like to be alone." As the crowd thinned, Trudie feared that more people would come to pay their respects. She demanded that David follow her even farther away.

Viktor ran frantically through the train station, grabbing and yelling at people to let him use their cell phone. His behavior was so bizarre that no one complied. If anyone had, Boris, dressed as a security guard, would have stopped any call from connecting.

Viktor approached the bank of pay phones he'd used to make the ransom demands. Boris arranged for every station to be engaged.

After searching his wallet for Trudie's burner phone number, Viktor shrieked at people to get off the phones.

Boris intervened.

"You don't understand! I must make a call, it's urgent." Viktor flung the phony attaché across the floor. "Get off the phones!" he shouted again.

"Wait your turn, sir," Boris demanded.

"Don't tell me to wait!"

"Come with me, sir." Boris took hold of Viktor's arm.

"Get your hands off me!" Viktor screamed, attracting the attention of the actual security.

"What going on?" they asked Boris.

"This gentleman refuses to wait his turn to make a phone call," Boris replied. "I'm new on the job and I am not sure how to proceed."

"Come with us, sir." They told Viktor.

"No…no, leave me alone," Viktor said to them as he straightened his clothing. "I'm okay; I'll wait my turn to make my call."

At the same time, Trudie's cell phone displayed Viktor's number. Ian held a digital recorder close to the phone to convey static across the line. While the voice wasn't distinct, Trudie got the message: "All clear," Ian said to her.

Trudie handed David the bag of coins. As she walked away, Trudie believed she had just clinched the perfect crime. The result varied from her original plan, but five-mil wasn't a bad haul.

She went in believing her take would be 100,000 Swiss francs. Now, if she played her cards well, her share could be so much more.

She congratulated herself. She felt elated. Viktor had been weak and screwed things up and, in her mind; she alone had held their scheme together.

Trudie allowed mourners to greet her and share their sympathies, but she couldn't hide her elation.

When questioned, she said, "I'm just celebrating Ash's life. My grandfather meant everything to me. Of course I am devastated, but Ash would want me to be happy." She slipped away from the crowd as fast as she could.

She planned to celebrate when she got back to Viktor's apartment. She had to put her disgust for him on hold for a while. *Perhaps it's in my best interest to get married?* she asked herself—a quick ceremony. After all, nothing has to last forever.

Although first, she'd have to face her family. They had waited until after the ceremony to confront her over Ash's death and the herbs he was taking.

*B*ack in his car, David called Sigmund and said, "Done."

"Good," Sigmund retorted, "I've got your attaché case."

"Is there any cash inside?"

Sigmund laughed. "It's all there, David, when will you have faith in me?"

"Getting the money back will be a start. Would you like to return my attaché over a drink?"

"I can't. William and Tiger will arrive home any time now. I will get the money to you tomorrow. The cash will be in our safe overnight. Is everything good between us now?"

"Time will tell," David said. "Only time will tell, but maybe I'll take your call the next time you're in trouble and need my help." David hung up.

18

Homecoming

William came into the house after putting Tiger into the field to stretch his legs after the lengthy trip back to Zürich.

"Welcome home," Sigmund said. "We're having coffee, would you like a cup?"

"I'd rather have a beer, please."

Alana entered the kitchen and greeted Zen with a hug. "I heard the horse van pass the house. How was the trip? Is Tiger glad to be home?"

"The flight went fine, although long. And, yes, he looked happy to be back in his paddock. I'm amazed how the horses adapt to flying.

"If I were a horse, I wouldn't want any part of it. Tiger was so relaxed. He munched hay the entire way home," Zen said. "Takeoffs and landings seem a bit dodgy, but the horses handle them well.

"It's amazing, really." William took the beer mug from his father. "Thanks, Dad."

"Ian told me the case is over," William said. "I can't believe how you tricked them. It was brilliant!"

"Yes, it's over," Andrew came in, saying. "I guess you've heard all the details on the sting operation."

"I'm not sure about *all*, but I got the gist of it. Now on to the next case," William said with a smile.

"Hold your horses," Sigmund stated. "You have school-work to finish before you start any next case."

"I know, but I'm ready to work at number Ninety-Six."

"And what would you like us to call you when you get there?" his grandfather asked.

"I don't understand," he replied.

"Alana made us aware that because you have been Zen in the horse world for so long, you might like to continue as Zen with us," Andrew said. "We've been so used to calling you William that we never thought to ask."

"I'm not sure what to say."

"Just say what is in your heart," his father said.

"Well then, I'll say I'm still the same William, no matter what anyone calls me, but I like being Zen. It's how I feel about myself."

"Then Zen it is," his father stated. "We'll see if it sticks and feels natural."

"All right, I like that idea. Let's give it time," Zen said. "What's on the agenda for today?"

"Nothing," his father replied. "We could all use a day to unwind...especially you."

"Since when do you unwind?" Zen asked his father.

"I'm learning." Sigmund poured himself coffee.

"No one's told me why Val wasn't on the flight home," Zen said. "Coach Lara said she wasn't going to be on the plane, but she didn't explain."

"Your grandfather went all Godfather on her, and she was afraid to come back to Switzerland," his father said. "Val couldn't contact any of her friends and feared we'd be waiting for her."

"She took a train to Montreal, and only after assurances from Remy did she book a flight home," Andrew stated. "Still, she was right. We met her at the airport all the same."

"I know you liked Val," Alana said. "Are you coming to terms with her deceit?"

"Yeah. Nobody enjoys being used, but I'm trying hard to put that piece of this ordeal out of my mind. Luckily, I am cautious about relationships. I hoped we would become a couple, but we weren't there yet.

"Speaking of relationships, is Elizabeth here?" Zen asked.

"She's still away with her family," Andrew said. "You're not implying I jump in too fast, are you? At my age, time is a precious commodity that can't be wasted."

Zen laughed. "Not at all, Elizabeth is a nice lady; I'm glad you found her."

Turning to Alana, Sigmund changed the direction of the conversation. "The Griegg people are getting together for dinner tonight, so spend the rest of the afternoon as you like, but plan on being here this evening."

Later in the afternoon, Zen came into the study where Alana was reading. "Now I understand how my dad and grandfather feel after closing a case. I'm drained," he said.

"Well, you're battling jet lag on top of everything else," she said. "Why don't you sit with me?"

Zen sat down and picked up a book on tai chi from the coffee table. "Were you reading this?"

"Yes, I was flipping through the pages," she said. "I was introduced to tai chi in college. You've inspired me to try it again. I see Tiger is named after a posture—Flying Oblique."

"Isn't that wild!" Zen exclaimed. "I knew him as Tiger when he came to the school where I rode in England. It wasn't until I received his registration papers that I saw his official name. Even then, I didn't know what Flying Oblique meant. The words seem at odds with each other.

"Prior to working with Ash, I had only learned a short sequence of the tai chi postures. He explained Flying Oblique was the name of a movement in the tai chi long form—it means rebounding chi or energy. The name is perfect for my horse, don't you think?"

"I do."

"When I pointed out the coincidence of Tiger's name to Ash, he said there was no such thing as a coincidence. He claimed I was always meant to be Zen and Tiger was always meant to be with me."

"Wow, what a cool story," Alana said. "I am fortunate to spend time with you and your family. Being asked to watch you ride in New Jersey meant so much to me.

"We've had little chance to talk, so I wanted to make sure you knew that."

"Thanks. I love having you here. You're like Elizabeth—a welcome addition to our family."

"There's no surprise that the Griegg men are historically short on female companionship. Except for my grandfather, now that he's seeing Elizabeth. I think she's a keeper."

"I wish you didn't live so far away. I think you are a good influence on my dad."

Alana smiled at Zen. "I'm not sure your dad could come to terms with my visions. I'd come with too much baggage."

"Well, you're friends, and that's what he needs," Zen said. "Speaking of friends, the one thing I don't want lost in the aftermath of the case is Ash. I'm disappointed that you never got to meet him.

"The Crime Club acted like they held some kind of moral high ground because their so-called perfect crime wouldn't hurt anyone, but that's wrong because Ash died. That should be a crime," Zen said.

"Sabine told us about his charming farm and the furniture he made. If it helps, I feel like I know so much about him," Alana said. "His wife's soap is in my bathroom."

"They were such a talented couple," he said.

"I love the photograph of you and Ash on the piano. The friendship on display is unmistakable."

"Ash usually dodged the camera, but he sat still for that one. It's the only photo I have of him."

"Do you find time to play the piano, these days?" she asked. "I remember how beautifully you played the last time I was here."

"I play a bit, but I prefer the violin," Zen said.

"I didn't know that. You must play for me."

Zen walked to the cabinet behind the piano and lifted out his violin. "I better do it now, since you're leaving soon.

"I play the piano because my mother played. I play the violin for myself. My favorite piece is a little-known melody from Shostakovich called *Romance*.

"It's better with accompaniment, of course, but I think it is very Zen-like as a violin solo…the way I do it, anyway," he said with a smile. "I'm not sure if others agree."

Zen played beautifully. Alana lost herself in the haunting sound that was melancholy yet carefree at the same time.

He played his solo for more than four minutes without opening his eyes. When he drew down his bow, he said, "Ash introduced me to Shostakovich when we first met, but I'm not a total geek. I like U2, Local H, and most classic rock bands from the Stones and Led Zeppelin era."

"I love that you are so connected to your music," Alana stated. "It's inspiring."

"Thank you," Zen said. "I get engrossed in music in the same way I do with my horses. I wish I could find the same connection to energy as you and Ash…I try, but I can't. It eludes me."

"I disagree with that. You just connect in a different way, your own way," Alana explained. "There is a unique link between you and your horses. It's not a relationship that other riders achieve…and it is all about energy.

"While I appreciate why you think I have a common bond with Ash, I'm not certain that's true. Ash could connect and communicate with pretty much any animal, right?"

Zen agreed.

"I can't trigger any connection. It chooses me. I have no control…it just happens. This investigation didn't produce any visions as dramatic as two years ago. Still, I'm glad I could contribute something."

"Well, you did. You envisioned the hidden coins, and then Tiger spoke to you. What did it feel like when you first thought Ash was dead?"

Alana shrugged. "It's like you said earlier, I sometimes connect to those subtle energies. I placed my hand on Tiger's neck and felt an immediate link. I didn't hear any words; I was just compelled to think them. *Ash is dead.*

"I've never felt a connection to an animal before. I'm so close to my dog, yet I've never felt him try to speak with me in the same way. As my hand touched Tiger's neck, there was a split-second where it felt as if magnets were pulling us together. I don't know what else to say."

"It's so weird that Ash experienced cardiac arrest at that very moment," Zen said to her, "and Tiger knew."

"Yeah, it was confusing to learn that Ash was alive, and then be told about the cardiac arrest and resuscitation the day before," Alana said. "Did you know he was ill?"

"No, I didn't. He had always been thin and rather pale, but he never let on that he wasn't well. I wish I had known. Perhaps I could have convinced him to see a doctor. Lots of people live with cancer for many years."

"Well, first of all, we don't know for sure that he hadn't seen a doctor. It seems to me that Ash was a smart man. If he wasn't under a doctor's care, it was because he didn't want help." Alana told Zen.

"But he let Trudie help him?" he questioned.

"The herbs gave him relief. That's very different from what a doctor would have prescribed. Maybe he already tried conventional medicine, we don't really know."

Zen acknowledged.

"In any event, never think Ash will be forgotten, you won't let that happen. When anyone has such a profound impact on another person's life, as Ash did with you, they stay with you forever."

"That's kind of what my father said."

After a pause, Zen said to Alana, "Earlier I said, rather cavalierly, that I wasn't going to let what Valentina did bother me. The fact is, I don't know how to let it go. I sense that you are the person who can relate to how I feel."

"She might haunt you for a while, they all will. Time will sift them from your memory. Once that happens, only Ash will remain." Alana told him.

"I hope so. It's only been days; I know it will take time." Zen conceded. "I need to check on the horses. Would you like to walk with me?"

"Yes, I'd like to get outside," Alana said.

As Alana stood, he watched her favor one leg for several steps before she could steady her stride. He'd seen the same thing happen before.

"I hope you don't mind me asking," Zen continued, "but does your ankle injury remind you about what happened to you and my grandfather?"

"It used to. Back when it happened, I assumed those thoughts would be with me forever. As I recommended to you, I decided that I wouldn't let it own me.

"Now," Alana said, "I only think of the good that came from my experience. We found the long-lost treasure, and it's getting back into the hands of its rightful owners. We solved a secret from my family's past, and in doing so, I got to know your family.

"There's just one thing I wish I could change, but I can't, so I don't allow it to rent space in my head."

"And you're not going to say what that is, are you?"

Alana smiled. "That would be renting space."

Zen laughed.

"If I could give you any advice, it would be to learn from your experiences, but live for the future. Leave any baggage in the past, where it belongs."

Alana said that truthfully, despite the guilt that she, herself, couldn't let go—the one mistake she continued to relive.

"I know that's what I have to do," Zen said. "By the way, thanks for mentioning the Zen thing to my dad and grandfather. Until my dad brought it up, I hadn't thought that I would be leaving the name behind. I *do* like being called Zen. I'd like to keep it, so I hope everyone will get used to it."

"I hope so, too," Alana said. "You know, when I think of Zen, I think of balance. That's not how the dictionary defines it, but I think that's the concept people relate to—balance or symmetry. It's why you were given that nickname.

"It came to you organically because that's what people saw in your riding...perfect balance, mentally and physically, between you and your horse. The two of you seem to form your own universe when you're in the saddle.

"That won't change as you move into another phase of your life. You can bring that same sense of equilibrium to everything you do. I think you will be just fine, Zen."

The terrace outside the kitchen door led to a cobblestone path that snaked its way down the hill to the barn. Lined with a mixture of evergreen trees and woodland shrubs, the walk of some 200-meters cleared at times to glimpse grassy fields on one side and the stable yard on the other.

By day, it was a lovely walk, but at night, the path could be outright dangerous to navigate at the pace Zen and Alana now traveled.

"I've been thinking about asking my father if we could build an indoor arena now that I won't be schooling away from the farm in the winters," Zen said, as they stopped at a clearing along the pathway.

"I've already plotted out the perfect location behind that fence line. I know it's extravagant, but I'd like to keep riding and our winters get so cold."

Zen's youthful exuberance made Alana feel her age for the first time. She would turn thirty-five on her next birthday. She loved her life and had few regrets, but it was a telling moment nevertheless.

Zen was so accomplished for his age, and his adult life had just begun. There's a time in everyone's life when the reality of age presents itself.

Alana was happy and felt fulfilled at home, but she couldn't deny the dynamism she felt in Switzerland with the Griegg family. *Was there more purpose for me here?* she wondered.

But why even think that? There was no reason for her to alter her life. Alana's thoughts jumped to the music Zen played. Shostakovich had come up in her case two years ago…*that's just crazy*, she thought.

Was it just a coincidence? Or was Ash correct to think coincidences didn't exist? She knew other people believe that…such are life's contemplations along the course of a 200-meter footpath. As they left the cobblestones, they saw Andrew fixing the gate on Tiger's paddock.

"I didn't realize you were down here Grandrew. Did Tiger break his gate?" Zen asked.

"Not yet, but he would soon if I don't change out these bolts." Andrew rattled around in his toolbox. "I'm sure you've noticed what goes on when Secret stands at the corner of his paddock…Tiger stretches his neck over the gate to have a little tête-à-tête," Andrew offered, still looking for the correct bolts.

Zen looked at Alana and said, "My horses keep Grandrew busy, especially Tiger."

"Oh yes, what would I do without them?" Andrew joked, but it was clear that he loved his role as a gentleman farmer. "Zen, will you hold the gate in place for me?" he asked.

Alana missed her father when she encountered a natural family moment like this one.

Andrew seemed completely at ease with growing older. There had been great stress when the case was active in New Jersey, but that was different. Here, he was in his element at home and on the farm.

Alana was jealous of anyone who had reached her age and still had their parents and grandparents in their lives. She wondered what her father would think of her now, all grown up. She wished he could have known about the mystery of the trap and how it was solved. She wanted him to have known the Grieggs…would they have liked him?

Like Sigmund, Alana's father hadn't accepted her visions. They surfaced when she was a young child. One day, she overheard him tell her mother that her "nightmares" were not normal. He said his grandmother had similar dreams and that members of his family called her psychic or clairvoyant.

"People would come to our house in Mississippi asking her questions about their lives," he said. He recalled those encounters as a "freakin' sideshow." It was one reason he joined the army after high school. He wanted a different life than what Mississippi and his family offered.

Alana had never wanted him to feel that way about her. Like any child, she didn't comprehend words like "psychic" or "clairvoyant," but she knew she didn't want to be either so, from then on, she kept her dreams secret.

Alana grew up never confronting her visions until the events in Germany involving "the trap." That's when she came to terms with the fact it wasn't something she could suppress. It wasn't a choice, it was who she was.

If her dad were here now, would he understand? She didn't know.

Alana's train of thought was broken when Zen asked, "Where's Dad?"

"Where do you think?" Andrew said, "He's gone to the Zürich office."

"So much for a relaxing day," Alana mused.

"In Sigmund's defense," Andrew said, "there was something he needed to finish. That's how he unwinds after a case. He likes to dot all the i's and cross all the t's. I was the same way, but today, he had an important mission. He had to get the sting money back to David."

"Oh, that's right. How soon the rest of us forget about the details." Alana laughed.

Zen added, "I guess we have to excuse him...no razzing tonight for going to the office."

"I think that would be wise," Andrew said.

"What time is dinner?" Alana asked.

"Six o'clock, I believe," Andrew responded. "Be warned, it can get raucous when we come together to rehash a case."

19

Aftermath

"Let's raise our glasses to another happy ending for the Gold Train treasure," Sigmund said with a smile.

"Here, here," Andrew agreed.

In a long-held practice, after closing cases, the Grieggs invited their staff to their county home for a festive dinner.

"David assures me all the coins are back in the tunnel vault in Poland. There was one extra coin from what we had estimated. They are now listed in the index and worth, conservatively, 13 million Swiss francs," Sigmund said.

"All but one coin," Ian added.

"Yes, while that's unfortunate, it's a happy ending all the same," Sigmund stated. "Although, David tells me the events have presented him with a dilemma."

"What's that?" his father asked.

Looking at Chris, Sigmund asked, "When we uncovered the name of Bruno Weiß as the owner of the double eagles, how much of his biography was anyone able to check?"

"Not much at all. If you recall, we were pretty busy at the time," Chris responded.

"Well, David confirmed that all the coins Palmer stole from OB came from Weiß's collection. The coins were all purchased legally, and all but one during the pre-war period.

"Since the collection was part of the treasure, I think we can assume the Nazis confiscated the coins at the time of his murder. Weiß was a mid-level industrialist, coerced to join the Nazi Party in order to preserve his business. In keeping with the times, I'm told, he was also a strong anti-Semite.

"Weiß's collection included more coinage than what ended up in the Polish tunnel. Perhaps some coins fell into the pockets of his SS assassins. No one knows.

"David's quandary is that the coins will be the first Gold Train distribution not being reunited with a Jewish family," Sigmund noted.

"Are they upstanding Germans?" Alana asked. "No one should be held to the views of their ancestors. We all stand on our own, as individuals."

"Yes, that's what I told him," Sigmund stated. "Although I didn't have to, David is a fair man. Operation Boomerang's function is to restore the treasure without prejudice, but you must admit that it would be problematic if Weiß had amassed his fortune illegally, or through a war crime. Happily, that's not the case.

"Mossad gave David permission to tell us that there was more to the legendary Gold Train than what ended up in their tunnel. It appears the *Der Goldzug* notebook alluded to another destination for the massive quantity of gold that gave the legend its name. Without details, however, there's no clue if the hoard still exists, or where it might be.

"It was a bombshell to hear, but I must admit it always seemed odd that there was no gold to speak of in the treasure under Porcelain House. The legend was, after all, coined the Gold Train."

Sigmund continued. "David said he'll share their evidence with us now that we've solved this case. Perhaps the Gold Train is reminiscent of a cat with nine lives…there could be more of the legendary mystery to solve!"

Andrew and Sabine came into the dining room carrying platters of saffron risotto and Berner Platte (a traditional Swiss meat dish). "Alana, we have fish too," Sabine said.

Zen placed loaves of zopf (braided bread) and butter at each end of the table.

"There is no need to compliment the chef." Andrew teased, "Well, you can, but that would mean calling the chef at Die Alte Mühle.

"I ordered Sven's Schogginikuchen (chocolate cake), so leave room for dessert."

After they passed the platters around the table, Alana started the conversation. "Does it bother anyone that these students won't pay for what they did?"

"Do you mean, because they weren't arrested?" Sigmund asked her.

"That, plus they benefited from the sale of that one coin," Zen stated. "So, yes, it bothers me that they took my horse, profited, and won't face justice or pay any penalty."

Andrew replied, "Patience, Zen. You don't know there won't be a price to pay for their crime. We haven't decided whether to share what we know with the police.

"It's complicated now that the coins are back at OB. The question is, can the case be prosecuted without all aspects of the crime being made public? It may not be possible."

"Besides, it is quite satisfying to learn, sometimes years later, that one of our bad actors has fallen into some well-deserved misfortune," Sigmund added.

"Life has a way of balancing out...call it karma, or just a belief that rotten people continue to make rotten decisions," Andrew said. "If one bad decision doesn't bite them, chances are the next one will."

"I expect you and Alana would believe in karma, Zen," his father stated.

"I *do* believe in karma. It's just that, as they say, 'karma works in mysterious ways.' I want to see it happen. The consequences should be out in the open. How do you stand not knowing?" Zen asked.

"Well, like your grandfather says, sometimes we *do* see an instant aftermath to events. Other times, you just have to wait. In the end, there is a day of reckoning for all of us," Sigmund philosophized.

"I hope you are right," Alana said.

"If I've learned anything in my life, it's that my father is always right." Sigmund smiled. "People get what's coming to them. It messes with your head to dwell on how or when."

"Speaking as someone who made awful choices in my youth," Ian said, "I don't find these students really bad. Don't get me wrong—they're dreadful—I'm just not convinced they're as evil as other people we've encountered in our line of work. Egon, in Alana's case, was an example of evil.

"Remember our reaction when we figured out the club's plan? It was really well done. Forget about the legality. I'm just saying that the plot to steal the coins was brilliant.

"The True Crime Club's mission statement was to plan and pull off the perfect crime. They came close to achieving that goal."

"I think you said it first, Alana," Sigmund said. "If they hadn't gone after the *Lady in Gold,* they would have achieved their plan and gotten away scot-free. Ian's right, there's a part of me that must admit the plan was impressive."

"Yeah, that is what I said," Alana agreed. "I understand the need to wait for karma…but I'm with Zen. I'd like to witness the justice."

Andrew said, "Karma isn't measured in tit for tat. You must have faith in a natural balance over time. I agree with Sigmund when he said that we all face a reckoning in the end.

"Remember, Palmer Harel put everything in motion—the brilliance of the perfect crime, if you call it that, comes from his plan to steal something that no one knew to exist…and now he's dead."

Andrew continued. "As Alana read in his journal, Palmer never expressed remorse, although he appeared tortured by his actions…and as we've said, the man is dead—there is no greater penalty to put on him.

"The students skillfully adapted the plan to the events they faced after Palmer died, but credit for masterminding the plan is his alone. I wonder what Palmer would have done had *he* lost the Lady in Gold…could he have let her go?"

Sigmund needed to pontificate: "As to Ian's point that the students aren't evil, I caution that evil can't be measured until it manifests itself into an action. No one can say for sure what any person would resort to when pushed to their limit."

During a lull in the dinner conversation, Alana said to the group, "I'm planning to fly home soon. I want to get back to Disraeli and the art gallery."

"Sigmund, haven't you told Alana your plan?" Andrew asked his son.

"No, Dad. I was going to do that after dinner," Sigmund said, and then he cleared his throat. "Alana, do you remember the company Gen Global coming up in the investigation?"

"Of course," she said. "That name was on the paper I took from the book at the grandmother's home."

"Well, that same day, I contacted Alain Barth. He runs Gen Global, a charter plane company. I wanted to know if our students had inquired about flights.

"Alain didn't recall their names, but as we got talking, I tentatively reserved seats on a charter scheduled to fly to Los Angeles. He was eager to fill the empty seats.

"I couldn't finalize meetings in LA until today…so long story short, you can join me on that flight, since the plane will land in New York to refuel. Would that work for you?"

"When are you flying?"

"Friday evening."

"Yeah, that works just fine," Alana said. "You spoil me."

"My pleasure," he said, reaching for the zopf.

Boris came in apologizing for his late arrival.

"I wasn't able to talk Niedermeyer into joining us this evening," Boris said. "He felt tired tonight. He asks for Alana to visit before she goes home."

"Okay," she replied. "It's about my family history. I'm so excited to see what he's found."

Andrew made his way around the table refilling wine glasses, but Sabine put her hand over her glass.

"I think this is a good time to announce that Chris and I are expecting a baby."

"Congratulations!" Andrew said, echoed by the others. "This *is* a festive evening."

"When are you due?" Alana asked, recalling that Sabine had also declined wine at the competition.

"In six and a half months. I know people usually wait longer to announce, but we're too excited."

"Well, we're just thrilled for you," Sigmund said. "Here's to our growing family." He raised his glass.

"Speaking of family," Sigmund continued, "you know that William will join the company soon. He has been known as 'Zen' amongst his horse pals for some time, and he'd like to keep that nickname, so I'd like us all to get used to calling him Zen."

"Oh, Zen, I love your nickname!" Sabine said. "I wanted to shout it out at the horse show, when your fans were chanting, but I restrained myself."

Zen said, "Since we're making announcements, I've decided that, as a Griegg employee, I should call my grandfather Andrew at the office…maybe outside the office, as well.

"Suddenly Grandrew sounds childish…and while it never felt that way before, I'm going to make the change now."

The group continued to gab and laugh with such joy for the future—then Ian's phone buzzed.

"Excuse me." Ian pulled out his laptop. "I've received an alert that the True Crime Club's chatroom has an active message. I guess I forgot to turn off the notifications. Sorry about this. If I don't do it now, it will just keep buzzing.

"Oh my," Ian said with caution. "It's Viktor's character, Tommy posting." He looked up, across the table. "The post says, 'Hilf mir'…help me."

"Is he messing with us?" Sabine asked.

"I don't think so." Alana looked at Ian's computer screen.

Ian typed in the chatroom: "What do you want?"

"12 Jralewagdn." Appeared on Ian's screen, he tried to pronounce letters that didn't form a word.

Alana warned, "Viktor is trying to type 112. He wants an ambulance—ein Krankenwagen, but, for some reason, he's hitting all the wrong keys."

Ian typed: "Seriously? Where are you?"

"Well, this is interesting karma." Sigmund walked over to watch the computer screen for another entry.

"If it's a genuine plea for help, why would Viktor go to the chatroom?" Andrew asked.

"The only thing that makes sense is that he has no access to any other form of communication." Ian guessed.

"Well, telling us is useless if we don't know where he is," Zen said with concern.

Ian typed again: "Where are you?"

Chris pulled out his laptop. "Viktor's address was listed as a resident hall at the university. He wasn't living there. That notepaper Alana found recorded three addresses for rental apartments, but we never found out where he moved."

"Can someone get one of the other students on their cell phone?" Sigmund asked.

"Already on it." Chris informed him.

"Remy, this is an emergency," Chris said. "Viktor is in the chatroom saying he is in trouble and needs an ambulance. I don't know where he lives. Will you tell me his address?"

"Who is this?" Remy asked.

"That's not important. I need your help."

"How do you have my cell phone number?"

"Please, Remy, just help Viktor."

The line went dead.

Neither Valentina nor Trudie answered their phones.

The group was silent. Their eyes stayed riveted on Ian's computer screen, waiting for the next post.

"Remy just logged in," Ian said.

Chris announced that Remy was calling. "Yes, Remy?"

"Viktor moved somewhere on Breitingerstrasse. More than that, I can't help."

As Remy spoke, another post appeared in the chatroom. It read: "Br uit im"

Ian looked up, "What does that mean?

Another line appeared: "452 B"

Followed by: "Br uit gggim…452 B"

Sigmund blurted out, "Breitingerstrasse, apartment 452 B. I know the location. Boris, you're with me."

"I'm coming too." Alana told him.

Sigmund posed no resistance.

Arriving at the flat, the lights were on, but no one responded to knocks on the door. Sigmund jimmied the lock in seconds. Boris unholstered his sidearm as they entered the apartment military style.

Viktor's body lay on the floor under his computer table. Boris checked for a pulse and shook his head to indicate no heartbeat. Sigmund walked through to the bedroom. Viktor was alone.

Alana called them over to a broken glass next to Viktor's body. "I know not to touch anything, but I can see tinted lip gloss on the rim. Trudie was here."

The three of them surveyed the apartment. They found Trudie's herb bag opened in the bedroom. It gave credence that Viktor had been poisoned.

Sigmund called the police to report a murder. "You two go back to the house. I'll handle things here," he said. "It will be less messy that way."

He handed his car keys to Boris.

It wasn't long before a taxi drove Sigmund home.

"In light of Viktor's death, I had to tell the police about Tiger's abduction and the *Lady in Gold*, minus any reference to the Gold Train." Sigmund walked over to Ian. "Here's the detective's contact info. Send her the cell numbers for Remy, Val, and Trudie.

"I'd like to find Trudie. She may divulge information that we should hear before the police," Sigmund said.

Sabine called Ash's wife. "I must locate Trudie as soon as possible, Mrs. Rechsteiner. It's an emergency."

"You woke me up. What is so important?"

"Trudie's boyfriend, Viktor, has been poisoned. We need to find Trudie to make sure she's okay."

"Poisoned with what? Is he all right?"

"I'm afraid he's dead," Sabine said.

"Guter Gott, we are living a nightmare."

"The police found Trudie's herb bag and your journal in his apartment. Do you know where she might go?

"No, but she was with the family earlier. We had an awful row, and she stormed off. She is a vindictive creature. Her parents don't see her the way I do. You don't want to cross her. She takes revenge."

When Sabine ended the call, she immediately aired her concern for Remy and Val. "If Trudie killed Viktor, she might turn on them," she said.

Sigmund said, "The police assured me they would contact them tonight.

"Viktor owns a car that wasn't at the apartment. They put out an APB on the vehicle, so the police will take action."

Chris said, "It's not just Remy and Val we should be concerned about. The students have information on us as well. We try to keep our private lives secure, but Trudie may know more than we would like."

"You're right," Sigmund said. "We all have good alarm systems, but let's take extra precautions until we know more. I'll call our security company and have them to post a guard outside each of our homes tonight."

The gathering broke up when Zen needed to shut the horses into their stalls for the night.

"Wait, son, I'll walk down with you."

Alana found herself alone with Andrew. "Do you know when the security will arrive?"

"It may take an hour or two to get people in place."

"This is very unsettling," she admitted. "After the events in Germany, I didn't feel safe. I bought a gun. I never thought I would, but I did. It gave me comfort to be in charge of my own security.

"I own the gallery, so I was able to acquire a concealed carry permit. I've carried the gun ever since.

"Until now, that is—obviously, I couldn't bring it with me. I'm protected with you, but still, it's worrisome."

"Follow me." Andrew went into the study and unlocked a wall safe. "This is the Walther PPKS380 that Sigmund gave you on our way to the church that night. I want you to keep it with you until you go home." He handed her two 8-round clips and the Velcro waist holster she had worn to conceal the gun two years ago. He removed another gun for himself.

The telephone rang, and Andrew busied himself answering questions from the police detective.

Alana listened in for a while, and then it struck her that Zen and his father had been gone a long time. She decided to walk down to the barn.

There was a full moon in the sky, but the path was dark. She couldn't see past a few meters. Zen had taken the flashlight left at the door.

As she neared the barn, Alana caught the lights flickering through the movement of the evergreens. Then voices in the darkened field drew her attention. A gunshot rang out, and the figure of a horse dropped to the ground. Zen cried out.

"Shut up!" Trudie cried, "You wrecked my life, and now I plan to ruin your family."

Sigmund appeared at the barn door. There was no cover for him to get closer. The sound had given him the direction of the shooter, but he couldn't see anyone, including his son.

Zen recognized Trudie from the investigation photos. He asked, "Why are you doing this? We did nothing to you."

Trudie's gun was set dead on Zen.

"I planned and executed the perfect crime. Then you and those so-called library people intervened. I just talked to Val. She told me your people were at Rob's school—then they met her at the airport...they had unraveled our plan."

Sigmund had snuck from the barn, and was now circling behind the sound of Trudie's voice.

"I'm going to kill you so your family will regret they ever messed with me," she said.

"You can't get away with it." Zen reasoned.

"I don't care," Trudie said.

As Alana's eyes adjusted to the darkness, she had a long, but clear, shot at Trudie, though there was no room for error. Zen's body shadowed Trudie, just a few meters farther away.

"Trudie!" Alana called out. As Trudie instinctively turned, Alana double tapped the trigger of the gun just as Sigmund had advised two years before: "Don't let the size of this gun fool you," he had said. "This is a 9mm; it's a powerful gun. While I don't expect you to use it, should it be necessary, aim for the chest and tap twice."

Trudie's body was on the ground.

Andrew ran down the path behind Alana. She turned to look at him, but neither spoke.

Sigmund found Zen kneeling by his horse.

"Pen's alive." Zen announced. "He's been hit in the leg."

Sigmund saw Alana on the path, "Alana, are you okay?"

"Yes," she yelled.

"I'm here too, Sigmund," Andrew stated.

"Can someone call the vet?" Sigmund shouted out. "Pen has been shot." He pulled off his coat and pressed it against the horse's wound.

Andrew checked Trudie's body for a pulse as he passed her. She was dead.

As he approached the horse, Andrew shined his flashlight on the scene.

"Is Trudie dead?" Zen asked.

"Yes," Andrew said, looking at Alana.

"How bad is Pen's wound?" Andrew asked.

Sigmund lifted his jacket to reveal a hole pooled in blood. The light now revealed blood seeping from the horse's chest.

"I don't think the bullet hit an artery—it must have gone straight through," Andrew stated. "The vet is on his way."

Then, with a great bound, Pen stood up on his own, holding his left front leg off the ground. Zen walked slowly as the horse insisted to hobble his way back to the barn.

Sigmund held towels over the wounds, as Andrew wrapped duct tape to hold them in place. Using a series of figure eight motions, he alternated between the horse's legs, around his shoulders, and chest.

Pendragon stood eerily still.

"Dad, I'm going to hook up the trailer, I'm sure he'll need to go to the clinic."

Alana held Pen and stroked his face.

Before long, headlights marked the vet's arrival.

"That was quick," Sigmund said.

"The doc was dining at Auf dem See. He was in the bar when I called." Andrew told him. "I said—drop everything."

"What sort of mischief has Pen gotten himself into?" The veterinarian sounded lighthearted as he entered the stable.

"I saw Zen hooking up the trailer; I'm guessing that means Pen will need to come home with me."

"I'm afraid he's been shot, Jonas," Andrew said.

"Shot? Oh my, what have I stepped into?"

"It's a long story that we'll share later," Sigmund said.

The vet acknowledged Alana with a nod.

"Let's have a look." The veterinarian spoke with the calm temper of a trained medical professional. "The wrapping is not a pretty sight, but you've done an effective job applying pressure to the wound.

"Where would we be without duct tape?" The vet asked rhetorically. "I almost hate to disturb anything until we get him to the clinic, so let's see if I can just peek underneath."

"There are two wounds," Andrew explained. "The shot seems to have gone straight through." He gestured an upward trajectory.

"Well, I think that's good," Jonas stated. "I understand that he's in pain, but he doesn't appear overtly stressed, given the circumstances."

Zen came back into the barn.

The vet shined his light into Pen's eyes, assessing the horse's level of shock. "Good boy." He pulled again at the duct tape covering Pen's leg and chest.

Jonas explained, "It appears the bullet entered the bicep, and then exited through the pectoral muscle. It must have stayed close to the surface.

"It missed the arteries, or there would be much more blood. Of course I'm worried about a bone chip or fracture, so I need radiographs to know the full story."

The vet opened his medical bag. "My initial thought is," he declared, "we're looking at one lucky horse. Let's get a blanket on him. I'll get some fluids and pain meds into him before we get on our way. He can stay with me a few days.

"I'd just finished my beer stein when you called, so I'll trust Zen to drive the truck and trailer to the clinic. One of my vets is on duty to treat Pen when we arrive. My wife is outside driving my car."

"We have had drinks over dinner, as well," Andrew said.

"I just had one beer, and it's been a while," Zen said. "Besides, there's nothing like having someone point a gun at your head to sober you up."

"Sorry to have spoiled your dinner, Jonas. You're the best." Sigmund patted the vet's shoulder.

Just as Jonas was ready to move Pendragon, the police pulled their car up to the barn. Andrew and Zen walked the horse out to the waiting trailer, leaving Sigmund and Alana to face the detective's inquiry.

As he closed the door, Jonas heard the police ask, "Where's Rechsteiner's body?"

After the coroner drove off the property with the corpse, Sigmund and Alana made their way back up to the house.

Sigmund poured two drinks. "Are you okay?"

"Yes," Alana said in a matter-of-fact tone. "What was there to think about…I just pulled the trigger before Trudie did. It felt quite mechanical."

"Yes, well, that's the short version. Where did the gun come from?" Sigmund asked.

"Andrew gave it to me when we came home after finding Viktor's body. I told him I had been carrying a gun since—well, since you know when."

"Thank you will never be enough, but it's all I have."

Alana didn't speak.

"I've been there, Alana. Please allow me." He put his arms around her and drew her in close.

The warmth of Sigmund's body was comforting. She felt safe. Alana didn't cry. She just felt numb. She had always proved herself to be a strong woman in the past, and tonight was no exception.

When Andrew and Zen arrived home, they found Alana and Sigmund sitting quietly in the study.

"Is Pen okay?" Alana jumped from her chair.

"He will be," Zen assured her. "It will be a long recovery, but he'll survive."

"Well, that's a relief," Sigmund said.

"Is it over now?" Alana asked.

"What else could happen?" Andrew asked, pouring himself a cup of coffee.

"I'm going up to bed," Alana said. "I've just been waiting for the two of you to get home."

"Alana." Zen looked into her eyes.

She gave him an empty smile. "We'll talk in the morning."

Sigmund glanced to his father, thinking, *there is nothing we can do. Alana wants to be alone.*

"It seems things happen for a reason." Andrew walked over to his son. "If Alana hadn't told me that she had been carrying a gun back home, I would never have offered her the PPK. It's unthinkable how this would have ended, had she not been curious to trek down to the barn."

Was it simply curiosity, or was she drawn to the barn by other means? Sigmund couldn't help but wonder.

"I blame myself. Even if it was out of character for any of the students to have a weapon," Sigmund said to his dad, "I should have carried a gun out to the barn. Still," he said, "I wouldn't have been in the right position to use it."

Andrew said, "As you mentioned at dinner, none of us could have anticipated the evil inside Trudie."

*U*pstairs, Alana undressed for bed. She reached into her pocket and pulled out the shard of glass she had taken from Viktor's apartment. She fell asleep clutching it in her hand, picturing the horrifying vision of his body on the floor.

Suddenly, Alana was in Trudie's head.

She heard her screaming, "I don't just not love you; I hate the sight of you, Viktor. You took our perfect crime and fucked it up. We came away with nothing…no paintings, no coins, no money. We got screwed, you bastard."

"Trudie, listen to me," Viktor argued.

"No! Getting the money was your only job." She kept walking away as he tried to get close to her.

Alana perceived Trudie wasn't just crazed over Viktor's incompetence. She also saw Trudie's family confronting her over Ash's death. They were brutal.

"Don't you know the side effects of lobelia?" her grandmother shouted. "Why didn't you ever tell anyone that your grandfather was sick?"

Trudie ran from the gathering. Her blanket denial of blame doubled down as she drove to Viktor's flat.

"I have to let this place go." Alana heard him tell Trudie. "I'm going back to school, I'll live at the university…I'll pick up my classes again and with any luck I'll graduate on time."

"You act like nothing happened. Where do I go?" Trudie screamed, "I can't go back to school. I can't go home. My family thinks I killed my grandfather."

"Why ask me?" Viktor shouted back. "You just said you hated me."

Alana's vision jumped to see Trudie in Viktor's bedroom, pulling her duffle bag from the closet. It was where she kept her herbs.

Trudie opened her grandmother's journal to the page marked *Atropa Belladonna*. It was a perennial herbaceous plant, belladonna—commonly called deadly nightshade. She read aloud, "It grows in the wild throughout Europe."

Trudie had known where to get belladonna. Her grandmother destroyed the herb whenever she came across it in the wild, but she cultivated one specimen plant for medicinal purposes. Trudie had helped encircle the plant with chicken wire for safety.

Mrs. Rechsteiner was a responsible herbalist. Her notes in the journal affirmed that the only effective use of belladonna was as an adjunctive therapy to treat irritable bowel syndrome or another condition called enterocolitis.

The grandmother had logged detailed notes each time she prescribed herbs and for what purpose. She respected the power of plants as medicine and never took it lightly.

Trudie, however, had added her own notes to the journal. Those remarks were not based on years of study, like her grandmother's, but just a cursory take of what she read in other books she had taken from the library.

Belladonna, Trudie recorded, is also an anesthetic and a poison. She searched her duffle bag for an ampoule containing a sample of the deadly nightshade root that she'd cut from her grandmother's specimen plant.

In Alana's dream, Trudie emerged from the bedroom with the slice of the root in her hand. It was far more potent than she supposed.

As Trudie held the root between her fingers, the smell of tomato tickled Alana's nasal hairs. When Trudie skimmed the root across her tongue, the bitter taste caused Alana to cough.

Trudie crushed the root into a glass and added kirsch. She never drank alcohol, but Viktor did, and there was always an open bottle of kirschwasser in the kitchen.

Trudie then lay on the sofa with her headset on, until she could drum up the courage to drink a tiny bit of the deadly concoction. She raised the glass to her lips several times, but never swallowed.

Viktor paid no attention. He assumed she would stew for some time before regretting the things she'd said.

He believed she loved him and only spewed her hateful rhetoric out of frustration. After all, they had both gone from an ultimate high to the depths of despair in the span of mere moments. Their belief in their perfect crime was shattered.

Viktor's phone call to say, "The money is gone. We've been scammed," had all but ended their future. He was just in denial of the facts. He couldn't face what had gone wrong any more than Trudie could. They just handled it differently.

Distraction for Viktor meant playing a computer game.

Alana envisioned him sitting at his computer desk logging on to better his high score in his favorite pastime.

Intuition told Alana that Trudie wouldn't attempt suicide. She was, however, playing a dangerous game.

Soon Viktor felt remorseful and wanted to see if Trudie would talk rationally; he clicked the pause button on his game and walked to the sofa. When Trudie heard him coming, she closed her eyes.

Viktor lifted the glass from the table and drank from it. Surprised to find her drinking kirsch, he just attributed it to the events of the day. Since Trudie was asleep, he took the drink back to his computer.

As Viktor played the game, he sipped on the kirsch. Within minutes, the glass was empty. Alana felt the poison take hold. The computer screen blurred. As he rubbed his eyes, his heart rate accelerated.

For Alana, it was as if her own heart was beating wildly. That's what made these dream sequences so taxing. She was in the room with Viktor, knowing what he knew and feeling what he felt…but he didn't know that he'd swallowed poison. He didn't know what was happening to him.

Viktor kept playing his game, but soon he lost control of his fingers. He pushed the wrong keys, even so, he didn't get why. *Am I having a panic attack?* he wondered. Was this his body's response to losing everything? *Am I in shock?*

Viktor called out, "T r u d i e." Alana saw his mouth move in slow motion…but Trudie didn't respond. Perhaps he made no sound—Alana couldn't say for sure.

His heart now felt like it would burst out of his chest. He tried again…"T r u d i e!" This time Alana heard him. Trudie did too. She opened her eyes and saw the kirsch was gone from the table.

"Viktor, what have you done!" she cried.

"Help me," he begged.

Trudie couldn't help. There was no antidote for deadly nightshade consumed in such a large measure. Anything but a swallow or two meant certain death.

Trudie panicked.

Alana watched as she freaked out.

She called Remy's cell phone. He didn't answer…then she keyed in Valentina's phone number.

Next, Alana saw Trudie grab the gun from the bedroom and take Viktor's car keys off the kitchen counter.

Viktor begged again, "Help me."

Trudie couldn't look at him. She ran from the apartment.

Viktor touched his pocket for his cell phone. It wasn't there. As he stood, he lost his balance and fell back down. He tried to think where he put his phone, but his brain couldn't process his thoughts.

His only option was the club's chatroom. As he pulled himself up to reach his keyboard…Alana saw Sigmund and Boris standing where Viktor lay dead. She awoke from her dream in a cold sweat.

Spotting a light under Alana's bedroom door, Sigmund knocked. "Alana, may I come in? Are you okay?"

"Come in," she said.

He opened the door to see her sitting on the bed with a glass of water in her hand. She motioned for him to come over and sit next to her.

"I know what happened at Viktor's apartment. I had one of my visions." She drank water and collected her thoughts before explaining.

"Trudie never intended for Viktor to die. She mixed the poisonous drink to make herself sick, but not dead. She wanted sympathy. Viktor unknowingly drank all the poison.

"His assured death sent Trudie into a frenzied mission of revenge. She blamed everyone but herself for all that went wrong with their perfect crime."

"You've cut your finger." Sigmund lifted her hand for a closer look.

"It's nothing," Alana said.

"Why don't you come downstairs? I'll get a bandage, and you can have a cup of tea," he said. "I can't leave you alone."

Otobang's Gift

Before Alana Leaves Switzerland

"I'm so sorry for your loss." Alana reached out and hugged Niedermeyer.

Alana wasn't usually a hugger, but it came naturally now because of his loss. During her case two years ago, she'd had little interaction with him. While everyone had been holed up in the Mossad safe house for days on end, Niedermeyer remained at the Griegg office on Hochbaumstrasse.

"Thank you," he said. "It's nice to see you. What do you think of these luxurious surroundings?" He gestured with his hand to welcome Alana into the house.

"It's just lovely," she stated. "It tells me so much about Alexander. I wish I had met him."

"Yes, I regret never introducing Alexander to my business associates." He struggled to say the words.

"Forgive me, I didn't mean to cause any upset."

Niedermeyer ignored his temporary loss of composure. "Well, come into the library, my dear. I am eager to show you my discoveries."

When Alana sat, Niedermeyer pulled a chair right alongside her. A lime green folder with her name on it lay on the table. He opened the file without revealing its contents.

"When you stayed here two years ago, you mentioned you wanted to learn about your surname. It lingered in my mind for the longest time, until I could do some digging.

"I wasn't optimistic, because African roots are notoriously difficult to trace. As Eastwood is a rare surname for a Black American to hold, I thought I would give it a go.

"Your father's Christian names, Spencer and Theodore, are also unique. Had it been more common, I fear I may not have undertaken the task, but the name Spencer Theodore Eastwood gave me promise."

He handed Alana the first page that included a picture of her father in his army uniform with his vital statistics printed below: Date of birth, marriage, military service, and death.

"Look how handsome my dad was. My mom married him on his army base in Germany." Alana said with pride, not telling Niedermeyer that the love Spencer felt for her mother was not fully reciprocal.

Alana's mother saw the marriage as a one-way ticket out of Germany. Her parents stayed married, but it had not been an idyllic relationship.

"Keep in mind that I've only been tracing your paternal Eastwood lineage. Your other ancestors are important, but they must wait their turn."

"Niedermeyer, hurry, I'm in such suspense!"

"Now, hold on. There is a method I have to follow. You must be patient, my dear.

"You know your father was born in Mississippi on 25 October 1942. He was a junior." He handed Alana another page, this one about her grandfather. No photograph was printed, but the page listed the records of his birth, marriage, a census page, and his death certificate.

"Your grandfather, Spencer Theodore Eastwood Sr., was born in Mississippi on 15 February 1918.

"Here is the census of 1920," he said, handing her the record. "It lists the Eastwood household, including the two-year-old child, Spencer. Your great-grandfather is two lines above, named Theodore Eastwood, with no middle name. Interestingly, it lists his birthplace as Toronto, in 1885."

"Canada! Oh my!" Alana fanned out the papers.

"And his wife was born in Galt, a town near Toronto." He pointed to the spot on the census.

Niedermeyer then handed Alana a copy of the Canadian census, dated 1890. "Your great-great-grandfather's name is," he said, pointing to the spot, "Nathanial Otobang Eastwood. The record gives his birthplace as the city of Nottingham, England, in 1835."

"They came from England to Canada to the United States," Alana said. "This is so fascinating. I can't believe you found all this information. It's just brilliant…but where does my dark skin come from?"

"Genealogy is exciting research. I've just begun to scratch the surface. Finding your ancestors is an awakening of sorts; you gain an intimate knowledge of past lives, and families can connect in surprising ways. Your story is most fascinating.

"In the 1800 census for Nottingham, England, a child with the single name of Otobang lived in the home of one George Fred Eastwood. It records the child as about four years old and his place of birth says Africa. Obviously Africa is a continent, not a country, but no country of origin has been given."

"They didn't know when or where Otobang was born?" Alana asked. "I am stunned by all of this. You would say gob-smacked, wouldn't you?"

Niedermeyer smiled.

"I can't thank you enough. I am speechless," she said, spreading the last of the pages across the table.

Niedermeyer methodically rearranged them all.

"I was curious about the name Otobang," he said. "I had seen it recently. The name had come up when I catalogued the books in Alexander's library. I searched through boxes packed for donation, and, sure enough, I found an author named Otobang Temitope.

"This man has no bearing on your story, mind you. My only interest was in the name."

He offered her the book, opened to the page listing the author's biography. "It says the name Otobang (pronounced Otobäng) translates as 'a divine gift.'

"Intrigued, I looked into the other names in your family tree. I found Theodore to mean a 'gift from God'. I find that most fascinating."

"Wow," Alana whispered. "Otobang's decedents were given an Anglo name with a similar meaning. What a lovely gesture to maintain their African heritage. Could his name indicate what African country he is from?" Alana asked.

"That I don't know," Niedermeyer admitted. "We must leave that answer for another time."

Alana perused the papers on the table.

"Does this mean that George Fred adopted Otobang?" Alana questioned, but then qualified that description. "Oh my, that could be all wrong…was he brought to England to be raised a slave?"

Without waiting for Niedermeyer to speak, she continued. "But England didn't endure slavery in the 1800s. I'm overwhelmed, I can't think straight."

"You're quite right. The English were a bit more civilized. Slavery disappeared from the British Isles after the Roman times. Indentured servitude continued in some professions, but that's not the case here. And, while slavery lingered in some British colonies, that doesn't concern your ancestors."

"What are you saying?" Alana asked.

"I'm suggesting that Otobang was a welcomed guest, brought up as a member of the family, and that he was eventually given the Eastwood name."

Niedermeyer added, "The census lists George Fred's occupation as Sea Captain. I was positively giddy to have that information because so much documented history exists around anything nautical.

"My cursory look found no sign that George Fred ran slaves. You can rest assured of that. Besides, I have proven that your Eastwoods arrived in America through Canada, generations after slavery ended.

"No, George Fred transported merchandise down the western coast of Africa to Cape Town and back to England, with ports of call in all the European countries along his way.

"Captain George raised the child for a reason I have yet to learn. I will continue my research. I just wanted to have this chat before your departure."

"Oh, Niedermeyer, I can't expect you to do more work," she stated.

"Alana, this is not work, it's what I love to do. Otobang grew up to marry a great-niece of George Fred. According to the Toronto records, Otobang's son, Nathanial, became a doctor. Nathanial's son, Theodore, your great-grandfather, was also listed as a doctor in later census records."

"I guess I'm astonished to hear of an interracial marriage in 1800s England," she explained. "It seems odd to even use that terminology today.

"Then, to learn my family includes two men educated as doctors is also unexpected."

"While not common, interracial marriage wasn't that rare within certain populations," he explained. "England, in the 1800s, was by no means a land of equal opportunity, the 'class system' ruled, but many Africans were prominent in society. It was the same in France and, perhaps to a lesser extent, in the northern states in America.

"Still, Otobang, as a child, would not have been allowed to venture out in public on his own over fears he might be abducted and sold into the slave trade.

"Obviously, that never happened. And under the watchful eye of a respected family like the Eastwoods, Otobang would have had a pleasurable upbringing. Perhaps even an influential one. I will know more before we talk again."

Niedermeyer continued. "The bigger question, for me, is why a doctor living in a racially progressive city like Toronto would move to the American Deep South in the early 1900s?

"No disrespect, but your grandfather, the son of a doctor, listed his occupation as 'farm laborer' on the 1940 census. It shows his highest schooling was the seventh grade.

"This is thought provoking, and I intend to uncover the truth. It's a puzzle I find most intriguing."

"Niedermeyer, I feel I must explain that throughout my life, whenever I ran into a roadblock of any kind, I just found my way around it, without making waves. That's who I am. My father taught me to let no one hold me back, and I never have," Alana said to him. "I've always accomplished my goals in an unassuming way. As I said, that's who I am.

"I'm aware that my Black ancestors had a much harder road to travel. Again, my dad taught me not to be angry, but to be proud. And I've been proud of my heritage, even without knowing the details.

"Perhaps I never researched my American roots because I was afraid of what I might find. Maybe I wouldn't be worthy of their struggle."

Niedermeyer related to her story.

"My dad was estranged from his family. He left home at eighteen to join the army. As far as I know, he never returned to Mississippi. I've never met any of my Eastwood relatives.

"I remember a phone call when his father died, but I don't think he went to the funeral. My dad was such a nice man, yet he didn't want to associate with his family.

"My German relatives were the strong influence in my life." She hesitated. "I don't know why I made that plural…it was just my grandfather that I was close to, Kirk Augsburg. It was his death that led me to find the mysterious letter that steered me to the Grieggs and to meeting you.

"I've always been comfortable in my own skin—part light-skinned European, and part dark-skinned African. The truth is, I just call myself an American.

"The Eastwood family history that you've documented is jaw-dropping; it's threading together a history is so different from what I imagined.

"Tracing my roots backwards from America, to Canada, to England, to somewhere in Africa has presented so many individual mysteries.

"Why was Otobang taken from Africa to live a life of privilege in England? Why did an educated doctor in Canada, as you say, move to Mississippi to raise a son with a seventh-grade education?

"If any name had deviated from this path, I wouldn't be here…and they're not just names, they were actual people with lives, and loves, and problems—just like us."

Alana held up the papers. "This is my Eastwood story, and I *do* want to learn more." She paused to choose her words carefully. "You know that I sometimes get a glimpse into history, right?"

"Of course," Niedermeyer said. "Believe it or not, I am not a skeptic."

"Then you'll understand that I foresee a perilous journey ahead. Just touching these documents has chilled my fingers to the bone."

"If that's true, the journey can be postponed, but I doubt it can be avoided," Niedermeyer said.

"You could be right. I fly back to Connecticut soon. So much has happened this week. I'm not sure how many more surprises I can handle. Would you mind taking a break from your research?"

"Not at all, my dear, I'm unaware of the current events in Zürich. Are you all right?" Niedermeyer watched as Alana's eyes filled with tears.

"There was a tragic occurrence at the Grieggs' home, a woman was killed...I shot her."

Alana burst into tears. "The last thing I want to do is burden you with my predicament."

"Here." Niedermeyer placed a handkerchief in her hand. "I didn't know. And here I was droning on and on about the past. You could have stopped me."

"I didn't want to. I just wanted to have a normal day. I haven't cried since the event. Now I can't control myself. I wouldn't have come to see you if I had known this would happen," she said.

"I should make you a cup of tea." Niedermeyer asked, "Will you be okay for a few minutes?"

"Yes, thank you."

When Niedermeyer returned, Alana had composed herself. He asked, "When we've had our tea, would you mind helping me gather some of my belongings? I'd like to drive back to Zürich with you," he said. "I have been out of the loop too long. It's time for me to go home, too.

"When you're ready to visit with Otobang again, just tell me. We will take the journey together. Precarious or not, I think you know it is your destiny."

"You are probably right, Niedermeyer. Whenever I've stumbled into an unsettled past, confrontation has been the only way out."

Epilogue

Karma

"*D*o you know what it's like to have the talent to be the best at something? It doesn't matter what that *something* is. It just matters that the only thing holding you back is money.

"You watch as less capable people succeed and it eats away at your very soul, knowing that, without money it will never happen for you.

"Then, this ingenious scheme comes along…like it just falls into your lap—bam—there it is, enough cash to answer all of your dreams. It's the perfect crime: No one gets injured, and even better, you can totally get away with it.

"You know the difference between people like you and me? I had the guts to go for it, while you are stuck in a stupid work-a-day job."

"I don't believe my job is stupid. I am a detective for the Polizia di Stato, the Italian police force. I love my job because I enjoy helping people. I want to help you."

"What makes you think I want your help?"

"I spoke with Sigmund Griegg. He confirmed that there was a plot to kidnap his son's horse. He also said that while it involved you, Viktor Harel and Trudie Rechsteiner were the key conspirators—and since they are both dead, the Grieggs have no wish to pursue charges against you.

"However, it seems that's the least of your worries, Ms. Abbatelli. There are now more serious charges for you to contend with." The detective asked, "When did you decide to drive to Rome?"

"What does that matter?" Valentina snapped.

"It matters a great deal. It's at least a nine-hour drive from Zürich. What did you plan to do upon your arrival?"

"What do you think?" she shouted.

"I know what you did; I'm asking what you planned."

Valentina didn't respond.

"Maybe you were overcome with emotion…making your actions spontaneous?"

"I didn't plan it," she said. "It just happened."

"Okay." The detective looked at her.

"Who would have thought I'd find him walking to his car just as I rounded the corner," Val admitted.

"The accusation is attempted murder. You face a lengthy jail sentence."

"I don't care. He stole my money."

"And how did he do that?"

"He cleaned out my bank account."

"Yes, we checked on that. Your father has proof that the account belongs to him. It is not illegal for him to withdraw money from his own account."

"Well, I didn't know that." Val pounded the table. "He gave the account to me. Seventy-five thousand Swiss francs were transferred into the account.

"That money was mine. It was there one day and gone the next!"

The detective asked, "You were so angry that you ran him down with your car?"

"I drove here to get my money back. When I saw him…" she shook her head.

"Luckily, your car merely ripped the prosthetic leg from his body, pushing him onto the hood of a parked car. He is shaken, but he'll survive. That's a miracle for a man his age."

"I don't care. He never cared about me."

"He gave you a bank account."

"You're kidding, right?"

"I have no idea how long you might have been living off his money."

"I never lived off his money. The account had a balance of a few thousand francs when he gave it to me. Do you know how much he's worth?" Val asked.

"That's not my concern," the detective said.

"I can't believe you are asking these questions. Did you get a hold of my boyfriend?"

"Do you mean Remy Abbatelli?"

"Yes, Remy Abbatelli—who else would I mean?"

"We couldn't locate him. It appears he vacated his flat in Zürich when details of your arrest went out over the news-wires and was broadcast on the local news."

"It was on the news?"

"Yes, it has been widely covered," he said. "I was going to say, since the Grieggs won't be pressing charges against you or Remy, there is no reason for any police department to track him down."

Valentina stared at the pictures of the accident scene spread across on the table.

"Has my mother called?"

"Not yet."

Valentina continued to look at the pictures.

"As I told you, the charges are pending and you will be prosecuted to the fullest extent of the law. I suggest you hire a talented lawyer."

"How do I do that?" she asked. "My father has stolen every penny I have." She then said calmly, "I need someone to tell me what to do."

"That's not my job, Ms. Abbatelli."

*B*ack in Connecticut, after she had enough time to process the shooting, Alana felt no guilt for Trudie's death…nor had she thought about the gun left on a desk in Germany years ago. The angst she had carried in her head for so long was gone. A catharsis had occurred to settle history.

Sigmund arrived in New York City to wrap up his Hong Kong project. Alana boarded a train to meet him. Once seated, she pulled her hair back into a ponytail and reached into her bag for the note he had sent.

It read:

"Meet me at Central Park West at 60th St.
I reserved a room for you at my hotel,
so you don't have to rush home.
With love, Sigmund."

Stepping from the cab at the address Sigmund provided, Alana opened the door to the restaurant named Karma.

To be continued…watch for *Otobang's Gift*, the third book in the Griegg/Eastwood Mystery series.

ABOUT THE AUTHOR

Andrea Wilson Steele was born in England and also lived in Canada before her family immigrated to the United States. An accountant by profession, she was a corporate officer in two insurance-related organizations during her business career.

A lifelong equestrian, she teamed with horse trainer Mark Russell to write *Lessons in Lightness: The Art of Educating the Horse*, published by the Lyons Press in 2004.

Andrea formed Mouse Hole Farm Productions in 2008 to create college-level DVDs and online educational experiences for riders and equine caregivers worldwide. These programs, called *Advanced Equine Studies*, received prestigious awards at the EQUUS Film Festival in 2015 and 2016.

In 2019 Mouse Hole Farm Press was founded. Her first novel in the Griegg/Eastwood Mysteries, *The Trap*, launched to critical acclaim in 2020. The series continues with book two, *Zen*. Watch for book three, *Otobang's Gift*, in the future.

Andrea lives on a horse farm in rural Connecticut with her husband, horses, and dogs.

www.facebook.com/awilsonsteele
www.AdvancedEquineStudies.com